Porn Star

LAURELIN PAIGE
and
SIERRA SIMONE

everafterROMANCE

EverAfter Romance
A Division of Diversion Publishing Corp.
443 Park Avenue South, Suite 1008
New York, New York 10016
www.DiversionBooks.com

Cover design by Sara Eirew

This is a work of fiction. Names, characters, places and incidents either
are the product of the author's imagination or are used fictitiously.
Any resemblance to actual persons, living or dead, events or locales is
entirely coincidental.

First edition March 2016.
ISBN: 9781682304686

The following story contains mature themes, strong language, and
sexual situations. It is intended for adult readers.

Porn Star

PROLOGUE

You know me.

Come on, you know you do.

Maybe you pretend you don't. Maybe you clear your browser history religiously. Maybe you pretend to be aghast whenever someone even mentions the word *porn* in your presence. Maybe you even wish you didn't know my name, just like you wish you didn't have that drawer with the lotion or the toy.

Yeah, I know about the drawer.

But the truth is you *do* know me. You know the shape of my hands when they're curled around a woman's hips, you know the way my eyes dance when I glance up at a woman from between her legs. You know the shape of my cock, the length of it, the thickness of it. You know my sandy brown hair and my bright green eyes, and you know the noises I make when I come.

I've won all the awards, racked up hundreds of thousands of social media followers, and get name-dropped everywhere, from *Cosmopolitan* to NPR to that hour on the *Today* show where those two ladies get drunk at nine in the morning.

Everybody knows Logan O'Toole, world famous porn star.

At least, everybody thinks they know me. For a country with the highest per capita porn consumption on the planet, a surprising number of people assume that I'm living like Mark Wahlberg's character in *Boogie Nights,* or like Hugh Hefner, or some weird amalgamation of the two. That every day it's nothing but sex and glamour and money, like I walk around in a Studio 54-esque bubble all the time, wearing a silk robe and dripping with gold jewelry, being followed by vacuous, fuck-me blondes.

But it's just not the truth.

Yes, I fuck women for money, and yes, I fucking love my job. Who wouldn't? I'm good at making women come, and for whatever reason, people like to watch me do it. I'm the luckiest guy in the world in that respect. But there are no *Scarface*-like piles of cocaine lying around, no train of needy women desperate to be fucked. No magic well of money either, courtesy of internet-fed piracy and the rise of amateur porn.

The truth is I work seven days a week for narrow profit margins, with a huge array of complicated, intelligent, sometimes damaged and sometimes delightful people. The truth is that I unabashedly love this business, and I love to fuck, even though I sometimes wish for *more*, for something bigger and realer and deeper.

The truth is that being a porn star is sometimes fucking awesome and sometimes fucking terrible, and sometimes just boring and sometimes so magical I want to cry. But despite the money headaches, the industry drama, and a state government hell-bent on driving our livelihood into the ground, I'm in love with my job. I'm in love with being Logan O'Toole, with being a porn star, and I plan on doing it until my pubes turn gray, no matter what happens.

So go ahead and pretend you don't know me, but the truth is, I'm not going anywhere.

CHAPTER ONE

The light is all wrong.

Normally, this wouldn't bother me. I am not bothered easily, especially not on a set and especially not on a day like today, when my day's work involves fucking two beautiful women.

But the problem is that this is *my* set. And the two beautiful women are my friends, who are admittedly getting paid to be here. But still. They could be off doing anything else and probably getting paid better, but instead they chose to give me their time. Which means, as a director and as a friend, I feel a lot of responsibility right now.

I want this scene to look good.

Don't get me wrong, the set already looks good because it's my house, and my house is amazing. High up in the Hills, lots of windows, lots of open space. It was the first thing I bought myself when I started making decent money, and even though I could probably upgrade to Bel-Air or North of Montana, I've stayed put. I like Laurel Canyon and I fucking love this house. But right now, light is pouring in like God himself is outside, and it's making everything over lit and high-key, and like a fucking Christian Singles ad, all bright and hopeful.

No Christian Singles here today, although I give myself a little grin at the mental joke and then glance over at Tanner, the twenty-four-year-old camera genius I've somehow tricked into working for my company. "What's it look like?"

Tanner shrugs, not looking away from the camera, where he's toying with a few settings. Ginger and Lexi are in the frame, both still in lingerie and both scrolling through their phones, looking like bored customers in line at the post office—save for the see-through bras and hickeys already blooming on their necks.

"We can fix some of this in post," Tanner says, eyes still on the girls, "but right now, it's kind of got a laundry commercial vibe."

I chew on my lip for half a second. The essence of this business is speed and quantity, specifically the speed at which you can create quantity. Which often means sacrificing quality. Most directors wouldn't give the lighting a second thought—in fact, there is a certain sense of tradition to the harshly lit scenes. What began as an accidental convergence of cheapness and lack of equipment had turned into an industry aesthetic. After all, who gives a shit what the mood of the scene is? The mood is fucking. The mood is always fucking. And if you can jack off to it, then mood achieved.

But that wasn't what I wanted O'Toole Films to be when I started it. I wanted to find a place between the high-end vanilla stuff that suburban couples rented on anniversaries and dirty dungeon porn. And there has to be a place in between, right? A place for the depraved porn junkie who also happens to have taste?

I make a snap decision. "We'll finish the kissing here. Then I'll pull them both into my bedroom. The windows in there are north-facing, so maybe the light will be less…"

"…1970's sitcom?" Tanner finishes for me.

"I was going to say *aggressive*."

"Ah."

With a sigh, I trot back over to the girls. "So I was thinking after we get done with the kissing—the part where I make you two kiss each other—we'll move to my bedroom."

"You should drag us by the hair," Ginger suggests, lowering her phone and narrowing her eyes past my shoulder at the door to the bedroom, as if blocking the scene in her mind. "That'd be hot."

"So hot," Lexi echoes, not bothering to look up from her Instagram.

That is one thing about this business. In about an hour, I'll have my dick up both their asses, but right now neither of them will look me in the eye. Not like they're ashamed to be here. But like I almost don't exist to them unless we're fucking.

Which is kind of a lonely thought.

Kind of a *really* lonely thought.

And I want to slap myself for that. I'm about to fuck two women who I love to fuck, and we're all going to make money doing it. When did I get so goddamn broody about everything?

Raven. That's when.

Today is a good day. It is also going to be a sober day. So I refuse to let Raven infect my thoughts, moving them instead to the pleasant way Lexi's ass curves into her girlish hips, the way her sleek blond hair begs to be tangled and tugged.

Tanner gives us a thumbs up and we move to my sofa. The phones vanish, Ginger's thigh-highs are adjusted, and then we're back to the kissing, which is one of my favorite parts of my line of work.

Well, all the parts are my favorite part, but this especially. Ginger—red-headed, tattooed, a ten-year industry veteran like me—crawls up to me on all fours, her full tits threatening to spill out of her bra, her pretty, overly made-up face schooled into a convincing pout. Lexi, small and slender, has nestled against my other side, petting my dick through my jeans, coaxing it to full-length as I impatiently grab for Ginger and pull her to me.

"Come here," I growl, delighted at the little squeal she gives as I yank her onto my lap. Ginger's a hardened pro, and so I've made it a private goal of mine to shock genuine reactions out her whenever I can. I like genuine. I like raw.

I like real.

Lexi transitions seamlessly into petting Ginger's ass now, tugging on Ginger's thong and spanking her for the benefit of Tanner's second camera directly across from the couch. He stays behind the one shooting from the side, so he can change angles or cut in closer when he needs; later we'll blend the footage between the two cameras to maximize all the elements of the scene. But the reason I have Tanner is so I don't have to think about this shit too hard when I'm actually in the scene—I tell him what I want, we discuss everything beforehand. After it's over, we'll edit the scene together, but right now I can just focus on the only thing I want to focus on, which is tasting the inside of Ginger's mouth.

I crush my lips to hers, and she tastes, fittingly enough, like Big Red gum. We kiss a few more times before I cup my hand around the back of her neck and hold her face fast to mine as I part her lips with my own and lick inside. She tries to pull back, since, like a lot of girls, she likes to stage kiss. But I don't. I deepen the kiss, stroking my tongue against hers and then pulling her lower lip between my teeth. She makes a little noise—a noise of protest or affirmation, I'm not sure which—but I keep going. As per our pre-game discussion, she'll reach up and subtly tap the outside of my arm if she gets emotionally or physically uncomfortable and I'll stop the second that happens, but until then she's mine.

No tap, no mercy.

Once I have Ginger panting, I turn my face to Lexi. I decide right away that I'm going to book a million more scenes with her as soon as we're finished today, because she's not afraid of tongue, not at all, and when I reach down to play with her pussy, I find it completely soaking wet.

"Good girl," I murmur against her mouth. She squirms against my hand, and I grin at her. "Is there something you want?"

"I want you to fuck me," she croons.

She says it with the rote intonation of an experienced performer, and I press the pad of my finger against her clit, rubbing a tight little circle that makes her gasp. "I don't believe you," I inform her quietly, moving my hand to spank her ass. She lets out a breath of real surprise.

"You better convince me or maybe I won't fuck you at all," I continue. "Maybe I won't let you come. How do you feel about that?"

She blinks at me, her mouth parting as I find her clit once again, stroking her in earnest now. She whimpers and I can feel her wetness all over my hand now. "Please," she murmurs.

And then there it is, that moment I love, when the performance starts to skid into the real, where her body is telling her *yes yes yes, you want to fuck him*, and it becomes about more than the money or the scene. It becomes about relieving the ache I've just created inside her. (I like to send my girls away happy. It's good business, and I'm impossibly addicted to the feeling of a girl coming on my dick.)

I give Lexi one final, lingering kiss, and then I guide my girls towards each other. They start kissing, Ginger grinding down on my erection, Lexi running her small hands over Ginger's tits, and when I look down, I see that Ginger is leaving a wet spot on the front of my jeans.

"*Fuck*," I groan. "Fuck yes."

They lick and nibble each other's mouths, Ginger taking charge as she slides her hand behind Lexi's neck and moves down to kiss her throat, then back up to Lexi's lips. I catch a glimpse of pink tongues and white teeth, and my dick would look so good in between their faces right now, sliding in between those lips and tongues. I can see it slipping into one girl's mouth, then the other's, and *oh my God*, if Ginger doesn't stop rubbing her pussy against me, I am going to flip her over and fuck her ass right now.

That thought summons another—a memory really—of different place and time, of two different girls. I bite it down, push it away, because it's a Raven thought…except not really, because even though Raven was there, it's the other girl I want to think about, it's the other girl I've been secretly jacking off to for the last three years.

It's Devi Dare that Logan O'Toole thinks of when he wants to get off by himself.

And then out of the corner of my eye, I see Tanner raise a finger, our signal that we've got enough of the foreplay and it's time to move on. I am so reluctant to stop all this when I have both girls kissing and grinding so nicely on top of me, with Devi and her perfectly plump ass hovering in my mind…

With a low growl, I fist one hand into Ginger's fire engine red hair and the other into Lexi's silky blond locks, and I stand up, dragging them both with me, forcing them down to their hands and knees where they crawl after me like the little minxes they are.

I let go of their hair and walk backward to my bedroom, going slowly enough that Tanner can join my backwards walk with a camera and so the girls don't bruise their knees clambering across my hardwood floors.

Neither Ginger nor Lexi get off on such overt submission, but that's fine because they are faking it so well for the camera, waggling their asses and batting their eyes as they prowl towards my bedroom door like cats. It's also fine because I've tried to stay away from the hardcore submission scenes for a while (three months) for a plethora of reasons (Raven, Raven, Raven) and playful, fake dominance is exactly the kind of facile, uncomplicated work I've been burying myself in lately.

"Okay, that's good. Give me about fifteen minutes to set up?" Tanner doesn't wait for a response as he trots back to the living room for his equipment. I go into my bedroom to make sure I don't have embarrassing shit all over the place, which I don't, just laundry and endless stacks of external hard drives and some tax stuff shoved haphazardly into a binder. I pull the covers tighter across my already-made bed (I make my bed every morning, just like my mom taught me) and almost step on a pile of DVD cases lying on the floor. I pick up the movie on the top.

By now, I can almost read Raven's name without flinching. *Raven's Real Playdates* was a feature-length film we made near the very beginning of our relationship, only a couple months in, and while I usually give all the DVDs I get from my films away as prizes and contest incentives, I kept this one. I flip the case over to look at the back, at the still of Raven lying back getting her pussy licked. The licking is being done by a smiling girl on her hands and knees, a girl with long cinnamon hair and golden-brown skin.

I'm already hard, but the sight of Devi Dare with her naked ass in the air is enough to make a man insane. Especially when that man remembers all too well what it was like to touch her, what it was like to push his cock into that smiling mouth.

"You okay?" I asked, right before the filming started and she, Raven and I climbed onto the bed.

"Yeah," she whispered. "It's my first real scene though, so…"

"Take it easy?"

A sunny laugh. "I was going to say make it memorable."

It was memorable for me at least. I've jacked off to both the memory of that scene and the actual thing on DVD enough times to have every gasp and moan memorized. And still I'm about to come just thinking about it.

I need to fuck someone. Where is Tanner with the cameras?

By the time I've kicked my dirty boxers and the *Criterion Collection* DVD cases under my bed and walked back out, Tanner is still breaking down equipment and the girls are already back on their phones. Ginger is apparently tweeting selfies of her tits, while Lexi giggles at something she's reading.

I accept the fact that fucking is still a ways off and I readjust my raging erection as I help Tanner bring in his camera stands and lighting boards.

"Are you going to Vida's party tonight?" Tanner asks as we work. "You should, you know. Networking and all that bullshit."

"I honestly haven't thought about it," I say, which is a lie. I've thought about it a lot. Vida Gines is the grand-maven of the porn scene right now, a former star turned producer, and her party tonight is celebrating her company's acquisition of Lelie, a popular Dutch feminist porn studio. And that makes this party a problem for me.

Don't get me wrong, I *love* feminist porn. The authenticity, the real women, the real orgasms, and I am a little obsessed with how creative and visual the directors are. Not to mention that my erection-fairy Devi Dare has only done the fair trade, female-friendly girl-girl stuff since *Raven's Real Playdates,* and I make it a point to watch every single one of those.

Plus, Vida's party is going to be huge, and while O'Toole Films is doing well, it never hurts to rub shoulders with affiliate managers, distributors, and new talent.

No, the problem is that the party will have the feminist porn crowd there. And the *art*-porn crowd, and the *alt*-porn crowd, and the locus at the middle of those three groups…

Raven.

My brain stutters to a halt, and I blink at the lighting board I just set on the floor.

Tanner reads my mind. "She may not be there, you know."

"I know," I say defensively, like my brain hasn't just been immolated by a thousand terrible, wonderful memories.

"And even if she is, maybe it's time you showed her that you're over…whatever it was that happened. You're one of the biggest names in the industry right now—this is your playground too. You can't hide from everything forever."

I take my time answering, fussing with the lighting board stand far longer than necessary. But when I do answer, it's only two words. "You're right."

This satisfies Tanner. "Of course, I'm right. I'm always right. I was right about tacos for breakfast this morning and I am right about Vida's party. You go, impress everyone with your smile and your dick, and you make Raven regret the day she left you."

Tanner makes it sound so easy, so direct, and for a moment, I see it in my head the way I would film it. An establishing shot of Vida's modernist mansion, richly lit, scored by something low but catchy. Me, laughing, making other people laugh. Raven, alone and glowering into a glass of mid-range white wine. There would be a moment—closely tracked, carefully scored—where I would pass her on the way to somewhere, the balcony maybe. And she would lift her eyes to mine, and see the easygoing confidence I'm famous for, and nothing else. She wouldn't see the empty scotch bottles or that night I saw *Goldfinger* three times in a row at a classic movie theater because I couldn't bear the thought of going home to an empty house. No, she would see the real Logan, the new Logan. The Logan who was about to kick everybody's ass (and then come all over those asses afterwards.)

Adrenaline pumps through me. For three months, my life has been a cycle of fucking, filming, and editing. I've only seen my friends if they happened to be part of my filming and fucking cycle. But tonight, all of that is going to change. Tonight, I'm going to take back my old life.

"Get the girls," I tell Tanner with a grin as I unbutton my jeans. "I'm ready."

Tonight, Logan O'Toole will finally come back from the land of the brokenhearted.

CHAPTER TWO

I can't even.

And not just because my mother is in the middle of naked yoga in front of me. I did just drop in, so I'm the one interrupting her routine, and normally her ritualistic meditation practices don't faze me. I'm used to her. She's my mother, after all.

But it is rather hard to concentrate on the bill in my hands from the student loan department when my mother's hoo-ha is right at eye level while she's in downward dog. Especially with a bush as full as hers. I respect my mother's hippie liberal ways and totally support the female form in its natural state, but I'm not convinced that Eve didn't do a bit of pruning first thing after she threw that apple core to the ground.

It's because I'm proud to be a woman that I spend so much time waxing and plucking. I know, I know, different strokes for different folks and all that jazz.

At the moment, it feels awfully apropos to be faced with her asshole when I've just discovered that life is dealing me a pile of shit. Goodbye new apartment in El Segundo. I can't even. This is terrible.

I must have said that last part out loud, because a second later my mother interrupts her ohms to ask, "What's terrible, Dev?"

"Everything," I answer. "Everything is terrible."

"*Whatever words we utter should be chosen with care for people will hear them and be influenced by them for good or ill.*" She's quoting Buddha. I swear that in a lifetime of being her daughter, less than fifty percent of everything she's ever said to me has been original.

I wish my words would influence her to stop her routine and tell me how to get out of the financial mess I seem to be in. Why did I decide to stop by to pick up my mail today anyway? I could have continued through the rest of the week, blissfully unaware that my one semester at UCLA was coming back to haunt me.

I look up as my mother moves into half downward dog, and immediately regret it. Shielding my eyes, I groan, "Mâmân, do you mind?"

As she glides into her next pose, she glances back at me and whatever she sees causes her to shriek—ironic considering that I'm the one watching a fifty-year-old woman doing naked yoga.

"Devil!" she exclaims. "Your aura's so murky it's practically black! Sit down, sit down. I'll get you some turmeric juice and then give you a Reiki treatment."

"Thanks, but I think I just need to talk for a minute." At least I'm now the focus of her attention. That's the way with my mother—she's either oblivious or doting. There's nothing in between.

"Nonsense." She's already pouring me a glass of her favorite elixir. "If you could see what I'm seeing, you'd know how badly your life energy needs healing."

"Actually, what needs healing is my bank account."

"*Contentment is the greatest wealth*,'" my dad says, coming in from the kitchen, the bamboo beads in the doorway clacking together as they fall behind him.

I try not to roll my eyes. "I bet Buddha would have thought differently if he'd had student loans," I mutter.

"Student loans?" my mother asks as she sets the turmeric juice in front of me, her voice rising with a hint of hopefulness.

"Are you enrolling in school again?" My father's tone matches my mother's.

I'm tempted to be annoyed—I know they only want what's best for me.

But if I'm annoyed at anyone, it's myself. It shouldn't be so goddamned hard to decide on a major, but somehow it is. It's not that I don't have any scholarly interests—I'm actually intrigued by a great many things. Just, committing to one subject and choosing it as a career is, well, daunting.

"Not yet, Bâbâ. Soon. But not yet." *Soon.* I hope that's not a lie.

"You'll figure it out," he says with a reassuring smile that almost makes me forget the terribleness of the paper in front of me. "You have your whole life to decide."

One of the most unbelievably amazing things about my parents is how completely they support everything I do. Even when they disagree with my choices, they smile and cheer me on wholeheartedly. As long as I'm doing what makes me happy, they're all for it.

My mother ushers me to sit down at the kitchen table, then moves behind me, and even though I can't see her, I know she's stroking the air above me, wiping the negative energy from my aura. Meanwhile, my father places a hand on my shoulder, channeling positive energy into my body.

I take a deep breath and sigh. This isn't what I need right now, but this is how they show their love, and it's the only way I'll keep their attention.

"Another deep breath, and then tell us what's troubling you." My father's accent slips out as it often does when he's practicing holistic medicine, even though he hasn't lived in Iran since he was ten. I love hearing it just as I love every snippet of Persian heritage he's passed on to me, including his coloring—dark hair, amber eyes, and olive skin. The "ethnic look," as my agent calls it, has gotten me a decent amount of work in the erotic modeling business. Well, that and my willingness to shed my clothes in front of a camera like it's no big deal, another attribute of mine I credit to my parents. For as long as I can remember, they've instilled in me the notion that bodies are most beautiful in their natural state. While I'm more conservative than they are, I can be nude without the slightest bit of self-consciousness.

I do as my father has requested and fill my lungs with air. Then I release it. "It's my student loans. My deferment has expired."

"Ah," my parents say in unison.

Another incredible thing about my parents is how in sync they are. Perhaps it's a side effect of doing everything together, and I mean everything. They work together, they cook together, they clean together. If my father wasn't recovering from a strained groin muscle, he would have been alongside my mother doing her yoga *au naturel.* Though I often poke fun at them for it, I hope to one day have a relationship with someone just like theirs. Perhaps with more clothing involved.

My father moves his hand to the base of my neck. "If you go back to school, won't the deferment kick in again?"

"Yes. But I still have no idea what I'd study. I also can't afford a payment like this—" I wave the bill in the air. "Not on top of my apartment." I was only able to afford moving out six months ago. My modeling jobs pay well, but not support-myself-in-California well.

"You know your room is always waiting for you." My mother would be happy if I lived with her forever. But, as much as I love my folks, a child has to spread her wings.

"I really don't think moving back home is the answer." Besides, living with them put a serious damper on my social life. Any time I brought a guy home for a nightcap, my parents would descend upon us with mushroom tea, pot brownies, and endless tips on how to achieve the best climax. They consider themselves experts in Tantric sex and aren't at all shy about sharing their personal experiences. It's awkward, to say the least.

Not that there's been a guy that I've wanted to bring home in a long time. The majority of my orgasms in the last year have come manually while watching Logan O'Toole porn. I imagine for a moment how he'd react to meeting my parents. Surely, he's the one person who wouldn't flinch at their carnal tales. God knows he could top any story they told.

Is it weird how often I think about Logan? We did a scene together—once—a threesome where I played the "extra." It was more than three years ago now, and I still fantasize about it on a regular basis. That's probably a sign that I'm not cut out to do full-blown porn. One on-camera scene with a man—sans intercourse, even—and I'm attached. Since then I've turned down any job that's strayed from my usual girl-on-girl.

It would be nice if I had more of that work coming in. That could make a dent in the student loans.

"Moving home *might* be the answer," my mother insists gently. "What makes you so quick to dismiss that option?"

"Is it pride, Devi?" There's an edge of lecture in my father's voice. Which is as close as he actually gets to lecturing. "You know what Buddha says about pride. *'Let go of anger. Let go of—'*"

"*—'pride. When you are bound by nothing, you go beyond sorrow,'*" I finish with him. "Yeah, yeah, I know and it's very sweet of you to offer. It's not about pride." It's *somewhat* about pride. "I just need to figure this out."

Mâmân is visibly disappointed with my response. I'm her only child and she misses me at home. "You know what? Let's tarot," she says. "The universe can tell you what to do." Eagerly, she prompts my father to get the tarot cards from the breadbox—because who doesn't keep a deck of Rider-Waite in their kitchen pantry?—and takes a seat at the chair next to me.

I blow out a hot stream of air, refusing to let my irritation show. Though I've been raised with the cards as a staple in my life, I'm less convinced of their divination properties and more convinced that my parents use them to convey whatever hard words they believe I need to hear. As my mother lays out the first card, I prepare myself for her interpretation to be, *"Move home, go back to school, be happy."*

And she'll make it sound so simple. If only that was how life really worked.

"We'll just do a three-card spread," she says, probably sensing my reluctance to give the reading any credence. "This is your pathway—*The Wheel of Fortune.*"

My father grimaces slightly over her shoulder. "Not my favorite card in the deck."

"Don't listen to your Bâbâ. That's a fantastic card. It's telling you to remember that things happen in cycles. You might be down right now, but the wheel always turns. You aren't doomed to stay at the bottom."

"And then when she's back at the top, all she has to look forward to is the ride back down." It's an uncharacteristically pessimistic viewpoint coming from my father, but it's one I've heard before. Every time this card has shown up in a reading for the last twenty-one years, in fact.

I put a hand up before they launch into further argument about the negative or positive aspects of *The Wheel of Fortune* and instead ask, "But how does that help as my path? I should just brace myself and know that eventually life will get better?"

My mother shakes her head. "No, of course not. It's a card that suggests you do exactly the opposite. Don't stand still and let the wheel push you down. You can actively work to get on the upside again."

I nod, pretending to take it in. "So think of a way to make some more money." Like I said before the cards came out. "Got it."

"Yes. Like you could move home. Temporarily." And there it is—the words she wants me to hear.

I grumble inwardly. "Next card, please."

"The greatest obstacle," she says, flipping another card from the deck. "Aw, it's *The Lovers*."

"Jesus," I mutter. "A relationship would definitely be an obstacle." Seriously, it's the last thing I need right now.

"*The Lovers* doesn't just represent a romantic relationship," my father says. "It can represent something more basic—an indicator that it's time to develop your own philosophy and belief system. It's time to decide who you are. What you believe in."

"What you want to do for the rest of your life…"

"Mother!" I groan.

"Don't get mad at *me*. I'm just a messenger for The Universe." She seems to correctly interpret my skepticism. "Going on. The outcome." She starts to flip another card, but halts when my father's phone sounds with Peter Griffin from *Family Guy* shouting, "Who's texting me?"

I smile as I always do at the notification tone I set up for him, then chuckle to myself when I think about how he most certainly has no idea how to change it. My anti-technology parents only have a cell phone to be notified when one of their clients has gone into labor, so both of them perk up anxiously while he reads the message.

"It's Astrid," he says, his eyes beaming. "Contractions are only six minutes apart. Got to hustle."

My mother shrieks with excitement. "I'm not even dressed!" She hops up, abandoning the deck on the table and rushes to don her doula attire.

I watch after her, wondering what it feels like to love a job as much as she loves hers.

My father stands behind me, putting his hands firmly on my upper arms, and I know he's directing his energy toward me. "Hang in there, kid. You'll figure it out. And you're right—the answer is *not* moving back home."

I'm a bit surprised that he isn't on my mother's side. And grateful. It's nice to not have that pressure from at least one of them.

He kisses the top of my head, and I soak up his affection, sending mine back to him. It might be hokey, but it makes him feel good, and *he* makes *me* feel good. "Thank you, Bâbâ. *Asheghtam*," I say, using the Persian words to say I love you.

He squeezes my arms and says it back to me. Then my mother has returned, dressed in her swimsuit. Must be a water birth.

"Good luck!" I wave at them, promising to lock up when I'm done.

As I scoop up the mail, an invitation-sized card addressed to me attracts my attention. I slice through the envelope and find an invitation to an industry party hosted by Vida Gines. The date says it's happening tonight. I consider for a moment. It's not the type of thing I usually attend—her parties are geared toward her crowd, the serious pornmakers—but if I want more jobs, even just the femme porn variety, this might be the place to make some new connections.

Wasn't that what *The Wheel of Fortune* was telling me to do? Look for new opportunities and the like. Not that I believe in that divination stuff. Not entirely, anyway.

It's merely out of curiosity that I flip over the next tarot card, the one that would have been the answer to my situation. It's *The Star*, my favorite card in the entire deck. As a child, I loved it because I loved the stars. I didn't care what the seers said it meant—for me it always represented the shining jewels that lit up the night sky. For hours and hours I'd stare at the bright dots through the telescope given to me on my tenth birthday, listening while my parents recited stories of the Greek gods who resided in constellation form above us. Even then I wondered what was beyond their tales, wondered what elements made the balls of fire, what made them burn and glow and fall.

Of course that isn't the message the reading is giving me now. In my parents' absence, I try to conjure up the intended meaning instead. *Hope*, I think. Yeah, that's it.

It's a universal message that could apply to anyone at any time. But as I gather my student loan invoice and Vida's invitation and head home to get ready for her party, hope buzzes inside me, and I can't help but think that the card was pretty apropos.

CHAPTER THREE

I suppose it doesn't take much to break a man.

Take me for example. My life checks a lot of boxes. Well-adjusted childhood, *check*. Successful business, *check*.

Healthy? Decently good-looking? Amazing dick?

Check, check, and *check*.

I had a great life. And I thought I had a great girlfriend to match it. For three years, I had this porcelain-skinned, dark-haired beauty at my side, and she was creative and smart and driven, and so goddamned sexy I couldn't keep my hands off her, even after a long day spent on set fucking other women. We had a purebred Yorkshire terrier that we named Prior. (After the character in *Angels in America*. Raven's idea.) We picked out towels and plates together. And she was so integral to the founding of O'Toole Films, helping me write business plans and apply for loans and shooting scenes with me that we knew we wouldn't get paid for until the company got off the ground...

And then I came home one night to an empty house.

No warning.

No goodbye.

I left her to her quinoa and fair trade coffee one morning and came back and she was gone. Clothes, makeup, dildos—anything that was hers, she took. Along with Prior, the furry little guy with his sweet little face and the habit of licking my toes when I tried to edit scenes in my office.

It didn't make sense. We were happy, right? We were having fun. I won't pretend that jealousy didn't stab me in the ribs when I saw scenes that she filmed with other people, but that was part of our business. I didn't stop fucking other girls and she didn't stop fucking other guys; we agreed at the beginning that our relationship wouldn't affect our jobs in any way, but for my own sanity, I set one simple ground rule: no off-screen fucking with anyone else.

There. Easy.

Except when she left, it became very clear that it was *not* that easy. Not only did she abruptly bow out of all of our upcoming projects—professionally embarrassing, since most of them were with outside studios that then had to scramble to find another performer to be with me. But the tall Italian guy that appeared in all of her Instagrams the following week indicated that I had probably missed a few key signs that Raven had checked out of our relationship long before she threw her dildos and our Yorkie into her purse and drove off.

I wish I could say that I dealt with this gracefully. That I didn't Google-stalk Italian Guy (some big shot producer over in Europe,) that I didn't listen to Damien Rice songs on repeat, that I didn't miss that dog so fucking much that I went to the pound every morning to pet the dogs there.

That I didn't drink my weight in scotch every week.

That I didn't withdraw from my family and my friends.

That I didn't fall asleep folded into a ball on my kitchen floor, because I couldn't bear looking at the empty bed, much less sleeping in it.

Those are not the kinds of things Logan O'Toole does. Logan is funny and friendly and worldly, too emotionally wise to feel heartbreak. Logan should have endured the departure (and probable infidelity) of his long-term girlfriend with a Zen-like equanimity, and wished her peace on her new journey or some bullshit.

And so that's who I am tonight. Worldly and Zen, flirty and aloof. My wounds have started to scar over, and I want to prove that I've moved on. And that is why I walk into Vida's like I own the place, shoulders back, grin at the ready, with a steady, focused gaze that makes it clear I'm *not* scanning the room for any hint of Raven's presence.

Tanner is in the main room—a large open space studded with low couches and ottomans that I'd be hesitant to shine a black light on—and he comes toward me with a drink in his hand.

"I got you some scotch," he says.

I sniff the glass. It's something smoky, probably an Islay Scotch, and although I prefer Speyside, I'm still impressed that it's single malt. Vida must have pulled out all the stops for this party.

While I sip, I finally take the chance to assess the room. Like I thought, it's mostly the feminists—tattooed, pierced, bespectacled. I do a lot of scenes with those types for O'Toole Films because we have a very similar ethos when it comes to consent and female pleasure.

Also I think girls with tattoos are fucking hot.

But there are other types here too—mainstream stars who frequently work with Vida's company, the indie crowd, the underground BDSM people in their vinyl corsets and thigh-high boots. And Vida herself at the center of it all—mid-forties, deeply tanned, platinum blond hair coiffed short and stylish. She looks exactly how you'd imagine an aging porn star to look—sagging plastic surgery, careworn face, too much makeup—but you'd be dumb to discount her business acumen or intelligence because of the way she looks. There's a reason even the most insulated, conservative Americans have heard of Vida: because she gets marketing and she gets content and she gets platform saturation.

I want to be her when I grow up.

"I like this party," Tanner says, taking a sip of his craft beer. "And hey, I'm not the only black guy here."

He's right about this crowd being more progressive than most, although it's still not ideal. "We're going to make it so all the parties are like this, but better," I tell him. When I hired Tanner two years ago, he was frank about all of the problems he saw within the industry—including the inherent racism embedded in the very foundations of mainstream porn. So I told him that if he came and worked for me, we'd fix it; we'd cultivate diversity without all the weird taboos and fetishes normally present in interracial sex work. And so I managed to snag an incredibly talented filmmaker right out of art school, and he managed to make a believer out of me.

He shrugs. "It's L.A.," he says, as if that's all the explanation required.

I am going to say something else but stop when I see *her*.

She's here.

My fingers tighten around my glass, and my stomach starts flipping over like a gymnast on the uneven bars, *swoop, swoop, toss, spin*—

"Breathe," Tanner coaches. "Everyone has to run into their ex-girlfriend for the first time since a breakup. You're just getting it out of the way now."

But it isn't Raven that I see laughing out by the pool. It's not Raven with the glass of scotch and the long caramel hair and the smile that could power the whole goddamn Valley if she wanted it to.

It's Devi Dare.

The balcony is lit up against the night, and the pool sends blue-white glimmers dancing across her face. She wears some sort of shimmery gold halter top that drapes low, exposing the smooth bronze skin of her sternum and teasing me with the hidden curvature of her tits, and leaving almost her entire back bare.

With her short black shorts and ankle-high gladiator heels, she doesn't just look fuckable, she looks beautiful, and I wish I had a camera right now. I want to film her here, laughing and golden with the sparkling grid of the city behind her, and then I want to take her to a beach and see what she looks like against a backdrop of inky sea. Maybe we could drive up north, find an empty stretch of highway, and I could film her walking on the dark asphalt. With that shining gold top and those fuck-me heels, the contrast of her with a desert highway would be so stark and so gorgeous and thought-provoking. The kind of shit you see gif-ed on Tumblr.

And then she turns and sees me through the floor-to-ceiling window. There's a moment where her eyes narrow, as if trying to make out my face in the dim interior of Vida's living room, and then her face blossoms into the kind of smile that makes me want to give her everything in my wallet. If my stomach was swooping before, it's a tornado now, whipping up emotional debris and lust and all the fantasies I've ever had about this woman, and I only barely remember that I'm supposed to be Worldly and Zen Logan in time to give her a flirty grin in return.

As she turns back to her friends, I realize my highway film would be all wrong. Devi is the living antithesis of asphalt. Devi is energy and health and vibrancy. She's sunshine and butter-yellow flower petals and the sweetly earthy smell of cinnamon and cloves. I was right before, with the ocean idea, or maybe the desert in the dark, when the night flowers are in bloom—

"Thinking about who you're going to fuck?"

A sharp voice jolts me out of my directorial reverie, and I blink to find Tanner gone and Vida Gines standing next to me, a bright pink drink in her hand. She arches an eyebrow at me as she cants her head toward the massive windows, indicating the balcony outside. "I saw you making eyes at Devi."

Worldly and Zen, I remind myself. Vida doesn't need to know that I'm mentally comparing Devi to the flowering night desert. *Be casual.*

"Devi's fucking hot," I say, taking care to keep my voice casual. "Lots of hot girls here." And then for good measure, I take a drink and look casually around the room. Casual Logan, that's me.

Vida takes a drink of her own, but that eyebrow stays arched and I know I'm not fooling her one bit.

"Great party," I volunteer, trying to deflect attention away from me and my overt ogling of Devi. The last thing I need after my insanely public breakup with Raven is rumors of a new fling. "Congratulations on acquiring Lelie, by the way."

Vida nods. "Lelie is an amazing studio. Great vision, great philosophy. Tons of potential for profit. Which is why we should talk."

I hear her, but for a moment, I zero in on the way her nails are painted the exact shade of her drink. Pink nails, pink drink, pink lips—the kind of thing a director would deliberately orchestrate. I make a mental note to toy around with this kind of visual sometime in my scenes. Surely, the girls wouldn't mind me choosing their lipstick color? If it was for art?

"Logan?"

I snap back to her. "Sorry, what?"

That eyebrow is practically touching her hairline now. "I said we should talk."

"I'm always happy to hear what such a smart lady has to say." And then I find the small of her back with my palm, leaning in to whisper, "Do you want to find someplace a little less noisy?"

Despite our age difference, and despite the fact that I know she only wants to talk business, my proximity affects her. She shivers and then laughs, pushing me playfully away. "You know how to make a woman feel young, Logan. This way."

"Yes, ma'am," I say in a mock-submissive voice, and she rolls her eyes, but a suppressed smile tugs at her lips as she walks past me. I drain the last of my scotch, set the glass down on a nearby table, and follow.

We go down an open flight of steps, all roughly welded metal and dark wood planks, and then we're in the heart of Vida's filming operations. As we walk down a darkened hallway to her office, I see rooms filled with St. Andrew's crosses, rooms furnished like high-school classrooms, rooms filled with nothing more than bare white walls and beds. And not all of these rooms are vacant; as we pass the last one on the right, I see that a small group of people have availed themselves use of one of the beds. They're all skin and mouths and sloshing drinks, and without thinking, I reach for the doorknob and tug their door slowly shut before I walk into Vida's office. When I first got into this business, I would have been right there with them, but maybe it's the threesome I had this morning or the fact that I actually want to hear what Vida has to say, but the whole scenario fails to interest me.

Now, if Devi was in there…

I drop into a chair by Vida's desk, crossing my long legs as she sits. She appraises me, and I find myself shifting a little. Her gaze is too perceptive…too *kind*. There's understanding in her faded blue eyes, and I remember that she's been divorced twice, that she's been in this business for twenty-five years. I remember that Vida's studio was one of those involved in the Great Logan-Raven Break-Up.

"It's okay to need time," she says, glancing past me to the door I just shut in the hallway. "We've all been there."

"I'm fine," I lie, maybe a little too convincingly, because she shrugs like she's ready to move on, and then a tiny, silly part of me wishes that she would keep asking about it. I've kept this heartbreak under wraps for so long, held it inside me, and suddenly I wonder if it would hurt less if I simply *talked* about it. Instead, I've trapped the pain inside myself, a hungry wolf that's long since devoured my heart and is now gnawing on my ribs, snarling and howling in the empty space where my heart used to be.

But the moment is gone, and Vida is all business once again. "Sinfully Vida has weathered the last year as best as can be expected," she says, referring to her production company. "But we took a hit with the rape stuff. I won't lie. It was a pretty big hit, and it left a huge gap in our content."

The rape stuff. It hit everyone pretty hard here on the west coast, the accusations that one of porn's biggest stars was a rapist, and then of course, the follow-up allegations that porn had fostered a rape-friendly culture. Studios had hurriedly re-drafted performer agreements, pulled down content featuring the accused, and splashed disclaimers all over their websites. Even I was affected, receiving fucktons of hate mail from people all over the world, even though I barely knew the guy who'd been accused, and I made consent a huge part of my work.

It sucked. It still sucks.

"Sinfully Vida had more content with him than any other studio," Vida says, and there's a note of betrayal in her voice. "And so we not only have a content gap, we have some image rehabilitation to do."

"Thus the Lelie purchase," I fill in for her.

She nods, tapping her fake nails on her desk. "Yes. Buying them is good for business. We need more 'feminist' porn, and we need it yesterday." She says *feminist* with air-quotes, as if it's some ridiculous, imaginary concept, and if Tanner were here, he'd lose his progressive shit. I bite back a smile as I imagine it, and Vida mistakes my expression. "So you're onboard?"

Uh, what?

"Pardon?" I ask politely.

"Logan, you are the obvious frontrunner to fill…*his*…shoes for Sinfully Vida." I notice how she doesn't say the other guy's name, like he's Voldemort or Rumpelstiltskin or something. "You're hot, you're insanely popular, and you've got the whole pro-women thing going on."

"So you want me to film a scene for Lelie?"

She leans forward. "More than a scene. I want *you*. We can partner with O'Toole Films of course, find a mutually profitable agreement, but I want you long-term. And I want it to be something big, something no one else is doing right now, something that engages a lot of the subscribing viewers we lost last year."

I like big and new and different, I like engaging, but I don't know about long-term. The last long-term thing I did ended with me crying naked in the shower while my ex-girlfriend fucked an Italian half a world away.

On the other hand, didn't I just promise myself this morning that I won't let Raven dictate any more of my life? That it's time for Logan O'Toole to start kicking asses and taking names?

"What did you have in mind?" I ask.

Vida sighs, turning her chair to stare out of the office window. Outside, the sky glows purple above the city, and lights sprawl for miles and miles. I suddenly feel lonely again, although I can't pinpoint exactly why—whether it's the city so massive and crowded and self-absorbed, or the sight of Vida Gines, Her Royal Majesty of Porn, looking so lonely herself.

Is this going to be me in fifteen years? Alone? With only my business for companionship?

"I'm not sure," she admits, and I can tell the admission pains her. "Porn is changing. And I'm used to adapting to how people watch it, how they pay, and how they steal, but adapting to these bigger things…"

She drifts off, her eyes pinned to the cityscape outside.

"We need something new," she finally says, and she turns back to me. "Something fresh. I don't know what that is, and that's why I need you. You're young, you're sexy, and most importantly, both men and women connect to your scenes. They don't just skip to the fucking and jerk off, they watch the whole thing, and then they come back and watch it again. They have *favorites*. Your subscription rates are through the roof and you're a social media darling. Logan, Lelie needs you if it's going to become more than art-house porn. *I* need you."

I think for a minute. Lelie has vision. Partnering with them would put me closer to my goal of creating unique and artistically driven films. And it sounds like Vida is basically giving me carte blanche to do whatever I want, so long as it bolsters Sinfully Vida's female-friendly reputation and ultimately makes money. There's no reason to say no, except…

"Vida, I'd love to work with Lelie."

She smiles.

"But I have no idea what to do."

She waves a hand, those nails like streaks of pink light through the air. "You don't need to know now. Just promise me you'll think about it. And when you're ready," she reaches for her smartphone and taps at the screen a few times, "contact Marieke de Vries. She's the head of Lelie, and she will get you whatever you need."

My phone lights up with Vida's text.

"Thanks, Vida."

"I'm looking forward to it," she says. "Now get upstairs and drink my liquor."

• • •

In that way that certain parties will, the mood has shifted and only half of the people here know it. When I make it upstairs, the unknowing half still laughs and drinks and dances, but the crowd in the common area of the house has noticeably thinned. I see the cluster of people in the upstairs hallway—crowding around the orgy that's undoubtedly happening in one of Vida's many bedrooms—I take in the unmistakable smell of pot and sex, and I know it's time for me to go home.

And that's okay, because all I want to do is think about Vida's offer. I'm excited about it, I'm nervous about it, I'm obsessed with it already, and so there's no room for an impersonal and drug-fueled orgy in my mind.

But then I hear her voice.

Not Vida's voice. Not Devi's voice.

Hers. My own personal Voldemort.

You know when you have a bruise and you can't stop pressing on it? Or a cut on your lip that you lick over and over again, even though you know it simply makes it worse? It's this impulse, this sick fascination, like you *want* to feel the ache, you *want* to hurt yourself, you want to be both the recipient and the giver of the pain all at the same time. And that is the only explanation I can find right now for why I'm walking toward the hallway, pushing through the crowd and standing in the doorway of one of Vida's bedrooms.

I'm not shocked at what I see in front of me. I've seen it hundreds, maybe thousands of times, both on set and off. There are five people on the bed and scattered couples around the room, all in various stages of fucking. Dicks, cunts, mouths. Legs spread, sweat glistening. Tonight there are more tattoos and piercings than normal, hair in blue or bright red victory rolls rather than sleek highlights, but it's all still the same.

But I'm not looking at them. I'm looking at the pale, dark-haired woman in the middle of the bed, who's riding one man while another fucks her in the ass, no condoms in sight. Her head is thrown back, her eyes are closed and she's moaning and panting as her stomach tenses up with her impending climax.

Raven always did like double penetration.

I don't need to see this. If I wanted to see my ex-girlfriend get fucked by another man—or two—all I have to do is crack open my laptop. I don't have to witness it like this, in this dark, smoke-wreathed room with Lana Del Rey droning in the background.

But I can't seem to make myself move. My traitorous dick jolts as she cries out and comes hard, her smooth thighs tensing and fingernails digging into the shoulders of the guy she's riding. God, she's a wonder to watch fucking, all those lithe muscles and that pale skin. Was it only three months ago that it was my cock inside her pussy? Only three months ago that I was the one to pull on that hair, kiss that neck, fight her for the blankets at night? Only three months since she broke my fucking heart?

She comes down from her orgasm with a breathy moan, looking coyly over her shoulder at the guy fucking her from behind, giving him the fluttering eyelashes and curled smile that I recognize all too well. It's her scene-smile, her *I'm-going-to-make-you-feel-like-a-big-strong-man* smile, and it's definitely not an expression she ever bothers to trot out when she's having real, off-screen sex.

She's performing, I realize. She's performing even though there are no cameras here, even though most of the people in the room are preoccupied with drugs or their own fucking. It hits me the minute those dark eyes flutter up to meet mine, and that curling smile grows bigger.

She's performing for me.

Shit.

I stumble backwards, the weight of her dark eyes so much heavier than anything else—than the two guys screwing her or her nakedness or her smile—it's those eyes. Weighted with...what? Revenge? Contrition? Scornfulness?

And then I recognize it.

Satisfaction. She wanted me to see this and now I have, and she's pleased about that for whatever twisted reason.

I'm pushing backward into people now, spilling their drinks and breaking apart kisses, but I don't care. Those eyes sear into my flesh, peeling away the shell I've maintained for the last three months and revealing the empty, shredded mess inside, and I can't stand it. I tear my eyes away, but the image of her is still burned into my retinas, and I press against the crowd, needing to make it out of here, needing to leave, needing to find a drink.

Needing to forget.

CHAPTER FOUR

I can still feel Raven's stare on me as I finally break through the crowd at the door and emerge into the hallway, my pulse pounding as if I just witnessed a grisly murder. As if I just came face to face with my own personal super-villain.

I walk numbly down the hallway, my mind racing. She must have known I'd be here tonight. And she wanted me to see her there, fucking in the raw, and I played right into her hands.

I grab an open bottle of scotch without even really looking at it, moving through the living room without seeing it, and going straight outside, un-stoppering my bottle as I do.

Though the pool is off the main floor, Vida's mansion is built on a steep slope, meaning that the pool terrace can extend into a ledge overlooking the city. I walk across the wide, white terrace with its sparkling water and curtained cabana—all of it currently devoid of party guests—and make my way to the chest-high wall rimming the edge of the balcony. I take a swig from the bottle as I survey the city—*my* city—and then wince.

"Fuck," I wheeze. It's Laphroaig.

I fucking hate Laphroaig.

I take another drink, a longer one this time. I don't deserve a scotch I like to drink right now—or maybe it's not that I don't deserve it, but it's more like I can't imagine any part of this night being pleasant or enjoyable. Not with my ex-girlfriend fucking just yards away from me right now.

No, I want my drink to taste like shit. I want my mouth to taste like old ashtrays, and I want to get dizzily, pukingly, disgustingly drunk. Because if I'm drunk, then I don't have to process Raven and her fucking mind games. I won't be tempted to scroll through her Instagram to find out when she got back to L.A., if she's still with Italian Guy, and I certainly won't be tempted to text her.

I pull out my phone, taking another long drink of the smoky liquor and open up my messages. I deleted her number long ago, but I still have it memorized, and maybe I could just send her one text. Just one. I could call her a bitch and tell her to go to hell. Tell her I knew exactly what she was up to.

Or I could beg her to come over to my house and just fucking *talk* to me. We haven't exchanged a word since the day she left, and all I've wanted these past three months is an explanation or an apology maybe, or even some fucking closure.

I tap in her number and open up a new message. My thumb hovers over the keyboard, the first golden glow of the scotch beginning to dull my anger. Maybe I *would* invite her to talk—that's what grown-ups did, right? Talk? And if it led to me fucking all the lies and deceit right out of her skinny body…

Jesus. I'm like the werewolf who needs to be chained to a radiator during the full moon. Of course I can't text her. Eliciting that kind of reaction is probably exactly what she wants, and fuck me if I'm going to do anything that she wants me to do.

I spin around and throw my phone as hard as I can into the pool.

It lands with a small splash, sinking like a brushed-aluminum stone straight to the bottom. My momentary satisfaction is eclipsed by immense regret, because I just got that phone a few weeks ago. Fuck it, I can get a new one tomorrow. If that's the price I have to pay to keep myself separate from Raven, then so be it.

I take a few healthy chugs of the Laphroaig.

"I hope you've got a good warranty," a cheerful voice says from next to me. Even over the smoky scent of the whisky, I smell her. Cinnamon and sunshine.

I inelegantly swallow the scotch still in my mouth, turning to face the person next to me. "Devi."

She flashes me her sunny grin, and then returns the greeting by playfully bumping her shoulder against my arm. Heat flares across my bicep, emanating from the place where our bare skin touched, and the heat slowly migrates towards my chest, independent of the blood now pumping to my groin.

I am suddenly very aware of the fact that Devi and I have never been *alone*. Strange, given that we've given each other orgasms, but *Raven's Real Playdates* was the only time we've worked together, and there are so many people on a porn set that it's impossible to feel any sense of *alone*-ness, even when you're staring someone in the eyes while they suck you off. And even though we've seen each other at parties and events since then, we've only ever said *hi* or *how are you* or *where's the bar*? Not exactly the basis for a deep understanding of one another.

So I should probably explain to her why I just chucked a brand new phone into the water, and also maybe not reveal the fact that I have a massive crush on her.

I try to muster the casual, flirty guy I was earlier tonight. "Devi, I…"

I jack off to you almost every day.

"…I, uh, didn't know anyone else was out here. Or I wouldn't have, you know." I mime throwing the phone.

She laughs and then bends down to unfasten her leather heel. "If it's in a good case, it might still be okay," she says. I watch, transfixed, as she kicks off both shoes, shimmies out of her shorts, and then walks to the edge of the pool. She's wearing what legally might qualify as underwear, but only just barely.

Have I mentioned Devi Dare's ass? Because I should. She has one of the best asses known to mankind. Plump and thick and juicy, the kind of ass that invites biting and squeezing, and the way it slopes out from her small waist is pure poetry. And those legs—despite the obvious muscles in her calves and thighs, they still move as she walks, like her ass does, and there's something so *healthy* about it, so tantalizing about her body with its wide hips and slightly soft stomach and full breasts. She's sexy in such a visceral, biological way, the kind of way that says *you want to make babies with me*. My cock lengthens as I watch her, tens of thousands of years of evolution telling me to haul her off and impregnate her.

She turns, hands on her hips. "Are you going to join me?"

"I was just enjoying the view," I say, and it comes out a little too raspy, a little too honest, but then I follow it up with a weak grin, and then she laughs and jumps into the pool. With a final gulp of whisky, I put the cork in the bottle and then fling myself in after her, clothes, shoes and all.

The water is cool and it's the best kind of contrast to the dry heat of the July night and the warmth of the scotch in my stomach—and to the new kind of warmth that's agitating in my chest, something frictive and thrilling pressing up against my anger and my broken heart. Something that started the moment Devi brushed against my arm.

I jumped into the deep end, so it's a few beats before my feet press flat against the bottom and I can push myself back up. I break the surface, sputtering, and awkwardly try to swim over to Devi with one hand still clenched around my scotch bottle. She treads water as steadily and gracefully as a water nymph, her long hair floating around her shoulders and her gold top drifting away from her skin, giving me just the barest glimpse of one nipple, dark rose and peaked into a tight furl. Water droplets cling to the thick fringe of her eyelashes.

"You're not very good at swimming," she points out as I make my way closer.

"Never liked it much," I say, swimming past her and moving to where my feet can touch. With a sigh of relief, I set my feet down, examine the scotch bottle to make sure no pool water leaked in, and then take a long drink. I'm on my way to being drunk, and I'm intent on sealing the deal. What can I say? I'm a finisher.

Devi drifts up next to me, holding something in her hand. It takes me a minute to realize that it's my phone, the entire reason we spontaneously jumped into the pool in the first place. And somehow, miraculously, the pricey case the Apple Store girl talked me into buying has saved the phone. The screen still glows with my unwritten text message.

Somehow, between the pool and the scotch and Devi Dare with no pants on, I've lost the urge to talk to Raven. I take the phone and toss it carelessly onto the concrete and then turn back to Devi.

"*You*, on the other hand, seem like quite the swimmer," I say with a smile, offering her the scotch. She takes it and raises the bottle to her lips.

"I was raised in California, you know," she says and then takes a drink.

"Well, so was I. But my parents are Boston transplants, so I guess they never saw swimming as a priority for me."

She hands the bottle back to me. "I think I had floaties before I had a bicycle. My parents are very, uh…" She searches for the right words. "*Natural* people. They think it's important to be periodically cleansed of negative energy, and flowing water is one of the best ways to do that. So we went swimming at least once a week."

I can see the faintest blush coloring the apples of her cheeks, as if she's embarrassed by what her parents believe. And then I wonder if she's embarrassed because she believes it a little too.

God, that blush is so sexy. I want to lick it right off her face. And then pin her down and lick her everywhere.

She tilts her head to the sky. "You can see Cassiopeia tonight."

I look up, following her gaze, but I see nothing other than the golden glow hovering above the city and a smattering of faint, twinkling stars. "Is Cassiopeia a constellation?" I venture.

She laughs and nods, and then she reaches over and takes my head in her hands. My pulse thrums, that warmth in my chest explodes into flames, and I want her to *kiss me kiss me kiss me*, but before I can turn my head to her, she trains my face to the sky, facing the right direction this time.

"Do you see it?" she asks. Her mouth is close to my neck, and I wonder what it would feel like if she bit me there. "It looks like a letter M." She traces the shape of it with her fingers, until finally I see it—an underwhelming handful of tired stars.

"You can't see it this far into the city sometimes," she continues.

"Cassiopeia sounds like a porn name," I say frankly and she laughs again.

"Ptolemy named it."

I give her a blank look. I got pretty good grades in school, but it's been more than ten years since graduation, and anything not intimately related to film or the kind of math I need to run my business has been filtered out of my brain.

"Ptolemy was a Greek astronomer," she explains, giving me an amused glance. "He named it after a famous queen in Greek mythology. She was so beautiful and vain and boastful that she brought the wrath of Poseidon down on her kingdom."

Beautiful, vain, boastful. My mind swerves back to Raven, possibly still in this very house, possibly still being screwed with that evil smile on her face. Where is Poseidon when you need him?

No.

No, I won't let Raven crowd into my happy, drunk moment with Devi and the scotch. I speak as much to drive away thoughts of my ex as to comment on Devi's astronomy knowledge. "You know a lot about this shit," I tell her, turning my eyes back to her face completely.

And now she really blushes. "I really like astronomy. Stars and galaxies and stuff. It makes life feel so…*big*…you know?"

The thing is, I do know. That big feeling, I mean. I get it every time I watch an amazing film, every time I imagine my own films with just the right setting and just the right cinematography and just the right score.

"I've never met a performer who's told me anything like that," I say. And it's true. Not once have I been around another adult film star and had them confess a purely impractical fascination. A call toward something that makes them feel like life is magical.

She blinks, and the way her long, thick eyelashes brush against her wet cheeks is arresting. "Really?"

"Really. Devi Dare, I do believe you are my first."

"I don't think any guy has ever said that to me before," she teases, as I take a step closer to her. I'm not sure why I do it; we're already so close. But the water is so pretty and clear, and the world is so soft from the scotch, and all I want on this earth right now is to count the water drops on her eyelashes.

Devi moves a little and her shirt pulls almost completely open, exposing those sweet breasts and even sweeter nipples. I'm suddenly very grateful for the pool, which hides my aching erection. It does not, however, hide the way I'm now staring at her tits, nor the way I bite my lip to keep from leaning forward and sucking one perfect tip into my mouth.

Her lips part, and she doesn't bother pulling her shirt closed. We are so close now, and I feel her bare toes brush against the front of my shoes. Her eyes are pure amber, liquid gold and warm, and they search mine now. Something has shifted with my step closer, and I feel like I'm going to combust, a pillar of flame in the middle of this sparkling pool.

I want to kiss her.

I want it like I've wanted nothing else in my life.

See, here's the problem. I know how soft and wet her tongue is, how warm and plush her lips feel, and I can recall every breathy pant she gave me when we kissed on set all those years ago. I know precisely how delicious and rewarding kissing her will be. And now her face is tilted completely towards mine, and her expression is open and inviting, and her hands slide up my chest, fisting in my soaking wet T-shirt. I let the corked, mostly empty scotch bottle bob away from us in the water.

"Logan," she whispers, eyes still searching, fingers clenched tight in my shirt.

Kiss her, you asshole! What are you waiting for?

But everything is smashed together inside of me—my anger at Raven, my determination to move on, my desire for Devi, Vida's offer—all of it is tangled and twisting, and I can't get my thoughts straight, I can't peel apart where my urge for revenge against Raven ends and my need to kiss Devi begins. Business is mixing with pleasure, pleasure is mingling with pain, and for just an instant, I wish Raven were right here, right now. I wish she were watching us. I wish she could see Devi and me and feel even a tithe of the jealousy and rage I felt when I found her. And God, I want to see her fucking face when she sees us…

I'm such a dickhead. How can I kiss this girl that I've liked for *years*, this girl I've idolized and fantasized about, how can I touch her with even a hint of Raven in my mind? More so, do I really want Raven to taint something I have wanted for so long? Give her ownership of the first off-screen kiss Devi and I will ever share?

No. When—*or if*, I think glumly—I kiss Devi, it will be without the ghost of Raven's betrayal hovering over us. And besides, if I kiss Devi now, everything will change. We might fool around or we might fuck, and then this won't be the night I stood in a pool and she showed me the stars, it will be the night that we did what everyone else does at these parties. It will be the night we turned the chemistry between us into something merely physical, and even the thought of that transformation is enough to wound me.

I want this to be our star night. And maybe, if I'm lucky and if I can get a fucking handle on myself, there will be a kissing night later.

Soon, my dick demands.

"Logan?" Devi repeats, and it's more naked now, pleading almost, and I reach up and cradle her elbows in my hands. I don't want to tell her about the Raven stuff—I don't want her to feel used or think that I've been mentally comparing her all night. And I can't articulate my fear about kissing without revealing my giant, epic crush on her and sounding like a creepy stalker.

So I say, "I think I should go now."

Her forehead wrinkles adorably. "You should?"

"Yeah," I mumble, pulling away and making for the edge of the pool. The loss of her skin, of those wide gold-brown eyes, makes me feel emptier than anything else that's happened tonight, and I almost turn back and do it. I almost turn and grab her and slant my mouth over hers and let all of the dark, tangled shit in my heart go.

But I don't.

I rescue the scotch from the water and hoist myself out of the pool, and then I turn and offer my hand to her, which she ignores, the lithe muscles in her arms easily working to pull her body onto the concrete. Her cheeks are red again, and she won't meet my eyes, and then when I say, "Devi..." not knowing what I mean or what I want or how to explain anything, she shakes her head. But I blunder on. "I—can I have your number?"

Fuck. Now, where did that come from?

She hesitates, still not meeting my eyes. After a moment, she bends down and grabs my phone from the side of the pool, and sends a blank text message to herself.

"There," she says, and there's so much in her voice that claws at my conscience; I hear her pride and thwarted lust and confusion. But how can I explain it all to her when I can't even explain it to myself?

God, I'm such a fucking mess.

"Thanks," I say awkwardly, and she gives me a curt nod, again without looking at me.

"Goodnight, Logan," she says and scoops up her shoes and shorts. Without bothering to tug them back on, she walks wet-footed and visibly upset into the house.

Shit.

CHAPTER FIVE

I wake up with longing on my lips and an ache between my legs, both aftereffects from Vida's party. With a hand thrown over my eyes, I press my thighs together and try to fall back into slumber, but the burn of desire is far too great.

Resigned and aroused, I roll over and grab my laptop from the side of my bed. I open it and within a couple of minutes I have it pulled up—*Raven's Real Playdates*. I hit play on the bookmarked scene and set the computer at the bottom of the bed, facing me. Then I push down my panties, lay back, prop my head up with pillows, and part my knees so I can see the screen while I relive the shoot—my favorite fantasy, my go-to masturbation material, guaranteed to deliver at least one self-administered "O."

The scene jolts into motion, picking up after the initial foreplay, after the characters have already kissed and sucked and fondled. Authoritative and controlling, Raven is directing the action, narrating what she wants to see happen, and what she wants to see next is the second woman—me—go down on the guy. Onscreen Devi is already naked, and though I've watched this a million times, I'm transfixed as she kneels before Logan O'Toole, unfastens his jeans, and tugs his briefs down far enough to unleash his dick. I hadn't done other shoots with men, but I'd been on enough sets to know what to expect. I hadn't expected him to already be hard. I'd expected he'd need a fluffer or that I'd need to prime him for a bit, either on camera or off.

But he'd been hard. Fully erect, his cock thick and heavy while it throbbed in my hands. I distinctly remember it—the weight of him in my palm—as I watch my onscreen self wrap her hands around his dick, lick up the length of him, and kiss the tip. She peers up at him, her wide brown eyes seeking approval.

The look Logan delivers in return makes me wet. Every Single Damn Time. It's a look that suggests he's on the edge, even this early in the scene, even before her lips part, and she slides them over his head and down the length of his cock.

If I were playing this from memory, I'd have chosen a section later in the scene to relive. When Logan lapped at my clit, most likely, his fingers buried deep in my pussy while Raven jacked him off.

But I don't need to watch that scene to remember how it felt and pretty much anytime I close my eyes and touch myself, I'm recalling the way he fucked me with his fingers and tongue.

So this is the part I like to view again and again instead. I get crazy hot watching how turned on I made him that day, watching him buck against my jaw, his hands threaded in my hair, pulling and tugging while he used my mouth for his pleasure.

I made him react like that. *Me.*

Now, I watch the screen, my finger circling feather lightly over my clit. Any more pressure, I'll explode, and I want to drag it out. I want to wait until he shoves his cock deep into the mouth of the onscreen Devi, so deep that she can barely breathe and her eyes start to water from the effort. So deep that his tip tickles against her tonsils—I can recall the sensation vividly—causing her throat to tighten around him. When she looks up at him this time, she means it to be a cue for him to relax his grip. But before he does, her eyes lock on his and for a handful of seconds, she's caught there, so blown away by the ecstasy marked on his features that she nearly comes herself without any manual stimulation.

This is the moment I was waiting for, and I press harder on my clit, sliding the fingers of my other hand up inside me. I hook them so they'll brush across the highly sensitive inner walls of my pussy.

Then I'm there. I'm everywhere, detonating in a massive blast of pleasure and release that causes me to curl inward and sends tremors down my spine. It's amazing, and the amazing lingers as I fall back on to the bed, limp and relaxed.

I let out a sated sigh.

Followed by a frustrated groan as I remember seeing Logan at Vida's party the night before. How adorable he'd been with his wet clothing clinging to his tight body. How searing his gaze had been on my skin. How he'd flirted and bantered.

How I'd gone home alone.

Damn, Logan O'Toole and his super hot hotness.

I'd truly convinced myself that I'd built the memory of him up in my head, that he couldn't possibly be as alluring and charming and sexy as I'd remembered.

I was wrong. He was all of that and more. So Much More.

We clicked too. Last night was the first time we really had a conversation, and I know I'm not imagining the spark between us. A spark that went beyond physical attraction. He listened when I talked. He looked at my eyes and my lips instead of my breasts and ass. Well, instead of just my breasts and ass. There was even a moment—a couple of moments, actually—where I thought he might kiss me. I tilted my chin up, I parted my mouth, I ran my tongue along my lips—had he really not gotten the hint?

Considering what Logan does for a living, it's impossible to think he missed my cues.

Which means he's obviously not interested.

I let out another sigh, lamenting, and sit up to shut the laptop. But, if he wasn't interested, I think, then why did he ask for my number?

That has to mean he wants to hear from me. Doesn't it?

With a burst of optimism, I reach for my phone and start to compose a text. It takes only a handful of seconds before I realize that: (a) I have no idea what to say; and, (b) I'd be too chicken to say it even if I did. I mean, he's Logan O'Toole. He's a star. He can get whomever he wants, whenever he wants. He doesn't need random ex-coworkers falling all over him, and he certainly doesn't need me texting him in a post-orgasm haze.

Anyway, he probably only asked for my number because he was being polite. Or because I'm a good resource to have when trying to round out a cast with ethnically diverse women, something I know Logan is conscious about in his work. And I needn't be so bummed about it because: (a) I believe in ethnic diversity in porn; and, (b) the whole reason I went to the party in the first place was to get a job.

Actually, I should be proud of how the whole evening went. I stepped out of my comfort zone and talked to a couple of producers, one of whom promised to reach out with a project soon.

So when the phone, still clutched in my hand, buzzes with an incoming text, I swipe the screen, confident that the message is from a prospective boss, ignoring the flutter of hope that it's from Logan.

I'm sure you know that in Persia, Cassiopeia rides a two-humped camel. And I didn't tell you this just so I could say "hump" in my first message to you.

Before I have a chance to respond, a second text comes through.

Okay, maybe that's exactly why I told you that.

I'm still giggling when the third comes through.

Also, aren't you proud that I spelled Cassiopeia correctly even though I obviously used spell check?

God, he's adorable.

And Oh My God he's texting me!

I hop out of bed, suddenly filled with a nervous energy that's driving me to pace the room. Logan O'Toole, the guy who I dream about, the guy who wouldn't lean down and kiss me even though he'd gone down on me on-camera three years before is texting me.

I don't know what to think. Or feel.

Is he interested after all? His tone seems flirty, but maybe I'm misreading. He's always a bit flirty. It's part of his job.

But he remembered Cassiopeia.

I made enough of an impression for him to still be thinking about it the next day. Enough for him to research it and then send a message about it. That has to mean *something*. What, I don't know.

What I do know is that now I have to think of a response, and I have zero clue what it should be.

What to say, what to say?

I pace and compose several responses in my head before attempting to type out a reply, and even with the mental prep, I'm anxious when I respond: **You said "hump."** I add a blushing emoticon because it feels appropriate.

I said it twice. You know why, right?

I'm too excited to even bother with a guess. **No. Why?**

Because that's how many times I thought about humping while I typed out that message.

I choke on a giggle. His response is juvenile and ridiculous, but what does it mean? Does it mean he was thinking about humping in general or thinking about humping *me*?

Then I come to my senses. Of course he wasn't thinking about humping me. If he had any interest, he would have made a move last night. And because I'm so certain he didn't really intend any innuendo, I type back: **It's because there are two humps on the constellation that Cassiopeia rides on. You thought about it once for each hump.**

There's a delay before he responds, and I bite my lip while I wait, my legs still jelly from the orgasm I had fantasizing about him just a few minutes before. I grow hot again thinking about it and when my phone buzzes with his latest message, my heart is hammering in my chest before I even read the first word.

Yes. That's right. Though, if there was a camel last night, I don't remember it. I only saw Cassiopeia.

For half a second I consider letting my fantasies bloom, letting the things I *wish* twist into things that *are*, and I imagine that he means I'm as beautiful as the mythological Cassiopeia, and that he only had eyes for me.

But of course he means he only saw the stars, and he's as far away from me as the Persian Queen on her two-humped camel in the sky.

• • •

The text he sends that night takes a much different tone.

After Stanley Tucci gives Captain America that shot and he gets all muscle-y and even more Captain America-y than before, do you think he could still have sex with a regular person? Or is his dick too powerful for mere mortals?

I'm already in bed because it's late. A glance at the time says it's just after one. *It's the middle of the night and he's thinking of me.*

Nope. Stop. I have to remind myself not to get giddy. He's probably drunk texting all the girls on his contact list. I should set down my phone and banish him from my mind like I did all day long.

Except I didn't banish him from my mind at all.

I refrained from responding after his final confusing text that morning, and threw myself wholeheartedly into trying not to think about him. Which meant I thought about him quite a lot. While I scrubbed my bathtub. During my rollerblading workout on Santa Monica Pier.

Through my photo shoot for *Tommy's Toys,* an erotic image website I pose for on a regular basis.

"You're on tonight, Devi, baby," Tommy said as he clicked shot after shot. "Radiant and fuck-hot. Are you knocked up or something?"

"Uh, no. It's probably my new face cleanser." I wasn't using a new cleanser, but I spouted the lie anyway, not wanting to put voice to the real reason I was glowing: Logan O'Toole.

Later, in the shower, I rubbed myself to orgasm thinking about him again. Then spent the next twenty minutes promising myself that tomorrow I wouldn't think about him at all.

Now I'm tired and vulnerable, and when his Captain America text arrives, I surrender to his game, whatever it may be. **Can a dick really be TOO hard? It's his stamina I'd be more concerned about. The power behind his thrusts. He'd need to restrain himself if he were going to indulge in sexual activity.**

But what about when he blows his load? See, I think he'd come too hard for her to take it. His sperm would shoot through her like a bullet.

Smiling from ear-to-ear, I roll over to my stomach to type my reply. **Nah. You men always think that your cum is more impressive than it is. It's really just a tiny little splurt. Even with increased force, that's not hurting anyone.**

We aren't talking about my cum—which IS impressive, by the way. We're talking about Captain Fucking America.

I grow warm all over at the mention of his cum, and I have to take a series of deep breaths before responding. **Does the idea of that turn you on? Coming inside a woman so hard that it kills her?**

Well. Sort of. Yeah.

I laugh out loud. **You're sick.**

Guilty. Another text immediately follows. **Goodnight, Cass.**

And for the second night in a row, I go to bed with an ache between my thighs because of Logan O'Toole.

• • •

For the next several days, Logan continues to send random texts. I've given up trying to interpret his motivations and instead just enjoy the banter. The fun conversation has put me in a surprisingly good mood, despite my money woes, and on Wednesday morning, I even get the nerve to open up the UCLA website for the first time in months.

"You can do this," I say out loud to myself. "Just go through the list and pick something. Anything. One thing that interests you." There are so many things that appeal to me. This shouldn't be that hard.

But after only a couple of clicks around the site, I end up on a page that shows the five colleges on campus: The College of Letters and Science, The School of the Arts and Architecture, School of Engineering and Applied Science, School of Nursing, School of Theater, Film, and Television.

And then I freeze because I'm equally drawn to each of the schools listed. Science? Love it. Architecture? I'm game. Nursing? My parents are doulas—I've been raised to be a caretaker. Film? That's totally what I'm working in now—if porn counts, that is, and it does in my book. So how the hell am I supposed to pick just one career path when I can't even narrow it down to a single college of study?

I shut my laptop in a panic, but perk up when I hear my phone buzzing on the kitchen counter where I left it after dinner. Hoping the message is from Logan, I hurry over to check and respond.

But it's not Logan, and it's not a text. It's a phone call and the caller ID says it's one of the producers I met at Vida's party—LaRue Hagen.

LaRue Hagen isn't someone I'd usually take a call from. He works for *Sinner's Playpen,* a hardcore heterosexual porn site, not my scene. But since my parents' tarot reading suggested I be more open to new opportunities, however, I gave him my number.

As I answer, I pray that I'm not wasting my time.

"Devi Dare. I'm so glad to finally get you on the phone," LaRue says, as though he's been trying to reach me for days and not just for three rings. "Got a minute to talk?"

"I have exactly that," I say, though I have no plans for the evening. "So I hope you have your pitch prepared."

"Damn. A woman who plays hardball. I like it." LaRue hasn't been around as long as some of the old-school producers, but he's not a newbie either. He's an astute businessman who has also managed to stay innovative and politically correct. If I did decide to venture further into the world of porn, he's one of the few producers I'd trust.

"Fortunately," he says smoothly, "I do have my pitch prepared because it's not a pitch, but fact. We at *Sinner's Playpen* have watched your career in girl-girl porn take off over the last several months. If you think no one was noticing, you're wrong. We sincerely believe that if you crossed over into traditional heterosexual porn, 'P in V' so to speak, you'd take the world by storm."

I stifle a stunned laugh. I am pleased with my rise in the industry over the last year, but this guy is blowing things out of proportion. My paychecks certainly don't reflect someone whose career has "taken off."

Though models and lesbian porn stars don't make much money even when they are successful.

I shift my weight from one foot to the other. "That's awfully presumptuous, don't you think, Mr. Hagen?"

"It's LaRue. And not presumptuous—perceptive. I've been in this biz for a decade, Devi. I've watched many a star rise and fall, and, trust me, I know what kind of trajectory your career is going to take from here."

I lean against the doorframe of my galley kitchen. "I'm flattered, LaRue. I've also got to be honest with you—though I'm currently entertaining the possibility of doing some light heterosexual porn, I'd still like the majority of my work to be girl-on-girl. I'm definitely not looking to be a star."

"No one's ever looking to be a star."

The image of *The Star* from my parents' tarot deck flashes in my mind then disappears. It renders me momentarily speechless.

LaRue steps into the silence. "Tell you what—our site is limited on the femme porn, but I think I can line up a few jobs for you."

I'm skeptical. "Why would you do that?" I don't want to be obliged to work for him in the future just because he's hooking me up now.

"Because, Devi Dare, whether you're ready or not, you're going to cross over into harder scenes. We want to be there when you do."

What if it's true? What if I am destined to be the next Jenna Jameson or Tori Black? Is that the direction the proverbial wheel of fortune is taking me?

Not wanting to rule out any path that might take me to a better life, I give LaRue my agent's information and agree to do a femme shoot with *Sinner's Playpen* in the next few weeks.

It buys me time to think about his other offer—the one that could be the solution to all my money problems if I just make that final step.

I'm not even sure what's holding me back. My parents would support me, and I don't really have anything against fucking with strangers.

Just.

If I decide to really commit to this career, the chances of ever going back to school diminish significantly. And though I still don't have any idea what to major in, I'm not ready to decide that I'll never finish my degree.

But with bills looming I may have to decide something soon.

I desperately long to talk to someone about my options, someone else in the industry. Another actor or actress maybe. The only person I can think of to reach out to is Logan.

I unlock the screen that has gone dark in the last several seconds and type out a text: **Need advice. Are you free?**

Just as I'm about to send it, though, I have second thoughts. We really aren't close enough to delve into career discussions, certainly not over text.

Regardless, he's the only one I want to talk to, period.

I delete the words and instead send: **Do you believe that God/a higher power/the universe answers prayers/bequests/needs through porn/smut/erotic modeling?**

It's the first time I've initiated the conversation, and my heart flutters when his response is nearly immediate. **Devi, the answer is always porn.**

I laugh, and though nothing is solved or decided, I feel better. I don't have to make any firm plans right now anyway. LaRue will throw me some light work, and if that doesn't bring in enough money, I have options.

And even if the universe isn't really trying to guide me, I can still recognize the turn my fortune is taking. Maybe it's LaRue's confidence that's contagious, but it feels like people and situations are lining up for me. Perhaps even Logan's appearance in my life is fortuitous since his friendship could lead to a surer footing in the industry.

I don't expect that fate has other ideas for us. But, still, there's that star card—so I *hope* it does.

CHAPTER SIX

By now, you might be wondering, *how does a sweet guy like Logan O'Toole end up in the porn industry?*

To which I say three things:

Firstly, I wasn't always a guy named Logan O'Toole.

Secondly, why not?

Thirdly, I get why you wonder. I mean, my parents are both pharmaceutical scientists. I grew up in the "right" school district, in a house with a big pool and a remodeled kitchen, with cable but not HBO, with family dinners almost every night and family vacations a few times a year. We went to a blandly pleasant Episcopal church on a semi-regular basis, we volunteered twice a month at a food bank in the city. I never touched drugs, I only slept with two girls in high school, the only trouble I ever had with the law was a speeding ticket one morning when I was late for class.

No, I was never destined to do porn. After high school, I was destined for an undergrad in film studies and the same sort of life my parents had before me and their parents had before them, except I planned to be wielding a camera instead of a microscope.

It was a series of accidents that altered my trajectory, that sent me spinning out of orbit and into the uniquely heavy gravity of the porn world.

It started with my theater teacher approaching me after school in the spring of my senior year. He had a friend who was filming a commercial for a local community college, and would I like to give him a call? It would be easy work and the first non-retail line on my flimsy resume, and even though I wanted to be a director or a cinematographer, it never hurt to explore acting too, right?

I did the commercial. And then I did another, this time for a dating website aimed at college kids, which led to a commercial for a "companionship" phone-line, a dying service in 2005, but apparently still strong enough to pay for a television ad. I never lied to my parents about what I was doing, and to their credit, they never tried to dissuade me from it, even though it must have been awkward for them to see my phone sex commercials while they were trying to watch *CSI* reruns.

And that's how I accidentally got into the commercial business.

This lasted about three months, and the day after graduation, while I was squinting at my computer screen, trying to parse my UCLA orientation email, I got a call from the director of the hotline ad.

"Hey kid, I've got a friend who likes your face, and he's short an extra for a little movie he's filming next week. You'd get fifty bucks a day, plus lunch. You in?"

The only thing I had planned for my summer was my part-time job at Best Buy, and honestly, getting paid to stand around on a film set sounded like a much better opportunity. I quit my Best Buy job and drove up to the set that next week, assuming a "little movie" meant an indie film or maybe a made-for-cable shlock-fest.

I was wrong on both counts. After meeting with the casting director—who was also the script supervisor—I was led back to the pool, where a woman lay on her back moaning, her hand buried inside of her lace panties. I remember watching, mesmerized, as the director occasionally called out instructions—more about the mechanics of her masturbation than about her acting.

"Spread your legs a little wider, Tara, we have a shadow."

"Okay, now use both hands."

"Rub your chest a little, please. Good."

I glanced back over the thin script I'd been handed. I hadn't read it over yet, because I knew I didn't have a speaking role, but now I read the lines with avid fascination. Lonely housewife. Seductive gardener. And me, "Pool Party Guest #2," who was scheduled to linger in the background with a red Solo cup and a veneer of partygoer merriment.

And that's how I accidentally got into the soft-core porn business.

From there on out, it was a series of gradual steps onward—or downward, depending on your point of view. The director liked me, and I came back the next week for a film about a naughty college cheerleader who falls for her professor. I played her jilted boyfriend—a role that required a scene where I received a blowjob, something that I initially had mixed feelings about. On one hand, no eighteen-year-old male has ever felt despair at the prospect of a blowjob, but on the other hand, it felt strange to be sucked off and then handed a check.

Not wrong, necessarily. But strange.

I don't remember much about that scene—my very first—but I do remember the actress, Traci Aliss, who's now married to a podiatrist and lives somewhere in Arizona. She was Asian-American, with glossy-smooth hair and flawless skin, and even with all the unnecessary makeup, the most beautiful woman I'd ever seen in my life. I'd never been touched in front of an audience, and so I'd been worried about staying hard with all those eyes on me. But when Traci trained her eyes on my face, licking her lips as she unzipped my pants, all of my apprehension vanished. I felt something I'd never felt before in my life, something deeper than lust, something essential, something akin to what I felt when I watched my favorite movies.

I suppose Devi would call it *bigness*. For a moment, I felt the entire expansive bigness of the world, of Traci's glowing skin, of the sunlight coming in harsh and bright through the window, of the subtle dynamic of power that coursed between us. I didn't feel like a boy who didn't have his future figured out, a boy who already felt limited by a path he'd barely stepped on.

I felt like a man. And I threaded my hands through Traci's hair and I murmured everything I felt to her, I told her what I wanted her to do to me and what I wanted to do to her, and for a moment, I could tell that she was as lost in the scene as I was. That despite the cameras—or maybe because of them—these sensations were galvanized into something exhilarating and intoxicating, and we both ended the scene filled with a sense of happy magic.

The director was so pleased with my performance that he asked to do another film, and another, and another, and by the end of the summer, I'd made five thousand dollars by having sex on camera, with the promise that I could make more if I was willing to segue into hardcore pornography.

I was.

After signing with a talent agency, I cancelled my UCLA classes, told my shocked but accepting parents, and rented an apartment in Burbank.

And that's how I accidentally became a porn star.

• • •

You're right. Porn is always the answer. No wonder those people keep losing on Family Feud.

That's the first thing waiting on my screen when I wake up. It's crazy what falling asleep without half a bottle of whiskey will do for a man's energy, and during the past week, the urge to go whiskey-numb has slowly diminished. Part of it is Vida's offer, an offer that I'm still trying to think of something for.

And part of it is Devi, my personal Cassiopeia, my Persian Queen.

But even thinking those words sends weird shivers down my spine, hot and cold flashes of lust and excitement, and also fear. Because what if she doesn't feel the same way I do? What if I'm just that friendly guy she did a scene with once?

Or worse, the guy who spurned her advances at a party?

Fuck.

Don't I give great advice? I text back to Devi, still lying in bed. **I can't believe I got fired from writing fortunes for the fortune cookie factory.**

No response. Not for the first time this week, I wonder if I'm bothering her with my texts, intruding on what I imagine to be her well-ordered, healthy, beachy life. Maybe she's just tolerating me because she doesn't want to be rude. Maybe she actually thinks I'm pathetic—too limp-dicked to kiss her at Vida's and now texting her like a boy in middle school.

I let the phone drop to the comforter and groan. I should leave her alone, I should bottle up this years-long crush I've had on her and give her space.

But then she texts me back and I'm diving for the phone again.

So tell me, O Wise One. I'm thinking about maybe doing some mainstream scenes. You know—with guys instead of girls. What do you think?

What do I think? I think I want to run over to her place now and make sure I'm the first male performer on her list! But no, I need to think like a friend and a mentor, not like a guy that jacks off to her every night.

Hardcore? I ask. A lot of people hear *hardcore* and think of extreme porn—BDSM and rough sex and all that, but really all it means is explicit. In hardcore porn, you get to see all the good stuff happening, pussy-eating and ejaculation and actual fucking. A lot of Devi's lesbian scenes could be considered hardcore, since she goes down on girls sometimes and they go down on her.

Yes, she texts back. **But nothing too intense. No kink or group-sex. I'm on the fence about anal.**

On the fence? No, no, no, you're supposed to be bent over the fence. I can't help myself. I'm only human.

Har har har. I don't have anything against it—but I really don't know if I could do it with just any performer, you know? I'd want to be with someone I trust.

I groan again, turning my face into the pillow. My dick is stirring from all this Devi-anal talk, and God, I wish I could be the performer she trusted. I would make her feel so good, I'd go slow, warm her up with all the orgasms she needed to relax, and then I'd make her feel like a glowing goddess. I'd use my fingers first, probing as I kissed and licked her cunt, and then I'd slowly work her open, sucking on her clit until her toes curled. I'd make her come with my dick inside her pussy, and while she was coming down, I would roll her onto her side, get on my knees and gently press inside. And then I'd make her come with my dick in her ass.

You're making me too hard to think straight, Cass.
Very funny, Logan. But really, what should I do?

Does she honestly think I'm joking about being hard? Does she not realize the impact she has on me?

Of course she doesn't, Captain Skinny-Dick. All she has to go on is how you pulled away in the pool.

I force myself to focus on her question. **You know me, my camel-riding queen. I'll always say do more porn. But make sure that it's stuff you feel comfortable with—stuff you feel safe and happy doing. Work with people you trust.**

This is unexpectedly serious for me, and I feel a little self-conscious pressing *send*. She doesn't respond, and I hope it's because she's mulling over what I've said and not because she's rolling her eyes at how suddenly pretentious and paternalistic I've gotten.

This doesn't solve the problem of me being hard, however. Hard and dying for a taste of Devi—her skin, her lips, her cunt. I reach down and circle my erection, using my other hand to cup my balls, which are heavy and aching for release.

I glance at my clock—eight in the morning. Ginger will be here in a few hours to shoot a scene, and as good as it would feel to rub one out right now, it might feel even better to use Ginger's wet pussy to get off. I squeeze my dick gently, imagining it now, Ginger tied up and helpless while I stroked in and out.

I would give my eyeteeth for it to be Devi, though.

With a groan of extreme restraint, I get out of the bed. I shower in some cold water to kill my boner and then brush my teeth. Once I'm all clean and minty, I trundle to my kitchen in only a pair of jeans to make a cup of coffee and wait for Tanner. He and I need to do some extensive blocking for the scene today because Ginger has decided she wants to try the harder, kinkier stuff, so we'll have some props going on and some cues that I'll mention in my monologue when we record it after the scene.

While I wait for the Keurig to power up, I open up my laptop and make a new Word document. I type in Ginger's name at the top, along with the date and the style of scene we're filming.

I film all sorts of scenes—sweet ones, filthy ones, public ones, scripted ones—and I try to make every monologue match the tone of the sex. I've become a bit famous for these monologues, which was a surprise to everyone when I started doing them a few years ago. Who wants to sit and listen to a guy talk for ten minutes before the fucking gets started? Who wants to wait for the penis-in-vagina, the *p-in-v*, just to hear the guy talk about the girl and what he loves about their sex?

A lot of people, actually.

A lot.

And I enjoy doing it. Honestly. What turns me on, what turns a girl on, what makes sexy, filthy porn—I could talk about that shit all day.

I limit myself to ten minutes though.

I won't draft the full monologue script until after the scene, but I go ahead and skeleton in several of the things I know I want to say. That right now, Ginger's newness to kink inspires me to be rougher than I normally am. That her submission fantasies and my domination fantasies dovetail perfectly, and that when we're fucking, I like to imagine dirty things, nasty things.

I won't say that I imagine Devi when I'm screwing Ginger, or that all of these dirty, nasty fantasies come to my mind when I'm alone in my bed with my hand under the sheets and one of Devi's girl/girl scenes on the laptop next to me. That would dispel the fantasy that I'm trying to create with my monologues, the fantasy that I sort of sexually fall in love with every girl I film with. But still, it's Devi I'm thinking about while I drag the bondage bed out of its usual corner in the basement and into the center of the concrete-floored playroom I had built here for filming scenes.

It's not nearly as elaborate as Vida's, but it works. Bare floor (easy to clean, plus it adds to that dungeon vibe people like), racks of toys and restraints, and chains and hooks dangling from the ceiling.

God, Devi would look good here, strapped down and waiting for me. Or maybe with those toned arms bound and stretched up toward the ceiling…

By the time Tanner and Ginger arrive, my hard-on is back and I'm more than ready to begin fucking.

• • •

Thirty minutes later, after we verbally run through Ginger's limits and make sure she's cool with what Tanner and I have come up with for the scene, she's flat on her back on the bondage bed and I'm buckling the cuffs around her wrists, subtly checking to make sure the cuffs aren't cutting off blood flow to her hands and fingers. It's something that I've done hundreds of times, and I smile affectionately down at her. Is there anything better than a great day on a great job with an old friend? And then out of the corner of my eye, I see my phone light up on the table behind Tanner, and my heart thumps with an electric judder, knowing it could be another text from Devi.

It really is a fantastic day.

"We're going to have fun now," I tell Ginger, practically humming as I move down to cuff her ankles.

Tanner's filming behind us, and there are a couple of other crew guys here today to help, and so Ginger is *on*, tilting her head so that the camera can't miss her seductive smile as she replies, "I know. I can't wait for you to fuck me."

This is the part where I should respond in kind, maybe growl something harsh and kinky, but I'm still in this bubble of goodwill and happiness, and my mind is full of Devi and stars, so instead I say, "I'm going to make you feel as beautiful as Cassiopeia today."

Ginger gives me a look that isn't just blank. It's blankness with shock and ignorance and the slightest whiff of humiliation. *She has no idea what I've just said*, I think. So I add, "Cassiopeia was an ancient Greek queen."

She looks a little taken aback by this, like she still doesn't know how to respond, like Greek mythology has no place in a BDSM porn scene, and after a couple of beats, she arches her back and purrs, "But you can't make me feel like a queen, because I've been such a bad girl."

And then she wriggles in her restraints, her mouth in a little moue of disappointment. "Stop talking, and punish me, Sir."

And my happy bubble starts to collapse in on itself.

Because of course Greek mythology has no place on a porn set. Of course Ginger doesn't want to make small talk or flirt or listen to my stupid thoughts. She's here to be flogged and fucked, and as friendly as we might be, we're not friends in the normal sense of the word. We're co-workers, colleagues, and Ginger is like the girl in the next cubicle at an office. As chatty as we might be in a meeting, we'll never be anything more.

And it's not just Ginger. Can I honestly claim that any of the other girls I work with are anything more than friendly co-workers? That they wouldn't get impatient with me if I wanted to talk about constellations instead of simply get on with the scene so we can all get paid and back to our real lives?

Devi wouldn't be like that, though.

Or would she? a worried voice in my mind wonders.

Tanner shifts behind me, and I snap out of my bubble-collapsing reverie. *Focus, Logan.* Now isn't the time for existential fussing.

I return all of my attention to Ginger and run a practiced hand down her bare stomach. She shivers, and I walk over to the wall and come back with a flogger.

"So you've been a bad girl?" I say with rehearsed menace.

She nods, biting her lip. One of the light guys follows Tanner as he moves around the table, and I see the shadow of the flogger outlined on her stomach. And despite all of my internal complaining, my dick is responding precisely the way it should, still a hard rod in my jeans.

"Then let's get started."

Ginger squirms as I begin flogging her—lightly. Since this is one of the first real bondage scenes she's done, I try to make it less about the pain and more about the subtle humiliation, more about the power dynamics between her and me. She doesn't have very many limits, but she brought up extreme pain as one, and I'm doing my best to keep her feeling safe and comfortable, just like I told Devi to do this morning.

So I keep the riding crop light, with small, flat-sounding slaps against her skin, just enough to redden her freckled skin the tiniest bit. Then I reach down to pluck at her nipples and slide my fingers into her mouth, and after ten or fifteen minutes of this, I reach between her legs and find her swollen and wet.

"Look at me," I tell her, and she does, her eyes glazed with lust and her hips moving on the table. She makes a small noise of frustration when I lift my hand from her pussy, and I know we've crossed the boundary between pretend and real, where the cameras and the contracts are starting to blur into the background as the needy hum in her core becomes all-consuming.

Which is perfect, because I'm hard as a fucking rock and aching to sink into her—into any woman, if I'm being honest—to get some relief.

I mean, there are other things I could do right now. I could bring out a different flogger, I could flip her over and paddle her, I could fuck her mouth until her eyes water. But Jesus fuck, I am so caught up in wanting Devi, in craving her, that I don't have the patience to wait any longer. That raw, gripping need to come is clawing at me, and Ginger is so lovely right now, with her freckled limbs and panting mouth, and wet, pink cunt.

I unbuckle the cuffs quickly and easily, intoning in my sternest voice that she is not to move until she's been given permission, and then I grab the spreader bar from the wall. There are a hundred creative things I could do right now—and should do, given that this is a bigger scene than usual—but I barely have enough focus left to flip her onto her hands and knees and attach the spreader bar to her ankles. I cuff her wrists to the spreader as well, which has the effect of forcing her head forward onto the table as her arms are stretched underneath her to the bar, and then I make a circle around the table. It looks as if I'm admiring my handiwork, which I am, to an extent, running a hand over her raised ass, biting my lip once I see how much her seam glistens in the dim, indoor light. But I'm also making one final check to make sure that she can breathe easily, that her weight is distributed comfortably, and to give her an easy opportunity to snap her fingers—our pre-arranged signal—if she needs a break or needs me to back off.

She's comfortable and there's no snapping; she even gives me a flirty wink when I walk around the side she's facing. I give her ass a slap, hop up onto the table on my knees, and I'm as giddy as a teenage boy when I unzip my jeans and push them low enough to free my erection, which has been straining against the denim all this time.

After sheathing myself with a condom, I line up the head of my cock with her opening and push inside, giving her ass a few spanks as I do. She's wet and warm and willing, all I need right now, and I can't help my mind drifting to Devi, to the fantasy of Devi pinned underneath me as I finger her ass and fuck her pussy.

It's filthy, but hey, I'm a filthy guy.

I get going, really get going, burying myself deep into Ginger's channel and stroking back out again. Yeah, that feels good. So good.

"You feel amazing on my cock, baby," I tell her, leaning forward to croon in her ear. I don't know if the camera can hear us, but I don't care, because I always talk to my girls, especially when they're edging towards the brink like Ginger. "You feel like you were built to have a big dick in this pussy, isn't that right? Don't big cocks like mine need to be taken care of?"

She nods and moans as I find her clit with one hand and work her mercilessly, rubbing until she has no choice but to come, and she does, so hard that her leg muscles quiver and she lets out a little shriek.

"Another," I growl, fucking her hard now, and I rub another climax out of her as I pound into her pussy, making her scream with pleasure.

And my vision splits and merges and splits again, sometimes Ginger's pale ass up in the air, sometimes Devi's bronze body writhing under mine, sometimes both. And then I'm grunting hard, pulling out just in time to yank off the condom and pump lashing jets of cum all over Ginger's ass. I milk myself with long, taut strokes, but the orgasm keeps barreling through me, and by the time I'm finally done, I'm barely able to keep myself upright.

I fall back on my heels, spent and also a little grateful that I didn't jerk off this morning, saving myself for this. It was worth it. Even if I wished it were Devi the entire time.

"Um…" Ginger says with a weak, post-orgasmic laugh. "I think I may need some baby wipes over here."

The laughter is contagious, spreading from me to Tanner to the crew, and I move to help her get uncuffed and cleaned up.

• • •

By the time mid-afternoon rolls around, my house is empty and I'm in my office, editing my monologue.

The digital version of me gazes out of the screen, raking his fingers through his light brown hair and grinning as he talks about Ginger.

"…always a new fantasy," the on-screen version of me is saying. "Today, I wanted to pretend that we'd just met at a BDSM club, and that she was a new submissive that I had to break in—gently at first, and then not-so-gently after." The Logan on the screen goes on to elaborate on the fantasy—being a skilled Master at a club, the thrill of meeting a new submissive, the satisfaction of feeling a stranger come around my cock.

For the first time, in a very real and concrete way, I wish that the scene had been a mirror to my monologue. Normally, my words complement the scene, act as a stimulating adjuvant, and the sex is still the chief enjoyment for me. But something's off today, and when I finish editing the thing and save it, I feel a sense of nostalgia, a slightly bitter pang of loss—both emotions so sudden and unexpected that I feel genuine shock once I realize they're what I'm feeling.

From the moment Traci Aliss wrapped her lips around my cock, I knew that I'd found my calling. I knew that I loved to fuck, and what's more, I knew that I loved to fuck around other people. I never forget while I'm filming that thousands of men and women will watch me at home—the women wishing it were me between their legs instead of their vibrator, the men wishing they *were* me, fucking a sweet pussy or a wet mouth or tight ass. And the thought of all that desire and jealousy heaped on me—it's more than a turn-on. It's a *raison d'etre*.

So what's wrong today? Why don't I have that post-scene high? I mean, of course there have been days where the sex was less than magical, where it honestly did feel like work, where the girl and I couldn't connect, or maybe I was tired or unmotivated or whatever. But I've never felt like this. I've never felt this peculiar emptiness, this odd disappointment, especially not after such an amazing scene.

So what am I disappointed about?

I have no idea.

I spin around in my chair a few times, rubbing my bare feet against the fuzzy-ass rug on my office floor, the one I bought even though Raven had hated it when we saw it in the store. I tap my fingers on my knees, I fiddle with a paperclip on my desk, and then finally, frustrated as hell, I stand up and walk out to the loft that overlooks my living room.

Other than a few low chairs and the waterfalls of golden sun pouring through the skylights, the room is vacant. An empty living room in an empty house.

Mentally, I direct the scene otherwise. I layer in the sound of Prior's paws scrabbling on the wood floors as he trotted around the house looking for his squeaky toy. I layer in the neo-punk music Raven played whenever she was here, and I layer in Raven herself, wearing something black and clingy, her phone wedged between her head and her shoulder as she stirred a pot of kale or something equally disgusting on the stove.

For the first time in three months, I consider—really consider—that maybe I wasn't as in love with Raven as I was with the idea of having a relationship in the first place. That it wasn't her I keened for in those bleak days in the movie theater or on my kitchen floor, it was that *life*. That life with noise and affection and connection.

The realization hits me like a freight train, freeing and terrifying all at once. I loved Raven, I know I did, but so much of that love was because she was filling a void for me, a void I hadn't known was there until three months after it yawned open and empty again. She gave me a fantasy, *the* fantasy, and I slowly begin to understand that it is the fantasy that underpins all the ones I film for my scenes.

The fantasy of being in love.

Jesus.

I scrub my face with my hands, feeling liberated and also feeling pathetic. Who in this selfish, indulgent, spray-tanned city would ever guess that Logan O'Toole has a chewy caramel center? That under his I'll-fuck-anything-that-moves veneer, there is a guy who just wants to love someone?

It's ridiculous. And bad for business. I'm the guy who thinks with his dick, not his heart, and maybe my brand is to be a little bit of both, but I can't give in to this inner boy band song. Maybe guys like me don't get to have love. Not the kind of deep, real, raw love that I want. We get casual fucks and friendships coupled with the occasional stoned blowjob, and if we're really lucky, maybe we meet a girl whose life will travel on parallel tracks to ours for a while. But those tracks always diverge, and then we're left alone. Again.

This love shit isn't just bad for business, Logan, it's bad for you, a voice tells me. And I agree.

I let the image of my life with Raven fade away, until there's only my ground floor again, every corner and every floorboard and every nook in the soaring ceiling screaming out the emptiness of my house. My hands grip the ledge tighter and then loosen as I let go of the memories of a life with love, let go of the fantasy.

But it all still tumbles around in my mind, tossed loosely around like clothes in a dryer, tangling with the texts from Devi that I keep re-reading, tangling with my strange disappointment over my scene with Ginger. And all of it tangling with Vida's business proposal, until a new thought emerges, unformed and flopping as all new ideas are. But the moment my mind seizes hold of it, I can't let it go.

I stand there for a moment more, blinking, and then I jog back to my office to find the card Vida gave me at her party. I dial the number on it, relieved to hear the Dutch-accented voice saying *Hallo?* after only two rings.

"Marieke," I say. "It's Logan. I have an idea for me and Lelie, and I'd like to tell you about it."

CHAPTER SEVEN

I'm standing in line at the post office when my phone starts playing "Pussy Monster" by Lil Wayne, and I realize that I hadn't fully considered this possible situation when I programmed all my contacts the night before to have distinct ringtones. At the time, assigning that song for Logan's number seemed like a secret sexy joke. But now that my cell is singing, "I'm the Pussy Monster, and you better feed me pussy, pussy, pussy, pussy, pussy" in a crowded public building, I think I quite possibly made a bad decision.

With cheeks hot from humiliation and nervousness (Logan is calling me!), I abandon my place in line and head outside to dig through my purse and find my cell. I'm breathless when I finally hit talk. "Hello?"

"Devi?"

"Hi! Logan. I…" *can't believe it's really you and ohmygod I can't believe you're calling me even though you text me pretty much every day.*

I won't tell him that. "Hello," I say again instead. "Hi." *I'm an idiot.*

Logan's so smooth that he almost makes me feel at ease, even as he laughs. "I think we have a greeting established. Should we move on?"

"Yeah." I cover my face with my hand. "Yes. Sorry. I was… distracted…when you called."

"Distracted? That sounds intriguing. Tell me more about that."

He has no idea that I have a massive secret crush on him, but sometimes, when his voice is layered like this with thick innuendo and comprehension, I wonder if he possibly *could* know.

Which is a ridiculous thing to wonder. He probably treats every woman as though she's madly in love with him, and every woman likely *is* madly in love with him. So of course he knows I'm harboring affection as well. Because, who isn't?

But hell if I'm admitting the ringtone I've assigned him.

"I just." I sigh into the mouthpiece, regrouping. "I was in line at the post office, and I hadn't realized my phone wasn't on silent. So your call surprised me."

"Ah. I see." He's quiet, and I decide he's as disappointed with my lame answer as I am. He probably regrets calling me.

"But thank goodness it wasn't on silent. Because then I would have missed you all together." Yep, I'm totally transparent.

And I totally want to die.

But it's not likely that I'm going to spontaneously fall dead, and also I'm curious about what he wants, so I ask, "Anyway, what's up?" He's never called before, and the reasons he could be calling now are swimming through my mind.

Or *one* reason is swimming—the reason that he might be calling for a date. The other ideas are drowning in my optimism.

"Actually, I…" He pauses, as though he's nervous too, which, of course, is impossible, but wouldn't it be nice if I could let myself think that? That he's as off-balance around me as I am around him?

In his hesitation, the hopeful tension grows until I can't stand it. "Yes?"

"I wondered if you were free later today," he says quickly—excitedly, maybe. "I need to see you."

"You do?" It's probably not cool to question it. "I mean, no, I'm not. Or…did you ask if I was busy or if I was free?"

"You know, I don't remember now."

I let out a chuckle that sounds an awful lot like a giggle. "Well, whatever you said, I'm not busy. I could see you. If you want." *Way to sound nonchalant, Devi.*

"I do want." His tone is so low I almost am unsure that's what he really said. Louder, he says, "That's great. I have a meeting right now, but I could do three-ish?"

Somehow I manage to speak like an intelligent human being as we arrange the specifics. Then we hang up, and I clutch the phone to my chest and let out an uncharacteristic squeal.

Two women jogging by throw me narrow glances, but who cares? I already have to find another post office to patronize, and I have a date with Logan O'Toole.

• • •

When I arrive at the coffee shop where we agreed to meet, I find him already in line to order. He hasn't seen me yet, and I take the opportunity to check him out. He's wearing jeans and a white T-shirt, not too tight, but thin enough to make out the muscles in his back. I'm overwhelmed with sense memory—the way he smelled, the way his fingers dug into my jaw as he held the sides of my face, the way his tongue felt darting over my skin, between my lips.

I shiver. It's been three years, and, yet, his is the only touch I remember.

I come up behind him in the line and nudge my shoulder against the back of his arm.

"Hey, there you are." He turns to give me the hug that's standard in Europe and Hollywood, and I have to force myself not to audibly sigh or cling.

I'm disappointed when he pulls away. But then he glides his eyes down my body, and I think I might not care if he never touched me again, as long as he keeps looking at me like he is now. His stare is invasive and warm and thorough.

I'm suddenly shy, which is strange. Because I've been naked with Logan O'Toole, and yet I've never felt as undressed as I do when he looks me over now. My outfit is casual—tan short shorts and a cream halter-top. I spent forever choosing it, but I glance down at my appearance, trying to see myself with different eyes, imagining what he sees, and I can't figure it out. The girl I see is curvy and lush with dark exotic features and piercing eyes. She's beautiful—I've never doubted my allure—but compared to the women he spends his time with on a daily basis, I'm same old, same old.

So why is he gazing at me as though he's never seen anything like me before? Why am I certain no one will ever see me this wholly again?

In an effort to break the delicious tension, I ask, "Am I late?"

"Nope. I'm early," and he's still looking at me like he could devour me, and the air in the shop is stifling, and my clothes feel heavy and tight, and I'm not sure how I'll make it through a minute with him, let alone a whole afternoon, and then it's our turn at the register, and he finally breaks his gaze and I can breathe again.

He orders first then gestures to me. I order my usual black Americano and give the barista my name. Logan pays then we step aside in unison to wait while our drinks are prepared.

Logan stuffs his hands in his pockets and gives me a curious glance. "So you go by Devi all the time?"

"Well, it's my name."

"For real? You changed it legally or…?"

"It's what my parents named me. They're sort of hippies." That's an understatement, but I don't want to scare him away on the first date. Then again, maybe it's best to be upfront. "Okay, they're actual hippies. No sort of about it. They believe in self-fulfilling prophecy—they name things what they want them to be."

"They wanted you to be a porn star?"

"They wanted me to be a goddess."

"So, yes." He waits for me to laugh before saying, "But Dare can't be your last name."

I shake my head. "It's not. It's short for Daryani. My full name is Devi Arezu Daryani." I've gone through periods of both pride and shame at having such a Middle Eastern name. I love that it's unique and exotic, but the stereotyping that comes with it, notsomuch. I've had racial slurs slung at me on more than one occasion—everything from camel jockey to mosquito to nightclub bomber. Airport security is always a pain in the ass. I swear I'm on a permanent watch list, pulled aside for additional searching every damn time.

But when I deliver my whole name to Logan, I say it with dignity. It's impossible not to feel self-respect with him. Even when his eyes wander to other parts of my body, he seems to be intently interested in what I have to say.

"What does Arezu mean?" He pronounces it pretty well for having heard it so quickly—ah-REH-Zaw—and the sound of him saying a part of my name that no one typically even attempts gives me goose bumps. I wish he'd say it again and again. Wish he'd say it in a more intimate setting. Wish I could hear him growl it and groan it and make it his own.

"It means 'longed for.'"

"How appropriate," he says quietly, and since he has no idea the struggle my parents went through to have me, the series of miscarriages and fertility rituals, I have to assume he's flirting, and I look away, suddenly warm.

"You know why I picked O'Toole for my name?"

I turn back to him. "Why?"

"Because I have plenty of O'Toole."

"How appropriate," I say, because it's funny and because I want him to know I didn't miss it when he said it.

The smile he gives me makes me ache in places I shouldn't be thinking about in public.

So I *don't* think about them. "Is Logan your birth name?"

"Nope."

"Then what is it?"

He stretches past me to grab the two coffee cups from the barista. "I'll never tell."

I realize he's serious about not telling when he immediately dives into another subject as he leads me to a sitting area in the back corner of the shop. "Hippies, huh? Then they're cool with your line of work?"

I take a seat in a wicker chair. "They're cooler than cool. They support me in everything I do as 'long as I'm happy and fulfilled.' Which is nice." I recognize how contrary my tone is, and I'm compelled to expand. "Just, I sometimes think it would be nicer if they would be more parent-y and told me what to do instead."

Logan's brow rises as he sits across from me and sets our drinks down on the table between us. "What to do about what?"

"I don't know. Anything. Everything. My career. School. My life." Listening to myself, I realize how young I am or how much older Logan is, and suddenly I feel awkward and immature. "Maybe I'm just not very good at adulting."

"Oh, adulting is terrible. I recommend only doing it when absolutely necessary. Like when you're out of clean clothes or when you're trying to decide whether or not to put on a condom. Beyond that, leave the adulting to adults."

I grin as I tilt my head to study him. "Strange that someone with that philosophy would choose to go into the *adult* film business."

"But that's a misnomer. Porn is the least adult-y line of work there is, except for maybe, say, clowning."

"Such respect for your job," I laugh. "Do you even like what you do?"

"Are you kidding me? I fucking love it. Pun intended."

I take a sip of my coffee, enjoying how easy the conversation is. I've watched pretty much every Logan O'Toole video out there—interviews and candid conversations as well as his porns. And while I realized he was charming, it's a lot different having his charm directed at me. It feels strangely intimate, more intimate than having his lips on my privates, and I want to explore this intimacy as long as he'll let me. "What do you love about it? Besides the fucking, I mean."

His brow creases as though he's thinking, but his answer comes fairly quickly. "The hours are good. The money's decent. The after-parties are the best time there is, and there's little-to-no stigma for sleeping with your coworkers."

My heart flips at the wink he gives me and any response I had escapes me.

Fortunately, he's still capable of conversation. "What about you? I've only ever seen you in lesbian porn, except for the film we did together." He avoids eye contact as he mentions our scene, and I wonder if he thinks that's polite or if it's because he's thinking of Raven. It hasn't been long since they've broken up, and I have a strong suspicion that she is to blame for his strange behavior at Vida's party.

I don't want Raven in his thoughts, so I decide to sidestep the reference to that scene, and the minute I do I realize he said he's seen my work. Which shouldn't be a shock since a lot of people have seen my work, and he *is* very in tune with what's going on in the industry.

But, oh my God. He's watched my work. How has that possibility never crossed my mind, and why do I find that so goddamned hot?

He grins, knowing he's thrown me off-balance. "So you mentioned maybe doing some more mainstream stuff. Have you decided? Will you go wider?" he asks, a devilish spark in his eyes. "Again, pun intended."

"Maybe. If I got the right offer." *Innuendo intended.*

He leans in and rests his elbows on the table between us. "What would the right offer look like? I'm curious."

It would look just like you. We're flirting, and if I were really brave, that's what I'd say. Or, if I wanted to be a touch more demure, I could say, *Make your bid and I'll tell you if you're close.* It's not a case of not having the snappy comebacks, because I do.

But even with the teasing banter, I haven't got a sense of what's going on between us, or what he intends to happen, or why he's asked me out, and the uncertainty prompts me to be cautious. "I still haven't decided what I'm looking for in a P in V shoot. You were right about one thing—even aside from anal, I'd want to feel safe. That's important to me. I have no problem taking my clothes off and fucking a stranger, but I've got to have complete say in what happens with my body both on and off set."

"Of course."

I relax muscles I didn't know were tense when Logan doesn't automatically get defensive about my insinuation that there are sets in the business that are not safe, especially for women. Too many times consent gets blurred when the camera turns off and an aroused male doesn't behave any differently than he did when the record light was on. It's not a pretty side of the industry, but it's also nothing new, and, actually, there are many professionals taking strides to change it.

"Other than that…" I consider. "I guess I'd want to feel like I'm doing something important or innovative. The girl-on-girl work that I do is important because the producers I've chosen to shoot with are all very pro-feminist and ethnically diverse. They're bold. They're progressive."

He nods. "That's not always as easy to find in the het environment."

"No, definitely not." I cringe inwardly as I realize that venturing into politics on a first date is not the sexiest of moves. I won't pander or downplay my convictions to impress a guy, but I need to be sensitive to the fact that I'm talking about his world. "I mean, it's getting better. I think. I hope."

"I think it is. There's still work to do," he says, and I'm relieved that he seems sincere. "There's always work to do, but I'd like to say I've seen a change even in the decade I've worked in the industry. I'd like to say I've been part of the change, and I want to help move it even further forward. Not just in terms of diversity and safety, but also in terms of artistic quality."

Artistic quality is not a buzzword I've heard from many of the producers I've worked with, and it hits me that even though Logan's films are always on trend, they also have a deeper level to them and tons of visual appeal. "Are you one of those people that misses old-school feature films?"

"Yes. And no. It's frustrating that anyone with a handheld can make a porno now. There are so many shitty homemade sex scenes, how can a regular Joe Schmo find anything with quality?

"But gonzo isn't completely terrible," he says, referring to the style of filming that puts the cinematographer in the production. "There are so many good things about it. The camera angles, the intimacy, the spontaneity—all of those are qualities that have advanced the industry and made it more accessible to the average Internet subscriber. So, what's missing from today's porn that should be brought back? Not the production costs. Or the bad acting. Storylines? John Stagliano insists that his films, even though they're gonzo style, have a story. And they do, but they're like the movies from the past. The plots are weak and unbelievable, and yes, I know they're supposed to be fantasies, but tell me, do you know anyone whose fantasy is *Debbie Does Dallas*?"

He pauses just long enough for me to shake my head. "Exactly. So we need to keep the camera techniques, the intimate filming quality, and the tight budget, and then get better actors and plots."

I'm transfixed as he talks about this thing he's obviously so passionate about, and while I'm hanging on every word, I'm also somewhere outside of myself, watching this man who is so nerdy and sexy and nothing at all like the "typical" porn star. He doesn't even have the look of the traditional film leads. He's toned but slim, not at all beefy like Rocco Siffredi or Bruce Venture, or hyper-masculine like Manuel Ferrara. Logan's clean-cut and tattoo-free with his endearingly boyish (and handsome) face, and maybe that's why he's such a force right now—because he's fresh and different and real.

Well, that, and also, he's a giver.

It strikes me that of everything there is to be attracted to about Logan, this is his sexiest part—this part of him I'm seeing now. This part of him that cares about his work beyond the sex. This part of him that isn't just physicality, but also emotion and heart.

"Then would you rather that more of the work you do is scripted?" I ask. The movies Logan produces already walk the line between improvised and plotted out. While the scenes themselves seem to be organic, they always begin with a monologue that he writes himself. It's another original aspect of his work.

"Hiring a good scriptwriter costs too much, so that's not the way to go. But reality TV has proven stories can be interesting when not scripted."

"But those situations aren't really 'real.'" I wonder if this is strange first date conversation. I've never gone out with someone else in the business, so my experience is narrow. "Those reality shows are all staged. Encouraged."

He sits forward, eager. "Right! The producers put together characters with whatever chemistry they're going after because they know that, based simply on psychology and human behavior, the 'actors' will react to each other in a way that's entertaining to watch."

He leans back in his chair again. "I mean, look at *The Bachelor* and *The Bachelorette*. People go crazy over watching men and women 'fall for each other' in real time." He uses air quotes as he says *fall for each other* suggesting he believes, as I do, that very little that happens on reality shows is genuine. "Imagine if we could capture that essence."

I squint my eyes as I follow his line of thought. "Then you're suggesting porn do *The Bachelor?*"

"Not a game show. But, yeah. A camera following a man and a woman over a series of dates. The sexual activity would be encouraged to progress at a natural pace and would be completely open door. Explicit. Hot. But it all happens organically, and if feelings develop between them, even better."

"That's actually a brilliant idea." I've never spent much time thinking about where porn could or should go, but hearing Logan talk about it is really inspiring. "It's cutting edge and yet right in line with where the trends are heading."

"That's what I think." He meets my eyes, and I have to concentrate to not squirm in my chair. His gaze is so hot and intense and demanding. It's as if he wants something from me, and if I knew what it was, I have a feeling I'd hand it over without a second thought.

"So what do you say?" he asks after a beat.

"What do I say about—wait." Everything starts to click into place. "Are you actually proposing this project?"

"Yeah."

"To *me?*"

"Yes. I am."

Then this isn't a date.

And the conversation wasn't candid and real; it was the preamble to this proposal.

I'm stunned. And speechless. Mostly because I'm disappointed.

But then he says, "I'm asking you if you'd like to be part of a revolution that takes the industry by storm," and I can't be quite as disappointed as I was because, even though this isn't a date, it's an opportunity. An opportunity to move into the het world. To make more money. To do more work with Logan.

To have more sex with Logan.

Take the industry by storm. Is it fate that he's used the same words that LaRue Hagen used?

I'm flattered and flustered. The whole thing is surreal, and I don't know what to say.

"Devi? What are you thinking?"

Before I can answer, I have to know, "Why wouldn't you ask someone with more experience? I haven't even done any het porn since the scene we did. Why me?"

I expect it's *because* of my inexperience. A project like this is best with a newbie that could be groomed along the way. My ethnicity probably helps too. If he's trying to be forward-thinking, an ethnically diverse cast is the way to go. And if LaRue Hagen is right, my career is poised to "break out." Naturally other directors would notice.

But he doesn't give any of those answers as his reasons. Instead his features grow somber and his eyes serious, and he says, "I want it to feel authentic."

"What?" I'm so surprised that the word falls out, breathy and astounded.

"I want it to be real," he says sheepishly. "As real as possible. So."

I don't know what to say. I don't want to say anything and ruin this incredible, awesome, strange, surreal moment. I mean, I'm in. How can I not be? But I'm still so flabbergasted that I can't answer right away.

Then he grins that charming crooked grin of his, the one that makes my knees shake, even when I'm sitting down. "Come on, Devi Dare," he says, and it's like he's purring. "Make porn with me."

And that's how I go from a stable career of girl-on-girl to making an arty, dirty reality show with a porn star.

CHAPTER EIGHT

Devi lives in El Segundo, in a stamp-sized bungalow that's been awkwardly chopped into two apartments. And despite the tidy landscaping and fresh paint, I notice that she locks no less than four locks before she skips down the driveway to my car. I knew the kind of porn she did paid less, but I guess I never realized how much less, and I immediately feel a wave of weirdness about my massive house up in Laurel Canyon and even the car I'm in right now. It's a Shelby Mustang Super Snake, and while it didn't cost as much as most of the other cars I see in the Hills, it would still be a few years' worth of rent in a place like this.

But there's no weirdness at all on Devi's face as she opens the door and slides inside. "Nice car," she says with genuine admiration, running her fingertips along the sleek dash. Her hair is in long beachy waves, tumbling over her shoulders and down to her waist, and she wears the shortest denim shorts I've ever seen, exposing long expanses of tanned and toned leg. I follow those legs up from her flat leather sandals, over the elegant curve of her calf, and up to her thighs, those firm slopes of muscle leading up to her juicy ass—which is only barely covered by the shorts.

I see the slightest hint of pink in her cheeks when she realizes I'm staring at her body, but I don't stop. Instead, I move my gaze up to her chest, where a thin orange tank top drapes low over her chest. She's wearing a light blue bra, the kind of bra that says *first date*, the kind of bra that doesn't anticipate sex but wouldn't shy away from it either.

She's this complete package of fun and summer and sex, of the girl next door and the girl of my dreams, and I want to pull her into my lap and kiss her neck while she straddles me. I want to wind my fingers in her hair and leave a trail of marks from her neck to her tits, and then I want to fuck her until she's trembling with the need for release, and then I want to give it to her…again and again and again. I shift in my seat, my dick now hard and insistent, and I resist the urge to start rubbing it through my jeans.

"See something you like?" she teases.

"Yeah, I do," I answer honestly. I meet her eyes without a trace of a smile on my face, and that pink flush deepens, and suddenly I am plunged back into Vida's pool, desperately wanting to kiss her and also knowing I would be a giant tool for doing it.

Get it together, Logan. This is still a scene, no matter how little sex you have tonight, so act like a goddamned professional. Not for the first time since I pitched the idea to Marieke, I wonder what my real motivations are here. This is supposed to be a scene, a fantasy, a fake date, and I told myself if I really wanted it to work, it needed to be with a woman I had chemistry with.

But what if I'm only doing this because I want to be close to Devi?

Because I do want to be close to Devi. A lot.

But how can I be sure that I'm really ready for that, that I'm not going after Devi as part of some rebound agenda? She deserves better than that. She deserves to be sought after because she's perfect, not because I hate my ex-girlfriend and I hate the loneliness that's chased me since she left. I want to give Devi what she deserves. I just don't know if I can yet.

Focus, goddammit. You need her for this project to be amazing and you can't scare her off.

Tonight is supposed to be our first shoot, our first fake date, and I want everything to be perfect, I want everything to feel real, but I also don't want to freak Devi out with how *real* things are inside of me right now. But still. Even just knowing that our project is going to lead to sex, that at some point next week or the week after or the week after that, I *will* fuck Devi Dare—I feel like my skin is about to combust.

Focus.

I reach over and grab her seatbelt, buckling her in the seat, the backs of my fingers brushing against her breasts as I bring the strap over and down and click it into place.

She shivers.

"We haven't even started filming yet, and already you're starting with the foreplay," she jokes weakly, trying to scrub the goose bumps off her arms.

"I'm always on the clock," I joke back, equally weakly, hoping she can't sense the conflicted desire pounding through my veins. I turn my body back to the front, start the car and shift into reverse. Soon, we're on our way north, driving through the city and towards Pasadena.

"So where are we going?" Devi asks, reaching forward to fiddle with my radio.

"A movie in the park," I say, a little proud of myself for coming up with this great date idea. "Zombie double-feature: *Night of the Living Dead* and *Shaun of the Dead.*"

She wrinkles her nose. "Isn't *Night of the Living Dead* really old?"

"Old?" I sputter. "I think the word you're looking for is *classic!*"

She giggles at my indignation, and it's been so long since I've made a woman really, truly laugh, and oh my God, I told her there wouldn't be any sex tonight and how am I going to hold myself to that?

I start talking about the movies to keep myself from saying or doing something stupid (like confessing that I have this crazy thing for her and that I beat off to her porn almost every night.) And by the time we get to the park, I've given Devi a forty-five minute lecture about the zombie film genre, ranging from Romero to James Bond to a little gem called *Zombie Strippers.*

"You should open your own film school," Devi says as I park the car and pull my camera bag from the back.

"I don't know enough," I admit. "I need to *go* to film school."

"Then why don't you?" she asks, sweetly puzzled, and I realize that I don't have an answer for that, actually. Other than money and convenience and the fear of failure and the fact that when you fall *into* doing something, it's so hard to fall *out* of it. I mumble something about not having enough time, and I'm glad she can't see my face as I look down at the bag.

"Okay," I say. "I'm going to start filming now, but don't worry about what you say or what you do. I was planning on tonight ending with our first kiss, but I'm not married to that idea, because I think it's better if the night has its own flow and rhythm and doesn't feel forced. And remember, I can edit anything out that I need to, so there's no pressure to get this right the first time."

"I think you just want to take me on more dates," she laughs, and God, I hope I'm not that transparent. Because I do want to take her on more dates. I want to bring her home. I even want to introduce her to my fucking family, and she can't know that, or she'll think I'm a stalker for sure.

So I just flash her a big smile, and say, "I bet I could make more dates worth your while."

I press a couple buttons, fiddle with a handful of settings, and then I get out of the car and walk around the front, opening the door on her side. I take her hand and help her out, and she's so beautiful in the hot evening light, sun-kissed and happy. My dick, which dozed off during the impromptu session of Logan's Zombie Classroom, wakes right up as she stretches and her tank top rides just above the low waist of her shorts, exposing a sliver of golden skin. God, those thighs with those surfing and hiking muscles, and those breasts, so full and high and perky all at once.

It hits me all of a sudden how young she is, only twenty-one, just barely out of girlhood. There's something so fresh about her, so unsullied, and then I remember her sucking me off when she was eighteen, remember how I was thinking the same thing then too. That it should feel wrong to be almost a decade older, that it should be wrong for a man my age to cradle the face of a barely-legal girl and fill her mouth with my dick, but help me, sweet baby Jesus, the wrongness only made it better.

When I finally speak, my voice has a subtle rasp to it. "Devi," I say, "won't you say *hi?*"

Devi waves, a little shyly, which is perfect, and I turn the camera to face myself. "I'm Logan O'Toole, and I'm here tonight to take this cute girl on a date. We met a few years ago, doing a job together, and then we reconnected…where was it, Devi?"

She plays along. "At a party a few weeks ago. You jumped into the pool with all of your clothes on."

"Well, I was drunk."

"You *were* drunk. And then I told you about a constellation and you didn't fall asleep, so I decided that you were a good guy. And I gave you my number."

I like this version of our meeting. It doesn't mention anything about Raven or about our aborted kiss; it makes it sound like we are just two normal people with normal jobs who go on dates in all the normal ways.

We banter back and forth as I unload the blankets and cooler out of the trunk, and then we search out a good spot with a view of the screen and a little privacy and no bees. (I'm allergic, but I don't mention it to Devi; in my experience, the minute you mention you're allergic to bees, people start mentally replaying that scene from *My Girl*, and that scene's a bit of a boner-shrinker to be honest.)

I have her film me spreading out the blanket and arranging our cushions, and by then, it's time for the movie to start, so I turn off the camera for a little while.

"Would you like some champagne?" I ask.

"Yes, please."

I dig out the champagne and get to work, and then I have one of those surreal moments, one of those moments that feels so perfectly scripted and blocked that it seems like a movie instead of real life. The *pop* of the cork and the dull *clack* of the plastic wine glasses that are mostly drowned out by the murmuring moviegoers and the wind ruffling through the palm trees and scrubby evergreens. The screen in front of us, where the black and white film shows a blond girl running down a dirt road to escape a suit-clad zombie. The brass-heavy soundtrack blaring through the speakers, and the evening breeze light and warm on our skin. Devi's hand hovering in mid-air, paused in the act of reaching for her glass, her face tilted up to the screen and her eyes wide and her lips parted in total absorption.

I watch her watching the movie, a smile tugging at my lips. She gives a little yip of surprise when the zombie bangs against the window of the farmhouse the girl is hiding in, and then she follows that with a self-conscious laugh, glancing over at me in embarrassment.

"Don't feel bad," I say, handing her the plastic cup of champagne. "It's only a fifty-year-old movie and you're sitting in a sunshine-filled park with five hundred other people. Any sane person would be scared in your position."

She sticks out her tongue at me, playful and inciting lust in me at the same time, because I remember exactly how that tongue felt on my cock.

"Careful sticking that tongue out there," I mock-warn. "Somebody might try to put it to good use."

She blows a raspberry at me and then turns her attention back to the movie screen, taking a drink of champagne. Within a few moments, she's gasping at the jump-scares again, jump scares that are clumsy and old and haven't actually scared people since 1968, if they scared them even them.

But Devi is completely caught up in the movie, gnawing on her lip as the main characters fortify the farmhouse, shuddering whenever a zombie shambles into view. I've seen this movie at least fifty times in my life, but watching it again with her is like watching it for the first time, and I remember seeing it as an eight-year-old boy late at night when my parents had friends over to play cards and had given me free rein in the basement with the VCR. I remember the fear, the anxiety, the constant assessment of whether or not I would survive if the zombies came and surrounded a house I was in.

"You know, all the blood effects were made out of chocolate syrup," I offer.

She flaps her hand and makes a shushing noise. And then another sudden zombie attack happens on the screen and she jumps right into my side, her fingers like claws in my thigh. I wrap an arm around her shoulders, amused, and she gradually relaxes, but her hand stays on my leg and her head stays against my shoulder, the sun and cinnamon smell of her filling the air. She's so intent on the movie, tension rippling through her back and arms, but I'm intent on her. On the way the fading sunlight catches in her honey-brown hair. On the way she fits so perfectly against my body, two halves of the yin and yang symbol slotted back together.

What was I so worried about earlier? I like Devi. I *like* her. In fact, I wonder if I'm falling in love with her a little as we sit here watching this zombie movie in the park, champagne still bubbly on our tongues and her hair spilling over her back and my arm, blowing against my neck and face in the breeze.

I've never felt like this, this relaxed and excited and nervous and giddy all at once, even when I was dating Raven, and it's as if just thinking that lifts a huge weight from my shoulders. What I feel for Devi is separate and apart from what I ever felt for Raven…and so much better.

All of the things I told myself earlier—that my heart wasn't clear enough to start chasing after Devi, that it would be unprofessional given that we were on a *fake* first date, it all blows away in the breeze.

Instead I'm left with this warm certainty, this feeling like a balloon is expanding in my chest. The movie-moment feeling is still here, still achingly, clarifyingly present, and the only thing that should happen next, that *must* happen next, is me kissing her. Tilting her face up to mine and finding her lips, and kissing her against the backdrop of the movie screen.

I forget about the camera, about the job we are supposed to be doing, about the fact that the ostensible reason I asked Devi to do the project with me was so I could make sure things like our first kiss had chemistry and so I should be making damn sure that I film this—everything is lost except the feeling of my skin against hers as I reach over and slide my hand up the long column of her neck.

I feel her swallow against my hand, and then she slowly turns her head up to me, her amber eyes meeting mine as my hand moves up to cradle her face. Her pupils are massive, huge pools of black rimmed with gold, and her lips begin to part.

"Logan…" she breathes.

I bend my face closer to hers, my heart pounding. "Yeah?"

I never find out what she was going to say because her phone starts vibrating noisily on the plastic lid of the cooler, *bzzz, bzzz,* while Rihanna's tinny, digital voice starts singing the opening lines of "Work."

Devi flushes a deep red and then reaches for her phone, pulling away from me and leaving my body aching with the sudden absence of her touch. A few people on blankets around us look over disapprovingly as Devi fumbles for the silent button on her phone.

"'Work'?" I ask, eyebrows raised, as she finally succeeds in silencing the call. It still lights up her screen, though, and just as I glimpse the name on the screen, *Sinner's Playpen,* she answers me. "It's my ringtone for business stuff. My agent and other performers and people like that. Hey, are you okay?"

She peers up at me quizzically, her phone still lit up in her lap, and I nod and clear my throat, as I move away under the pretense of getting her more champagne, but really to give myself space.

Sinner's Playpen is one of the biggest web-only studios out there right now, and if they're calling Devi, then that must mean either they're interested in her or her agent has let them know that she's interested in them, which is only significant because Sinner's Playpen specializes in hardcore porn. Hardcore *het* porn. She really is moving wider with her career, not just with me.

Devi will soon be getting fucked by other men.

And the moment I saw that name on the screen, my blood ran hot with the most intense jealousy imaginable, jealousy like acid eating up my veins. And the moment I recognized the jealousy, regret and shame and logic barreled into me. Who the fuck am I to care what other jobs Devi works? I already knew that she was thinking of moving away from the lesbian porn, that's why I felt like I could ask her to do this project with me, and it would be beyond unreasonable—it would be creepy and insane—to assume that our project would be the only one she would do. She's got bills to pay, after all, and even if we did have a *thing*, we would never expect the other not to work. Raven and I never slowed down our careers for each other when we were dating; if you dated another porn star, you both had to respect the job. I would never say that it is an easy thing to do, but what's the alternative? Leaving a career you enjoy and make a living at? I don't know when I'll ever meet someone worth that.

Except.

Except except except.

Except right now, when I can't force the adrenalized anger out of my blood, when I can't force my breathing to return to a normal, non-caveman-like state. I've never felt this intensely jealous over even just the possibility of a girl I liked doing a scene, and all I want to do is drive her to some beach cabin where we can live forever without either of us ever touching another human being again…and *get it fucking together, O'Toole!*

I take a deep breath. I'm being a total fucking hypocrite. If I pulled up my calendar on my phone right now, I would see scenes booked for almost every day of the week. How did I have the fucking nerve to be jealous of Devi working when I was planning on screwing seven different women in the next five days?

I clear my throat. "I'm fine," I say, handing her another full cup of champagne. "Just thirsty is all."

"Okay," she says, her eyes and voice full of this gentle implicit trust that I haven't fucking earned, and *fucking hell*, that punches me right in the chest.

What is happening to me right now? I need to get my shit together, mentally and emotionally and also spiritually, since *spiritual* is the only word I can think of to define at exactly what level Devi Dare affects me.

I grab for the camera, because that's the one thing I know for sure will put me back on level ground. But while I'm turning it on, she touches a hand to my shoulder.

"Logan," she says. "I just wanted you to know…this is the best fake date I've ever been on."

The sun is setting behind her, painting her in oranges and lavenders, and I can't help the words I say next, any more than I can help my aching erection or still-hot jealousy. "Me too, but…I guess I just also wish this were a real date."

Maybe it's the faint bitterness in my voice or the obvious lust, but her eyes widen and as they do, I realize what a giant fucking mistake I've just made. She thinks she's here as a peer, a colleague, a friend maybe, but I've just made it clear that I have feelings for her, and that's so unprofessional, not to mention dick-ish, and *fuck fuck fuck*.

"Logan?" she asks.

I have three options. I can run away—pretend I have to piss or something—or I can ignore her and mess with the camera some more. Or I can face her and apologize. And as much as I itch to run away, I turn to face her. "I'm sorry," I manage. "That wasn't okay for me to say, and I shouldn't have said it, and we should just forget it. Can we just forget it?"

Her mouth opens and closes, and she looks away, and I feel even worse about myself, and more unprofessional bullshit pours out from my mouth. "You remember our scene three years ago?"

Her expression shifts, a flash of exposed hope immediately schooled into something closed-off and cautious. She gives me a single nod that, yes, she remembers.

I know what I want to say. *I think about it all the time—I think about you all the time. I've had a crush on you for three years, and now in the span of two hours, I've decided that I'm falling for you.*

But my sense of self-preservation finally reappears, and I think quickly, equivocating around the truth. "I've wanted to do another scene with you ever since then." That's the truth, at least, if only part of it. "You are so fucking sexy, Devi, and that's why it had to be you for this project. I've been wanting to film with you again for three fucking years."

If I was hoping this explanation would distract her away from the *I wish this were a real date*, I was wrong. It doesn't satisfy her questions, I can see it in her eyes, in the way she gives me another nod as she presses her lips together.

She gives me a thin smile as she turns back to the movie. "I'm happy to be filming with you, too," she says, facing the screen and not looking at me. There's a solid six inches of empty blanket between us and she hugs her knees to her chest, as closed off as a person can possibly be to another.

She looks so young again, young and vulnerable. It only makes me more miserable.

"Good," I say faintly, pointlessly, and try to turn my attention back to the movie too. Except there's this new distance between us, this new strangeness, and I can't tell if she's angry with me for so obviously being dishonest with her or angry with me for being so unprofessional. For all I know, despite her sweet flirtatiousness, she may look at this as just another job and I've just made her extremely uncomfortable by confessing my feelings. I'm like the 1950's boss ogling his secretary to her.

Shit.

I turn the camera on and occupy myself with filming for the rest of the evening. And even though she's obviously upset and distant, she turns it on for the camera, smiling and bantering in all the right places. I film her jumping at the movie's scary parts, toasting champagne with me, lying on her back while I rub her bare feet with one hand. *Night of the Living Dead* ends and *Shaun of the Dead* starts, and I get several great shots of her laughing, of her watching the movie with her head in my lap.

But it's all with the camera on, all for the project.

When I plotted out this project, I planned for tonight to end with our first kiss, but I can't imagine it will happen now. I don't even want it to happen when there's this weird tension between us…it will have to be later. Another day, when she's forgotten how I creepily came on to her when we were supposed to be working.

Around midnight, the movie ends and huge floodlights come on, illuminating every blade of grass and tree trunk in sharp, harsh relief. Together, Devi and I pack up our things and I carry them back to the Shelby, making sure I open the door for her when we get to the car.

The drive back to El Segundo is quiet. Devi finds some Halsey on my phone and plays it through the car stereo. The freeway is wide and easy, white light pooling on the concrete, the sky a gentle purple above us. We drive through the city and down to her neighborhood, which is still fairly awake at this time of night.

We don't talk.

I back into her driveway, putting the car in park, and the ensuing silence has the kind of weight that can collapse bridges.

"I, um." My voice is loud in the quiet car. "I need to film us saying goodbye."

"Of course," she says softly.

I get out the camera and turn it on. "I wish I knew what you were thinking," I say suddenly, my finger hovering over the record button. "I feel like I've made an ass out of myself tonight, and I want to fix it, but I'm not sure how to do that. Can I say I'm sorry again?"

She turns to face me. Her eyes are inscrutable in the dark. "Logan, you told me you think I'm so sexy that you've been wanting to work with me for three years. There's nothing to apologize for."

"I feel like maybe it was unprofessional, and I don't want to be the creepy guy hitting on you while we're supposed to be doing a job, and if you don't feel comfortable doing the kiss tonight or even continuing—"

"Logan." Her voice gives me pause, it's so grave and serious and unlike her. "Please stop. You didn't do anything wrong, and I don't want to leave the project."

"Okay," I say, heaving a relieved breath. "I still think that maybe we should wait for the kiss. I don't want it to feel...contrived. Maybe just a goodbye for tonight?"

"Whatever you like," she murmurs. Is that disappointment in her voice?

I know that it's disappointment I feel, even though I know it's for the best. But this is our second aborted kiss, and I don't know how much longer I can keep myself from kissing her.

I hit *record* and put the handheld on the dash, aimed so that both of us are in the frame. "Devi, I'm so glad you came out with me tonight. Do you feel like an expert in zombie movies now?"

She gives a little laugh. "I guess you could say that, although biologically I find the entire scenario a joke. Zombies are corpses and their decomposing stomachs wouldn't be able to metabolize nutrients...and you need nutrients for muscle function. Even if something did reanimate a corpse, it wouldn't be able to have directed, long-term movement."

I blink at her. "Wow."

She shrugs, like it's no big deal that she just knows all this stuff about metabolic function and reanimation.

"You know, you didn't mention any of this during the movie."

"Well…during the movie, I was actually a little scared," she admits.

"I hope that doesn't mean I've scared you off of another date, though." I look at her from under my eyelashes (I have damn good eyelashes for a man.) "I really had a good time tonight, and I'd like to see you again, if you'd let me?"

For just a moment, I try to pour everything into my gaze, to show her that I actually *mean* these words, that I'm not just saying them for the show. If things were different and this was our real first date…

Her eyes are gold-dark and soft as she returns my gaze. "I'd like that," she replies shyly, and my heart leaps once before it remembers that she's acting too.

"Okay," I say.

"Okay," she says back with a smile. She breaks our gaze, reaching down to unbuckle her seatbelt. She puts her hand on the door handle and then looks back at me. The light from her porch is soft and yellow, filling parts of the Shelby with a subdued glow that burnishes her caramel skin into a dark bronze. "For what it's worth," she says quietly, "I would've still wanted to do the kiss tonight."

And then the door opens and she's gone, and I'm staring blankly ahead, the red *record* light of the camera blinking at the edge of my vision like a silent recrimination, a glaring marker of every second I let Devi walk away from my car with those as the last words spoken.

Because when she said it, she wasn't using the jaded voice of an experienced porn model, she wasn't using the affectionate voice of a friend. She was telling me something real, something personal.

Of course she is, you idiot. She wanted to kiss you that night at Vida's, remember?

I bring the flat of my hand down hard on my steering wheel, frustration surging in me. I wanted to kiss her that night too, and I want to kiss her right now, and there's no reason that I shouldn't run after her and show her exactly how I feel, except maybe there is every reason that I shouldn't do it—

I slam my hand against the steering wheel three more times, a low growl building in my chest. Fuck it. Fuck trying to do the right thing, because there's only one thing I want to do right now and Devi just told me that she wants it too.

I unbuckle my seatbelt and open my car door in record time, calling Devi's name as I close the door and walk forward. She is almost to her front porch but stops and turns to face me. "What is it?" she asks, taking a step toward me.

I take a step of my own, not sure what to say, so I just hold out my hand. She looks at it and then up to my face, which I know must be a mess—lust and hesitation and worry and raw attraction. But I see the pulse pounding in her neck, the way her lips part just from looking at me, and she comes forward and slides her hand in mine.

I use it to tug her a little closer to me, playfully, carefully, and then I say, "I've been wanting to kiss you all night." And I press my lips to hers.

I feel her hand trembling in mine, feel her lips yield to my kiss, and for one perfect, suspended moment, we are kissing the chaste kind of kiss you see on PBS historical shows, the Disney Channel kind of kiss, where it's just our lips touching, just our hands joined together. It's pure romance, and I feel very genteel and distinguished as I pull away and she blinks up at me with a dazed smile.

"I guess I'll be seeing you," she says, a little breathlessly, and I rejoin with a really articulate, "Yeah," and then she squeezes my hand and walks back to her door.

And then I'm standing there by the trunk of my car like an idiot, because my lips are still hungry for hers, my body is still clamoring for her touch, and my mind is this churning loop of our date and her amber eyes and our scene from three years ago, and that kiss wasn't enough, it couldn't possibly be enough. And then I'm eating up the distance to her front door in long, quick strides; she's facing the door trying to sort through her jangling mass of keys; I grab her shoulder and spin her around, slamming her back into the door and bringing my mouth down on hers with the kind of ferocity that would terrify most women.

Devi Dare gasps into my mouth, and I step into her, my hands roaming aggressively from her neck to her tits and then finally down to her ass, where I scoop her up effortlessly. She wraps her legs around my waist, and I push her hard against the door, both of us groaning the moment my erection finally presses against the spot where she wants me the most. And then I part her lips with mine and finally, finally taste her, her kiss the same sweet flavor I remember from three years ago, with just a dash of champagne added in.

Her hands are in my hair, pulling hard, and the next thing I know, she's yanking my head to the side and biting my neck like a vampire, leaving a trail of deep fire from my collarbone to my jaw, and if I was hard before, I'm like granite now, my cock trying to bore a hole through my jeans.

I return the favor and move to her neck, biting and sucking until she's grinding on my cock so hard that I know I'll have friction burns later, although I would pay that price and so much more to have her pinned up against a door again. She's saying my name over and over, *Logan, Logan, Logan,* and for the briefest second, I wish she knew my real name (and then I'm glad she doesn't because it's a stupid, terrible name.)

I find her mouth again, and I take my time with this kiss, etching every detail and sensation into my memory. The softness of her lips, the wet satin of her tongue, the way she gasps for air when we part. Her fingers in my hair and her heels digging into my back, and everywhere, all around me, is her cinnamon smell and the feeling of her hair brushing my skin. I've fucked hundreds of women, literally hundreds, and never, ever have I shared a kiss like this, never have I felt like a woman was pulling my soul out of my body through my mouth, like a woman could know my entire mind just by pressing her lips to mine.

But that's what I feel now, like Devi has magnetized something inside of me, and now every atom in my body is pulling itself to her, an ionized attraction that can't be fought, can't be helped, can only be witnessed.

And so I witness myself right now, my hand palming one perfect breast, my shirt rucked up to my chest while her fingertips run eager, desperate trails up my abs. And that's when I realize that she's just as caught up as I am in this. That's when I realize that she's as hungry, as needy, as turned on, and the thought drags the caveman out from hiding. I rock my hips against her again and her thighs tighten and she cries out, her eyes fluttering shut.

I could make her come like this. Hell, *I* could come like this, like a teenage boy, rutting into her fully clothed, grunting and panting. And I'm so far gone that I almost give in, my balls throbbing for release, my mind aching to see her face when she comes.

I don't know where I summon the control to stop, to gently lower her to her feet and to plant one last, lingering kiss on her mouth, but I know it comes first and foremost from my reluctance to use her, to push her. This kiss was already so outside the bounds of what's okay, professionally and emotionally, and even though I finally feel like I can touch her without Raven's vengeful ghost haunting my thoughts, I don't want to go from zero to sixty in one night. That's the problem with my job sometimes. I'm so used to quotidian, workaday sex that I've forgotten how to take it slow. Yes, in a scene I may take my time…for a couple of hours. But I haven't taken days or weeks to build up to sex since—well, since high school.

I want to make sure Devi is comfortable with this—with *us*—before we go any further. And I want to make sure that, if she is okay with it, I make every second of this thing as mind-blowing and delicious as possible.

We slowly pull apart and her eyes gradually open, though they're still half-hooded with arousal and unsatisfied need.

"Jesus Christ," she breathes. "You really know how to kiss a girl."

I try not to preen, but I do a little. "I know," I say, flashing her a grin.

"I mean it. I could die now and be happy. *Here Lies Devi Dare, Murdered by a Kiss.*"

I honestly think I could die right now too and be just as happy, and I tell her that. And then I add, "But mine would say: *Here Lies Logan O'Toole*, and then there'd be like seven eggplant emojis underneath it."

She laughs, a floating, happy sound that does nothing to help the squeezing in my chest or the ache in my groin. I am so wrecked by this girl, which means I'm so very thoroughly fucked right now.

Totally fucked.

I lean forward and brace my hands against her door, one hand on either side of her head so that she's trapped without me even touching her, and then I bring my face down to hers and give her the smallest, lightest kiss possible—just a brush of lips really.

She shivers, her breathing quickening.

"I'll see you soon," I murmur against her lips. "I promise."

"Okay," she murmurs back, and I straighten, tucking a stray lock of hair behind her ear as I do. "Goodnight, Logan."

"Goodnight, Devi."

And even though it's physically painful to do it, I turn away and leave her on her front porch. It's only when I get back into the Shelby and start the car that I notice the camera's *record* light still flashing, and also realize that it was aimed at the rear window, which would have given it a direct view of Devi's porch.

I pick up the camera and rewind through the footage, a huge smile splitting my face as I realize that the entire moment—the first chaste kiss and then me chasing after her—were perfectly captured on camera. A little distant maybe, a little out-of-focus through the window, but it just adds to the reality of the moment, *cinema verité* style.

The smile doesn't leave my face the entire drive home. I kissed a girl I really like and I filmed an awesome scene. What could be better than that?

CHAPTER NINE

I can still feel the power of that kiss the next day. And the next night too.

The day after that, I swear my lips are still swollen, and my legs feel like they're going to give out every time I think about Logan's mouth invading mine while his body pressed against me with such obvious, raw desire. I would have invited him up—hell, I would have let him fuck me against my door—and I almost did.

But. The show.

There's a contract, and while it doesn't say anything that would prohibit fucking against my door after filming the first episode, there are stipulations that suggest that it wouldn't be in the best interest of the project. And this project is so important to Logan. He spent several days hammering out the details via my agent, and I'm happy with the resulting arrangement. There will be seven episodes in total, each roughly forty to sixty minutes in length, and progressing in sexual and romantic activity. The story of a young L.A. couple will be unscripted and improvised, but the director/screenwriter/cameraman (aka Logan) will explain briefly where and how far he'd like each scene to go at the beginning of each shoot. And if I have any objections, I am to bring them up then.

The series, which is to be filmed in its entirety before airing on Vida Gine's website, will eventually earn the label of hardcore porn—unless the scenes don't naturally reach that. And they will, if Logan or I have anything to say about it. There will be little to no kink or fetish, and all sexual activity is to be exclusively between the two of us. The usual safety clauses were written in to protect both of us (but mostly me—women in the industry are generally the victims of nonconsensual assault), and we each submitted and approved each other's limit lists. Mine detailed the fluids I considered acceptable, his specified no tickling, particularly of his feet. Apparently when tickled, Logan O'Toole cries.

When I read that last bit of information, I immediately had to text him. **I never fantasized about tickling you. And now it's all I can think about.**

His response had been, **At least you're thinking about me.**

Was I ever not?

So, with the flirting and the texting, and the way he looked at me throughout our date with hungry eyes, I was already pretty certain he wanted me. Even when he almost let me walk away, I knew it was only himself getting in the way.

And then that kiss…

Damn, that kiss. It was unreal because it was *so real*. It wasn't acting or performing. It wasn't a show of any sort, even though the rest of the night had been all about the series, all about the camera. Our dynamics and dialogue at the park dictated by that little red light. But then I'd gotten out of the car and left, and he chased after me without the camera in his hand. The scene was over, but he wanted my lips just as much as I wanted his, and so he'd left the camera behind and claimed me for his own. Not for Vida or Lelie or for *art*, but for Logan.

Fuck, it makes me wet just thinking about it.

Maybe I could have asked him to stay. Maybe it wouldn't have hindered the show's storyline. We could have spent the night together off-screen, and then simply pretended it hadn't happened when we filmed the next episode. After all, that's what would have to happen with this kiss; since it wasn't filmed, we would need to film a fake first kiss for the project still.

But despite the hiccup of this first kiss, we agreed the show would be best if we let the relationship progress *in front of the audience*. And I'm head over heels with the concept. I'm head over heels with Logan's desire to create something authentic.

I am even, possibly—probably—a little head over heels with Logan himself. Or a lot.

Which is why I let him say goodnight. I let him walk away. I let him leave me with the promise that we'd see each other again soon, and I haven't stopped thinking about him since.

So when he sends over a rough edit of the footage two days after he left me on my doorstep, I don't need to see it to remember how amazing he is and how incredible our date was, but I rush to play it all the same.

And wow. It's fantastic. More than fantastic—it's breathtaking. It's art.

Too eager to wait until I'm at my computer to watch it, I stare transfixed at the screen of my iPhone and swoon all over again. It's good. So, so good. I know I'm biased because I personally experienced what he's captured, but it's more than that. The angles he chose to shoot from, the way he cut the footage together—it's beautiful and captivating and different than anything I've seen both in and out of the industry. I knew it was going to be good, but I'm surprised by *how* good.

I'm also surprised how well he captured the sexual tension between us. It's so thick it's palpable, and I'm certain that if I were a stranger watching these two people on the screen, I'd be dying for them to bang. Just like I'm dying for us to bang. I'm dying for it so badly I'm in agony.

But I'm excited too—about how good the footage has turned out, about being a part of this incredible and innovative art, about what's happening between Logan and me on a personal level. So excited that my cheeks hurt from grinning by the time I reach the part of the video where I get out of the car.

The part that's supposed to be the end.

But it *doesn't* end there. It goes on, and soon I'm watching Logan run after me—not once, but twice—and then he's ravishing me on my doorstep in what I'm certain has to be the hottest kiss ever captured by a camera.

My heart sinks with disappointment—not with the speed of a comet or a falling star, but with the slow descent of a hot air balloon. It takes me a minute to process that the most utterly thrilling moment of my life so far has been tainted by its preservation. Because now I'm uncertain whether he ran after me for *me*...or for this.

I slump onto a dining room chair. He couldn't have faked that kiss. It's impossible. Isn't it? He was definitely aroused—I know that for a fact. His cock was a steel rod through his clothes.

But this is his job. He knows how to deliver a kiss. He has his dick trained to respond, too.

And what does it matter if it wasn't real? It looked real. That's what's important. Nothing else.

Logan must have assumed I'd watch the clip as soon as he sent it over, and he must have kept an eye on the clock, because not two minutes after I've finished, he's texting me. **Well????**

I haven't quite pulled myself together, and all I can think is to answer honestly. **I didn't realize you filmed the kiss.**

I left the camera running in the car. It could have turned out like shit recording through the window, but doesn't it fucking rock?

He's happy with the outcome—and he should be. It's good! I just forgot for a moment that this isn't a relationship; it's a show. Anything else I thought it might be was just a misunderstanding on my part.

I text him what I should have said to begin with. **It's incredible, Logan. All of it. You're so talented. Even I was convinced by the storyline.**

Then I pull up Halsey on Spotify, turn my speakers on so the music will play via Bluetooth, and flip my phone upside down so the screen is facing the table and I can't see it light up with calls or texts. It's possible Logan will want more feedback or will want to chat, but he'll have to wait. There's laundry to put away and dishes to be done and a whole slew of "real" things that need my attention.

• • •

Tonight, let's try to aim for oral.

I reread the text several times as I get ready for my next date with Logan. My stomach flutters like I'm in an airplane that's taking off, and I have goose bumps in anticipation. I probably shouldn't be this excited, but I've been looking forward to giving Logan head again since, well, since the last time I gave him head. Despite my disappointment over the last date's footage, I'm psyched.

As I step out of the shower and towel off my hair, though, a voice inside asks, *Are you sure getting excited is a good idea?*

I wipe the steam from the mirror and stare at my reflection. "There's nothing wrong with looking forward to going to work," I tell myself. Especially when work is sex. "You just have to manage your expectations."

Tonight, I expect that everything will be filmed, everything that happens will be for the show, and as long as I remember that, it's going to be fun.

Satisfied with my pep talk, I use the night's agenda to plan my wardrobe. Since it's too hot for pants, I choose a short black skater skirt to wear paired with a loose blouse with spaghetti straps and a low neckline. My cleavage will look awesome when Logan looks down at me bowed before him. My knees are likely going to get scuffed or else my thighs are going to strain from squatting, but that's fine—it's part of the job.

It's not until I start applying my makeup, and realize I've been grinning for almost an hour, that I start to reevaluate my anticipation. The thing is, it's not just the sex I'm looking forward to. And it's not just the job. It's Logan—I'm looking forward to seeing him. I'm looking forward to seeing him a lot.

And maybe that's a problem after all.

"This is fine," I tell the Devi in the mirror. "It's probably completely normal to have a crush on the first guy you had sex with on camera." The *only* guy. And perhaps that's the problem—I need more mainstream porn experience.

Logan's project paid me a decent advance, but it's a good idea to have something else lined up.

So when my agent happens to call a few minutes later with details about a lesbian shoot I have, I tell her I'm ready to book more. I'm ready to take the next step and commit to a hetero scene with Hagen. "Can you please make sure he's aware of all my limits and restrictions?"

"Do you want me to give him the same guidelines you gave Logan?"

The honest answer is no. I want things with him that I want with no one else. Which is why I tell her, "Yes." Because I need to treat Logan's job like any other, and that means treating every other job just like it's a scene with Logan.

• • •

Logan already has the camera on when I open his car door twenty minutes later. It's propped on his dashboard, and the minute I slide in, he slips his hand behind my neck and pulls me toward him. His kiss is fire and salt, and I'm dizzy when he eases up.

"Hello," he says, his mouth still against mine. "I think I'll be needing to do that a lot tonight."

It's for the show, but I melt. "Say hello?"

He grins and nods and then presses his lips around my lower one.

"Hello," I say, breathless when we part again, and I suddenly don't care if it is just for the camera because it has the same effect on me either way. And damn, the effect is amazing.

"I brought a picnic again." He sounds apologetic. "It's just so hard to obtain permits for most public places. Especially when I don't have any intention of behaving."

"Sounds good to me." He's the only thing I'm interested in putting in my mouth anyway.

He pulls out into traffic and then reaches over to lace his fingers in mine. "The picnic? Or not behaving?"

I shrug and smile coyly, partly for the camera, but mostly because I'm afraid if I speak, the only thing I'll want to say is hello a few more times, or a thousand.

Logan doesn't tell me where we're going, save that it's a ways out of town but totally worth it; he drives north and east, and two hours later we're pulling off Templin Highway outside Angeles National Forest onto a wide gravel shoulder.

"Good. We're alone." He gives me a quick peck before turning off the engine and gesturing for me to get out of the car.

Logan sets up our picnic on the hood of his car, and even with his handheld a distinct presence, our meal of sushi and tsukemono paired with plum wine is absolute perfection. Between popping California rolls in our mouths, we kiss and make-out like any two normal people who are attracted to each other and are newly going out.

Is that what we are—normal people? When I'm with him like this, and he's touching me, and my blood is boiling in my veins, I actually believe we might be.

When the sun has set and we've finished both dinner and the bottle of wine, I realize why he's brought me to this spot. "The stars," I gasp. "They're so clear here."

"Impressed? Hint—you should say yes."

My smile is so wide, I'm sure I look like a dork. "Yes." I lose myself in the sky above me, searching out the patterns I know best, identifying their pinpoints silently in my head. *Polaris, Orion, Rigel, Betelgeuse, Antares...*

"Stay here." Logan slides off the hood and disappears behind the car. I hear the trunk pop and a minute later he returns with a tripod. After extending the legs, he sets it on the ground, facing toward the hood of the car, and I swear my temperature rises a whole degree in anticipation of what he's planning to film next.

I sit up, propping myself on my elbows, and watch him.

He can feel my gaze. I'm sure of it. But he doesn't react to it, and as he begins to fasten the camera to the tripod, he glances behind him at the horizon and nods. "What stars are those?"

I follow the line to find the two brightest lights at the end of it. "They're actually not stars at all. That's Jupiter," I point to the one higher in the sky, then at the lower one, "and that's Venus."

"Planets, then. Are they always that close to each other?"

"No. And they're not really close. It's an illusion. Venus is our closest neighbor and is about the same size as Earth. Jupiter is far away, but since it's so big, it looks the same size at this distance. As the Earth rotates, they can look like they're closer or farther apart depending on how the horizon lines up."

I realize my scientific explanation probably sounds serious and bland so I add, "My father says they're the lovers Layla and Majnun, immortalized forever in the sky. The two have been dancing nearer to each other all month. Later, they'll get so close they'll look like they're kissing."

Apparently done fiddling with the camera, he straightens and moves toward me. "Kissing's nice," he says. Then he leans down to kiss the inside of my knee.

Electricity shoots through my body like a bolt of lightning. "Yes." Does my voice sound as thin to him as it does to me? "Especially because Layla and Majnun never actually touched on Earth."

"That's tragic." His fingers graze the spot he kissed then begin trailing the line of my leg.

I shiver. "Very."

"Tell me about them."

"Well." I take a breath, using the sky to center myself, to focus on what I'm saying instead of the blistering scorch of his touch. "The story dates back to seventh century Persia with Qays, the son of a wealthy and powerful descendent of Muhammad known as a Sayyid. When he's just a boy, Qays meets Layla at school and they immediately fall in love."

"As boys do."

"As boys do." Goose pimples skate down my arms even as I try to ignore what *this* boy is doing. It's hard to think while his hands—both of them now—caress a pathway up the inside of my thighs.

But he urges me to go on, so I do. "Qays is so inspired by his love that he writes her endless letters and poems and songs and then recites them on the street corners for anyone who passes by to hear. Soon, the community starts referring to him as Majnun, which means madman, because his passion for Layla is so great it's mistaken for insanity."

Right now, I'm about to mistake my own passion for insanity because Logan's journey has reached my panties and the nearness of his caress to my most wanting body part is driving *me* mad. His fingers wrap around the waistband, and I lift my hips so that he can draw the thin garment down my legs and over my sandals.

With a sly smirk, he stuffs my underwear into the pocket of his jeans. "He's crazy with desire?"

"Yes," I say on a hiss.

"I think I might know something about that." He pushes my skirt up, and my legs spread automatically to bare my pussy for him. His stare is intense as he brushes his fingers across my trimmed curls, lust burned into his expression. "Go on," he says, tracing up and down along my slit.

"Uh." I'm so wet, so aroused. "Mm. Majnun gets the courage to go to Layla's father. And he asks for her hand in marriage, but he's denied. How could any father allow a union between his daughter and a crazy person? It would ruin the family reputation. Instead, she's wed to an older man in a neighboring village."

"She marries someone else? That's terrible." Logan dips inside my hole and pulls my wetness up to paint my clit with it.

"Devastating," I moan.

"So what does Majnun do?"

"He's, uh." My body is already tightening with pleasure as Logan draws constellations on my clit with his fingertips. "He's overcome. With grief. He spends the rest of his life mourning their love. Wandering the wilderness in solitude. Composing poems for Layla. If he hadn't been mad before, he surely is now. Driven there by a broken heart."

Logan is driving me crazy as well, delivering a touch so precisely gentle that it makes me wriggle and buck up against him, begging for more with my body.

He responds by reducing his pressure even further. "And what does Layla do about Majnun's broken heart?" he asks. "Does she even care?"

"Yes, she cares," I whisper. "She loves him. Secretly." I'm so quiet he has to be almost still to hear me, his only movement now the rise and fall of his chest and the probing of his fingers. "So she lives 'between the water of her tears and the fire of her love.' She hears the songs and poems that he's written for her because they're everywhere now."

His eyes lock on mine. He's enrapt and I can tell that he's as tortured as I am.

"One day," my voice is low and shaky like my legs, but it still commands his attention, "she meets an old man who, uh, mm," (Jesus, I'm going to come!) "wants to help them. Help them exchange letters. Then, for one night only, he helps them meet. But they have to stay ten paces from each other."

"He can't even touch her from ten paces away." Logan's voice is as quiet as mine is, as threadbare.

"No, he can't." My palms are sweaty against the hood of the car, and my control is slipping. I'm so worked up that I know my release is going to be tumultuous.

"So sad." With palms braced on my inner thighs, Logan bends down and draws my clit into his mouth.

This—this is definitely *not* sad.

"Oh God, oh God, oh God."

He licks and sucks, and I fall apart, coming in a sudden rush that is both unexpected and a relief. With a moan, I curl upward in a crunch and clutch onto his hair for support.

I thought I remembered what this felt like—how his mouth on my most erogenous zone turns me into pudding and short-circuits my senses.

I was wrong. This is so much more than I remember. So much more incredible/arousing/overwhelming/perfect than I remember. It's a feeling that's too intense to be able to commit to memory, I realize, and the fragments that I can preserve are feeble souvenirs. No wonder Majnun was so prolific where Layla was concerned—he wanted to remember everything, every bit of their time together just like I want to remember every bit of this time with Logan.

When my stomach muscles relax, when I can finally fit air in my lungs again, I lay back on the hood, sated and spent.

But Logan's not done.

He blows a warm stream of air over my damp pussy. "What happens next, Devi?" He traces a line around my hole with his finger. "Tell me what happens with Majnun and Layla when they meet but can't touch. What does he do instead?" He blows again, this time plunging two long digits inside me.

And, fuck, I'm already winding up again.

I start to writhe, but Logan holds me in place. "What does he do, Devi?"

"He tells her the things he wants to do to her," I gasp. That's not exactly how the story goes. In traditional versions, Majnun spills his heart out in poetry, and I'd never assumed it was sexual language.

But now I'm certain that was what he spoke to her—how could he finally be so close to her and not let her know all the ways he wanted her?

"What things?" Logan crooks his fingers, rubbing the area I like to call the Control Panel because once I'm touched there, I lose all control.

In a rush of words, I say, "He tells it all—how he wants to put his hands on her, how he wants to lick her and kiss her and be inside her and twist her up and break her down. He tells her with such vivid description that she comes just from his words."

"Yes," Logan says before circling his tongue around my clit.

"He tells her everything, in every word, in every way. Then, at dawn, they go their separate ways."

"And then?" He continues to tease with his finger and his mouth.

"And then Layla dies, and Majnun dies of grief beside her tomb. The legend says that they meet each other in paradise and spend eternity together."

"That's not where you say it ends." Logan's lips tickle against me as he talks, and I shudder.

"No. It's not. My father says that's a foolish ending, told only as a moral lesson for those who fear worldly lust. He insists instead that the lovers remained star-crossed, even in death, and that they exist now as Venus and Jupiter, far, far apart in the night skies. But every now and then, they meet and spend a night of love and passion together before parting again at dawn. Like tonight."

Logan stands up, but only long enough to fold my legs in toward my stomach. His eyes scan hungrily over my cunt. "Keep going." His words are marinated in heavy desire. "You stop, I stop."

"The story is over." I sound desperate because I am. I don't think I can take any more of his torture, but I'm certain I can't stand it if he stops.

"Then tell me another," he says, and so I do. I tell him another and another and another, dredging up every myth I've ever been told about the constellations and the planets and the balls of fire that flicker and flame above us until I release again. And then again. And I can't talk anymore, drunk on coming. Drunk on Logan and this night and the poetry he's written in my most private parts.

Still, he doesn't let up.

I'm limp and sweat-soaked when he straightens and tugs me up to meet him. With his fingers still buried inside of me, his mouth finds mine, his lips are smeared with my wetness and his tongue is thick with my taste, and the kiss he gives me turns me inside out.

Soon he pulls away and mumbles at my ear, so softly that I wonder if he's forgotten that he's filming or if he's just gotten too caught up to care, because there's no way the camera is picking up these words. "You're making me so hard, Devi." He grinds against the curve of my ass, proving his point. "My cock is fucking lead because of you."

Unbelievably, this turns me on even more. I tighten around his finger, and he groans. "You should pay for this. For being such a tease. For making me this goddamned turned on."

I close my eyes as yet another climax crests, but he jerks my chin up toward him.

"Look at me," he says, and I do. His features are strained as if he's the one close to orgasm instead of me. As if giving me pleasure is as intense for him as it is for me to receive. It's shocking and thrilling and perfect and I can't look away, both because he's told me not to and because he's too beautiful not to look at. Especially with his face framed by the night behind him, the tiny dots of stars twinkling like candles he's lit just for me.

But the brightest lights before me are the twin sparks in his eyes as he urges, "give it to me. Give it to me."

And then the stars are falling, shooting across his face, across my vision, and I understand why Juliet paired her thoughts of orgasm with Romeo cut up into stars and preserved forever as a constellation.

Because I will now forever pair this bliss with Logan and the heavenly bodies above me now.

I'm gasping against his mouth, tears are falling from my eyes, and every muscle in my body is vibrating with this release—this orgasm so violent, so intense, that I'm sure my heart has stalled.

"Jesus, Devil! Yes! Yes." He's pleased. Excited by the potency of my climax. "More. Give it to me. Give it all to me."

I shatter around him, until I'm nothing, nothing, nothing,

I'm also desperate to do to him what he's done to me, so when I'm able to move my limbs again, I sit up, into his kiss, and fumble to get into his pants. Eagerly, he gropes my breast, half climbing on top of me as he bucks against my hands, muttering for me to hurry with my task.

But before I even have his belt undone, red and blue lights streak through the now pitch black night, and the headlights of a police car land on the road beside us.

"Fuuuuck," Logan says, sliding off of me. He turns away toward the camera and a second later I see the red record light disappear.

I sit up, and smooth my skirt over my thighs then run my fingers through my hair, so that I'm—hopefully—presentable by the time the cop gets out of his car and approaches us.

"Good evening," he says in greeting.

"Hello, officer." I give him my flirtiest grin. In my periphery, I see Logan pull down his shirt to cover his erection.

The cop narrows his eyes, surveying the scene in front of him. "What are you two doing out here tonight?"

"Just looking at the stars," Logan says, turning to join the conversation. He points to the sky. "That's Jupiter and Venus over there. Do you want to see my Wilderness Pass?"

"Not necessary." The officer never takes his eyes off us. There's no way he's fooled. The scent of sex is clinging heavily to me, and I'm sure my hair is even more mussed than Logan's.

With a knowing shake of his head, the policeman says, "It's probably best you get moving on now."

"Yep. Going." Logan is already loading up the camera and tripod. I clean up the remains of our dinner, and within a handful of minutes, we're in the Mustang, driving down the highway back toward the lights of the city.

And then another minute, and we burst into laughter. I laugh so hard my eyes water and my sides hurt by the time I can speak. "Wow. That was a first." I wipe at the tears running down my cheeks.

"I've had cops shoo me away from locations before, but always because I have a hard time remembering to carry a permit. Or to get one in the first place."

Another fit of giggles rips through me.

"Pretty sure this is the first time my dick didn't go limp the minute I saw the lights though." He lifts his hips to adjust himself, and a pang of guilt runs through me, silencing my laughs. He got me off so many times, and he's still stone hard.

The guilt is gone in a flash and replaced with a yearning so deep, so intense, I've never felt anything like it. My mouth waters, and suddenly I have to have him in my mouth. Not because I feel sorry for the blue balls he's sporting, but because I need to please him. I need to stroke his cock and suck him off and watch him fall to pieces in front of me.

Or, perhaps, not quite that far. He's driving, after all.

Without any preamble, I undo my seatbelt and lean across the console to work on his pants. His cock leaps as my palm grazes his granite erection. Damn, he's *hard*. My chest flutters with anticipation.

But even though Logan groans at my touch, he says, "You don't have to do that, Devi."

"I want to." Translation: I'm greedy for it. "I can't leave you like this." Translation: I can't leave *me* like this.

"Don't worry about me." Then, when I'm still fumbling with his zipper, he puts a hand on my shoulder and gently nudges me off. Nudges me away.

Slowly, I sit up. Confusion follows surprise, and I study him with disbelief.

He glances toward me, and my expression must be transparent, because he says, "I think this episode will have more of an impact if you don't reciprocate this time. You know, it's more of a romantic gesture this way. It's better. For the show."

"Right. The show." That sinking feeling from the day before returns, but then I glance at Logan's profile, and it hits me—he's as mixed up about all this as I am. It's written all over his face. He's longing. He's conflicted. He's nobler than he realizes.

It's possible that I'm making it all up, that I'm seeing things that aren't there. But the camera's off. That look on his face is genuine, and I know that expression. It's the same one that met me in the mirror when I got ready tonight.

I settle back into my seat, and with my elbow propped on the door, I chew on my knuckle and try to dissect the strange discontentment that has crept over me. Yes, I like the guy. There's no dancing around that fact. But what's going on with *him*? Why is he pushing me away when his body language and his body parts are telling me he wants, wants, wants?

Is it me? Is it my age? Is he still hung up on his ex? Has the industry jaded him against relationships in general?

The truth is, I don't know him well enough to begin to form any real answer. What I do know, is that no matter how real this chemistry is between us, he's a closed set. No matter what he reveals on camera, he's not letting me in any further than that.

"Star-crossed," I say, breaking the silence that's stretched between us. "I think that's what you should call the show."

"Star-crossed?"

"Yeah."

"It's good. I like it."

I don't have to wonder why he accepts my suggestion so readily. I'm sure it's because he realizes as well as I do how fitting of a title it is to describe us—two lovers never meant to be together who meet occasionally in the night.

CHAPTER TEN

Devi's quiet when we approach her apartment, and I'm not sure what to say. I'm not sure I *can* say anything, because I'm still hard as a rock, and every time I breathe, I breathe in the smell of her. It lingers everywhere—my hands, her thighs, my lips—and it's driving me fucking crazy. When she reached for me earlier, her hands fumbling eagerly with my zipper, I had almost climaxed right then and there. I may be a man renowned for his control, and my scenes usually highlight this about me, but with Devi, I have nothing. *Nothing.* No shred of patience or restraint, and going down on her on the hood of my Mustang had already driven me into a fucking frenzy. (Because what man doesn't fantasize about that at some point—a beautiful woman spread open on the hood of a muscle car, cunt exposed, hair like tousled cascades on the sleek metal?)

And fuck if getting caught hadn't made me harder, sent my mind spiraling into the filthiest, most depraved fantasies possible—watching Devi try to "convince" the officers to let us go, first with her mouth and then with her pussy, the kind of fantasies I would never admit to anyone else. And then we got on the highway and she dove for my dick like a madwoman, and I hope God was watching what a fucking gentleman I was, because it was the hardest thing I've ever done in my life to push her away.

Except now I'm in her driveway saying goodbye and I'm throbbing with misery and I can tell she's a little hurt, and shit. Why did I push her away?

I wasn't lying when I told her that I thought it would be better for the show for her not to reciprocate tonight. I do think that, and also I'd like to plan another visually dynamic venue for the blowjob, not just the interior of my goddamn car (even though it's the best car in the world.)

But that's not the real reason, and the real reason is so fragile even in my own mind that I know I have no hope of explaining it to her. Because those thirty minutes with her on my hood, when I tongued her to orgasm over and over again while she told me Persian and Greek fables in that breathy, faltering voice, the *big* feeling had come, and I was drunk on it. It came with my mouth on Devi's silken skin, with her words drifting into the desert, and it was more powerful than I'd ever felt with anyone, *ever.* More than my first scene, my favorite films, or my most elaborate and creative ideas.

No, this was something beyond anything I've ever felt, so powerful and elemental that I could feel it coursing through my body and into the rocky ground underneath me and into the speckled, glittering sky above me, and the world dissolved into pure, celestial magic.

Sparkling.

Atomic.

Holy.

And then the world came together again, normal once more but still charged with the ionized memory of our magic, and we sped into the dark, laughing at our near-miss.

So why did I push her away?

Because I couldn't bear the thought of something so unbearably sexy, so indelibly perfect, being brought down to earth with something as mercenary and trite as forcing her to suck me off in my car. I mean, I knew at the time that I wasn't forcing anything, that she would have been happy to do it, but it would have ultimately been me leading the transition from the stars to the slurping, and it felt wrong.

It still feels wrong. I chose the right thing, I know it, even as I sit here listening to Devi gather up her things and unbuckle herself.

"I'll walk you inside," I say suddenly, unbuckling too.

"Okay," she says. Her voice betrays nothing, and this is one of the strangest things I've learned about Devi in the past few weeks. She can be so friendly, so straightforward, so adorably young, that it would be tempting to think that she's an open book. But she's not always, only when she chooses to be, and there are times when she's just as unreadable as the stars. More Queen Cassiopeia than Layla.

We get out and I follow her up the walk, up to her front door. The moment is pregnant as she unlocks it, as we both recall our searing first kiss here, and I wonder how she remembers it. She wanted it, I know, just like she genuinely wanted to blow me tonight in my car. Devi is a modern, sex-positive girl; she enjoys having sex and she likes me as a friend. And there have been a few moments where I've thought I've glimpsed something more, kernels of yearning in her voice, a bite of the lip or a quick blink as she looks away from me.

But I still think it might have just been a hot kiss for her and nothing more. Not the revelation it was for me.

The moment passes and then we're walking up the old wooden stairs to the upper floor and unlocking another door there.

She flicks a light on, and a yellow CFL bulb illuminates a cozy living room lined with bookshelves and dominated by the ugliest couch I've ever seen in my life, a hulking thing of orange velvet. It's either the kind of couch you find in your great-aunt's basement or the kind of couch you pay too much money for at a place like Anthropologie.

I walk over to investigate it further, and then I hear Devi clear her throat like she's going to speak, like it's easier for her to speak when we're not looking at each other. I brace myself for whatever it is she's going to say.

"Why wouldn't you let me blow you in the car?" she asks softly.

Dammit. The one question I would pay real, American money for her not to ask.

I turn to face her, my filmmaker brain having tiny seizures when I see how sweet and vulnerable she looks framed against her sagging, overwhelmed bookshelves. "Devi, it's just about the show, it's not because I don't—"

"Bullshit." There's no menace or heat in her voice right now, just the matter-of-fact voice she would use to tell me about star formation.

I hesitate. She tilts her head at me.

I speak after a long moment, trying to fumble my way towards the truth without exposing how deeply, crazily, ridiculously I am caught up in her. "I didn't want to use you, Devi. I didn't want to cheapen what we shared in the desert."

She raises an eyebrow, and I realize suddenly I've said something wrong.

"For one thing," she says, using her fingers to tick off her words, suddenly not looking like a girl at all, but a confident—and irritated—woman, "there's nothing cheap about my choosing to do any sexual act with you. I make the choice—I *choose* to use my body, either for work or for pleasure, and tonight I was *choosing* to go down on you, even though I knew the cameras were off. When you call that choice cheap, it makes me feel cheap."

Shit shit shit.

"That's not at all what I meant," I hurry to explain. "I just meant—"

"And for another thing," she continues, as if I haven't spoken, "I feel like you're holding yourself back from me, and I don't get it at all. Logan, your body isn't a machine, and I don't expect it to be—I don't expect you to turn yourself off like a switch when the camera turns off. You're human, you're going to keep needing and craving even after a scene ends. Of course, you don't want to use women, and of course you aren't the kind of guy who tries to fuck around with girls onset when the cameras aren't rolling. It's one of the things I like best about you."

I don't know what to say to this, because I'm so floored and grateful that she has noticed those things about me, but I also know that she's not finished talking yet and that I'm still in trouble.

"But Logan—" she steps forward "—I *offered*. I was offering because I wanted to. I wanted to and I chose it, and you wouldn't have been manipulating or even coaxing me into it. Please…as we move forward… please open up to me more. I'm your friend and I think I'm—" she breaks off, swallowing and glancing away. "I'm so turned on for you all the time," she finishes, and it makes my dick ache and my heart beat hard, even as my mind recognizes that she changed course at the last moment.

She changed course…why? My heart beats harder and faster. What was she going to say? Because what if she was going to say that she is falling for me? That she has feelings for me?

What would I say back?

The answer rises to my lips immediately: *Me too me too me too.*

She drags my mind away from those thoughts with a soft sigh, the kind of sigh that makes me remember the noises she made on the hood of my car. Something snaps inside of me, something big.

"Sit on the couch," I command. My voice is firm, loud and a little harsh in the small, warm space. Some distant part of me wonders if I've crossed a line.

But she sits.

I walk over to her. "On the edge," I say, and she obeys, and then I kick her legs apart, so that she's not only sitting on the edge but has her legs splayed wide. Her skirt rides up, baring her pussy.

She peers up at me with those golden eyes at the same time that I smell her scent again. My pulse thuds in my neck and wrists and groin, and it hits me.

I'm not just caught up in Devi, I'm truly, honestly falling for her. I have feelings.

Capital F Feelings.

Somehow my crush has gone from "casually obsessed with" to "move in with me," and I have no idea what the fuck to do with that, much less what Devi would do with it if she knew. She's obviously attracted to me, but that in no way equates romance, especially in our line of work. It's too soon for me to feel this way, and it's not right to drag that into the middle of a project. And if I'm being honest, I'm scared. Not a little scared, but a lot scared, because the last time I had *capital* F Feelings, I lost my dog, my heart, and my sobriety in one fell swoop.

But I can't just ignore this, and clearly, I can't hide it from Devi, nor do I want to.

There has to be a middle ground, right? Between pretending it away and proposing marriage?

I drop to my knees in between her legs, not missing her small shiver as I do.

"You're turned on for me all the time?" I ask her. "Well, I'm worse. I'm fucking miserable with the need to touch you and taste you. I'm obsessed with it. I'm obsessed with *you*." I meet her eyes. "You have to tell me if that makes you uncomfortable. Because the way I think about you, the way I crave you, it's not just like two performers. It's not just like two friends." My hands find her ankles and wrap around them, more to keep myself from touching her in more interesting places while she answers. I can see her pulse hammering in her throat as she swallows.

"Do you understand what I'm saying to you?" I ask tentatively.

"Yes," she whispers.

"And are you okay with it?"

A pause. And then a nod.

Well, it's not the most enthusiastic response I could have hoped for, but what did I expect? Even holding back from going full Romeo on her, it's still a lot to lay on a girl, that I think about her all the time, and not in a friends-only way. I start to get up from my kneeling position, but she stops me with a hand on my shoulder. It drifts over to my throat, where her thumb caresses lightly across my Adam's apple.

It's my turn to shiver.

"I'm sorry," she murmurs, "you just took me by surprise. What I mean to say is that it's more than okay with me. I'm…I'm a little obsessed with you, too."

I feel like my chest is going to explode. "Really?"

She smiles. "Really."

"But you also understand why I want to bottle up some of… whatever this is…and use it for the show, right?"

She nods, but the smile fades. "I understand. We want it to feel real."

"Because it *is* real. The heat between us, it's special, Cass, and if we play our cards right, everyone who watches us will feel it."

"I get it."

But something is off in her voice, and I don't know how to fix it. Except to do what I planned on doing originally when I made her sit: lean down and bury my face between her legs.

She lets out a low noise—half moan, half sigh—and I go easy on her, knowing she's probably a little sore from all the times I made her come in the desert. I go soft and steady, long strokes of my tongue and light flicks over her clit, and her build-up is slow but inexorable as she squirms in front of me, her fingers laced in my hair and pulling hard. And when she comes, she cries out my name, and I nearly lose all my resolve and fuck her right there.

"I just needed another taste before I went home," I explain as I straighten, wiping my mouth.

"I like that," she mumbles dazedly. "I like when it happens without the cameras…it makes me feel like you want me."

"Jesus, woman. I can prove that I want you every second of the day, if you want. But for tonight, I'll be happy with my taste."

She falls back against the couch with a tired laugh. "You can have all the tastes you want."

"I might take you up on that, Cass."

And later that night, when I'm undressing, I discover that I still have her panties—pink, silk, teenage boy's wet dream panties—in my pocket. And so I finally, finally relieve the ache, stroking my neglected cock with the silk until I erupt in thick ropes of cum. I film the entire thing on my phone and I send it to Devi.

Told you I was obsessed, I text right after it sends.

Can't type, my fingers are too busy, she responds after a few minutes.

I fall asleep to the image of her masturbating to a video of me jacking off with her panties, and maybe my depraved porno heart has never been happier than it is right now.

· · ·

I can't stop humming. It's becoming a problem, apparently, at least according to Tanner, who has started grumbling about staging a humming intervention. I hum in between takes when filming scenes, I hum while I'm editing, I hum when I crack open a beer for Tanner at the end of our workday.

"You okay, man?" he asks, taking a drink of his beer.

It's Wednesday, four days since I went down on Devi in the desert and told her that I had more-than-friends feelings about her. We've been texting every day, mostly banter and industry gossip, but at night, our conversations devolve into absolute raunch, usually ending in us sending each other naked selfies and videos of us masturbating to said selfies and so on and so forth until we fall asleep. I've been importing some of the selfies and texts and videos to incorporate into the *Star-Crossed* series (Vida and Marieke both loved Devi's idea for the name.) All with Devi's permission, of course.

But even as I work our late night messages into the series, I feel like we're edging into this exhilarating gray area where the rules don't apply; where what's happening between us happens off-script, off-camera first, and then makes it into the project later. We're skidding off the road in slow-motion, and all I want to do is press down hard on the gas, barrel headlong into this thrilling thing together.

And to that end, I've been desperate to see her, but I had to stay in Las Vegas for a few nights for an extended shoot, and she has to work tonight. But tomorrow I get to see her again, and I feel like someone has injected me with pure, uncut happiness. Even right now, while I'm on my knees with leather upholstery cleaner wiping down the couch I just had sex on this morning.

"I'm more than okay, dude," I reply to Tanner's question. "I'm magnificent. I'm brilliant. I'm—"

"Are you using drugs?" he cuts in. "I don't think I've ever seen you so…animated."

"The only thing I'm high on is life," I say with as much dignity as I can muster while scrubbing semen off my couch cushions.

"It's that girl, isn't it?" he asks. "Devi."

Thinking of Devi sends my thoughts tumbling down a spiral of affectionate depravity. I want to do the filthiest things to her and then I want to take her to meet my parents. Is this normal? Is this how normal relationships work?

Can we even call it a relationship, given that the only thing we've actually admitted is how desperate we are to fuck each other?

"So let me ask you a real question," Tanner says, setting down his beer and walking over to me with a fresh roll of paper towels. "I don't have sex with women for money, so I'm not sure how this all works—but do you feel weird at all about fucking other women while you like this girl?"

His question burrows into me, sharp and shaming, joining the other thoughts I've been suppressing for the last few weeks. I'm a typical man, I'm good at compartmentalizing, but I'm also this sentimental bastard with all these gooey feelings, and I'd be lying if I said this doesn't bother me when I think about it.

"I don't know how I feel," I start, not really sure how to frame what I want to say. I stop wiping at the couch for a minute and sit back on my heels. "Sex isn't love, Tanner. It's not even about *liking* someone. I respect all the girls I fuck, and I enjoy fucking them, but I don't always want to hang out with them when the shoot is finished or wake up next to them in the morning. No more than eating a good sandwich for lunch makes me crave my actual dinner any less."

"But sex isn't food," Tanner points out. "It's not the same as scratching an itch or taking a nap—it's not purely physical, and even you can't deny that."

I sigh. He's right. "I know. But this isn't my first time falling in love as a porn star. Even *she*—" we both know I mean She-Voldemort here "—wasn't my first girlfriend in the industry. I know how to do this now, and it's to have really clear boundaries and to keep some things special for each other."

He looks doubtful. "Most couples have 'no sex with other people' as a boundary, you know. That's like…a super-common boundary."

"But that's what I'm saying—porn people aren't like other people. We're not common. I mean, on some level, don't you think that maybe we're more evolved because we *can* separate sex from love? Don't you feel like that's noble? That I can have sex with so many different partners but still set aside my heart for someone else?"

The doubtful look hasn't left his face.

"Okay, and yes," I concede, "it does feel strange. All I think about, all I want, is Devi, and so it felt weird to fuck Candi and Ang today and it felt weird to fuck Jen and Nina yesterday in Vegas, but at the same time, my job is to fuck beautiful women. I can't just abandon my job whenever I meet a girl I like. And I *love* my job. My feelings for Devi don't change that, and I would never expect her feelings for me to change her own career path."

"If you say so," Tanner says, draining the last of his beer and walking over to the recycling bin to chuck in the can. "I just don't think I'd even want to touch another woman if I was in love with someone else."

"That's very chivalrous," I say, and I don't say it mockingly. I mean it. I admire that, because despite my warm, gooey center, despite my fantasy to love and be loved, I also know that while it's still my job to fuck women, I'll do it happily. Maybe with some complicated feelings, but never with any regrets. It's not as if I'm going to start going limp on set because my heart's in another place.

It's just that I don't think my heart and my dick have to be connected, at least not all of the time.

"And I think you know yourself pretty well, Logan," he says, grabbing his keys and phone off the kitchen counter. "I don't doubt that you've got it all figured out. But what about this Devi girl? Do you think she feels the same way? You think she'll really be cool letting you fuck your way up and down and sideways around the Valley?"

"Of course," I scoff. "She's a professional! And I guarantee she won't stop fucking other people either. I know for a fact that she's ramping up her career as we speak."

Tanner shrugs. "Alright, man. Whatever you say. I'll see you Friday?"

"Yeah. Whenever you want to come over is fine—we don't have a scene booked and I'll be editing all day."

"And don't forget to 'gram those pictures you took of Candi and Ang today."

"When have I ever forgotten to post on social media?"

He laughs. "Okay, okay, you're right. But you do have to occasionally promote yourself, you know, not just talk about the lunch you're eating or whatever show you're bingeing at the moment."

"Yeah, yeah, yeah."

He tosses me a wave as he leaves out the front door, and I throw myself onto my newly-sanitized couch, digging out my phone to post the pictures on Instagram and Twitter, and tease up the scene a little, even though it probably won't go up until next week.

When I'm done, I check Devi's Twitter feed on a whim. We follow each other, but Devi doesn't leave much to follow…her most recent tweet is from last month, and it's a selfie taken inside the flagship Good Vibrations store in San Francisco, where she's giving a giant dildo an exaggerated, adorable wink. No hashtags, no caption. Her Instagram feed is equally sparse, usually shots of the beach or the desert, never with any words attached.

What was she thinking when she posted those pictures, I wonder. How was she feeling? For all that we've done together, for as intimate as we've been, I have no idea what her inner life is like. I don't know if she felt lonely when she looked out at that ocean sunset she posted, or if she felt complete. I have no idea whether her lack of online presence is because she's shy or because she lives so fully in the moment that she doesn't even think about sharing it publicly.

I stare at that Good Vibrations selfie for a long time, at the way her hair tumbles around her shoulders and her mouth opens playfully. And then my chest squeezes hard and my mind floods with uncertainties and doubts, and I jam my phone back into my pocket.

I wish Tanner hadn't asked me all those questions, even as I also realize that they're necessary. I've been avoiding thinking about it, trying to put Devi in a mental box as I filmed my usual scenes, as I leaned down to whisper all my dirty, intense thoughts in the ears of other women, as I came on them and inside them, as I wrote monologues inspired by them.

But it was messier than that. The boxes I'd put Devi and *Star-Crossed* in were porous, and they seeped into everything else, creating these confusing scenarios where I fantasized about Devi as I fucked other women but I was still turned on and completely engaged by the other women. Is that a thing? Being able to want one person so utterly and consumingly, but also being able to throw myself into sex with other people without missing a beat? If porn wasn't my job, I have no doubt I'd be monogamous. But porn *is* my job, so where does that leave me?

I stand up, suddenly determined not to think about this anymore. I don't even really know that Devi has *capital F* Feelings for me; I don't know that she'll want me after *Star-Crossed* is over. Right now, the only thing that we've established for certain is how much we want to fool around with each other and that we maybe like each other in a more-than-friends way. Hardly the time to start thinking about the future.

Even if it's all I want to think about.

God, she'd look good in my house. Sleeping in my bed, swimming in my pool. Sharing my life…

But no. I'm not going to think about this anymore. For all I know, I'm just setting myself up for heartbreak when I discover she doesn't feel the same way.

My phone rings, and I fish it back out of my pocket, hoping against hope that it's Devi and then letting out a world-class sigh when I see that it's my mom.

Dutifully, I answer. "Hey, Mom."

"Hi, honey. Am I interrupting…anything?"

I can't help but smile. My parents have been mostly supportive of my career choices—not as enthusiastic as Devi's parents seem to be—but supportive enough. Except that neither of them, Mom especially, like to mention anything about my job by name. The words *porn, sex, scene,* and even *adult* as an adjective coupled with anything else, are never words you'll hear around my family's dinner table.

"No, Mom. I'm not working right now."

"Good, because I need to talk to you," she says briskly. "Dad and I are selling our house."

I frown. "Why?"

"Dad got a job offer near Portland and he's decided to take it. We never meant for California to be our forever-home, you know. We thought maybe we'd head back to Boston, but then this Portland offer came in, and we've always loved Oregon."

I'm still frowning. "But…"

"But what, honey?"

"But I kind of like you guys being here and stuff. What about when I want to come visit my old XBox? Or my high school computer?"

She laughs. "Well, of course we will give you a chance to go through all your old stuff. Which reminds me, Phil from down the street said his grandson is about the right age for that old game set you had, the one with the plastic guitar and drums and stuff."

I pinch the bridge of my nose. "*Rock Band*, Mom. It's called *Rock Band*."

"Anyway, I gave it all to Phil. It's got to be almost ten years old now—isn't that like ten thousand years in technology time?"

"Yes, but still! I don't like this. The giving stuff away and the moving stuff. What am I supposed to do for Thanksgiving? I can't make a turkey by myself!"

"You're supposed to book a plane ticket to Portland, *or* accept that you are almost thirty and that your dad and I have lives outside of being available for your turkey needs."

"I guess."

"Are you really upset about us moving?"

I think for a moment, standing up and drifting over to the huge window that looks out from my living room onto my sparkling blue pool. "No, I'm not. But I'll miss you guys," I say honestly.

I know. It's gross and un-masculine. But I like my parents, and I have dinner with them at least once a month, and I guess I've also never really thought about my childhood being so ephemeral—that the biggest fixed geographical point in my life could shift so suddenly.

Plus, this means my mom is really right. I am an adult, and *fuck*, I hate being reminded of that. It makes me start thinking of questions I can't really answer, like what am I going to do with the rest of my life? Will I ever really pursue film as a dream? And don't I someday want to have adult sons of my own whining on the phone about *Rock Band*?

"We will miss you, too," Mom assures me. "I'll call you later next week to set up a time for you to come by and go through your stuff, okay?"

I decide to put my parents moving into a mental box, just like I've done with Devi. I'll figure out how I really feel about it later. "Okay, Mom. Love you."

"Love you, sweetie. Goodbye."

She hangs up, and as she does, I hear a strange clicking noise, clicking like little dog claws on the hardwood. It's a sound that used to be as familiar as the washer running or traffic outside. Out of habit, I squat down and pat my leg, not even thinking about what I'm doing until Prior is actually butting up against my hand and giving me tiny, effeminate yaps to let me know how happy he is to see me.

As I pat his furry gray and blond head, my mind gradually catches up.

Prior.

My old dog.

The dog She-Voldemort took.

Here in my house.

I look up towards the entrance to the living room, already knowing whom I'll see there. And I hate to admit it, but she looks as gorgeous as ever, pale skin accentuated by a red crop top and a yellow tulle skirt, dark hair in a tight ballet bun on the top of her head. As always, she looks a hundred percent New York, a hundred percent fashionable, and a hundred percent unattainable. There used to be a time when I felt like the luckiest guy in the world.

"Hi, Raven," I say, scooping the Yorkie up in my arms and standing.

"Hi, Logan."

They're literally the first words we've said to each other since she left.

She steps forward into the light, and I see her face clearly. Delicate, almost European features. Bright red lips. Eyes limned with the blackest kohl.

"So did you just let yourself in or what?"

"I still have a key," she says primly. "And I thought it was time that we finally talk. After all, you didn't come find me after you saw me being fucked at Vida's."

Entitlement, manipulation and a dose of guilt, all in three sentences.

Yep, it's definitely her, all right.

"What is there to talk about, Raven?" I ask, willing myself to put down the dog and escort her to the door. Except I can't put the dog down because I've fucking missed the shit out of this dog, and I'd bet everything I own that Raven knows that, and brought him for the sole purpose of throwing me off-balance.

She takes a step forward. "Don't act with me, Logan. We both know that you were never a good actor."

Jesus. Going for the balls already.

"I've never pretended to be a good actor," I say as pleasantly as I can while still gritting my teeth.

"Oh, that's right. You wanted to be Logan O'Toole, *erotic auteur*, am I right?"

"What did you want to talk about again?" I repeat, my eyes sliding away from her to the door, wondering how I could make her move towards it. "Because if you came here just to make me feel shitty, I think I'd rather you left."

Raven glances down at the floor, rubbing the back of her right calf with the toe of her left foot, encased in some expensive ankle-boot thing that straddles the line between *haute couture* and Skid Row. "I didn't come here to make you feel shitty," she says after a minute. "I'm sorry about that. I guess I'm feeling defensive because…well, you know why."

There's silence. If this is her apology, her actual play to win over my time and energy, then it's not enough. "I think I do know why, Raven. You left me. You didn't talk to me about it, you didn't leave a note or a voicemail, you just left. I couldn't even tell people that we 'broke up,' because you did all the breaking. You broke my heart, you almost broke my career, and you certainly broke my mind, at least for a little while." Prior reaches up to lick my neck. "Oh yeah, and you took my fucking dog. And all so you could gallivant across Europe and fuck some Italian?"

"It wasn't that simple," she insists. "And it wasn't fucking easy. Do you think I woke up one day, and was like, 'Oh, I'll just throw away three years of my life because I want someone who can read the menu at a pasta place'? It was the hardest decision of my life, walking away from you, and I thought it would be better for me if I left with a clean break."

"Well, I'm so glad you made the decision that was better for *you*," I say bitterly.

Raven throws up her hands. "You're deliberately twisting my words. I only meant that if I had tried to talk it over with you, if I'd lingered in your house—in your bed—then I would have ended up staying."

"And what would have been so terrible about that?" I say, and it comes out broken and hushed, a deathbed whisper, and I hate myself for it. I don't want to show her a single iota of weakness. She doesn't deserve to know how thoroughly she wrecked me.

But as soon as it's said, her face changes. Not into an expression of pity—I probably would have lit my own house on fire if I'd seen even the barest trace of pity on her face—but of pleading.

"Logan," she says, begging. "Please understand. I had to leave for my own sanity, for my own *life*. Everywhere we went, I was your girlfriend. Every industry party, every joint shoot…every *solo* shoot for that matter, I wasn't Raven Fleur, I was Logan O'Toole's fuckdoll. Rumors started that I was only getting jobs because of you, that I would never be able to work if we broke up, and I started to think they might be right. I've been working in this business since I was seventeen, and for the first time in twelve years, I doubted every decision I made. I started to lose a sense of who Raven was, the work she liked to do, because it was so hugely eclipsed by your…" She gestures to me, to the freshly cleaned couch behind me. "Just you. Not only your business—I could have handled that. But your vision. Your *you*-ness. You didn't leave any room for me to create my own world."

I am immediately defensive. "I never, not even once, told you what kind of jobs to take or what kind of scenes to film. I never pressured you to be any more involved with O'Toole films than you wanted to be. And I would certainly never—"

"Logan," she interrupts. "You've never had to pressure anybody in your life. Don't you fucking get it? People fall all over themselves trying to make you happy. One tweet reply from you, one smile across the room at a party, and you win friends for life. And me?" Her mouth twists up in a rueful smile. "I was so desperate for your smiles, to be inside that playful but intense inner circle, that I was sacrificing myself in advance."

"You should have told me," I maintain. "'You should have talked to me!'"

"And said what? Exactly what I just said, and then have you say exactly what you've just said, and then feel both reassured and ignored at the same time? Or worse, ready to go willingly back to my personal prison?"

I turn away from her, walking back towards the window overlooking the pool. I'm too angry and hurt to think clearly, even though I recognize the grains of truth in her words. I *can* be a little monomaniacal about my projects, and I do have a bad habit of wanting everyone I care about to be involved with all the same things I care about too. And maybe if I'd been a more sensitive boyfriend, I would have seen that Raven felt stifled in our creative partnership even as our domestic partnership still sailed steady atop smooth seas.

But it doesn't excuse her cowardice. Or her infidelity.

"You did so much more than try to renew your career when you left. You didn't even pay me the courtesy of a goodbye, not to mention the Italian guy."

She clears her throat, and I realize she's come up very close behind me. "I was wrong to do that. Luca and I…we were seeing each other for a while before I left."

I know this. I have known this for months. So why does her admission spark so much rage inside of me? It should be old news, and besides, it took some courage for her to admit that. She never did like admitting she was wrong.

Once I can trust my voice, I speak, still keeping my eyes on the pool. "I wish you and Luca the best. And I suppose I feel more enlightened now than before we talked, so thank you for that."

"Luca and I broke up," she says quickly, before I can get to the part where I ask her to leave. "It wasn't real, Logan, it never was. He was just in the right place at the right time, able to tell me all the things I wanted to hear."

I swivel my head to look at her. She's standing beside me now, her eyes on the pool as well, one pale hand pressed against the glass.

And then she says it.

"I'm still in love with you." Her dark eyes meet mine. "I know I've fucked things up, but I'm not too proud to beg."

For a moment, I remember why I loved her once. Her sharp beauty. Her stubborn pride. "You don't still love me," I tell her. "You're here because things didn't go according to plan, and I'm the last person you remember being happy with. Whatever you're looking for though, I can't help you. I've moved on."

She takes this on the chin, her only sign of disturbance at my rejection of her a slight sucking of her top teeth.

"You've moved on," she echoes. "Who is she?"

Devi flashes to mind, but no fucking way am I willing to tempt fate like that. Instead I say, "There's not another girl. I just mean that I've moved on personally. I'm past what happened, and I'm looking to the future. I've got a great new project lined up, too."

"A new project?"

I have no interest in pitching *Star-Crossed* to her, but my latent enthusiasm for it bleeds into my words anyway. "It's a new project with Vida and that Dutch studio Lelie, like a reality show where two people are falling in love, but all the sex is also open-door, which makes it better than reality TV. Plus I'm making it with Devi Dare—remember that girl from *Real Playdates*? She's fucking amazing. Like, her body melts my brain, and her actual *brain* could melt my brain, she's so smart."

Raven chews her lip. "Sounds like quite the project."

I shrug. "I'm super pumped about it, but yeah. It's needing pretty much all of my free time."

"That's a shame. I was kind of hoping we could at least work together while I'm in L.A. this month." She drops her hand from the window and smooths her skirt. "You know, some clear-the-air kind of fucking. Even if we don't get back together, it would still feel good, wouldn't it?"

She steps so close to me that I can feel her breath on my chest. Prior squirms to get down, but I hold him tight.

"Don't you want to fuck me?" she asks in a low purr, her mouth in that performance pout I witnessed at Vida's. "Aren't you mad enough at me that it would feel so good to pin me down and take me hard?"

I hate how well she knows me; hate how well she knows I itch for exactly that. But what she doesn't know is that even as I itch for it, I'm also repulsed by the idea of ever touching her again. "No, Julie," I say, using her real name. "I'd rather not."

Her jaw drops and I can't tell if it's using her real name or my outright refusal to work with or sleep with her again, but I don't care. I keep going. "I'm sorry that you felt lost and I'm sorry that you felt like you couldn't talk to me. But for future reference, that's only a good reason to cheat on your partner in indie movies and book club novels. It doesn't excuse what you did, and while I will work on forgiving, I would be an idiot to forget."

I put Prior back in her arms. Her stunned expression is slowly giving way to fury.

"Fuck you," she hisses. "Fuck you, D—" And I see it coming, hear it on the tip of her tongue, but I block it out. She can say my real name in all its twangy and possibly ironic grandeur, but it doesn't change anything about how I feel.

"Goodbye, Raven," I say, and then she shoots me a look of such livid fury that I actually feel its acidic heat prickle against my skin.

She leaves without another word, and after a moment's thought, I shuffle into the kitchen and root around for some scotch. I finally said goodbye to Raven, I finally got all the closure I had once so desperately craved, but I don't feel satisfied. I don't feel at peace.

I feel like getting drunk.

CHAPTER ELEVEN

Thursday dawns with the kind of aggressive sunshine only California in late August can muster. I open one eye, then the other, fully appreciating how much like shit I feel, from my scuzzy mouth to my roiling stomach to my pounding headache.

Yep, I sure showed Raven last night. I drank half a bottle of scotch and sang Ben Folds Five's "Song for the Dumped" at the top of my lungs for about two hours straight, and then I think I went swimming with my clothes on, guessing from the strong smell of chlorine around me and my still-damp clothes.

So what's on the docket today, Your Honor?

Devi. We have a scene today.

I stumble into the bathroom, where I drink approximately seven glasses of water and swallow a handful of Advil without bothering to count out how many.

Well, Cass. I think it's about time you returned a certain favor for me.

I can't wait. Can I come over now?

I glance up at the mirror, wincing at my reflection. I look like Deadpool without his mask.

Sure thing, gorgeous. I partied a little too hard last night, so I'm going to hop in the shower and scrub the top layer of skin off my body, but go ahead and let yourself in. I've got a key under the potted succulent plant by the door.

The three telltale dots appear on my screen while she types and I use the lull in our conversation to brush my teeth and find a clean towel.

Then my phone pings. **I can't believe you didn't make a joke about the word succulent.**

I groan. She's right. I'm off my game.

I think I killed a few brain cells last night. They must have been the funny ones.

Jesus. What—or who—did you do last night?

It involves Ben Folds and mid-level scotch. It doesn't matter. Drive here so I can give you orgasms.

Okay, Cyrano. I'm on my way.

I brush my teeth several more times in the shower and scour my body with soap and a washcloth until the drunk-last-night feeling starts to wash away. "I'm never drinking again," I promise myself in a mumble. And I actually kind of believe it. The truth is that I was never a heavy drinker—I preferred being buzzed to being drunk—but after Raven left, I had no emotional tools to cope with it. No tools except for liquor, that is.

But I feel released from Raven now, released from my complicated emotions about her. I meant what I said yesterday. I'm not in love with her anymore. And I've moved on. In fact, on the other side of things, it's incredible to believe that I was so devastated. Yesterday proved just how different we are, and how I ever thought what we had was actually sustainable happiness is astounding.

Finally clean and awake, I turn off the shower and pad into my room, settling for my usual uniform of a T-shirt and jeans. I scrub at my hair with the towel, don't bother brushing it, and then walk out to my living room, where I find the patio door open and Devi Dare out by my pool. Hopping into my pool, actually.

And she's completely naked.

I walk over to call out to her, to tell her that I'm finished getting ready, but then I pause as she breaks the surface of the water, slicks her hair back, and starts backstroking easily across the pool. She has no idea I'm standing here, has no idea that anyone is watching, and she's so unself-conscious right now, so natural. So fucking sexy.

I lick my lips as I watch her, water droplets shimmering on the soft curves of her breasts, on the taut lines of her stomach. A small pool of water has gathered in her navel, highlighting the dip it makes in her trim but still feminine stomach. Her skin is a dark bronze in the bluish-clear water, and her hair is like a coffee-colored cloud around her head.

Her eyes are shut, her nipples are hard, and God-fucking-damn if I'm not more turned on than I've ever been. My cock is already pushing against my jeans, my pulse speeding up, and never have I wanted to fuck someone so badly that it's like I want to crawl inside of them, like I want to fuse my soul to theirs.

But that's how I feel now.

Quietly, like a sailor trying not to disturb a mermaid, I move closer to the door and pull out my phone. I start filming her.

It's mesmerizing, the way she effortlessly cuts through the water. The grace, the supple lines of her body, the sharp contrasts in color coupled with the occasional tantalizing glance of her pussy—

It's not porn, I know that, otherwise I'd be running for my actual camera. But it's undeniably, powerfully, painfully erotic; it's that slow burn of desire that reminds you with subtle but insistent nudges that you are a sexual being. It's the kind of image that lodges in your mind before it nudges your dick, and makes it that much harder to shake, that much more consuming. My theater teacher in high school liked to talk about the unities, where time and place and action all converged into one point. Well, Devi is my unity right now. Drawing my body and my mind and my heart into a single, crystalline point, fusing all the disparate Logans into one bewitched, infatuated man.

I was wrong earlier—I'm not *falling* for her.

I've already fallen.

I don't know how, given that I can count the number of times we've hung out on one hand, and I don't know why necessarily, given that she's so vastly different than the other career porn stars I've dated.

But it's true, nonetheless.

I tap my phone screen and end my private video, my throat tight for no reason other than the display of beauty in front of me. I want to jump in there, I want to fish her out of that damn pool and make love to her right here in the sun, but I don't, because I'm a coward. Because I still remember how it felt to be abandoned, rejected by someone I loved.

Instead, I clear my throat. She drops her feet to the bottom of the pool with a sheepish smile. "Sorry," she grins. "I couldn't resist."

"I can't resist *you*," I rejoin, but the joke is half-hearted because she's climbing out of the pool, and I'm having trouble breathing.

Water streams off her firm, curvy body as she walks towards me. She seems so casual, so open about being naked, and then I wonder if it's because she is always like that or if it's because she trusts me and feels comfortable with me.

The thought gives me a little puff of pride, with a simultaneous jolt of affection, and I'm determined to keep her comfortable around me, no matter what the cost. Even if it means keeping my inner Romeo caged up for the time being. I'm sure she has guys claiming to be in love with her all the time. The last thing she needs is her co-worker doing it.

"Do you want a towel?" I ask.

"Yes, please."

I go fetch her one, but—I can't help myself—I don't hand it to her. I towel her off myself instead, drying her limbs before I stand up and dab gently at her face.

She's smiling. "Full service pool. I like it."

"It's not the only thing that's full service. Come on inside."

Without bothering to scoop up her clothes, she follows me, and while I talk, I try to drown out the voice in my mind that's screaming *she's almost naked she's almost naked, under that towel she's naked.* I'm around naked women every day; it shouldn't be something that affects me. But it's Devi, and so it does. Not only because her body is delicious and perfect, but because this marks the first time I've seen her completely naked in person since *Real Playdates* all those years ago.

Somehow, I manage to keep it together—at least on the surface. "So, I have a little something special planned for our oral scene tonight. Do you have any plans late tonight or early tomorrow?"

"Tomorrow?" she asks, and her cheeks darken. "Um, no. I'm pretty much completely free until morning."

"Excellent," I say, walking backward into my room. I re-emerge with a bag stuffed full of shit—film equipment but also clothes and toiletries and a giant-ass sleeping bag hanging off the side. "Our scene might be filmed late at night. Is that okay?"

She swallows. And nods. "More than okay," she gets out.

God, I want to fuck her right now. Watch that delicate throat move as I take a nipple into my mouth. Watch that mouth part when I finally push inside of her.

Patience, patience, I coax myself. *All good things come in time.*

• • •

"I don't think you can handle it," I say doubtfully an hour later. After Devi dressed and I packed the car, I decided that I needed hangover food—stat—so I took her to a bar on the edge of the suburbs. Ungentrified, unglamorous, without even the cozy, warm feeling of a dive hangout. Nope, this place is as cheap as it is soulless, and that's why I like it. No lawyer bros on lunch break, no hipsters basking in a "genuine vibe." Russell's caters to one clientele and one clientele only—people willing to put up with surly service and scuffed drywall for cold beer and the best wings in the city.

Right now, Devi Dare, in her naive innocence, thinks she can handle a dozen wings on her own.

"Why don't you start with a half dozen?" I suggest diplomatically.

She looks up from the laminated menu. "This is not my first wings rodeo, son."

"Devi, I only like to tell women what to do in bed. But I'm telling you, a dozen is too many."

She smirks at me. "Want to put money on it?"

"I can think of things more interesting than money."

"Like what?" Her eyes are sparkling.

"Okay, if you can't eat all the wings, then I get to take you to the most arthouse, painfully subtitled movie playing right now."

"And if I can eat them all?"

I shrug. "I don't know. What's something that would be totally new to me?"

She thinks for a moment, looking at the ceiling and slowly tapping her mouth with one, slender finger…

….And that is how I end up on Venice Beach two hours later walking towards a small psychic's shop.

• • •

Devi leads the way down the boardwalk, her fingers laced loosely through mine as she half pulls me forward. "I can't believe you doubted my ability to eat wings," she huffs, the breath catching in her throat the precise same way I'd like it to when I'm fucking her.

Even her scoffing is sexy. Jesus, I have it bad.

"You just seem so healthy," I argue. "Like the kind of girl who only eats chia seeds and that kind of shit."

She giggles as a gust of wind blows her hair around her face, and fuck, she's so young. I know eight years isn't the biggest difference in the grand scheme of things, but it feels big right now. It feels important.

Worse, it feels exciting.

"I eat pretty healthy most of the time," she admits. "Mostly because my parents are always dropping stuff by. A fresh batch of kombucha or leftover kale from their co-op or whatever. But at least once or twice a week, I eat something terrible and amazing. Like a triple cheeseburger. Or a dozen wings. After all, this ass won't stay thick on its own."

She gives her ass a playful smack. I almost perish on the spot.

"Anyway," she continues, "I think balance is important, right? A little bad sprinkled into good makes everything so much more interesting."

"You have to stop talking like this or I'm not going to be fit to meet the psychic."

She laughs again, and then we're at the bead-covered door of *Madam Psuka's, Psychic Extraordinaire*. Neon moons and stars vainly attempt to compete with the bright beach sunlight.

"We're really lucky," Devi says in a hushed voice. "She spends half the year in Michigan. Whenever she comes back to L.A., she's usually too swamped with her repeat customers to see anyone."

A ray of hope blossoms inside me. "So maybe she won't be able to see us today?" I ask, trying not to sound too relieved.

Devi just points to the sign hanging in the window. *Walk-Ins Welcome Today.*

"Shit," I mutter.

Devi swats at my arm. "You lost fair and square. Be a good sport."

"You can't really believe all this stuff, right? It's so silly. And you're so...science-y."

She pushes me inside, into the thick, dark air within. While my eyes adjust, I hear Devi digging into her big slouchy shoulder bag, and when I can finally see again, I realize she has my camera. I gave it to her just in case we wanted to capture any moments for *Star-Crossed*.

She turns it on. "I think this is worth filming. It's like we're on a fake date again! Wings and now psychics."

"You know, when I gave you that, I was really just imagining us finding a place to make out or something."

She tuts at me and flaps her hand, indicating that I should sit in one of the chairs packed into the tiny waiting area where we are now. "It smells like pot," I observe, taking a few more experimental sniffs. "A *lot* of pot."

Devi grins. "It's sage. People burn it to purify a space of negative energy."

"*This* is considered purified? I think that is an excellent way to cover up smoking pot. 'Oh no, officer, I wasn't smoking marijuana, I was just purifying my car of negative energy.'"

Devi giggles, and then I hear an older woman say, "Boombalee!"

It's not precisely English—or any other language I know—and I wonder if it's psychic-speak for something important, or if maybe this woman is speaking in tongues or having a stroke, but then she pushes past the beads separating the inner space from the waiting room and scurries toward Devi, arms outstretched.

"Oh, shit," Devi mutters, looking at me with something akin to panic. "I'm so sorry about this."

"Sorry about what?"

But she can't talk now because the woman has pulled her up from her chair and wrapped her in a massive hug. She's in her late forties, with thick gray-blond hair tied back in a utilitarian braid, and a petite but willowy build. She's wearing a long skirt and blouse that have an unmistakable "Sedona, Arizona" vibe. For a minute, I think she's the psychic but then she pulls back and I say aloud, "Holy shit."

They both turn to look at me beamingly, and it's so apparent now that I feel retroactively stupid for not having seen it before. The woman looks exactly like Devi, but without the Persian coloring. The same high cheekbones and pointed chin, the same heart-shaped faces with identical, beautiful smiles.

It's Devi's mom.

I stick out my hand. "Logan O'Toole. Nice to meet you."

"Sue Jones-Daryani. What brings you to Madam Psuka's today? And how come I haven't seen you in over a week, Boombalee? I miss you."

"*Mom,*" Devi says, a little embarrassed. "I've been busy. And don't call me that in public!"

"Boombalee? Devi, I labored for twenty-seven hours with no medication to bring you into this world, and when you came out, you tore my—"

"Mom!" Devi looks seriously alarmed now. "Can you *not* in front of my colleague?"

"My point is, I'll call you whatever I want." Her gray eyes fall back to me and she softens. "It's nice to meet you, Logan. Are you making pornography with my daughter?"

I can't help but laugh. "Yes, ma'am. I am."

"I'm glad to hear it. You have very virile energy, you know. I can feel the pulsing of your sacral chakra from here."

"Uh…is that something I should get checked out by a doctor?"

Sue tuts at me in just the same way that Devi tutted at me earlier and reaches behind me, pressing her palm against the very top part of my ass. Beside me, Devi makes the kind of groan someone would make if they were willing themselves to die, and when I look over, she's got her face buried in her hands in mortification.

I, however, am having a *great* time.

"Ms. Jones-Dayrani, you're trying to seduce me, aren't you?" I tease as she gives my chakra a few extra pats for good measure.

"Young man, I've never had to seduce a single sexual partner in my life, and I'm certain that you've never needed to either."

I give a modest half-shrug.

"Mom, can you please get your hand off Logan's ass now?"

Sue sighs, as if her daughter is the biggest prude in the world. "Devi, your sacral chakra, on the other hand, is completely blocked. And *something's* going on with your heart chakra." She frowns. "We need to do some reiki, or maybe you should see Dr. Tammaro for acupuncture. But in the meantime, I recommend some meditation and maybe some vigorous sex to unblock that chakra."

"I'd be happy to help your daughter with that, ma'am," I chime in with a wide grin.

Devi's hands are still on her face. "Isn't there like a midwifery conference or something that you need to be at?"

"Actually, your father and I have hot yoga class, so I should be off. But you need to come over this week for dinner sometime. We just got a whole box of manioc roots from our co-op and we'll need help eating them all."

"Okay," Devi says with the exact level of excitement you'd expect from someone agreeing to eat manioc root. "I'll call you."

Sue gives her a big hug, and then leans in to kiss my cheek. "Honor her," is the firm intonation she delivers in my ear, but the sternness is softened by the affectionate caress she gives my sacral chakra. And then she opens the door and leaves the shop.

"I am *so sorry,*" Devi groans as she throws herself into a nearby chair. "I knew about this place because my mother comes here, but I had no idea she would be in today, and I am so, so embarrassed right now."

"Why?" I don't sit. I stand in front of her and nudge her knees with my own. "I thought she was great. More than great; she's awesome. Just like you."

Devi lifts her eyes to mine. "Really? You don't hate me now that you've met my wack-a-doo mom?"

"The exact opposite. The more I learn about you, the more I want to know." *The more I fall in love with you.*

I don't say that, obviously.

She bites her lip to keep from smiling too wide, and my pulse speeds up. I'm suddenly and painfully aware of how her bare knees rub against my jeans, of the way the thin cotton bodice of her mini dress pulls away from her skin, revealing to an explicit degree how very much she is not wearing anything underneath.

I lean down. The camera's still dangling in her hand, the standby light blinking, but I ignore it and use my thumb and forefinger to guide her face up to mine.

She blinks those long, dark eyelashes once, twice, and then I bring my lips to hers. She is all soft warmth, sunshine and cinnamon, and I breathe her in even as I kiss her, even as I dizzily wonder if this is how it happens for other people. Do they eat wings and see psychics and have awkward run-ins with parents? Do they spend days on random adventures, treasuring every single second spent in each other's company?

This isn't a fake date at all… I realize. *This is a real date now.*

"This is not a kissing parlor," a brusque voice informs us.

We straighten up, and I turn around to see a woman with scratchy-looking blond hair and more beaded necklaces than I would have thought possible.

"Madam Psuka?" Devi asks, standing up from the chair and straightening her clothes. "Hi. I'm Sue's daughter."

"Yes, I know who you are," the medium says impatiently. Her accent is of indiscriminate origin—definitely former Soviet Bloc—and when she waves her hand, I smell Aqua-Net and the kind of perfume that you buy from a grocery store.

"We're actually here for my friend Logan," Devi explains. "I wanted him to come get a reading."

"What kind of reading?"

They're both looking at me. "I, uh, don't know?"

Madam narrows her eyes at me. "No palm reading today, I think. No horoscope or rune stones. You need tarot. One card."

Devi practically jumps up and down. "Tarot's my favorite!"

"This will be quick," Madam says in a way I find weirdly ominous, and then she vanishes into her inner chamber and returns with a wicker basket filled with velvet bags. "Pick deck," she orders in that clipped accent of hers.

I pick a velvet bag at random, right there in the foyer, and then Madam nods, as if that's the deck she expected me to pick all along. There's a glass counter in the corner with an ancient register on top and flyers for psychic fairs and New Age conferences pinned up on the walls all around, and she walks over there now, setting the bag down on top.

She pulls the cards out and indicates that I should come stand by her.

"Knock once, then shuffle with the question in your heart. After that, hand the deck to me." She hands me the cards, and I glance over at Devi, who nods in encouragement, and I think, *why the hell not?* I'm on this sort of accidentally real date with a girl I'm in love with, why not see where this takes me?

So I rap on the deck with my knuckles and then I pick the cards up to shuffle them. They are larger than playing cards, but my hands are big enough to make it work. (That's what she said.)

As I shuffle, I get glimpses of the art on the cards, which seems to be comprised of lots and lots of naked people. Fitting, I guess, but maybe a little too fitting, judging from Madam's smirk as she notices me noticing the cards.

Just a coincidence. I don't believe in this shit, and Devi doesn't either. Right?

"Think of it as focused meditation," she says, as if she knows what I'm thinking. "It will give you a new frame of reference for your question."

Oh, shit. The question. I cast around for anything I want to ask, but actually my life is really solid right now. Good money, steady work I enjoy. Closure over Raven (if not over my dog.) Really the only thing up in the air is Devi, and she's not so much a question as a…

A what? A hope? A possibility?

I don't know what to ask, so instead I just think of Devi. I think of Devi and I think of *Star-Crossed* and I think of all the times I've felt that big, magic feeling with her. And I hope the tarot deck can make sense of all that.

I finish shuffling and hand the deck to Madam Psuka, who briskly cuts the deck into three stacks. "Point to pile."

"Um…"

"She means that you need to pick a pile to go on top," Devi whisper-explains.

I point to the center stack, and again Madam gives that nod, as if that's what she expected all along. She gathers up the deck, with the stack I picked on top, and then she slides the card off the top and with great flourish lays it on the counter.

"*The Hanged Man,*" she announces dramatically, as if I'm supposed to know what that means. I look over at Devi, but her face reveals nothing.

I don't know much (or anything) about tarot cards, but a card called *The Hanged Man* doesn't really imbue me with confidence. I'd rather get a card called *The Frequently Fellated Man* or maybe *The Incredibly Wealthy and Amazingly Endowed Man*. But I guess there's no helping that now. With a resigned sigh, I lean over to examine it.

It's a beautiful but disturbing illustration of a naked man hanging upside down from a tree, ropes wrapped shibari-style around his body. He hangs primarily by one leg, the other leg fastened in a bent position so that his left ankle is behind his right knee. His arms are lashed behind his back, and rope crisscrosses his body in banded patterns, cutting into the firm muscles of his stomach and legs.

Most striking of all is his face. If I were to be hanged upside down from a tree, I think I'd be considerably upset, but he seems to be enduring his fate quietly. Pensively, even. He stares straight ahead with a clear, almost curious, expression, and the corners of his mouth are tilted in what appears to be a small, knowing smirk, as if he knows something I don't.

"He is at peace because he hung himself from the tree," Madam Psuka tells me, her voice startling me upright. "He chose this path. Like Odin or Dionysus, he has sacrificed himself for greater cause."

"I don't have any great causes in my life," I point out. "Certainly not any that would require me to hang from a tree."

Madam Psuka briefly shuts her eyes, as if my ignorance pains her. "Is metaphor," she says, a little defensively, her accent thickening. "Is not literal."

"So I have to *metaphorically* hang myself from a tree?"

She taps the card. "This card means that you are coming to time of great choice. You will be asked to sacrifice something intensely personal and important."

Hmm. I don't like the way that sounds at all. "Do I at least get something awesome in return?"

Madam Psuka gives me a shrug that is so very, very European. "Who can say? Is not job of *The Hanged Man* to know. He knows only that he must have faith. But he also knows that he may perish instead, without having gained anything at all."

All this talk of perishing and sacrifice and death is a bit of a boner-killer. I turn to glare at Devi. "You told me this would be fun!"

"I said no such thing!" she exclaims. "I only said it was my favorite."

"Getting creepy cards is your favorite?"

"They're not all creepy," she says, jutting her lower lip out in a way that makes me want to bite it. "They just reflect different stages of a journey. That's all."

"She is right," Madam affirms. "This card is not meant to frighten. If you are disturbed, it's only because you sense—deep down—is truth. Here," she says abruptly, pushing the card across the counter. "You must take this with you. It belongs in your care now."

The pain and sacrifice card? No thanks. "That's kind, Madam, but I—"

Devi elbows me, and I realize that I should shut up. "How much do we owe you for the reading?" she asks sweetly.

Madam looks me over. "Nothing," she pronounces, her *g* sounding like a *k*. "Is favor for Sue."

"Thank you," Devi says, giving Madam Psuka a hug. "Come on, Logan."

Madam Psuka picks up the card and holds it out to me. There's no way to refuse it without looking rude, so I grudgingly take it from her fingers.

"Sacrifice is just another word for change," she tells me, her thick brows drawn together. "Change that requires letting go."

I give her a nod and then I let Devi tug me back into the blinding sunlight outside.

CHAPTER TWELVE

"So you never told me where we're going for the blowjob," Devi says a few hours later. With Madam Psuka's card jammed in my back pocket, we walked all over the boardwalk, eating shaved ice and hot dogs and cotton candy, and watching the street artists. Then Devi led me down to the beach and we walked ankle-deep in the surf, gossiping about the porn people we knew and speculating about what would happen in the next couple of years with our industry. And then we made our way to my car, where we are now, heading back into the city.

I look over at Devi. As usual, she has the window cracked, the hot wind ruffling her hair. For a brief, tiny moment, I panic that the tarot card Madam drew for me might mean that Devi and I can't make it, or won't make it, for some important but unseeable reason, and my veins are flooded with an anxious adrenaline.

It's not real, I tell myself. *It's not real.*

But what if it is? What if this is some sort of sign that Devi doesn't love me back? Or that I'll have to give her up?

It's not real.

Despite my mental pep talk, anxiety coats my voice when I say, "It's a surprise where we're going."

She hears the change in my voice and turns her head to stare at me. "Are you okay?"

"Yeah. Fine."

"Okay," she says gently, letting me have my space without the slightest hint of resentment, and then I feel bad for shutting her out.

I take a breath, and then confess. "That tarot card is a little disturbing, don't you think?"

She laughs. "Is that really what you're thinking about right now, Mr. This Stuff Is So Silly?"

"Well, it's hard to think it's silly with all the death imagery," I say, a bit grumpily.

"*The Hanged Man* isn't dead, he's suffering. There's a difference."

"Well, that cheers me right up. Thank you."

"But in the end, he sees the world completely differently. Sometimes perspective is painful."

"You know, maybe you should also be fired from the fortune cookie factory."

She puts a hand on my thigh, her fingers warm and slender, and I relax under her touch. "It's not divination, Logan. It's not prophecy. It's just something to think about."

Sigh. "Sure, Cass."

"I think I know what would cheer you up."

"What's that?" I ask, but then her seat belt is unbuckled and she's kneeling on her seat and leaning into me, her lips against my neck. And then she's sucking, soft and wet, sending shivers down my spine and straight to my balls, which start feeling heavy and constrained in my jeans. I want to slide my hand up her thighs and see what else is soft and wet, but my stupid car is a manual transmission, and the thick L.A. traffic means I'm constantly shifting between gears as I slow down and speed up.

"This isn't fair," I murmur. "I can't touch you back."

"Mmm, good," she croons into my ear. "I get to be the one in control."

"Don't say that stuff to me, Cass, or we may not make it to our destination."

She doesn't respond, just keeps kissing and licking all around my neck and earlobe and jaw, and it's only by the grace of God that I don't crash the car. As it is, I still arrive at our filming spot with a hard-on straining the seams of my jeans. I can barely focus enough to get the car parked and turned off.

"Where are we?" Devi asks, finally relenting with the necking and peering out the windshield. We're outside a small mural-covered warehouse near the river, with the skyline towering in the background, shimmering in the evening heat.

My skin dies a little when she pulls away, but it's probably necessary unless I want to walk in there with a giant erection tenting my jeans. "It's an art gallery, a new one. They're doing an exhibit I thought you might like." I'm a little shy when I say this, mostly because I'm worried she'll think it's lame, and I want to impress her, dammit, and not just with my ability to make her come in under two minutes. "The gallery owner let me rent it for the night, so after it closes to the public at nine, it's all ours until morning."

Her face splits into a huge smile. "That sounds amazing. Porn in an art gallery?"

"Yeah, I'd like to say that I have this meta vision for juxtaposing high art and low art, but really it's because I thought the exhibit was something you'd like, plus it was cheap to rent."

"I won't tell if you don't," she says with a wink, and then gets out of the car. I get out too, grab our bag, and walk to the front door to open it for her, catching a glimpse of the inside through the glass as I do.

It's still eight o'clock, meaning that the gallery is open, and to my dismay, I see that there's some sort of reception going on, so the space is crowded with people drinking free wine and milling around. I was hoping to get some shots of Devi walking around the exhibit, since I got permission from both the owner and the artist to use it as a backdrop, but filming her will be difficult with a bunch of randos walking into my shot and needing releases or whatever.

I quickly decide it's okay, and that I can always film her later. I'm too excited for her to see it to wait any longer. I open the door all the way, unleashing the normal gallery onslaught of music and voices. I gesture for Devi to walk in and she does.

I follow her in, admiring the way her ass moves under her dress as I do. Rich orchestral music reverberates throughout the space, deep strings and discordant piano keys, and I see the exact moment that Devi realizes what the exhibit is, understands why I thought she'd like it.

"Logan," she breathes, reaching for my hand without taking her eyes off the display in front of us. "This is…you…I can't believe…" She finally stops trying to put her feelings into words and simply squeezes my hand, overcome. My heart soars so far above the ground that I'm certain it's reached lunar orbit.

If this is all it takes to make her so happy, then I'm taking her to an art gallery every day.

The exhibit is called *Zodiactive* and is laid out in a large circle. All throughout the gallery, tiny light bulbs of various brightness are arranged, in a manner that looks completely random and discombobulated to me, but that I know from the gallery's website is designed to mimic the constellations visible from Los Angeles at this time of year. The bulbs are strung up high, but also line the walls, creating the dazzling effect of being surrounded by stars. Gauzy strips of fabric in deep lavenders and pinks hang from the ceiling, wafting with the movement of the guests, the ephemeral panels representing nebulas and gas clouds. And punctuating the gallery space at regular intervals are huge, magnificent paintings, each one representing a sign of the zodiac, with more light bulbs studding the canvas to show where the actual stars are in each constellation.

The artist in me appreciates the effect of the light and the color and the spacey music, but the Logan in me, who doesn't know shit about the zodiac or the constellations they come from, is deeply bored. So instead, I turn all of my attention to Devi, watching her eager eyes drink everything in, watching the way her lips move as she murmurs quiet things to herself that I can't quite catch. We make our way around the circle, stopping every three feet for Devi to examine the light bulbs and declare which constellations they are supposed to be, and once for me to grab a couple cups of free wine.

At one point, she stops and slowly spins around, as if lost. "It's like being *in* the sky," she tells me with excitement in her voice. "It's easy to forget that the sky isn't flat, that the stars are actually light years apart. But it doesn't feel cold or distant at all when rendered this way. It feels intimate."

I lift my hand and gently sweep some hair out of her eyes. She pauses and looks at me, our eyes meeting, and it's as if every atom in my body is thrumming with electricity. There's something about her, some indefinable *thing*, that supersedes her lovely face and sexy-as-hell body and even her top-notch brain. It's strange, because even at the height of my relationship with Raven, I could list logically all the reasons I enjoyed being with her—namely sex and shared interests—and loving her was more of a sustained choice than a feeling. But with Devi, it's more than a choice *or* a feeling—it's fact, just as much a universal fact as gravity, or the speed of light.

Because with Devi, it's different. It's like there's something beyond the quantifiable, easy-to-name reasons she affects me. My pull to her is something above the sexual, above the intellectual, and maybe even above the emotional, and all of a sudden, I feel myself at the edge of a vast abyss. My stomach drops as I continue looking into those dark gold eyes, because what I feel for Devi is a thousand times stronger than anything I've ever felt, even after three years with Raven, and I'm scared. I'm scared by the intensity of my own feelings, and I'm scared that she doesn't feel the same way. I'm scared that this speed of light feeling is going to blast a hole right through me, and I'll be left gutted in a way that Raven never could have gutted me.

It's this fear that makes me swallow and look away. "Do you want more wine?" I ask Devi, even though I know she's barely touched the wine she already has.

"No, I'm good." She puts a hand on my wrist. "Logan, this is more than I could have ever expected. *This* is the best fake date I've ever been on."

Her words prick into me like needles.

Fake date.

Right. Because now we're on location. But then why can't it also be real? Why can't something be real *and* planned? Real *and* recorded? Why can't it be both?

I can't help myself, I say the words pressing against the inside of my lips begging to be let out. "It's not a fake date, Devi. Yes, we're recording what happens later, but it's real." I plead with her with my eyes. "I want us…I mean—I want there to be an *us*. I want to take you on actual dates. I want this to be a real date."

Her lips are parted ever so slightly, and they tremble now as she searches for a response, and oh my God, I am going to devour her mouth if I watch it any longer. With a quick glance around us, I grab her hand and pull her in between two of the zodiac canvases, and suddenly the noise dims a little and we are by ourselves, sandwiched between canvas and exposed brick. I lead her a little farther around the outer edge of the exhibit, until we're near the back of the gallery space. Here, the narrow gaps between the canvases are covered with a cluster of gauzy fabric panels and the comparative dearth of lights in this corner gives an extra shroud of shadows. In other words, though only a few inches of fabric, canvas and paint separate us from the other people in the gallery, it won't be easy to be seen, unless somebody took the trouble to look at the six-inch gap between the floor and the bottom of the canvas, but I honestly doubt that will happen.

Once we're sufficiently hidden, I take her cup of wine and set it down a nearby ledge with mine, and drop my bag to the floor. Devi looks like she's used this interval to compose herself somewhat.

"It can't be a real date if we're filming it," she says, her chin rising slightly. "This is amazing, Logan, don't get me wrong. No man has ever done anything like this with me. But once we turn on the camera, it's different. You have to see that. Even if it's not solely performative, it can't be completely genuine."

I'm already shaking my head. "I don't think there has to be barrier between art and life. I don't think capturing a moment makes it any less authentic."

She gives me a sad smile. "But when that moment's being captured to make money? When that moment is being made for sale? How can that not retroactively affect the moment itself?"

A tiny voice inside of me wonders if she has a point, but I push it aside. I want to prove to her that we can have it all—the realness and the camera—and that all it takes is a shift in perspective. After all, wasn't that what she was trying to explain to me about *The Hanged Man*? Perspective?

I step closer to her. "Will you let me try to convince you?"

"Convince me of what?"

I lean forward and brace myself against the wall with my forearms, caging her between the wall and me. "Let me turn on the camera," I say, using the tip of my nose to trace the line of her jaw. She shudders and goose bumps erupt everywhere on her skin. "Let me film us doing our thing tonight and show you how real it can be."

"I'm not saying I don't want to film," she says. I take her earlobe between my teeth and she lets out a soft groan. "I just…"

"I know what you're saying," I breathe into her ear. "And what I'm saying is I want you to be open to the idea of it feeling real. I want you to forget about the camera while I'm touching you."

"I can't," she protests faintly.

"I think you can. At least let me try to help you?"

She sighs, half resignation, half pleasure because my mouth

is now on her neck. "Okay," she relents. "I'll try to forget about the camera tonight."

I give her neck one last nip and then straighten up, reaching for my bag.

"Wait, *now*?" she asks, sounding horrified. "While there're still people here?"

I give her an evil grin. "Are you being modest, Devi Dare?"

"There's a difference between modest and law-abiding," she shoots back.

Undeterred, I dig out the camera and turn it on, setting it on the ledge so it's aimed at our corner. While I adjust the settings to compensate for the dim light, Devi lists off all the reasons it's a bad idea to film right now.

"We could get caught. We could get thrown out. We could get arrested. They'll find out you didn't have the right permits and you could get fined. Even Vida could get in trouble."

Satisfied that the camera is set up well, I walk towards her and slowly back her into the wall. Her voice falters and her words trail off as my stomach touches hers, and then she gasps as my hips move forward and I press my growing erection into her.

"I'm not ignoring your concerns," I tell her, sliding one hand around her waist and the other up her neck to hold the side of her face. "But I want you to trust me. Let me take on your concerns, and I promise to take care of you. I'll be responsible for you—for us—and I'll make sure we don't get caught."

I feel her hesitate, and even though I want nothing more than to seal my lips over hers and kiss the resistance right out of her, I have to know whether or not this is an actual limit for her.

I use my hand to guide her face so that she's looking at me. "Devi, it's okay if this is a boundary. Being in public. All you have to do is tell me."

She worries at her bottom lip with her teeth, and then she finally shakes her head. "As long as you listen for anyone…"

"I give you my solemn vow."

"…then I guess it's okay."

"You guess? I need more than that, Cass."

She takes a breath. "I'm sure it's okay."

"I don't know how much better that is." I'm full hard now, and all I want is to start, but I have to know that she feels safe and comfortable.

Otherwise, no dice. "It seems like you're uncertain…do you want to try it and then if you need to stop, we can stop?"

Her forehead wrinkles. "Like with using a safe word?"

"Right, but you can just snap your fingers if you'd like." I've found that many girls struggle to vocalize their limits, even with permission, and sometimes things like snapping fingers are easier.

"Okay. I'll snap my fingers if I want to stop. But I don't think I'll need to." She gives me a small smile. "I trust you."

"Thank God," I exhale. "I didn't know how much longer I could keep from kissing you."

"Then don't wait any longer," she says, and I don't. I do have something to prove, after all.

I lower my face, brushing across her mouth once, twice, three times before I firmly settle my lips against hers. For a minute, everything seems singularly slow and distinct: her small inhalations and exhalations tickling the skin above my upper lip, the way her hand finds the back of my neck to pull me even closer to her, the way my heart pounds in my chest as I cradle her face against mine. And then time catches up with us all in a rush, Devi's fingers finding my hair and pulling, my hand dropping down past her hip. I ruck up her skirt until my hand finds the bare skin of her ass and then I'm grabbing and squeezing the delicious curve of firm flesh, my cock leaping every time my fingers dig into her skin.

She's just as busy, her other hand finding the bottom of my shirt and then sliding up my stomach to trail lines of light scratches across my abs. I hiss as she finds a flat nipple and pinches it, the sensation traveling straight to my dick.

I deepen the kiss, parting her lips with mine and licking inside her mouth. It's sweet, like the cotton candy she ate earlier, and warm—and like a lightning strike, I remember that she's going to suck me off with that sweet, warm mouth, and I have to pull back for a second to clear my head.

"What?" she murmurs, using the break in the kiss to move her mouth to my neck, sucking and biting hard enough to bruise, and I have to wrap my hands around the brick ledge to keep from shoving her to her knees right then and there.

Keep control, you asshat.

After all, I am supposed to be proving something to her, right? Not simply proving how much I want her to go down on me. I'm going to prove to her how real and how organic we can be, even with the camera.

Resolve renewed, I take a step back. "Turn around," I say, keeping my voice quiet to account for the people enjoying the art mere feet away.

Biting her lower lip, she pivots so that she's facing the wall. I lean forward enough that my mouth comes close to her ear. "Brace your hands against the wall," I whisper.

She shivers and more of those delightful goose bumps appear, and she obeys, her slender hands spread wide and flat against the brick. The thin dress she's wearing has ridden up slightly in back, and I place a hand in the middle of her shoulder blades and push her forward even more, so that the hem of the dress barely clears her ass.

And then I drop down to my knees, my palms sliding up the back of her thighs to her rump. I inch the hem of her skirt up until she's mostly uncovered and then I spread her cheeks to see a thin strip of lace covering her pussy. She's wearing a thong, as white as fresh snow, and I get the most maddening glimpses of what that lace is hiding—tiny curlicues of glistening pink, small semi-circles of smooth bronze.

Without hesitation, I bury my face there, the flat of my tongue running over the lace to press against her clit. She gasps above me, her legs widening to grant me better access, and I oblige her unspoken request, repeating the motion over her clit and then moving my tongue to her entrance, she and I together thoroughly soaking the lace all the way through. I can taste her through the fabric, and the taste is a perfect balance of sweet and female, a taste that triggers all of my most primal, male impulses.

I hook a finger in her thong and pull it aside, and the moment my tongue makes unfettered contact with her cunt, she sucks in a breath and raises up on her tiptoes. Finger still holding the thong aside, I lick from her clit to the small button of firm flesh between her cheeks, and I repeat the process several times, until I can sense her breathing speeding up. Then I add a finger, then two, curling them against the sensitive front wall of her pussy as I bite and suck on her ass.

She's breathing hard now, her thighs tense, and I abandon her entrance and start rubbing her clit fast and hard. She throws her head back, her fingers turning into claws against the brick, and then I withdraw. Completely.

She spins around, dazed and angry. "Don't stop," she pants, and I shrug with one shoulder. I bring my fingers to my mouth to suck her taste off them, and her eyes narrow. I do a little internal victory dance when she doesn't glance at the camera once as she steps forward. I knew that to distract her from the filming would mean making her focus only on me, and making her angry and needy seemed like the best way to do that. Looks like I've succeeded.

"Finish me off," she says in a furious plea.

"But you're so cute when you're angry."

"Don't fuck with me—finish fucking me."

"What about," I offer mischievously, "you give me head, and then I'll *think* about finishing you off."

"You bastard. I can finish myself off." She pulls up her dress and then moves her hand underneath her thong, slumping against the wall when she finds her clit with her fingers. God, I'm so fucking glad I'm filming this, even if she's forgotten.

I stare at her hungrily, watching her fingers move under the lace and her nipples bead and strain against her dress. I don't have to look down to see that my dick is practically sobbing at me to do something; I can feel the wet spot growing on the inside of my jeans.

But still I wait, wait until her cheeks are flushed and her eyes are closed, when her orgasm is imminent, and then I grab her wrist and pull her hand away from her pussy. Her eyes snap open and an expression of beautiful, incandescent rage lights her face. Behind us, I hear the gallery music change into a soft melody, which makes the footsteps on the gallery hardwoods and the animated chatter seem even closer, like any minute people could push through the fabric and find us.

I fucking love that.

Devi, however, looks like love is nowhere near what she's feeling, and she tries to wrench her wrist away from me. When I don't let her, she tries to push her other hand down to her cunt, and I don't let her do that either, sandwiching her body between mine and the wall and leaving no room for her to touch herself.

"Fuck," she groans, trying to squirm against me, and I grin.

"You seem like you want something," I say cheerfully.

"Fuck you."

"Hmm," I respond, slowly guiding her hand to her mouth. She doesn't resist, letting me push her fingers past her lips to touch her tongue. She licks her own taste off her fingertips in curling, deliberate licks, like a cat, and I watch her tongue obsessively. Fuck, I can't wait until it's on my cock.

"I think that you might want something," I repeat, my eyes still on her mouth. "And you know else what I think?"

She raises an eyebrow at me but not very high. Her eyes are glazed with lust and her pulse pounds hard in her throat, and I think she's at the edge of coherent thought right now.

"I think that thing you want would feel even better with my mouth than with your fingers." Her tongue darts out to wet her lips, and to demonstrate my point, I carefully suck one of her fingers into my mouth, nibbling and licking.

She moans quietly.

"Don't you want me to use my mouth? Put my mouth on your pretty pussy?"

She nods.

"I want to do that too. At least, I think I do. Maybe you should convince me."

As soon as I say it, I have a quick moment of clear-headed panic. Even though we planned tonight's scene to be a blowjob, I think I've done a pretty effective job of disorienting her and pulling her out of the typical scene mentality. Which was what I wanted, obviously, but I also need to make sure she isn't so dazed that I'm coercing her into anything.

I lean forward, my lips moving against her ear. "Remember, you can snap your fingers at any time, okay?"

"I know," she murmurs back and when I move my head to look at her, her eyes are clear and lucid.

Perfect.

Keeping my fingers curled around her wrist, I reach down with my other hand and work my belt buckle open. She keeps her eyes on mine as I unbutton my pants, as I tug my zipper down with a faint *purr*.

"God, I've been wanting this," I mutter. "So fucking much." My dick is finally free, and Devi gives me a naughty little nip on my jaw before she moves down to her knees. Jesus fuck, even just that is almost too much, with the way the bite sends a small zing of pain straight down my spine, with the look on her face as she kneels, as if she's about to give me the fiercest blowjob in history.

Yes, please.

She tugs my pants down more so that my whole shaft is exposed, and she takes me in her hand. Normally at this point, a porn actress would pump my dick a few times, maybe even smack her lips with it, and I always like it fine whenever actresses do that, because hey, a woman playing with your dick is a woman playing with your dick. Don't look the gift-horse in the mouth and all that.

But Devi does something different, and it does something to me, drives me crazy. She holds my cock and looks at it, her lips parted and her eyes wide, as if she can't believe that she's actually holding me. She slides her fingers up and down slowly, not to stimulate me, but to feel me and touch me, measure me and weigh me. Learn me and memorize me.

Everything about her hands and her expression makes it seem like she's stunned and eager and grateful, and goddammit, it's so fucking sexy. And by the time she presses her lips to the underside of my dick, I'm ready to explode.

More than ever, I'm aware of the people shuffling around near us, of the fact that if someone looks under the painting they'll see the legs of my jeans sagging around my ankles, Devi's knees on the floor. But as long as they stay on their side of the art, I don't care. In fact, it makes it that much hotter, but never mind that now, because Devi is kissing my cock.

Not sucking. Not licking.

Kissing.

Sweet little kisses, from my base to my tip, soft and warm. And then that *she's so fucking young* feeling comes back, but I'm too far gone to care or feel anything about it now. Instead, I revel in it, revel in the small, innocent kisses and her wide, dark eyes, which have gone from angry to imploring.

And like a flash, my mind is back to *Raven's Real Playdates*, to the eighteen-year-old Devi worshipping my cock with her mouth. As soon as I saw her on that set, I was entranced. She was beautiful, fresh, soft and firm all at once, and after watching her go down on Raven, her thick ass in the air, I didn't need any prep whatsoever when it was time for me to walk on. Watching her with my then-girlfriend had made me rock-hard, and then when she knelt in front of me, licking and kissing my cock with the kind of inexperienced and hesitant eagerness that told me she hadn't given very many blowjobs before…

Well, the director almost got one more pop shot than she'd paid me for.

I used to justify my body's response to Devi that day as a perverted reaction to her youth or maybe just a natural reaction to a new woman, but the truth is staring me in the face right now with dilated amber eyes: it's none of those reasons. It's Devi. She does this to me, brings me to the edge, and it won't matter how many times she sucks me off, how many times she touches me or I touch her, it will always be like this.

Hell, at this point, even I've almost completely forgotten about the camera, and I know I should make this blowjob last longer, should back off a little, because if I'm this far gone without her even taking me in her mouth yet, if I'm this close just with these kisses…

But fuck it. I want this. I want it like this.

I reach down and stroke her hair back from her face.

"Lick it," I instruct, and she does, starting with my base and licking up towards the tip. Over and over, teasingly, maddeningly, and I realize she's mimicking how I tongue-fucked her earlier with the long, taunting strokes.

"Very cute," I say. My thumb finds her lower lip, and I pull her mouth open. "But you know what I want."

She smiles, my thumb still on her lip. "Then why don't you take it?" she teases.

Well, then.

I fist myself near my root and nudge my crown against her lips, tracing the heart-shaped pout once—and then once more again—before I lazily push past that pout to the wet heat inside. For a moment, she does nothing but stare up at me, her tongue soft and still against my dick. And it's not as if she's being passive out of inexperience or reluctance or even naughtiness…once again, I get the feeling that she's trying to commit this to memory, the way my face looks right now and maybe the way I feel against her tongue.

I can't blame her. I want to commit this to memory too, every detail, the stray lock of hair on her forehead, the way her lips stretch around my girth, the way her eyes search mine, asking for permission or affirmation or absolution.

And then her hands slide around my hips and her fingers find my ass, digging in as she starts sucking me.

"Holy fuck, Devi," I say raggedly (and maybe a little too loudly) but I can't help it. Her mouth is like this Valhalla of wet silk, her lips sealed tight to create the kind of suction that would make a man weep. And believe me, I'm near weeping.

She holds my ass and swallows against me, making me groan, and then she pulls off to focus her attention on the tip, sucking and swirling.

"I want to go deeper," I manage after a few deep breaths. "Can I go deeper?"

"Yes," she whispers with her lips still mostly occupied, smiling as if I just offered her a brand new car instead of asking to shove my dick down her throat.

What a woman.

I reach back to find one of her hands and then I move it to my front so that it's braced against my hip and she can easily stop me if I go too deep. And then I cradle her face with one hand as I feed my cock to her with the other, pushing past her lips and teeth and tongue until I hit the back of her throat, and fuck me, she's so perfect, even more perfect than I remember from *Real Playdates*. She takes me so willingly, so easily, and I feel the armored plates of my control beginning to chink open and fall away.

I pull back, giving her a minute to breathe, and then I shove in again, a little rougher this time. Kneeling is not the easiest way to deep-throat, and I don't want to hurt her or make her gag. But even though her eyes water a little, she swallows me without issue, her eyelashes even fluttering up at me coquettishly. Trusting that she'll stop me with her hand or snap her fingers to signal if she needs to slow down or stop, I pick up the pace, driving in deeper and faster now. My hands look so large wrapped around her head like this, large and powerful, and I'd be lying if I don't say this fuels my lust even more. The power exchange, this young woman kneeling in front of me while I fuck her face, it turns me the hell on, and the fact that it's a young woman I love and respect—that makes the pretend degradation even sexier.

I thrust in again, this time so deeply that I feel her nose press into my stomach, her lips and tongue reflexively swallowing and tightening around my base, and I could come like this, just like this, feeling that nose against my stomach and her head in my hands, and my tip being squeezed so tightly.

My balls draw up in anticipation, but I'm not ready to come yet. I want this to last forever.

Even though she's not snapping or pushing, I sense she needs a breath and I pull back, letting her breathe, and she does with a gasp, tears gathering in the corners of her eyes and smudging her eye makeup. She looks so beautiful right now, her makeup blurry and her hair impossibly tangled, and I take some of that hair in my fist now and pull her up—not hard, but hard enough that she scrambles to her feet.

My mouth crashes down on hers, and I taste traces of myself—salt and soap—and her mouth is wet and gasping. She kisses me back messily, desperately, as if she's struggling against her own need to breathe, and I am practically clawing at the lace on her hips to yank her thong down. I finally manage to get it past her knees and then my fingers are there in her secret place, which is so impossibly wet right now. She's so wet that her thighs are slick, and it's pure instinct that makes me step forward and grind my dick against her. I feel the taut skin of her stomach, the silky curls between her legs, and then her hands are sliding between my slumped jeans and my ass again, pulling me even closer.

It's an accident, or at least I think it is, the first time she raises up on her toes and my cock slips between her thighs. One second, I am grinding on her like a horny teenager, and the next second, my dick is squeezed between her wet thighs, which are so wet that I can slide in and out of them easily.

"Fuck," I mumble, because it feels good, because I want it to keep feeling good, but thigh-sex isn't exactly the hottest category on my website, and also it's dangerously close to the real thing and that's not the plan for tonight.

But then it happens again, and I stop caring. My hands are everywhere—inside her dress, on her ass, thumbing her nipples—and it feels so good to push between her thighs, especially with that wet pussy moving against the top of my shaft. Without me saying anything, she brings her feet together and crosses her ankles, making it tighter for me.

I hiss out a string of swear words, and she giggles, and I decide that I want to know what it sounds like when her giggles dissolve into moans. So I hook a hand around one of her thighs and haul it up to my waist, raising her up enough that I can bend my head and take a nipple into my mouth through the fabric of her dress.

She does indeed start to moan, and I'm sucking the tip of her breast as hard as I can, and we are both unconsciously squirming and grinding, and then all of a sudden it happens. I feel my swollen crown not just brush past her folds, but for the barest of seconds, push in.

"Shit," I whisper, raising my head to look at her.

"Shit," she agrees in a moan, and her face is a mask of desperate, frantic longing.

I can't seem to pull out, even though I'm barely *in*, and then she says, "What if you did it just once? Felt the inside of me just once and then pulled right back out? That wouldn't count, right?"

"Cass…" I say, my voice stretched to the breaking point. I can feel how wet she is against my tip, as if her pussy is kissing my crown, and I'm about to ignore everything I know I should do—like stop and step away and really, seriously stop—and just thrust home. But I can't, and the reasons are legion: the show, plus we haven't discussed sex yet, plus even if I were going to do this, I need to get a condom…

"Just once," she pleads. "Then we can stop. But I can't—you can't stop now. Just once, Logan, *please.*"

And then she's pulling me closer and murmuring all those dangerous words, *just once just once please please please.* And there's no way in hell I can win this battle, even if I wanted to.

Which I don't.

I never advocate not-thinking when it comes to filming porn, I never advocate shifting a scene's acts outside of the agreed-on list beforehand, but I'm so far gone and we are so far outside of what constitutes a normal scene now that maybe God and the county of Los Angeles will forgive me for what I'm about to do.

I wrap an arm tight around her waist, press my hand to her cheek, and lock eyes with her as I shift my hips and then slowly, so slowly that it almost feels like I'm barely moving at all, press inside. The minute I truly breach her, she lets out a loud gasp, and I clap a hand over her mouth to keep her quiet.

Her head drops forward to lean on my shoulder and I keep going. I have to bend my knees and angle myself, reach down and hike up her leg again, but it feels so fucking good that I wonder how mad she'd be if I came right now.

Her pussy is tight, tighter than I could have ever imagined, and so wet that even with the squeeze of her channel I can slide in with almost no resistance. The flared edge of my crown drags against her g-spot and she moans and shakes against my hand, and then I'm pushing up and up and up, deeper and deeper, until her pussy is stretched wide around my base, her pelvis flush with mine. I grab her other leg and pull her up so that she's got her legs wrapped around my waist and I'm supporting all her weight with my hands under her ass. I lean back a little so that I can look at where we're joined, and then I look up at her.

"Cass?"

Her mouth is open and her pupils are huge and black. "Move in me," she begs. "Just for a minute."

Jesus fuck. I squeeze my eyes shut for a minute to stave off the waves of fire her words ignite in me. "Okay," I murmur, eyes still shut. "Just for a minute."

I push her against the wall and move, the kind of deep, rolling movements that cameras don't capture well, but goddammit my body can feel perfectly, and hers too, judging by the amount of noise my hand is blocking. I can feel my tip tracing circles and lines and angles in the deepest parts of her, can feel how tightly she's stretched around me, and every time I move in her, she moans against my palm.

I shift, ever so slightly, moving my pelvis against hers so that my lower abs knead her clit as I grind into her. The effect is instantaneous—her muffled moans rise in pitch and frequency and her thighs clench tight around my waist.

"Are you going to come, Cass?" I whisper in her ear.

She nods.

"Because…I don't think I can make it through you coming," I confess. "If you come, then I'm going to come so fast…" Saying it aloud helps me think, helps me figure out what to do. I can't come inside of her. This is already so outside of the bounds of pornography film restrictions and what I consider personally okay, and I assume she's on birth control, but what if she's not? That would be an asshole assumption to make, when I have just as much power to exercise caution as she does.

On the other hand, now that I've felt her pussy, I'm hungry to make it come, eager to feel it squeeze and flutter around me. And the idea of holding her so close as I pump my own way to climax…*appealing* isn't nearly a strong enough word.

More like necessary.

Luckily for us both, I'm a good problem-solver.

I lift my hand from Devi's mouth, and then I back away from the wall and maneuver us so that we separate and I can set her on her feet. It's the third time I've denied her an orgasm in the space of twenty minutes, and her wild eyes and stunned pout tell me all I need to know.

"Don't move," I tell her, and then I reach for the slender wallet in my back pocket. I locate a condom and pull it out, dropping my wallet to the floor, where it lands with a flat-sounding *smack*. My patience is so ragged-thin that my hand is shaking as I raise the wrapper to my teeth to tear it open. Devi's feral eyes are on me the entire time, as I roll the condom down my dick, which is so hard now that the crown is a swollen and angry maroon color. I give it a few hard pumps as she watches, and I feel the last of my control evanesce away, disintegrate into nothing.

"Turn to the wall, like before," I say. My words are short, staccato rasps, and I hope she forgives me for being brusque, because I can't be anything else right now. Not with that wet pussy within reach. Not knowing that I can fuck her without any worry or reserve.

The minute she turns and spreads her legs, I'm behind her and it only takes half a second for my sheathed cock to find what it needs. I slam in, letting out a low hiss at the same time she lets out a guttural groan, and I think I hear someone ask, "Did you hear that?"

But there's no stopping now. I wrap her long coffee-colored hair around my hand and yank her head back to me. "If you want to come, you have to be quiet. Can you do that?"

"Yes," she breathes. "Oh Logan, I'm so close, make me come, make me come."

I use my other hand to find her clit and start rubbing her there. I'm pounding into her hard now, her ass cheeks shaking, the wet, sweet sounds of her pussy getting loud and distinct against the backdrop of music and conversation.

I keep a hold of her hair, forcing her to arch her back and keeping that ass at such a delicious angle to me, and I rub her clit harder and faster, until I can feel every muscle in her body tense up, her legs and her shoulders and her stomach, all of her tightening and tightening like a guitar string. And I'm so close now too, so close to exploding inside this girl I've craved for so long, and I feel the years of tension, the years of secretly jacking off to Devi when Raven was asleep, twisting at the base of my spine.

"Your pussy is so good," I tell her in a low voice. "I'm going to come so hard for you, going to come so fucking hard..."

"Logan," she gasps. "Oh, fuck, Logan, that's it, that's it, oh my *God*—"

I feel her crescendo, the split second before all the tension unravels, and then she's unspooling around me, clenching and releasing and clenching again, and I look down at where my cock disappears in and out of her, and I remember what she felt like raw and think of how good it would feel to come inside her without a condom, how satisfying it would be to see my cum dripping out of her, and then my balls draw up tight and then I'm coming so fucking hard that my vision goes fuzzy and my hearing fades out and there is only the tight heat of her cunt and the surges of roaring pleasure and the mindless drive to rut as hard and as long as I can.

My cock convulses, and I'm grunting, still fucking my way through the orgasm, and I feel her peak again, her hands flying out to grab at the brick ledge as she tries to keep on her feet, but her knees are buckling and she's going to collapse. I wrap an arm around her stomach, holding her upright as she rides out the tremors, as I finish releasing my pent-up lust inside her, and we gradually come down together, panting and sweaty and I realize I'm not sure how loud all that just was.

I don't care. So worth it.

Once I'm certain she can stand on her own, I circle the bottom of the condom with my fingers and slowly pull out of her pussy. Everything is wet—her, the condom, me on the inside of the condom—and this is one of the moments I usually love least in a scene, pulling out with all my cum still contained. I know, it's probably domineering and wrong of me, but there's something so gratifying on this deep, primal level about seeing my cum in a woman's pussy or on her tits or on her ass. The condom makes things safe, and I respect that, but at the same time, it makes things sterile, and Devi Dare is the last woman on earth I want to be sterile with.

But, despite all that, despite the sterility, as I pull out, I mostly only feel this intense gratitude and wonder. I got to be inside Devi, I got to feel her come on my cock, I got to touch and experience her in the most intimate way possible, and it's like fucking her has taken the torch I carry for Devi and fanned it into a fucking wildfire.

It's so strong that I'm not even going soft right now. I could put on a fresh condom and go again…and probably again a few times after that.

I'm still staring down at my dick and Devi is still braced against the wall catching her breath as the footsteps approach, and there's no time, no time at all, and then a tiny white-haired woman—bespectacled and lost-looking—rounds the corner with her quad cane. We freeze and she keeps walking, mumbling something to herself as she does, and then all of a sudden, she sees us, her head snapping up and her eyes going wide like dollar coins.

"Um," I say, my hand still around my cum-covered dick and my jeans around my ankles. "Howdy."

"Howdy," Devi parrots, still bent over with her dress hiked over her ass.

For a few seconds that seem to stretch into infinity, the old lady blinks at us, too stunned to speak. And then she makes a hasty retreat, shuffling backwards around the canvases until she's out of sight.

Devi explodes into snorts and giggles, and I start panic-laughing as I frantically tie off the condom and try to pull up my pants and grab all my stuff at the same time. My pants are zipped but not buttoned and my bag slung over my shoulder as I take Devi's hand and pull her towards the fire exit door, where we emerge into the California night wheezing with the giddy laughter of people who've been caught having raunchy public sex by a tiny old grandma.

And then I drop everything to the ground and pin Devi into the fiercest, longest kiss I've ever given, wishing she could know with every trace of my tongue and every brush of my lips how much I've fallen in love with her.

· · ·

The old lady must have kept our secret, because when we presented ourselves to the gallery owner after closing after all the other patrons had left, she didn't say a word of censure or reproach to us. And so we were able to have the night I planned—some wine and snacks I packed, and a campout on the gallery floor, the camera trained on us from a perch at the foot of the sleeping bag, recording everything.

This is possibly the silliest thing I'll ever admit to, but right now, the mere fact that Devi and I are sharing a sleeping bag makes me feel floaty. A side effect of being a porn star is that I don't have very many firsts to share with women. I hardly have *any* firsts, actually. But I've never spent the night with anyone in a place other than my house. I know, that's insane, but it's true. Raven and I were always so busy with work that there was never a chance of our travel schedules matching up...so no hotels. And because I'm so busy, she (or the girlfriend I had before her, Tessalie), always came to my house after a day's work. I have fucked women in every imaginable space, public and private, but when it comes to actual, honest-to-God sleeping, when it comes to snuggling and spooning and talking about whatever random stuff floats to mind, it's only ever been in my bed. The novelty of sharing this first with Devi is better than a whole bottle of eighteen-year-old scotch.

"You don't seem like the kind of person to have a two-person sleeping bag," Devi points out dreamily as we lie on our backs and look at the strings of fake stars above us. "Do you camp a lot?"

"I've only been camping once with a church group and I hated it. Showers are very important to me."

She gives a rueful sigh. "I think I've been camping more times than I can count."

"That doesn't surprise me. No, my parents got this for me a couple Christmases ago because they never know what to buy. What do you get the man who has everything—or at least gets to fuck everything? And the answer is usually the kinds of gift you see in catalogs on the airplane."

Devi rolls over onto her elbow, her face suddenly serious. "Do you think that you want to be the man who fucks everything forever?"

I turn my head to look at her. "You mean, like do I ever see myself quitting porn?"

"Yeah."

I think for a moment. "Maybe?" I finally say, after my thoughts refuse to order themselves out of the incomprehensible jumble they are right now. "Like, I know logically that the job depends on my body, and my body only has a lifespan of being nice to look at for another decade or so, unless by some magic, I age like Robert Downey Jr. or Terry Crews or something. I guess I just keep thinking that I'll have my shit figured out by then, and I'll know what to do when the time comes to step away."

"If you could do anything, what would it be?"

Her brow is adorably furrowed right now, as if the answer to her question is the most important thing she'll ever hear. I reach up with my thumb and smooth it out, bringing a smile to her lips. "I'd make movies. Not just sexy movies, but all kinds of movies. But that's not really the kind of thing I can just jump into, and I don't know enough about it even if I wanted to jump in anyway."

"You could go to film school."

"That used to be the plan." I roll up on my elbow too so I can look at her better. "Hey, Cass?"

"Yes?"

"Tonight—did it feel real? With the camera?" As I ask, I glance over to the camera trained on us now, recording in silence.

Even in the dim light, I can see her cheeks color. "Yes, Logan," she says quietly. "It felt real."

"Does it feel real now?"

A pause. Then: "Yes."

I trace the curve of her shoulder, my fingers dancing over her skin to find the slope of her rib cage, and my hand settles in making circles in the dip of her waist. "I want things to be real between us all of the time," I say, and I didn't realize how nervous I would be saying this until I'm saying it now. "I know we've admitted that we like each other in a physical sense. That we're attracted to each other and want to be more than friends. But it's even more than that for me."

I feel her tense up underneath my hand, and I have a brief debate—backpedal or continue? But I have to continue. If she decides that my feelings make her too uncomfortable to go on with *Star-Crossed*, then I have to accept that. But I don't think I can hide how I really feel from her any longer.

But to make myself more comfortable, I revert to what I know best—sex. My hand skims around her waist to the curve of her ass, and then I find her pussy warm and soft between her legs. She moans as I start playing with her.

"I like you, Devi. Not just in the porno way, but in the mushy hearts and flowers kind of way. I like being with you and hearing you talk and just watching you exist. I know that makes me a stalker, but…well, I guess I don't really have an excuse for that. Almost every night since we filmed *Playdates*, I've beaten off to your scenes…"

"Jesus, Logan," she murmurs.

"Is that a good Jesus or a bad Jesus?"

"So good," she mumbles, rolling onto her stomach and spreading her legs so that I have better access to her pussy. "Rub me."

"Yes, ma'am." I comply with her request and search out her clit, kneading it gently in case she's sore. "So I know I'm being manipulative by fingering you while we have this discussion, but I guess I want to know if I'm alone in this. If you like me in the mushy way too."

I can hear her smile in her words even though I can't see her face. "I like you in the mushy way too. A lot. You're definitely not alone."

The wave of sweet relief hits me so hard that I'm surprised to find that my eyelids are burning a little. I clear my throat to cover it up. "Really?"

"Really." She turns her head to look at me. "I masturbated to you almost every night too, you know. And the sex tonight was so good. You make me feel—I don't even have words for it. Reckless. Alive. Ecstatic. I was so caught up in you that I let you fuck me without a condom." She shakes her head in disbelief. "I would fucking never do that in my right mind."

By now I should be used to the fact that Devi doesn't make emotional leaps without a healthy dose of logical caution, that there will always be a gap between my impetuous declarations and her admitting that she feels the same way. But I'm not used to it yet, I guess, because relief and joy and giddy excitement are still thrumming through me with tornadic force. I drop my head to her shoulder blade, breathing in her cinnamon smell. "I want to make you out of your mind all the time," I say against her skin. "Like the way you make me."

"I'd say you're off to a good start." She squirms against my hand, and when I tease her folds open, I find that she's completely soaked.

I peer around to see her eyes. "Does this mean I can—" I search for the right words. "—try to be your boyfriend?"

"Try?" Her voice and expression are unreadable as she repeats the key word to the request, and shame bolts through me. I want to offer her so much more than *try*, I want to *be*, but at the same time, this is Devi. Perfection embodied. My goddess and queen of the night, and what if I'm not able to be good enough for her?

What if, like Tanner suggested, she's not okay with me continuing with my porn career?

Try is safest for now, even though it's the least of what I want to give her. I'm the older, (theoretically) more mature party in this, and I've also recently traveled through the conflagration of a ruined relationship. I deserve better, Devi certainly deserves better, and that means treading thoughtfully for now.

"Yes," I say carefully. "I want to try a boyfriend-girlfriend thing with you."

I see her mind running through my words, weighing them and

judging them, and then the biggest, most bashful smile spreads across her face. "Yes, Logan. Let's try to have a boyfriend-girlfriend thing."

"Oh, thank God," I say, and I should tell her I love her now, I *want* to, but then I think of my logical girl with her cautious eyes. It's fascinating to me how she can seem so carefree, so sunny, but at the same time, she's got a mind that ticks through thoughts and decisions like a Swiss watch. I can't spring the love thing on her now without making her watch mechanisms work overtime, so instead, I say, "I've got to fuck you again, you know that right?"

Her body makes a sinuous arch as she stretches off the sleeping bag to find my wallet. She extracts a condom, and I raise up on my knees, a big dopey grin on my face. My thoughts run something like this: *sex is happening, yay! With my new sort-of girlfriend, yay! Sex sex sex!*

She tears the wrapper open with her teeth, expertly pinches the tip and rolls it down my thick erection. When she's done, she gives my cock a little teasing squeeze and looks up at my face.

"You look so happy," she says shyly.

"Because I get to fuck my sort-of girlfriend right now."

Spontaneously, she raises up and gives me a deep, searing kiss. I kiss her back until she's panting and squirming against me.

"On your knees and smile for the camera," I say.

CHAPTER THIRTEEN

The number one question I get when people find out I do girl-girl porn is, "So you're a lesbian?"

The short answer is, "I'm bi."

The long answer is, "All women are bi."

The reason that answer is long is because there's usually a discussion that has to take place after someone makes a comment like that. But here's the thing—science pretty much proves it.

Now, no reason to get your panties in a wad about this. I'm not trying to start an argument; I just want to be able to explain how I got into this line of work, and part of that explanation requires understanding the basics of human biology, which, surprisingly, many people don't.

Lesson time—woman can identify one hundred percent heterosexual, live a completely straight lifestyle, and still be aroused by another woman. It's a fact. By arousal I mean pupils dilate, pulse quickens, blood flow increases to the genitals. The female might not even recognize that these physical changes are happening, and I'm not talking about these things occurring when she's kissed or caressed—I'm talking about when women are shown pictures of other attractive women, their bodies react.

Read the studies if you don't believe me.

But, see, arousal is not the same as sexual orientation. Arousal is something that occurs on a physiological level. It's natural. Base. Primal.

Sexual lifestyle is determined by things that are harder to measure and explain—cultural conditioning, emotional attachment, socioeconomic factors, religious affiliation. That's a much more controversial topic to delve into, and all I'm going to say on that matter is that the way I was raised has a lot to do with how I feel about sex.

But I'm getting ahead of myself.

The point is if we're going by physical arousal, research suggests that women are most certainly never completely straight. We're turned on by varying degrees of both male and female sexual stimuli. And why wouldn't we be? We're wired to procreate, but we're also wired to seek pleasure. There's so much pleasure in the female form—their hips, their breasts, their lips. Women are soft and beautiful and sexy in ways that men just aren't.

So if the studies show that women are aroused from viewing same-sex stimuli, then how much more aroused are they going to be if they have a physical encounter? Then the stimulus becomes more than just sight and sound. Now it's also touch and scent and taste. Say what you will about the gender you would prefer to get it on with; if you were blindfolded, could you honestly tell the difference between a man stroking your hair and a woman? Both feel good. And feels good is feels good. What gets in the way of enjoying it is all mental.

I told you it was a long answer.

Maybe a better answer is the explanation of how I got started in this business. Short answer is, "I blame my parents."

Long answer is, "No, I mean, I really blame my parents."

From as early as I can remember, I was taught that bodies are beautiful and sex is natural. It was practically a daily prayer, one that my parents strove to reflect in their daily lives. Before I'd hit puberty, I'd been exposed to so many different variations of free love and nudist living that I had no chance of growing up to be a woman afraid of showing a little skin.

Let me be clear—it wasn't like my parents were harmfully inappropriate. Sure they were lax about the amount of clothing they wore in my presence, but I wasn't molested or forced to participate in sixties-style orgies. I was actually taught very firmly to respect bodies—others' and mine.. I was taught consent. I was exposed to people engaged in liberal lifestyles, and both my mother and father were very open about sex and the human form.

So when I was seventeen and approached by an erotic modeling agent, I figured, why not? Bodies are beautiful. Sex is natural. And erotic modeling sounded a whole hell of a lot better than any of the other job options I had. For those first shoots, I'd had to dodge the question of my age, but it brought in decent money, money that might have gone further if I hadn't spent the entire summer after high school backpacking through Europe.

One day after I'd returned from my extended vacation and I was bemoaning the cost of a college education, my agent said, "You know, there's more money in erotic pictures when they're movies. And there's more money in movies when you're having sex."

Again, I figured, why not?

I started with a couple of masturbation shoots, both of which went smoothly. Hell, I got a vibrator for my fourteenth birthday; I was already a pro at masturbation. Then I was offered my first girl-girl scene—a finger-fuck and pussy-lick. I was to be the receiver. Except for the heavy petting I'd done with Teresa Murray at her sixteenth birthday sleepover— we were young, we were curious—I'd never had any lesbian experience.

But Teresa had been pretty fun to make-out with, and if she'd wanted to go down on me, I'd have let her. Feels good is feels good.

So I accepted the job. And that's when I discovered that yes, I could definitely be aroused by another woman. I booked a few more scenes and discovered that for me, lesbian sex wasn't like the sex I'd had with my boyfriends. This was more primitive. My body reacted, but my emotions didn't get involved. Part of me wondered if it was because of the camera. Part of me wondered if maybe I was really into women after all.

I'd done four girl-girl shoots before my threesome with Raven and Logan. And that's when I learned that (a) I could still have feelings, even in front of a camera, and (b) I was definitely straight. Or, at least, I was straight for Logan O'Toole. That man did things to me…and not just physical things, but mental things. Emotional things. Spiritual things, even. After that scene was over, I was twisted inside for days. My head was wrapped up in Logan. He invaded my entire being like a virus. Like he was in my bloodstream. Like he was a rash that made me itch on the inside.

I cashed that paycheck, glad for the experience, and went back to filming strictly girl-girl. I'd recovered from Logan, for the most part, after a week or two of pining. But I didn't know if my reaction had been to the hetero sex or to Logan. I didn't have enough experience to be sure, and I wasn't interested in collecting the data to find out. It seemed safer to just stick to what I knew.

I'm not quite that honest when he asks me why I haven't done any het porn since the shoot with him and Raven. He's asked once before; this time it's for the camera. "I realized it was cleaner."

"Cleaner? As in, no cum shots to clean up?"

I pause my eyeliner application to chuckle. He's filming me while I get ready for a girl-girl scene I booked with a producer I've worked with several times before. Logan decided it would be great footage for the Lelie project, seeing me "at work," so he got permission to shoot while I'm prepping. Like most of the films I do, this one is low-budget. We're shooting in a studio that's tucked inside an infrequently patronized strip mall in West Hollywood. It was formerly an artist's studio. My dressing room consists of a cracked mirror hung above a leaky basin that looks like it was used to clean paintbrushes, but it's private and has a door that closes and locks, and that's what's important.

It's silly, but even though the set is shit compared to the ones Logan usually works on, I'm excited for him to be here. I'm excited for him to see me at my job. Of course he understands what I do better than any other guy I've slept with, but he hasn't seen me *do* what I do since the shoot three years ago.

Well, except for what we've shot for *Star-Crossed*. But that's different.

"I meant cleaner in the figurative sense. I've learned that I'm a woman who, like all women, is easily aroused by various stimuli but prefers to have relationships with men. Even though I can have a good time making out with another girl, I only ever fall in love with boys." I focus unnecessarily hard on my lipstick application as I say this last part. We've said we like each other, and that's all I'm ready to say for the moment. But I mentioned the L word because I want him to know this about me—want him to know that there's no danger of me having an emotional connection to Kendi Korn, my scene partner for the day.

Of course, telling him this might make it harder to justify my het scene with LaRue Hagen's studio booked for later today, but I'm not thinking about that right now.

"So, you consider yourself straight, even though you lick pussy all day? Do you fake all your orgasms, or…?"

"Actually, since I mostly film soft porn, it's kissing that I do all day—I only lick pussy in the afternoons." In my periphery, I don't miss Logan adjusting his pants. "I'm straight because I'm only drawn to men off-camera. But, biologically, I'm perfectly capable of having an orgasm with a woman." I turn to deliver my next line directly to the camera. "And I've never had to fake it."

Logan groans. "You know what you're doing to me, don't you? It's going to take all my strength not to jack-off while you're filming."

"I'm pretty sure that will get you kicked off set." It would be crazy hot, though, knowing he was jerking off while I was performing, knowing he was stroking himself, pretending that my lips or my body were around him. If I weren't concerned about either of us getting in trouble, I'd suggest he do it, and, admittedly, the idea of breaking the rules makes the whole scenario even hotter. Like when we'd fucked the night before at the gallery—I'd been leery because of the consequences, because the last thing I want is for Logan to face charges for indecent exposure. It could have an extremely negative impact on his career, and I would hate myself if I were partly to blame for anything like that.

But, Jesus, last night, knowing we were doing something so "wrong," so naughty—it about blew my mind. And then Logan actually *did* blow my mind. Over and over again, with the sex and the talk of making it real, and the way he was super cool with my mom, and taking me to an art show based on constellations! And then telling me he wants to try to be my boyfriend—whatever is going on between us is magical and amazing and *big*, and I'm really into it.

But I have doubts too. I can't figure out if they're based in my head or my heart, but they're definitely there. I've tried to rationalize through it and haven't gotten very far. On the one hand, he makes porn for a living. On the other, that doesn't mean he's necessarily a playboy—he was with Raven for three years, after all. But their breakup is still new. So maybe I'm his rebound girl. Or maybe I'm the girl he was really looking for when he started dating her. Or maybe he's like this with everyone. Maybe what we have between us is nothing special.

Or maybe it is. Maybe *he* is. Maybe *I* am. He sure makes it feel like I am.

I could probably spend an entire lunar synodic cycle trying to figure it out and still not be any closer to knowing.

And, that's probably best. Because I admire Logan's skills, and I, as a viewer of his work, love believing that he's into the women he fucks as much as it looks like he is.

But as the woman he fucked last night? As the woman who he's calling his sort-of girlfriend? As the woman who slept with his arms tucked snugly around her? As the woman who's developing very real, very intense feelings for him?

Yeah, I'm not thinking about that either.

I drop my robe and, naked now, do a quick inspection of my bikini area, making sure everything is nice and groomed before donning the white cotton panties that the director chose from the handful I brought as options. I pair it with a baby-blue tank top, no bra, then I pull my hair into two pigtails. "How do I look?"

Logan balances the camera on the edge of the sink, aiming it so that it will still catch us in the frame. "Come here," he says, grabbing the hem of my tank to tug me to him. "You look so fucking hot, it's killing me." He presses my hand against his bulge to prove it.

Then he kisses me—sweetly but hungrily. It's a short kiss, yet I'm flushed when he pulls away. He gives me a stupid grin. "Lick some ass."

I want to ask if it bothers him that I'm about to get off with someone else. I want to ask if it bothers him that I let girls make me come. I want to ask if it will bother him when, later, when Bruce Madden makes me come.

But I don't. Because I don't want to hear that the long and short answer is "no."

• • •

There's lots of kissing in Lynne Femke's lesbian porn. Though I do a variety of heat levels, Lynne's tend to be the sweeter scenes.

"You're just so curvy and soft," the Swedish director told me once. "I could spend hours watching women touch you."

So it's no surprise when today Lynne's direction calls for an extensive make-out session. "Lots of breast play, please. Then, Kendi, I want you to fuck Devi with your fingers." She shows us the position she wants us to be in for the climax—*literal* climax—and then we're ready to shoot.

Logan has his camera packed away now and is sitting by himself on a folding chair in the corner of the room. He wants to stay out of the way; as if I'll forget he's there if he's farther from me.

I'm certain I won't be able to forget. He's the kind of guy that's unforgettable.

But, to my surprise, I'm really not as distracted by him as I thought

I'd be. He's there, and I'm constantly aware of that, but I'm good at my job, good at focusing on the person in front of me.

Kendi's a pro, too. We run quickly through the cheesy dialogue that sets up the scene—two college girls who have been assigned to be roommates. It's our first night together in the dorm, and Kendi's character, the returning student in the scenario, has taken it upon herself to teach my character how to…well, how to "get fucked by a girl."

Admittedly, I'm not that great of an actress. If I were, I'd probably be performing in a completely different kind of film. My lack of skill doesn't bother me—porn isn't about acting. It's about providing just enough visual and verbal cues to establish a fantasy and then genuinely focusing on the other person.

Figuring out how to turn someone on is like figuring out a math equation. How much of this will equal this? How many kisses before her breath gets shallow? How many flicks of my thumb over her nipple before it's hard? How many strokes of her clit before her thighs start to tense?

Today, the math is easy because Kendi, in her role as teacher, is giving me all the answers. She's telling me what feels good in words as well as body language. Naturally dominant, she's good at this part, and I willingly submit, giving into the command of her soft lips and firm tongue invading my mouth. She tastes like mouthwash and the Skittles I saw her munching on before we started filming. Until she doesn't. Until we've kissed so long, so deeply that our tastes have mingled and the only flavor in my mouth is want and pleasure.

We move through the steps of seduction organically, hands roaming over curves and slopes, under shirts, over cotton panties. Our clothes come off and, while I caress and grope the softest parts of her body, she makes love to my breasts, her tongue laving first one nipple then the other, turning them into sharp, rosy peaks.

I'm lost in delight. Before her fingers even find my clit, I'm wet and throbbing with need. Kendi's a good lover, and I'm desperate for her to get me off. And, yes, I'd be into this no matter what, but I'm even more desperate for her because I know Logan is watching. Because I suspect that Logan is just as hot for this as I am.

If only I could watch him back…

But the cameras are on, and the story is just Kendi and I, so my eyes are pinned on her as her mouth roams lower and lower, as her tongue finds my most sensitive parts, as she brings me to delicious climax.

We shift positions, kissing for long moments before, at Lynne's direction, Kendi turns me so my back is pressed up against her front. Her breasts push into my skin as she wraps herself around me so her hands can stroke my pussy. She swirls a fingertip across my clit, and when she slides her longest finger inside of me, I look up. I catch Logan's eyes.

And the whole scene changes.

Logan is still as he watches, riveted, and the expression on his face is so wild and hot, so intense, so provocative, that I'm as transfixed as he is. I can't look away. It's Kendi who's stroking me, Kendi who's finger fucking me to orgasm, but all I can see is Logan. All I can think is Logan. All I can feel is Logan, Logan, Logan.

Images of the night before come back to me, vivid and alive. *"Your pussy is so good."* The memory of Logan's raspy words fills my head. The way he looked so greedy and driven and starved as he shoved inside of me. *"I'm going to come so hard for you, going to come so fucking hard…"*

The memory transforms into fantasy, and the words I hear aren't ones he spoke then, but ones I imagine he's speaking to me now. *Greedy, greedy girl,* he says from across the distance.

Please, I beg. *Put it in me. Put it in me now.*

That's not how I want you to come.

But I need you.

He's unflinching. *This isn't about you right now.*

And he's right—this isn't about me. I can see clearly that he is as swept away with this fantasy as I am, whether or not the words he hears in his head match the ones that play in mine. It doesn't matter. We are in this together. This scene is about us. This moment is about us.

It could be like this, he tells me. *Our world. Filming with each other, for each other. This could be the future you were looking for. This could be us.*

I'm coming, my pussy throbbing, my hips stuttering as they buck against Kendi's hand, my breath frozen as Logan encourages my climax. *Give it to me, Devi. Give it to me, Goddess. Layla. Cass, the Queen of the Night.*

The fantasy swells with my release, pieces of the puzzle shifting into place—the star I could be with him, the movies we could make, the art. How we could go on working together, how we could go on seeing each other. How we could go on…*together.*

I'm completely spent when it hits me—I don't just want to make porn with Logan O'Toole; I want to make a life.

CHAPTER FOURTEEN

The scene goes long.

Lynne says it was too beautiful, and she couldn't bear to call cut. "Absolutely the best thing I've seen from you," she says, and I look past her to Logan, who has surely heard her, and I wonder if he knows, like I do, that he's the reason my performance today was so superb.

I don't have time to find out because now I'm running late for the P in V scene that I have booked with LaRue, and I barely have a chance to gather my things and kiss Logan goodbye before I have to be on the road.

It's not a long drive, and instead of using the little time I have to prepare mentally for the next scene, I spend it thinking about the one I just left. Thinking about last night. Thinking about Logan, and how he's burrowed inside me, how I should have maybe built more walls to keep him out. How I don't know what my career will look like now that he's in my life. Wondering how I will ever be able to work again without him.

It's not until I'm parked in the driveway of the mansion that LaRue has rented in the Hills that I finally pull my thoughts into focus and realize I'm about to film my first het sex without him. A male/female scene without Logan.

Oh shit.

Seriously, oh shit.

I'm being silly. I've done lots of scenes without Logan. I've had lots of sex that wasn't with Logan. I can have sex now in a scene without Logan.

I start to get out of the car, and my stomach lurches. For half a second I wonder if I can pretend I'm sick, but I quickly dismiss that plan. The phrase "the show must go on"? I'm pretty sure a porn director coined it. After a performer has been booked and the contracts have been signed, there's almost nothing that could prevent the show from being filmed. Even if the performer is on the rag, even if she's puking her guts up, even if she's got Montezuma's Revenge and they're shooting an anal scene—the show goes on. There's too much money on the floor not to; a crew and other actors that have to be paid. It's too expensive to forego a scene for just one person.

I check the time. I have a few minutes before I need to be inside so I get back in the car and phone my agent. The call goes to voicemail. I groan as it plays but sound my usual chipper self when I leave my message. "Hey, it's Devi. I'm at the LaRue job, and I can't…" My voice trails off.

Any way I explain this is going to sound terrible, especially left in a voicemail. Besides, I don't know exactly what it is I want her to do for me. Talk me down? Remind me of my obligations? Tell me its okay to cancel? "Just call me. Please. As soon as possible."

I hang up and stare at my cell for several minutes—four of them, to be precise—willing it to ring.

It doesn't. Now, officially late for my call time, I start to panic. What if I can't get aroused? What if I *can*? Is this cheating? Can it even be cheating when I'm not officially anything to Logan? Only a sort-of girlfriend? Can you even cheat on a porn star?

I'm overwhelmed with doubts and anxiety and this isn't like me at all. I'm level-headed, dammit. I'm calm, cool, collected. I'm a professional.

So get your shit together and act like one!

I take a deep breath.

A professional would pull up her big-girl panties, go in and do the scene. It's one scene. One hour of my life. I can imagine the guy is Logan. I can pretend it's for him like the last scene was. Afterwards, I don't have to book another het scene again until I figure out, well, everything.

Right. Yes. I can do this.

One more breath, and I'm out of my car. Three more, and I've made it to the door. A sign on the door says to come in quietly in case the camera's running. I turn the handle and step in.

And run smack into Raven.

And it's embarrassing because I run into her with such force that the reusable shopping bag I'm carrying full of wardrobe choices spills and my panties are strewn all over the entryway and on top of Raven's Jimmy Choo ballet slipper-style shoes.

Yes, *that* Raven. *The* Raven. The *only* Raven. *Logan's* Raven.

He's never talked to me about her and I'm not sure what all went down with Raven and Logan, but everyone in the biz, as well as a lot of people *outside* of the biz, knew about their relationship. They were an "It" couple. For nearly three years, they made *XBIZ's* as "Porn Pair We Ship" List and frequently graced the cover of *Adult Video News* together. They played on the same charity softball team. They had an Instagram account for Prior, their Yorkie. They held hands at the O'Toole Films press conference where he announced his commitment to respect women in the industry. When Logan won his last AVN award, he thanked her with an intimate wink that suggested they had a whole secret language between them.

Then, one day, without any explanation, Logan's name wasn't on Prior's social media accounts anymore, and Raven posted a vague Facebook status about having to deal with movers. The media immediately assumed they'd broken up. Neither party confirmed or denied it, but it was obvious to everyone that the love bubble had burst.

I can't say that I wasn't happy about it. And curious. But I respected Logan's privacy.

Now, seeing her, I realize that by never asking him about her, I am just as unprepared to face her as I am for this scene. What's happening between Logan and me is brand new and still undefined, but I feel certain that I'm moving toward girlfriend status. And yet, I know nothing about the ex.

I should have asked.

He should have told me.

I ignore the tightening knot in my belly. "Sorry," I say, bending down to scoop up my underwear, hoping she'll walk past, and we can circumvent the whole ex-girlfriend encounter.

But she says, "Devi," and she's not warm or surprised, and she's not trying to get by me, and it almost feels like she's been waiting for me.

"Raven." Still squatting, I glance past her and see the crew setting up to shoot in the dining room. The cameras are off, and the director, for now at least, doesn't seem to be anxious to get going.

I stuff my clothes back in the bag and stand up to give Raven the attention she seems to be waiting for. Except for her lipstick, which seems newly applied, her makeup is mussed, and her hair's a mess, and under the heavy scent of perfume, I catch the smell of sweat and sex. She's just done a scene. And she still looks absolutely fuckable. I'm positive I don't look the same after being on the set with Kendi.

But whatever. "Were you shooting with Sinner's today too?" I ask, trying to be polite.

Raven nods with a tight smile, her red lips bright against her creamy pale skin. "I saw your name on the call schedule and thought I'd stick around and say hi. It's been—what? Three years since we've done any work together?"

I'm immediately suspicious of her motives because: (a) she's the ex, and (b) what she said is not true. We've done a couple of movies together since then; we just haven't been in the same scenes and have somehow managed to never bump into each other on set. Maybe she's not the type to pay attention to details like that, but if that's the case, why would she pay attention now?

Unless it's because of Logan.

So I don't exactly correct her. "Three years since *Raven's Real Playmates*. Time really flies, doesn't it?"

"Wow." She looks me over, her gaze over me as hungry in condescension as Logan's was hungry in lust earlier. "You're so grown up."

It's been three years. Not thirty. But I nod and accept her statement like it's a compliment. "Yep. Crazy how that happens."

"Logan tells me you're working on a series together."

And there it is. There *he* is, making himself known, saying *I'm the guy that will cause you girls to fail a Bechdel test.*

Well, now I know I was right—that her interest in me today is because of him.

Also, I know that he's talked to her. Recently. About me. And I have no idea what that means or how to feel about it except unsettled.

I know I need time to process, so I'm careful to leave emotion out of my response. "Yeah, we are."

"Hmm." She draws the *mmm* out, and it's seductive and sexy and I understand why she's such a star. Because Raven isn't just beautiful—she's bewitching. And glamorous. And sophisticated.

And I'm the girl who carries her cotton underwear to the set in a bag from Ralph's.

"What's the show about, anyway?" She's fishing, which means Logan hasn't gone into details with her, and there are several possible reasons for this. The ones in the front of my mind are the ones that bother me to think about.

Regardless of his reasons, if Logan remained vague, I want to remain vague as well. "It's still shaping, actually. Lots of improv. Probably won't really know what it is until it's done."

Behind her, the director catches my eye. "Excuse me, Raven, if you don't mind, I need to—"

She ignores my cue of dismissal. "If Tanner isn't on set with you, you should be carrying an Epipen. Logan will never think to bring it himself."

I blink. "Epipen?"

"For his allergy. You know how to use it, right?"

"I…" I didn't know Logan had any allergies. I didn't know he needed an Epipen. I didn't know that he wasn't the type to address his own serious medical conditions.

I'm sure that Raven can read the ignorance all over my face, but I try to remain composed. "I'll make sure he has one on set," I say. "Now it was really good seeing you again, but I'm late."

I brush past her but she stops me with her next words. "You don't normally do het scenes, do you? Did you take this job because of Logan? If you're hoping to make him jealous…"

My nails dig into the Ralph's bag as I hug it to my chest. *Deep breaths, deep breaths.*

I turn back to her and tilt my chin up. "I took the job for me."

But I don't sound very convincing because even I'm not sure anymore why I took the job, and there's a good chance it *was* for Logan just like the reasons I don't want to do the job now are for Logan.

Raven lets out a laugh, then immediately covers her mouth with her hand, as if she hadn't really meant to laugh out loud. "Oh. You're really adorable, Devi." She looks me over again and this time her gaze is sympathetic, the kind of look that says, *You're so young; you're so naïve; you'll learn when you're older.*

I desperately want to know what it is she knows that I don't, and I don't want to know all at the same time. Because being young doesn't necessarily mean I'm ignorant. But, also, because it doesn't necessarily mean I'm not, and the worst part about my age and lack of life experience is that there's no way to know which is true in this moment.

I'm off-balance, and I'm sure Raven knows it.

She takes a step toward me. "Word of advice?" She poses it like a question but doesn't leave a space for me to respond. "Logan doesn't care where you're sleeping. In fact, he's happier when he knows you're fucking other people because then he figures he won't have to deal with any shit about *him* fucking other people. And, take it from me—he's *always* fucking other people."

It's a knife in my gut. Which makes no sense because this isn't any sort of revelation. Of course Logan is always fucking other people—it's his *job*.

But she's said it in such a way that makes me think she's insinuating that Logan fucked other girls off set when she was with him. And maybe he did. But I can't know that unless I ask Logan. And suddenly I'm painfully aware of all the things I've never asked Logan, all the things I don't know about him or about us, things I'm not sure I have the right to ask. Things I'm not sure I want to know the answer to.

Someone calls from the set behind me. "You Devi Dare?"

"Me?" I twist my head and see both the director and Bruce staring at me. "Yes."

"Gotta run," Raven says, and she's gone before I can even say goodbye.

As much as I didn't want a confrontation with her, I'm almost disappointed that she's left. Or, rather, I'm disappointed that she's left and I'm still agitated.

"I want to shoot in five," the director says in a tone that suggests he wants to shoot now but knows I'm not ready. "Do you know what you're wearing?"

With Raven gone, I have nothing keeping me in the entryway. I cross to him. My knees feel weak, and I'm distracted, and I wish I could focus on the things distracting me instead of on what I should be wearing before I'm not wearing anything.

But I can't.

When I reach the director, I hold out my Ralph's bag. "I have other options."

Without looking at my clothes, he shoos the bag away. "Not necessary. We're already running long on some of the other scenes. This one needs to be concise."

"What are you thinking?" The buddy-buddy way Bruce confers with the director puts me immediately on guard.

For the first time since I've arrived, I scan the room. The crew is entirely comprised of men. Middle-aged white men, to be precise. The director's assistant is a blonde in a short skirt. The gray-bearded lighting guy's T-shirt reads, "*It won't suck itself.*" The cameraman is ogling the girls dressing in the next room—the kitchen, which seems to be the makeshift dressing room. There's no door, so everyone can watch the performers dress, which might seem like no big deal since we're shooting porn, but it is a big deal. To me it is. This set is a total boy's club—the kind of set I have managed to avoid in my three-year career.

"I'm thinking we lose the clothes," the director says to Bruce. "Cut the time it takes her to strip. Let's put her in a robe and maybe she's cleaning up after dinner and then you come in and fuck her on the table."

"Ooo, I like that," Bruce says, his pupils dilating as he leers at me.

"Debs, see if there are some dishes in the kitchen cabinets we can use for this scene."

"How does that sound to you, Devi?" LaRue Hagen puts his hand on my arm startling me with both his touch and his presence. I hadn't seen him until just now and hadn't been sure he'd even be on set today.

I'm grateful he is—not only is he a friendly face, but he's the only person who seems to care what my opinion is about the proposed changes to the scene.

"It sounds—" *ridiculous, unrealistic, and grossly male-centric.* The dishes the director's assistant is already setting out on the table aren't dirty— why would I be clearing them? Yes, I know, porn isn't about making sense, just...

Ugh.

But, honestly, if it shortens the scene, I'm game. "It sounds okay to me. Thank you for asking. Is there another room where I can get undressed? A room with a door?"

The director doesn't hide his eye roll, but LaRue smiles reassuringly. "Definitely. Why don't you use the office? I believe there's a mirror above the mini-bar. We're running late, though, so get yourself changed and back out here quickly."

"Sure."

I scurry into the office and shut the door, which doesn't lock, but I don't have time to be annoyed. It only takes a minute to undress and put on my robe. Then I take another minute to center myself. My head is all over the place, and I need to be focused to do my job.

The breath goes in, the breath goes out, I say to myself, concentrating on the air as it fills my lungs then as I release it. *The breath goes in, the breath goes out. The breath goes in, the breath goes out.*

I bet Raven knows Logan's real name.

The thought is sudden and paralyzing, but before I can recover there's a knock on the door.

"Devi?" LaRue says through the wood door. "We're ready for you."

I'm not ready for them. I'm not ready for any of this.

I open the door about to give an excuse to stall, but before I can say anything, LaRue's ushering me back to the set. "Everything okay, Dev?"

I'm not sure that he's really interested in my answer, and I get it. It's his money we're burning with every minute the camera isn't rolling. He's a good guy, though, and I think he'd genuinely want to know that I'm having issues.

So I decide to tell him. "Actually," and then LaRue's phone starts buzzing in his pocket.

"Excuse me," he says as he pulls it out to look at the screen. He clicks the talk button saying, "I'm sorry, I've got to take this. Jerry, hi!" Cell to his ear, LaRue makes his way through the naked women in the kitchen and steps outside on the back lanai, closing the sliding door behind him.

With his boss gone, the director, who has yet to introduce himself, gets more assertive. "Okay, Devi, babe. Drop the robe, will ya, so we can set light levels. Debs tried to step in for you, but you're darker than her."

It's not a racist comment, yet he sounds like a douche when he says it. Possibly because he's telling me to take my clothes off in the same breath. Yes, I'm comfortable with my clothes off, but typically the directors I work with still respect that I'm a person, not just a body. They're courteous and nurturing, and conscious of what I need to feel safe while performing.

Maybe this is just the way het sex works, though. Maybe I really am as naïve as Raven seemed to suggest I was.

At the thought of ultra-pro Raven, I undo my belt and shed the robe.

"Nice," the director says with a wink. He continues to chat with me while the bearded guy checks the light levels against my skin. "When the camera rolls, you'll be gathering these dishes. Bruce will come in behind you and pull off the robe. The dishes are plastic so it's okay if you drop them. Bruce and I have worked through the choreography, so you just let him lead."

I throw a glance toward Bruce who's staring at me while Debs is fluffing his cock. *So he'll be hard when the scene starts.* That means he won't need time to get aroused, and since we've already cut the undressing, I'm afraid foreplay is going to be cut all together.

The idea makes me uncomfortable. "I'd rather know the sequence for myself. Could you go over it, please?"

The director shakes his head curtly. "If you wanted to know the sequence, you should have been to the set on time. Okay, everyone, we're ready to shoot."

As I tie the belt of my robe again, Bruce zips up his jeans and gives me a predatory grin. "Go ahead and make it tight, sweetheart. It's not going to stop me."

And then I realize—I can't.

I can't do this.

I can't tune out the warning bells in my head. I can't dismiss this sexist environment. I can't pretend I feel safe on this set. And I can't have sex with Bruce Madden.

And even if Logan will always be fucking other people, and even though I don't know if I can handle that, I do know with a fair amount of certainty that a good part of the reason I can't have sex with this caveman alpha in front of me is Logan.

So when the director calls places, I shake my head, and without an apology, I quit.

CHAPTER FIFTEEN

The director yells behind me as I run from the room. "You can't quit! You're already here. You're already naked. Just do the fuck—"

I make it to the office and slam the door. The director's voice turns into muffled noise, and I let out a sigh of relief.

It's not like me to make emotional or spur-of-the-moment decisions, but I feel justified. The list of reasons I can't do this scene is comprehensive and rational:

1. I don't feel comfortable on this set.

2. I don't feel safe on this set.

3. The director refused to explain what my performance partner would do to me in the scene.

4. I don't trust my partner.

But as logical and sensible as I am about this, as clearly as I can state my complaints, I'm lying to myself if I don't admit that the biggest reason for quitting is Logan. The other reasons just make it easier to follow through with my heart on this one.

Footsteps outside the office spur me into action. Eventually someone will come after me, and I'd prefer to be clothed and ready to leave when they do. I head to the desk where I piled my belongings when I'd stripped earlier.

The door opens as soon as I move from it. I peer over my shoulder to find Bruce. Gritting my teeth, I pretend his presence irritates me rather than makes me nervous. "I'm getting dressed in here."

Ignoring the hint, he enters the room. "That's a shame."

"I'm asking you not to come in here." I step into my panties and pull them up under my robe, wanting desperately to be dressed.

Bruce swaggers over to me. "Calm your tits, sweets. I'm just coming in here to make sure you're okay." He reaches a hand out and rests it on my upper arm. "Okay?"

I let out a breath of air, willing my shoulders to relax. Maybe I'm being paranoid where he's concerned. The only thing Bruce is guilty of at this point is being a man in a man's business. He just wants to do his job, and here I am fucking with that. "Yes. Sorry. I'm just not in the right mindset for this. Things weren't presented to me quite accurately."

I pull at the knot at my waist and accidentally make it tighter. "Jesus Christ," I mutter, frustrated.

"Here. Let me help you." He grabs the ends of my belt and drags me toward him. Immediately I tense, not sure if I should be wary or not. I barely breathe as he works the knot. When it's loosened, I start to pull away, but he pulls me back, opening my robe completely. His lip curls into a devilish smile. "Told you this wouldn't stop me from getting you naked."

I tug at the garment, trying to close it, but Bruce wraps each end of my belt around his hands, drawing me even closer to him.

My heart is hammering so loud in my chest, I wonder if he can hear it. "Stop it." My voice is quiet and strained. "Please. I want you to go."

"Hey, I'm just playing around." He lets go of the belt, but before I can move away, his hands grip my bare hips.

"Don't touch me." I try again to pull away, but his fingernails dig into my skin.

His eyes are dark and full of greed as he smirks. "God, you're such a fucking tease. It's really not nice when you tease like you do."

"I'm not a tease." Again, I try to push him away, but Bruce is stronger than me.

"You are. You took your clothes off and made me want you." He leans against the desk and positions himself so my legs are caught in his. Now he has more freedom to rove his hands over me. He jerks me forward so my pelvis bumps against his cock. He bucks into me. "Feel that. You did that."

My throat goes dry as I suddenly become aware of the gravity of the situation. If I don't start seriously fighting back, there's a good chance this could end with me bent over and Bruce having his merry old way with me—the very thing I'd left the set trying to avoid.

I struggle in earnest now.

"I think you should lick it."

"I'm not licking anything. Let me go."

"Come on, Dev. Just a little taste. Lick me." With his leg coiled around me and one hand snaked around my waist, he tries to push my head toward his crotch. "Are you going to make this easy? Or are you going to make this fun?"

My eyes are watering now. My throat's tight. "I'll scream."

"Fun then." Bruce pushes my head down again, this time with more force. I can't fight him—he's too strong—but I try anyway, flailing and kicking.

I'm gathering my voice to let out a scream when there's a knock on the door "Devi?"

Bruce freezes and, before he can think to prevent me, I shout, "Come in!"

The door opens, and LaRue walks in. Bruce still has his hands on me, but this time when I pull out of his grasp, he lets go. I wrap the robe around me, holding it tightly at my neck and waist.

The producer looks from me to Bruce and back to me. "Everything okay in here?"

Fuck. No. Not okay in the least.

Bruce is the one who answers first. "Thought I could make her a little more comfortable before filming. That's all." He lifts his hand to draw two fingers down my cheek. "See you on set, Devi."

I shudder and wrap my arms tighter around myself. My lips are trembling and I can't tell if I'm about to cry or throw up. I want to get out of here more than ever, but I can't move. I can't speak. If LaRue hadn't come after me, if he hadn't interrupted….

"Hey, what's this I hear about you quitting?"

I barely register what he says, practically crying as I let out a tremulous breath. "Thank you. For coming when you did. Bruce…he…he just…"

Concerned, LaRue steps toward me. But I flinch when he reaches his hand out. "What is it?" he asks.

"He tried to come on to me. He wouldn't stop." I'm shook up, completely unsettled, and it's difficult to form my scattered thoughts into sentences so I just repeat myself. "He wouldn't stop. He wouldn't stop."

My skin burns where Bruce touched me, as if his fingers had been doused in acid, and I feel the urgent need to shower and scrub, though I also never want to take my clothes off again.

LaRue drops his hands to his sides, and the look on his face is both cautious and perplexed. "Bruce Madden just tried to come on to you?" he asks slowly.

"Yes!" *Didn't I fucking say that?* "After I said no!"

"Well, Devi." He pauses as if about to deliver news he thinks I don't want to hear, and I can already tell he's right. "You *are* here to make porn. What did you expect would happen?"

My heart feels like it's in my throat, and it was already pounding so hard I was sure it would bruise my insides. I blink up at LaRue several times. "Jesus, are you kidding me?"

LaRue cocks his hip against the desk. "I was going to ask the same about you. You signed a contract to do a certain type of work for me, and now you're not only walking out of that contract, but are crying foul when other people on my set expect you to live up to what you agreed to? That's not how this business works."

His tone is calm and reasonable, and for a fraction of a second I think he may be right—that I am obviously the one in the wrong, that it's my choices that have put me in this situation, that I'm being too sensitive. What had Bruce Madden really done, anyway? Touched my skin? I'd come here today with the intention of letting him doing so much more.

But then the moment of doubt passes and a lifetime of lessons in self-respect and personal rights takes hold of my emotions, turning them to blind rage. "First of all," I channel my anger into talking points. "I quit because the terms I agreed to were not being met. Second of all, this room is not your set. Third of all, even if it were, I still get to decide what happens to me. Just because I signed a contract doesn't mean I give up consent. That's not how my body works."

LaRue shakes his head, incredulous. "Damn, I knew you were young, but I didn't think you were so naïve. Do you realize what you've cost me today? I've already had to pay the crew for thirty minutes of standing around because you were running late and now because of your cold feet. If you're not careful, you're going to get a reputation for being a diva, and that's no way to launch the next part of your career."

I'm still angry, still indignant, but LaRue's chiding is an echo of

Raven's earlier words, and self-doubt forces me into an apology I don't mean. "I'm sorry that I've wasted your money. That wasn't my intention."

"Doesn't matter what your intention was. I've lost money and I expect you to help recuperate my expenses."

I turn my head sharply in his direction and tighten my arms around my chest, instantly wary of what he expects in the form of retribution.

He waves his hand, seeming to understand what I assume he's suggesting. "I'm sure you give a fine fuck, but even if you have a golden cunt, it's not going to translate to cash unless you wipe your eyes, pull yourself together, and go out there and shoot this scene. Give me a dynamite performance, and I'll forget that we had a rocky start."

He turns to leave as though the conversation is over, as though the matter is settled.

I'm flabbergasted. "Like hell, I'm shooting anything with you. I don't care what I cost you. I'm out of here."

Though I'd prefer to dress without him in the room, that want is a far second to the need to leave. I pull my cut-off shorts on then turn away from him to shed my robe and put on my T-shirt, foregoing a bra in favor of speedy dressing.

For the first time he's come into the room, LaRue's voice sharpens. "You walk out of here without doing that scene, and you've just kissed your career goodbye."

I slip my feet into my flip-flops and gather up my Ralph's bag. "Well, let's just see what happens when I tell people what happened today."

"Tell who what? Who's even going to care what you have to say? Naïve, Devi." His words hit my backside as I rush out of the room. "Your agent will be hearing from me," he shouts after me.

I manage to make it out of the house and to my car without anyone stopping or bothering me, but I'm on the road before I finally take a real breath. And then I burst into tears. I don't know where to go. I don't know what to do. I don't know what I want or what to think, so I drive aimlessly as the sun sinks lower in the sky, trying to gather my thoughts together. I've spent three years in the erotica industry and have never felt so violated. I've heard stories from other performers, stories of abuse and harassment, and yet it always felt so far away from me. And it *was* far away from me—because I'd carefully chosen my projects and producers, because I'd made sure that the jobs I'd taken had been vetted by people I trust.

Until now.

And why? Why did I take this job without investigating it further? *Logan.*

Because I'd wanted to prove to myself that my emotions for Logan wouldn't affect my work. Instead, I've proven just the opposite. I've proven that what he makes me feel is frightening enough to cause me to ignore my usual thorough standards. I've proven that these feelings are the strong kind, probably strong enough to be given a label. Strong enough to call love.

I'm still too dazed from everything that's just happened to fully feel the impact of this realization, but I want to feel it. I want to feel something that isn't this dirty, terrible, violated feeling.

So I say the words out loud, seeing if it makes a difference. "I love Logan. I'm *in love* with Logan."

The acknowledgment helps. I'm still cold and numb, but there's a light now, something hopeful, like the first star in a night sky. Like something I can cling to in order to keep from drowning in the darkness.

My phone starts singing the ringtone I've assigned for my agent and thank God I'm at a stoplight so I can dig through my purse to find it. "Thank, fuck," I say skipping a formal greeting. "The shoot with LaRue? Fucking terrible. It was unsafe, un-female friendly. The director—I still don't know his fucking name—treated me as inferior. The dressing room didn't lock. Bruce Madden walked right in and made himself at home with my body. I swear he would have raped me if LaRue hadn't walked in." Talking about it renews my anger. I'm shaking by the time I get through everything. "I just…I'm so upset, Lucy, I can't even."

"Take a deep breath," Lucy says calmly. "Now, are you driving? You're upset. Should you pull over?"

"Probably. But I need to keep driving." I'm not sure where I am. There are places I could park—a gas station, a McDonald's parking lot—but the thought of stopping makes me panic, as though Bruce might be driving right behind me, just waiting for me to let my guard down.

Lucy doesn't try to argue. "Understood. Be careful, okay?"

"Okay."

"Now, first. Are you hurt?"

I shake my head before realizing she can't see me. "No. I'm just worked up."

"Would you rather I call you back?"

"Don't hang up!" I didn't realize how desperate I was to talk to someone until now. "I just. I might not be very coherent. But I want to talk. Please."

"I'm not going anywhere. Do you want to tell me what happened with Bruce?"

"He harassed me. He scared me." I tell her the whole thing in as much detail as I can muster. I hear myself as I'm talking, and I know I sound melodramatic. I begin to doubt myself again.

But Lucy is supportive and reassuring, treating my every emotion as valid and legitimate.

"And Bruce is the reason you quit the scene?" she asks eventually.

"No—wait. How do you know—?" I try to remember if I mentioned quitting, but can't recall.

"I just got off the phone with LaRue," she explains.

Of course he called her immediately. I probably wasn't even out of the house before he'd dialed her number. "Whatever he said to you is full of shit. That situation was one hundred percent not appropriate."

"I understand, and I'm sorry." There's a beat before she goes on. "But you left me a phone message before you even got to the set, didn't you? Saying you couldn't do the scene?"

"Oh, great. You think I'm being ridiculous too."

"I didn't say that, Devi. I'm trying to get a clear picture of the situation so that I can get you out of this the best I can."

"Get me out of what? I'm not the one who did anything that needs getting out of. Is LaRue trying to sue or…?" I trail off, overwhelmed by the prospect of a legal battle.

"Yes, he wants to be reimbursed for money lost." *Well, fuck. There goes my apartment.* "But I'm pretty sure I can get him to drop that, Devi. I'm more concerned about what he's going to do to your reputation going forward."

"He can shit on my rep all he wants. I'm not doing het porn. I thought I was cut out for it, but I was wrong." I know it's not fair to assume all hetero sets are alike, but I'm not about to take the chance of repeating this afternoon's experience.

And there's the other reason I won't consider doing het porn again anytime soon. The reason that has nothing to do with Bruce or LaRue and has everything to do with Logan.

Lucy is silent for a second. "It's not just P in V scenes I'm concerned about. Hagen has a lot of pull in the industry. I'm afraid you're going to see fallout in your regular jobs as well."

Shit.

Shit, shit, shit.

I bite the inside of my cheek and fight the new set of tears that are threatening to fall. "Do you think I did the wrong thing by walking off the set?"

"No." She lets out a heavy sigh. "But there are rules in this industry. Rules I don't agree with, but they're there all the same. They're unethical and illegal, even, but very few people take sex workers seriously. If you're not making any formal allegations then we have a better shot at coming out of this, but it's going to be hard to not point fingers at something if we're trying to get out of your contractual obligation to LaRue Hagen's company."

I bite my cheek harder, taking in what she's said. Nothing here is a revelation. I know what kind of world I'm part of. I'm *not* this ignorant.

"I really fucked up, didn't I?" And I don't mean by walking off the job but by pushing to take it in the first place. By staying in this business instead of figuring out what I really want to do with my life. Because is this really what I want to be doing in five years? In ten? Is porn my passion? Is all of this bullshit worth it?

And wasn't it just this morning at my shoot with Lynne that I thought I could do this forever?

Well, maybe I could have if I hadn't fucked it up.

"Hey. Don't blame yourself for this. We should be able to salvage a career, though it might be a good idea to focus on just print work for a while."

"Whatever you think is best." I'm not so sure. I'm not so sure about anything anymore.

"Out of curiosity—was there a reason in particular that you were wary before you arrived on set?"

There's a part of me that wants to tell her about Logan, about how I've fallen head over heels for him, about how I kind of only want to have sex with him now.

But if I thought I sounded naïve complaining about Bruce, I can only imagine how naïve it will sound to declare that I'm in love with a porn star.

So I say, "I just had a bad feeling. That's all."

If Lucy senses I'm withholding something, she doesn't let on. "Sounds like you've got good instincts. But it's probably best we not mention that you had any issues before you walked in. It weakens the argument for the inappropriate work environment. Let's meet next week, and we can prepare a formal record of complaint to rebuttal against LaRue's accusation of breach of contract."

"Okay. But, Lucy? If Hagen tries to make bargains—like, even if he hires a new crew or changes the rules for the set behavior—I don't want to do a reshoot."

"I understand." And though I can tell she truly does, I can also tell that this would be so much easier if I would just agree to do another shoot. Thankfully, she doesn't say that. "Don't think about this too much tonight, Dev. Be proud for sticking up for yourself. That took guts. A lot of women wouldn't have been able to do that."

I tell her I'll try to focus on the positive and agree to call her in a day or two. We hang up, and I'm back to where I was before she called—lost and drifting. I need a shower. But I don't want to go home—I need to not be alone. I need to be somewhere I feel safe and supported.

I'm not sure when or if I actually decide where I'm going, but at some point my driving turns from aimless to purposeful, and before long I'm pulling into his driveway and using the key under the succulent plant to let myself into his house.

Logan's stretched out on his front room couch. He's wearing nothing but jeans; his bare feet are crossed at the ankles in front of him as he edits some footage on his laptop.

He sits up, surprised, when I walk in the room, but then I think he must get a good look at me, and his features quickly wrinkle into concern. Instantly, he's on his feet. "What's wrong?"

Instead of answering him, I fall into his open arms and let out a raspy, "I need you." Because, the truth is, now that I'm wrapped in the cocoon of his warmth and his scent and his touch and his *him*-ness, the answer to his question is, "*nothing.*"

CHAPTER SIXTEEN

Devi's face is buried in my shoulder, and I want to pull back to look at her, but then I feel the unmistakable warmth of tears on my skin, and so I don't. Instead, I hook an arm behind her knees and scoop her up into my arms and carry her into my dark bedroom, where the drawn shades keep out most of the afternoon sun. I sit on the edge of the bed with her still in my arms, and simply sit, rocking her slowly and resting my head on top of hers.

I don't ask her what's wrong again, even though I'm itching in the worst way to know. When I last saw her this morning, she was dewy-faced and flushed from her scene with Kendi (and, I secretly hoped, the moment we shared on set). And when she kissed me goodbye, she seemed happy and chipper, if a little nervous. I know she had a scene scheduled after the one I saw—could that be what's upsetting her? Something that happened on set?

I rack my brain, trying to remember if she told me any details about the shoot she was going to. Generally, her scenes don't get much rougher than some dildo play and maybe the occasional light bondage, but certainly not the kind of punishing scenes some actors film. So maybe she fought with someone on set? Another performer? A director?

"Devi," I say. It's an invitation for her to speak, but it's also an affirmation, a reminder that I am here for her and only for her, and that she is completely safe and cared for in my arms.

"I—I didn't tell you something," she gets out.

I frown, my eyebrows pulling together. "Whatever it is, babe, it's fine."

She shakes her head against my chest. "It wasn't fine," she says, the tears flowing faster and harder now. "I—I thought I could do it and then he was so aggressive and he cornered me—"

He?

A fucking *he?*

What the fuck was she doing this afternoon? While I was missing her and feeling lonely as I worked on my couch, she was on a set with a *he?*

My mouth reacts before my brain entirely catches up. "What?" I ask sharply. "Who is *he?*"

I feel her shrink in my arms, retreating into herself and curling into a ball. "I booked a het shoot with LaRue Hagen," she whispers tearfully. "That's where I was going today…not for a girl-on-girl scene, but for a scene with Bruce Madden."

"Bruce Madden?" I demand, five different kinds of anger rising in my chest, the chief one an insanely protective instinct, because Bruce Madden is notorious for shitty onset behavior and *fuck that guy.* My blood immediately boils, conjuring the worst possible scenarios and elaborate fantasies that involve me going on vigilante murder sprees, but I try to breathe myself into a state of patient calm until I know what actually happened. It's just that I know my girl, and I know that she's not the type to cry. She's not the type to let emotions overrule her control, and so whatever happened must have been big.

And bad.

I think about some of the worst stories I've heard happen on porn sets, all the rapes that happened on camera and were never prosecuted. Raven and I advocated hard for those performers—and we still do, albeit separately now—but I never ever thought that it might happen to someone close to me, someone I love…

Oh God. If something like that happened to Devi today, there will be no end to the hell I will rain down on everyone even tangentially connected. Hell and handcuffs and blood and money, and I will personally see to it that Bruce himself is castrated.

You don't know what happened yet—set the mental castrating knife down.

"Yes, Bruce Madden," she sniffles. "He was…oh God, Logan, he was awful."

"Did he…?" I can't even get the question out, because I'm asking two questions—*did he assault you?* and *if not, did you still fuck him?* But even in my protective rage, I can't bear to ask anything that makes her feel for one second like she's to blame or did anything wrong. Whatever happened was one hundred percent that shit-bag's fault. "Did it happen during the shoot?"

"I couldn't even start the shoot. But then he found me while I was trying to leave…" She breaks off abruptly and starts sobbing, the kind of sobs that tell me that words can't happen right now, and so I just hold her and rock her, stroking the back of her head as she cries.

Then as I'm rocking her and murmuring reassuring words, something else hits me and hits me hard.

Devi booked a het scene. When Devi kissed me goodbye this morning, she was driving off to go fuck another man. And even through the veil of my rage at Bruce Madden and my desperate fear that she's been terribly hurt, another emotion surfaces, ugly and undeniable.

Jealousy.

I remember our first fake date in the park, when I saw that Sinner's Playpen was calling Devi, and I remember her asking my advice about doing more mainstream porn, and I remember telling Tanner that of course we were both professionals and would keep filming all the scenes we wanted to. And somehow none of that matters right now, because before now it was all in abstract, just things that could potentially happen, things that didn't feel real. I told myself and everyone else it was okay.

But it's not.

It's not okay.

Because I'm holding this woman in my arms, and I want to be the only one to hold her, fucking ever, and you know what? That goes for the female performers who get to fuck her too, because I want it just to be me me me, and have her all to myself.

I try to remind myself that it's just sex, it's just fucking, and it doesn't mean anything, but if it doesn't mean anything, then why didn't she tell me about it? Why would she keep it a secret?

And then the twin sister to jealousy shows up.

Suspicion.

I hate it. I hate every inch of that emotion, I hate feeling it crawl over my heart and rifle through my thoughts, wondering if there's some reason Devi kept it a secret, wondering if I'm going to wake up one day soon to find Devi posting pictures of herself with some Italian. I hate wondering if I care about her more than she cares about me, if she's been fucking other guys all this time, if I'm about to have my heart broken again.

And then I shut it down—all of it. The jealousy and the suspicion and the rage. I don't have a right to care if she's fucking other guys because I've been fucking other girls, and even if I hadn't, "sort-of boyfriend" isn't a term that has to mean explicit monogamy. We never talked about being exclusive.

We're porn stars. We shoot porn. We fuck other people. That's just how it is.

And right now the woman I love is hurting, and that's where all my attention needs to be. I can figure out the rest later.

After a few minutes, I feel her begin to relax in my arms, her tears slowing and her breathing returning to normal. She wipes at her face with her hand, and it comes back black with mascara. She pulls back to look at my shoulder and chest, which are smeared with the same.

She barks out the kind of laughter that only comes in the midst of tears. "I got your chest all messy."

"We can fix that," I say as cheerfully as I can while I'm still trying to contain all of the residual bitter pangs of jealousy and the over-protective boyfriend instincts that are telling me to go burn shit down. I stand up and carry her into my bathroom and set her down on the wide bench in my shower.

My shower is big—the size of most people's entire bathrooms big—and has a million showerheads and jets and nozzles that I don't normally use, because, as you may have heard, we don't have water in California anymore. But today is an extenuating circumstance, and I turn everything on, hot as it will go.

Devi blinks at me from the bench, suddenly very young and forlorn-looking. And then all of my jealousy and suspicion melt completely away, washed down the drain. Instead, I feel an overwhelming need to shelter her and protect her, to erase whatever bad thing has happened, but it's too late for that. I can only hope to atone for not being there, for not being able to help her.

I approach her slowly through the water, ignoring the way my jeans are getting soaked. You've probably already guessed this, but I don't mind getting my clothes wet—a porn habit, I guess. But I leave my jeans on for another reason: I don't want Devi to think that I brought her in here to fuck her. I don't want her to think that this is about sex or about me, or about anything other than helping her feel better.

She watches me with curious, tired eyes as I get closer, until I'm over to the bench. "Can I undress you?" I ask.

She bites her bottom lip and then nods. "Yes, please." Her voice is barely audible over the hiss of the water.

Steam billows around us as I work her damp T-shirt off of her body. My dick jolts as I see she's not wearing anything underneath and those delicious tits are just hanging out, ripe and plump, but I move my focus elsewhere, helping her out of her flip-flops and then her denim cutoffs, tossing everything to the edge of the shower.

Once she's naked, I take her elbows in my hands and guide her to the waterfall showerhead, where I make her stand while I go get a washcloth and body wash.

"You're going to smell like a dude, I'm sorry," I apologize as I start washing her.

"No," she corrects me. "I'll smell like you."

The way she says it, like it's the best possible thing I could give her, twists my heart. I quickly look back down to the washcloth so she doesn't see how much this affects me, paying extra attention to non-sexual places like her hands and feet. Even so, being this close to her body, watching the water pour over her breasts and hips and ass, is doing uncomfortable things to my jeans. I wait until I go get shampoo and conditioner to surreptitiously adjust myself—not easy in soaking wet denim, but I manage.

I take my time washing her hair, massaging her scalp and rubbing the tresses clean between my fingertips. *I love you*, I think, wishing she could feel the words radiating off my body. *I love you so much.*

But of course I don't say them, knowing now is not the time, not with whatever is hanging over her like a dark cloud. I rinse her off, wrap her in a giant fluffy towel and carry her to my bed.

I go to shuck my wet jeans and grab another pair when she finally speaks again. "No, don't put another pair on. Come here."

"Cass, it doesn't have to—"

"I know," she says firmly. "I know what you're trying not to do, but it's what I want."

Somewhere inside of me, I know I should protest more, but I can't.

Not only because of how aroused I am after washing her body, but because the warm confidence in her voice is undeniable. I strip off the wet jeans and walk towards the bed, crawling up next to her. She reaches immediately for my cock but I grab her hand.

"I know I look horny as fuck right now—and I am—but Cass, if something… really bad…happened today, I need to know about it." I don't use the *r* word, but it hangs in the air between us nonetheless.

She takes a minute to answer, struggling for words. "I wasn't—it's not—" She swallows and looks down at my hand, large and strong, wrapped around her wrist. I quickly let go.

"I want to know what happened, but I understand if you don't want to talk about it. We can just be here. But I'm not comfortable doing anything more until I'm sure that I'm not taking advantage of you."

Devi groans loudly and suddenly, flopping onto her back. "I wish you wouldn't be so goddamned circumspect. I want you; I *need* you. Only you can make me feel better in the way I need."

"Then you have to tell me why."

She blinks up at the ceiling. "As long as you touch me while I'm talking."

"Cass…"

"It doesn't have to be sex. But Logan, I need to remember what it feels like to be touched by the person I've chosen to give my body to. I need a man to touch me in the way I like and want, because I don't want today to make me forget."

In a flash, I understand. I mean, not entirely, because I've never been touched in a way I didn't have control of, and because I'm a man, I'll probably never be powerless in that way. But her plea is so deeply human, so deeply vulnerable, and I can't deny her. I can't deny her anything, when it comes down to it.

I roll and crawl over her, resting my body weight on my knees and forearms, letting our naked chests and stomachs touch and my stiff cock press into her lower belly. I kiss her neck and her shoulders and jaw, and I feel her melt into my touch and let go of her last remaining shreds of control. She starts crying again, slow and silent tears, and she keeps crying as I drop kisses everywhere, light lips-only kisses, and gradually, haltingly, the story emerges. She tells me about the set, about her discomfort with the director and with Bruce.

And then when she gets to the part where Bruce cornered her in the office, my open hands clench into fists, and I turn my face away so she can't see my expression. Because all I can think about is murder. Castration and murder and then castration again. Double castration.

She finishes and then reaches for my face, gently turning me so that I'm forced to meet her eyes. "What are you thinking?" she asks, uncertain and vulnerable.

My heart breaks, but I'm honest. "About how I want to hang Bruce Madden and LaRue Hagen from the Hollywood sign."

She presses her lips together in what might be a smile. "It would be too difficult to get up there with two bodies in tow."

"Not for a determined man."

She sighs underneath me, and I stroke her hair away from her face. "I don't know what to say, Devi. Except I'm so desperately furious and heartbroken for you. I wish I could have been there to protect you!"

"I wish that, too," she murmurs, but then she falls silent, as if she's troubled.

I hesitate, but then I say it anyway. "Devi, why didn't you tell me about the scene? I have never lied about the work I'm doing. It makes me worry that we aren't on the same page…?" My voice lifts in a question at the end, betraying all of my unfounded fears.

She glances away, new tears in her eyes. "I'm so sorry, Logan. I didn't mean to lie to you. But telling you about it—it would have meant having a talk with myself that I didn't know I was ready to have. And it's all so stupid because now I've ruined everything."

I'm not sure what she means by the first thing, but I can help with the last. "Please don't worry about the fallout. As long as I'm around, you will have work if you want it, I swear. And I will personally see to it that Bruce Madden is destroyed. That fucker won't get away with this. Neither will LaRue."

Another sigh. "Even you would be hard-pressed to take on LaRue. And thank you for the offer of work, but I also want to work on my own terms, you know? That's important to me. As it is, I'm not sure how much I want to work at all…" she trails off.

I'm confused. "Like, not work while you sort all this out? Or leave porn? Because this was shitty and horrible, but you know that there are safe places to work. You've been working in them for three years. And you're so fucking amazing at it! Don't let an asshole like Bruce drive you away from something you love to do and something you fucking rock at doing."

"It's not…" She takes a breath. "It's not that I feel driven away, Logan. But there's something else, something I haven't told you, and I don't know what it means for me or my work yet."

I'm listening, but she doesn't continue talking. She seems to shut down, something in her eyes shuttering closed and her mouth pressing together.

"You can tell me anything," I say, leaning down to kiss the delicate skin near her ear. "Anything. Devi, please. You asked me not to shut you out…don't shut me out. Tell me."

Her voice is cautious. Logical. "I don't think I'm ready to tell you. I haven't thought it through yet."

"You don't have to have a thesis paper written about it, babe. If we're going to try this boyfriend-girlfriend thing, part of that is talking with one another about things that might be messy or hard. It's okay if you haven't gotten it all figured out yet. I want to hear about it because I care about you, and I—"

I stop myself right before I say it. *Not the time, Romeo*, I remind myself. This is not the place for my tendency to jump into shit heart first, head later. Devi is too precious for my usual messy, full-throttle approach to love.

But something I say seems to unfreeze her. Her lips part and her eyelashes flutter and all of a sudden her chin starts trembling.

"What were you going to say?" she whispers.

I shake my head. "It's not important."

"Is that true?" she asks. "Or are you just saying it's not important because you don't want to talk about it? You just talked about shutting each other out, but you're doing it too!"

Shit. Why do I keep fucking this up?

"I don't want that," I say, "but I also…you're so young and I don't want to fuck this up and I'm worried that I'm pressing on the gas too hard for you."

"No," she murmurs. "You're not."

"But it's okay to take things slow, I mean, that's kind of what we talked about at the gallery—"

"I'm in love with you," she says abruptly.

There's nothing but static and sparks in my brain, and an expansive hot glow igniting in my chest. "What?" I manage.

"I've been thinking about it, and I think I've been in love with you for a while, but this morning, it became completely clear. I'm so much in love with you, that even the thought of coming for another man, of him touching me where you touched me, it bothered me. Scratched at me. I almost walked away from that set before I even entered, because I realized that I didn't want to make that kind of porn without you."

She doesn't deliver this news to me as if celebrating a huge revelation or confiding a hope. She shares this like she's confessing a sin to me, a weakness, and then I realize why—she doesn't know I love her back. She thinks she's being the irrational one because she's normally so incredibly rational, and I've done too good a job hiding my feelings from her. She must think that she's gone too far, and that's making her insecure and nervous about telling me these things.

"I know that sounds like something the worst, clingiest girlfriend on earth would say," she continues. "I know it sounds prudish or narrow-minded or something, but the whole experience, the way Madden handled me and LaRue dismissed me, it made me realize that not only are you the man I feel safest with shooting porn, but you're the man who makes me *want* to shoot porn. If any man is going to touch me, I want it to be you. I don't want to settle for anything less. But I also understand how completely out of line this is emotionally, and how unwelcome it might be to you, and if you want me to go, I understand."

In fact, she even starts to roll out from under me, as if to leave. But I keep her caged against the bed, and I lean down and claim her mouth with a rumbling growl in my chest.

"You're mine," I say against her mouth. "You belong to me and you're not going anywhere."

She pulls back a little, her brows furrowed in worry. "You're not grossed out by what I said?"

"Devi, I'm desperately in love with you too. Maybe I have been since the day we met. I didn't say anything because I didn't want to scare you or overwhelm you." I move my hand so my thumb can trace her bottom lip. "But you said it first, my brave girl. You said it first, so I know that I haven't pushed you into it or that you're lying to make me feel better. You really love me, don't you?"

She nods, those gold-brown eyes huge and limpid. "I do," she whispers.

"Thank fucking God," I breathe, my thumb pulling her lip down just a tad. My erection, which abated while she described Madden's assault, stirs back to hot life against her stomach. "I love you so fucking much."

I move my mouth against hers, and she kisses me back hungrily for a minute, her hands sliding up my torso and staying warm and firm against my chest, but then she breaks off the kiss. "Logan, I need…"

"Anything, Cass. Name anything."

"I just—" she blinks up at me, and her eyes are wet with new tears, her face open with hope and pain. "Is this real? You're not saying this for *Star-Crossed?*"

"Do you see any cameras in here?" I ask roughly.

"No, but—"

I crush my mouth to hers, cutting her off. "This is real," I growl in between kisses. "It's just you and me in this bed, and I'm going to show you exactly how fucking real it is."

A tear spills out of one eye and traces down her temple. I catch it with my lips before it reaches her hairline. She reaches down and then I feel her hands cradle my swollen cock. I let out a low groan.

"Please make me forget about Bruce," she begs. "Show me you love me."

"My brave girl," I say, brushing her hair away from her face. "So brave on the set and then so brave with me." It's her bravery that drives me down, moving backwards until I can settle between her thighs and begin nuzzling the soft skin there. I want to lavish her with piles of money and jewelry; I want to buy her a new house and a new car. I want to give her something—anything—that shows her how fucking grateful and torn up with happiness I am. Not just that she loves me, but that she told me first, because every other step forward in our relationship has been me, me coaxing and me leading, and her cautiously thinking things through before she says yes.

But not today.

Today, she plunged in and bared her soul, with no guarantee that I felt the same, and without her usual safety net of logic and analysis. And seeing my Devi all reckless and unsettled because of *me*—then she has to love me. She must. She must feel the same turbulent, all-consuming pull that I do, and that makes me so desperate to thank her, to touch her, to show her exactly how fucking much I love her back.

Since I can't give her piles of money, I'm determined to worship her body to show her my adoration instead. The moment my lips brush against the soft, neatly trimmed curls just above her clit, she shivers and widens her legs.

I settle in, sliding my arms under her thighs and then curling my hands over the top to keep her legs spread as widely as I want. And then I dive in, running my tongue everywhere and tasting everything and stopping at nothing to make her squirm and whimper. She smells like clean water and my body wash, but when I spread her open even further and let my tongue trace circles inside her entrance, I taste a sweetness that is hers and hers alone.

She writhes on the bed, her hands reaching for my hair, and it's one of my favorite things about eating a girl out—maybe my favorite thing—feeling her fingers curl into my hair and pull, feeling her hands on the back of my head while her hips lift to rub her pussy against my face.

In my porno career, I've shot a few scenes where I've been playfully tied up, but they've never been anything but the loosest shadow of submission. But when I'm between a woman's legs like this, heels digging into my back and hands rough and forcing around my head, I think I understand the appeal. Because while I may be the one on my belly, from my vantage, I'm the one with all the power. I'm looking up over the rise of Devi's public bone and up the slope of her stomach to her face, which is currently scrunched up in abject pleasure, and *I'm* the one doing that. Maybe her hands are the ones tugging and she's the one urging—*harder, faster, inside, please lick me inside*—but it's my mouth, my tongue, my skills. I'm the one unraveling her, and that makes me feel more powerful than I've ever felt with a crop in my hand.

I'm not saying I want to give up the crop, mind you. But this is just as amazing.

I look up at her again, still sucking and licking, and I watch her as I move my hand from under her thigh to find her seam. I stroke everywhere—her ass, her thighs, her entrance—but it's when I finally slide a finger inside of her that I see her start to truly come apart. This morning, she was coming for Kendi, and now she's coming for me, and I just think that's fucking beautiful, like some sort of cunt-licking circle of life, but then I wonder for a minute if she feels a difference between me and Kendi. If not in her cunt, in her heart or her mind—because it's got to be different, right? When someone you love touches you?

I'll make it feel different, I vow. I'll make it so that she has no doubt that I love her, that her body learns ways to respond to me and only to me. I want to own her fantasies, I want her to think of me whenever she closes her eyes on a set. Whenever another actress fucks Devi with her tongue, I want Devi to imagine my mouth, and whenever she's fucking herself with a dildo, I want it to be my cock she dreams of.

Devi tugs me up over her, and I oblige, wiping my mouth with my arm as I settle back on top of her.

"What is it, Cass?"

Her gaze meets mine, the pupils so dilated that her eyes are pools of black. "I love you," she whispers, searching my face. "I love you and I wanted to say it again. I wanted to make sure it was still real—you loving me too."

Her honesty breaks my heart. "Never doubt that for a fucking second. It's always real." And I lean down to kiss her and she kisses me back hungrily, licking and sucking her own taste off my mouth, which makes my cock so fucking hard that I can feel it leaving a wet spot against her belly. I love her and I want to fuck her until she can't walk. I want to know her soul and I want to tie her down and fuck her for days at a time. I want to worship her like a temple slave and I want to come in her so hard and so often that she's reminded of me every time she walks. It's taking everything I have not to stab my cock into her right now, to keep my mind present when my body and heart are so singularly united in the goal of fusing myself to her.

I'm shuddering with restraint, my muscles literally fighting against themselves, when she whispers, "Please."

"Are you sure?" I force myself to ask. "Just because we've shared things doesn't mean we have to…" I'm so hard that I can barely breathe and my voice is stuttering and raspy. "We don't have to today."

"I meant what I said," she tells me with those dark eyes. "About needing your touch." She closes her eyes for a minute. "Show me it's real," she begs. "Fuck me like it's real."

"Okay," I say hoarsely. "Gimme a minute." I reach for my bedside table, where I keep a small glass jar of condoms, but then she stops me.

"No," she says earnestly. "Bare. I want you bare."

I look down at her. "Are you sure?" I ask. I'm tested every two weeks, and I know that she is too, but it's still a big leap of trust. "I know you're clean, baby girl, and I know you're on the pill, but it's a big step, and we're just getting started. We have lots of time for big steps."

She shakes her head. "I want it—you. All of you. Nothing between us."

I'm braced up on my hands and I hang my head for a minute, trying to catch my breath and decide if I can say no to this. I don't want to and there's no logical reason to, but this feels big. The special kind of big that only Devi and film make me feel, and it fucking terrifies me.

"I'm scared," I admit. "Devi, being with you bare, with no barriers and no cameras...I'm scared. Whatever is between us, it's so real that it hurts."

"I'm scared too," she says. "But I'm with you. If we fall, we fall together."

If we fall, we fall together.

My heart pounds with both relief and terror at the same time, and I dive back down to capture her mouth in a searing kiss. "God, I love you," I say fiercely. "So fucking much."

"Do it, Logan," she breathes. "Please. Need it. Need you."

I inch just a tiny bit lower, and—with our eyes locked on each other's the entire time—I reach down and take myself in my hand and guide the swollen crown to her wet entrance. I only push inside to the flared edge of my helmet and then I stop. I take another deep breath, almost unable to bear how tight her pussy is around my crest. It squeezes me, it fists my crown better than any real fist ever could, and I almost want to stay like this forever, with her wet and begging, and me rendering both of us practically insensate and nonverbal with just the barest penetration.

And then I slide in deeper.

Her thighs tremble and her hands dig into my back, and I feel my cock stretching her so tight, forcing its girth deeper into her wet, soft warmth, until I'm nestled all the way. I'm in between her legs, our pelvises flush together, our stomachs touching and my chest brushing against her stiff, dark nipples. I lower myself to my forearms and I kiss her again, not moving inside of her yet, letting her adjust and letting myself cool down before I embarrass myself and explode like a teenage boy before making Devi come.

We kiss long and slow, and she moves soft and sighing underneath me, until she's practically glowing with happiness, until she's moving herself against me and wearing the kind of open, warm expression that radiates pure love.

She's rubbing her clit as she undulates under me, and I see a dark flush rising up her chest and cheeks and I know it will be any second now, and sure enough—despite the fact that I'm not moving at all—she's grinding herself to orgasm underneath me, the balls of her feet moving against the sheet as she searches out friction and depth.

"You're so fucking beautiful," I murmur to her, watching her face blush as she works herself on my thickness, watching those fleeting sex smiles chase themselves on and off her lips as she approaches the edge. It occurs to me that I haven't fucked a woman in missionary position in I don't know how long, because it's not a great position to film with. I prefer the positions where the viewers can see my dick and the pretty, pink pussy it's fucking, and missionary hides so much of the good stuff.

Except it feels fucking incredible—for me and for her—and there's something else. I forgot how intimate it is. Our skin is touching everywhere, *everywhere*, our thighs sliding together, our stomachs, our arms and our lips. I'm so close to her and I can see her every expression, her every unspoken thought, and I know she can see mine. There is nothing between us—no condom, no camera, no invisible walls of denial or fear. There's only us moving together as one, an intimacy so deep and feverish that I almost feel outside of myself, like my soul really is leaving my body to search out Devi's.

It's the closest I've ever felt to any woman, ever.

But right as she begins to peak, I have this uncomfortable thought, this thought out of nowhere, that this is the best it's ever going to be. That I'm going to look back at this moment one day and realize that it was when we were the closest, the most uncomplicated, the most in love. And I realize I think that because there's no camera on us right now, no camera to capture this moment forever. It makes the moment feel so fragile, like it could vanish at any moment, and how do people bear this? This feeling like love and ecstasy are slipping through their fingers? With a camera, I could hold on to it, freeze it in time. But without one, there's nothing protecting this moment from being swept into oblivion.

And then a dawning realization of oblivion comes as she shatters around me, as she cries out and flexes and shudders with waves of release.

I want all these moments. I want only these moments. Because the only way to hold on to them is to hold on to her, and the way I want to hold on to her is something like I've never felt before. I want to give her all of me, all the time, always, and what the fuck does that mean? Does that mean I don't want to fuck other women? That's ridiculous, of course, but the answer is right underneath me, coming down from her orgasm glassy-eyed and breathless.

I think I might only want Devi.

I think I love her in a way I've never loved anyone else before.

I think I want to give her all of me. *All* of me. Meaning I don't give myself to anyone else.

Because that's one thing that the economics of porn can't erase—you are sharing yourself, endlessly, over and over again. Private slices of yourself, and I want Devi to have all my slices, all the parts of me that I have to share.

A ball of panic clenches in my stomach, because I don't know how to digest any of this. I try to push it all aside, but as I start rolling my hips into hers, I catch sight of my camera on my bedside table. It's dark and unseeing now, but its presence soothes me and worries me all at once. Who is Logan O'Toole, really? And what does he want?

I bury my face in Devi's neck, smelling her skin and my body wash and the slightest note of cinnamon, and I may not know all of the answers to those questions yet, but I know that all those answers start with the same woman.

"Did it feel good to come on my dick, baby?" I ask her, still rolling in and out, nice and easy.

"Yes," she says dazedly. "So good."

I move up onto my hands, nudging her legs open wider. I watch her as she watches me, her eyes on where we're joined as I start pumping in and out, the thick ridges and veins of my cock glistening from her pussy. Her gaze transforms from contented to hungry, and I look down too, loving the sight of my cock stretching out her hole, of her legs open for me and just for me.

But no, that thought brings back the unanswerable questions, and so I instead focus on the fucking, picking up the pace and jabbing into her faster and faster, until I'm grunting and she's gasping. Color is high in her cheeks, and I feel my balls tighten at the thought of coming in her like this, but I'm not ready, not ready at all. I want this moment to last forever.

So I slow down and change my strokes from short stabs to long, deep thrusts. I go so deep that I feel her cervix, and she lets out a half gasp, half moan.

"You like that?"

She closes her eyes and nods. "You're so big," she says in a tight whisper. "Even after I came. I thought it might be less tight, but I feel so full…"

"Such a brave girl," I reassure Devi in a low, deep purr. "Such a brave girl to take such a big cock."

She flushes under the praise, looking so bashfully proud and young that I have to duck my head and bite her shoulder to keep from looking at her face, because I'll come in an instant if she keeps wearing that look.

"It's the biggest cock you've ever felt inside you, isn't it? Tell me how big it is. Tell me how big I feel inside you." To punctuate my words, I thrust in deep, loving how tight her cunt feels around me, like a slick, hot vise.

Her eyelashes flutter when I hit that deep spot, and she moans. "It feels like you're splitting me in half," she says in a strangled voice. "I can feel you everywhere."

I guide her legs up so that her ankles are hooked past my shoulders, and then I lean forward on my arms, driving down into her cunt. I can get so deep in this position, and I use it to my advantage, stroking and rubbing that special spot.

"Fuck," she groans, turning her head from side to side. "Logan, oh my God."

"I'm gonna make you come so hard, Cass."

"Logan, I—I don't think I can—oh God, oh God, oh God--"

"Look at me, baby. Just keep watching me, okay?"

She's trembling hard, and I can feel the hard tip of my cock massaging her cervix, kissing up against it over and over again, and I pull out just enough to drag the wide, crest against her g-spot before I push back in to press against her cervix. Her head is tossing, her thighs shaking against me, and I can tell she's fighting it off because it feels too big, too intense.

"Devi, look at me," I urge, and she finally does, her eyes wide and desperate looking. "That's it," I coax her. "Let me take care of you. Let me make you feel good."

"I don't think I can," she says, a little wildly, but I keep going, crooning words of encouragement to her, *you're gonna feel so good* and *such a good, brave girl* and *I'm so deep, baby, so fucking deep* and then I see her hands clawing at the sheets and the cords in her neck strain.

And then it happens. Devi's stomach starts visibly tensing and every muscle in her body tremors and her back arches clear off the bed, her face contorted in the throes of ecstasy. She can't speak, can barely make any noise other than the soft keening that comes from somewhere in her throat, and she's on another plane, in another world, her body convulsing in long, deep, slow contractions that consume her, swallow her, transform her.

Cervical orgasms, ladies. They're a thing, and they are *intense*. Devi has completely fallen apart underneath me, oblivious to everything but the deep waves of release rolling out from her womb to the tips of her fingers and the soles of her feet. And unlike her clitoral orgasms, this lasts an eternity. Seconds and minutes and what feels like hours that I get to watch (and feel) the most beautiful woman in the world quiver and fracture into billions of glowing pieces. No man can last feeling that around his cock, watching that happen underneath him, and I'm no exception, because it's never been this good, it's never felt this good, and God fucking damn it if I haven't completely lost myself in her.

"Do it," she pants. "Come inside me."

"I'm gonna," I grunt, letting her legs fall back to the bed and driving into her fast and hard. "Gonna come so good for you, Cass."

Her hands find my ass, her fingers digging into my cheeks and urging me to go harder, faster, and she feels so good and she looks so good, all soft and sated underneath me. Her cunt is so fucking tight, squeezing me and squeezing me, and holy fuck, I want to marry this woman, and then with a juddering groan, my balls contract and I explode.

I rut into her hard, pumping hot jets of cum deep inside her, our eyes locked and the air heavy with magic. My whole torso is spasming, my entire pelvis a fiery, burning sun of release, unleashing waves and waves of deep, roiling pleasure. I pump and thrust and fuck my way through the climax, feeling high and drunk and dizzy, intoxicated by Devi, empowered by her, totally alive and exhilarated because of her. I feel the wet heat of my orgasm inside of her, I see the dark points of her erect nipples and the scorching lust on her face, and it draws it out. And the pulses keeping coming, again and again and again, and I empty myself inside of her, drain my balls until she's filled with me. Until she's dripping around us both.

When the pulses finally subside, the room smells of earthy sex and cinnamon, and we are messy everywhere. Sweat on our stomachs, and cum and arousal smearing our thighs. Devi's long hair is tangled as fuck, my bed looks like a hurricane tore it apart, and I can feel scratches blooming into light, teasing pain on my back and ass cheeks.

I'm so fucking in love.

I lean down to kiss her, a deep, soul-felt kiss, without the urgency of earlier. I take my time exploring her mouth, lavishing attention onto every crease of her lips, every silky slide of her tongue. She's making a humming noise in her chest, a happy, contented noise, and I pull back with a smile.

"Are you…purring?"

She giggles. "Yeah. I guess I am."

My chest puffs a little. I've given many women many orgasms, but I think this is the first time that I've actually made a woman purr with satisfaction.

"Let's see how long I can make that purring last, kitten. Flip over."

• • •

After Round Two, dinner, and a shower (which turned into Round Three), we are back in bed. It's nighttime now, and we're cuddling, Devi's back pressed against my chest and my arms around her. We're both drowsy, even my cock, which is content to be semi-hard and nestled against Devi's luscious ass. I think she's finally drifted off when she asks, "Do you have an Epipen in here?"

"Yeah, somewhere," I say sleepily. "There's one in my medicine cabinet, I think."

"Oh. Shouldn't you have it with you at all times?"

"I'm allergic to bees, Cass. It's not something I worry about happening in my bedroom."

"But do you carry one on set? Shouldn't you have had one in the desert the night we went out there?"

More awake now, I prop myself up on one elbow and look down at her. She doesn't turn to look at me. "I was planning on eating you out, not foraging for honey. At least not that kind of honey," I say with a smirk.

She doesn't smile.

"Why are you asking me this?" I poke her shoulder gently. "Are you planning to introduce bees into our sex play? Do you secretly keep bees in your pussy?"

Still no smile.

I sigh. "If it really worries you, I always keep one in my glove box. And why did this come up, anyway? Did I mention the bee thing to you?" Because it's not something I normally talk about, not because it's some sort of painful secret, but because it's really not a big deal. Honestly, sometimes even I forget about it.

She doesn't answer right away, and when she does, her voice is measured. "Raven mentioned it today on the set."

Her name drops like an anvil, thudding and lifeless.

Raven.

Ugh.

And the moment my personal distaste fades, a sense of protective anger flares up. How dare she talk to Devi? How dare she bring me up to Devi, in what I can only assume amounted to a sick sort of power play?

"What else did she say to you?" I ask, not bothering to hide my anger. "Did she upset you?"

Devi starts to shake her head but then stops. Then she gives a little nod. "Yeah," she admits. "I guess it did upset me. And she didn't say anything that wasn't true, Logan, That was the hard part. She said that I was doing het porn to make you jealous, and that it would never make you jealous, it would just make you feel better about fucking other people." A pause. "And that you were always fucking other people."

I have to close my eyes against the white-hot anger that boils inside me. I know, cerebrally, that Raven's not evil, that she's just honest and probably hurting right now. But I don't feel that way. Instead, I feel like I want to build the highest, thickest wall around me and Devi and hold her tight and protect her from all the fears and insecurities that Raven forced her to look at.

And if I'm being totally honest with myself, Raven wasn't entirely wrong. I was using Devi doing even lesbian porn as an excuse not to feel bad for continuing to shoot scenes. And more—as an excuse not to feel guilty for *enjoying* shooting them. It's our lifestyle, right? And as long as it's *our* lifestyle, not just mine, then there's no need for guilt or jealousy.

Except.

Except I *am* fucking jealous. I was jealous when Kendi licked her to orgasm this morning and jealous a few hours ago when she told me that she went to a set planning to fuck Bruce Madden. I'm jealous of every minute she spends writhing under somebody else's touch.

And I am guilty. Whenever I fuck someone else, I think of Devi. But it's almost like my guilt makes me hornier, fiercer, and I use it as fuel for my fucking, each pump and jab of my cock layered with lust and longing and the kind of shame that burns under my skin and makes me restless for release. Since that shame only rears its head while I'm balls-deep in another girl, it's so easy to give in to its restlessness and try to fuck it out.

And all of this is just bringing up those questions from before and I can't answer them. I can't, because if I actually answer them, I might have to face that my entire life has to change, and suddenly I remember Madam Psuka's tarot card still shoved in an unwashed pair of jeans. The Hanged Man, the card of suffering and sacrifice.

But what do I have to sacrifice?

And what do I have to suffer for?

I push those questions to the side and lean down to kiss Devi's cheek. "She's wrong, Devi. I'm not always fucking other people, and I'm not happy to see you fucking other people. But I respect our jobs, and I respect your right to make decisions about your body and who you fuck."

Devi looks uncertain, sad. I tug on her shoulder until she rolls onto her back and I can cup her face with one hand.

"We need to make some boundaries, Cass. What are we okay with and what are we not okay with? What will we keep special just for each other?"

She gives a small, fragile shrug and she looks so young and defenseless right now. My heart aches. "I've never done this before, Logan," she says. "I've never been with a porn star. And I've certainly never been with one of the most famous porn stars in the world."

"You don't have to decide right now," I reassure her, stroking her hair back from her face. "We have so much time, Devi. We'll get it figured out."

"Yeah," she says, but her voice is full of doubt.

"Want to hear a joke?" I ask, trying to cheer her up, cajole her back to her normal sunny self.

"I guess."

"Why does Santa Claus have such a big sack?"

She shrugs again.

I grin. "He only comes once a year!"

No reaction.

"Okay, okay, not my best work. How about this: what's the difference between a lentil and a chick pea?"

"What?"

I wait a beat to let the punch line fall with maximum effect. "I wouldn't pay a hundred dollars to have a lentil on my chest."

Devi's eyes widen and then she starts snort-laughing, slapping my bare chest hard. "You're disgusting!"

But she's smiling again. I resist the urge to preen.

She's still giggling a little. "Okay, I have one for you. What's the difference between jam and jelly?"

I play along. "What?"

"I can't jelly my cock up your ass."

I burst out laughing. "Why, Devi Dare, you dirty woman."

"You have no idea."

She grabs for my ass, and we start wrestling and laughing, both of us naked and still a little emotional, and then the wrestling turns to grinding and the laughing turns to kissing, and you know what?

Suddenly my cock isn't so drowsy anymore.

CHAPTER SEVENTEEN

I wake to sunlight streaming through the curtains, a rough thumb brushing across my nipple, and soft kisses on my shoulder. I'm immediately wet— or I'm still wet from all the sex we had the night before—and I could easily part my legs and make room for his already hard cock to slip inside me. But I don't.

Instead, I pretend I'm still asleep. Because even though I'm the type of person to usually roll out of bed with a smile on my face, today I need a few minutes. I need to wake up enough to be sure none of this was a dream. I need a moment to process what we did, what we said. How we feel.

He loves me.

He told me he loved me, and I don't even question it. I *know* he does. I felt it in the way he ravaged me. I felt it in his lips and with his tongue and in the orgasms he drew from the deepest parts of my body, orgasms that ripped and tore through every muscle, every cell, every bit of energy that makes up my soul.

He loves me. And though that love can't undo or erase the incident that occurred on Hagen's set, it does make surviving it better. Easier.

Logan moves his mouth up my neck to my ear. He nips my lobe— *hard*—and I squeal.

His arms fold around me, and he pulls my backside into his body. "I knew you were awake. Were you faking because you're too tired for me?"

"Never," I mumble, turning into him to press my mouth along the curve of his jaw. "I was just thinking."

"About how much I love you?" He buries his face in my bosom and does something with his tongue along the skin between my breasts and oh my God I had no idea that was such an erogenous zone for me.

"Actually…" I gasp as he pinches a nipple between his fingers. "Yeah, I was."

He lifts his gaze back to mine, and it's serious now. "I do, you know. Love you."

I nod. "I know."

"And you really do love me. Don't you? So much." He's teasing, pulling the words from me for fun, but I catch a glimpse of something in his eyes that says he really wants to hear it too. Like, maybe he's as much in awe of the newly discovered shared emotion as I am.

So I'm serious when I answer him. "So much."

And then, when the way he looks at me becomes so hot I begin to melt underneath him, I tease him back. "Do I need to prove it?" I wiggle my hips, rubbing against his hard-on, working us both up.

"Yeah, I think that's what you're going to have to do." There's a hint of mischief in his tone that disappears when he adds, "Hold on just a sec." He stretches past me, reaching for something, so I peer over my shoulder to see what it is and spot his camera on the nightstand.

I sigh audibly with disappointment. I'd hoped last night would linger into this morning, that we'd still be "Logan and Devi" instead of "the show."

But instead of grabbing the handheld, Logan hits a button on his bedside clock.

I'm relieved, and I quickly school my features to hide my initial reaction. Unfortunately, I'm too late.

"I'd set my alarm," he explains. "What did you think…?" He looks from me to the nightstand, trying to determine what had upset me. His eyes land on the only other item on the table. "You thought I was going for my camera."

My silence is his answer.

"Ah, I see." He pulls away, suddenly distant.

"I just…I haven't showered. Or anything." I know I sound like I'm making excuses, because I am, and I'm one of those people that's too transparent to lie. So I shake off the pretext and admit the truth. "I wanted it to be just us."

He tenses, and I know I've upset him. He sits up to lean against the headboard before running a hand through his hair, struggling with some battle he's not ready to share.

Finally, he speaks. "I can want to be with you genuinely, and still want to capture it. You get that, right? I told you this before, and I thought you understood."

I sit up too, ignoring the impulse to pull the sheet up over my breasts. That would be hiding, and I want desperately to be open with him, which is part of the reason I was so eager to not have an audience this morning. "I do understand, Logan. I really do. It means so much to me that you are so into us that you want to share it with the whole world. I'm flattered, and I support it.

"But sometimes I want to be completely unguarded with you. I want to be able to bring down all my walls and let you into all the secret parts of me—granted, I don't have many because I'm an open book—but there are things I'd prefer to share only with you." I lower my voice and my eyes. "There are parts of you I wish you'd only share with me."

"There *are* parts of me I only share with you. I talk to you about movies and art. I slept with you in a sleeping bag. I've never done that with another person. I share things with *only you*. Things not related to sex."

"Sometimes I need them to be sex too." I swallow then raise my gaze to his, tentatively. "Can you understand that?"

He holds my stare for several seconds. Then he scratches the back of his neck. "I wasn't reaching for the camera." He says it in a way that says he does understand, says he feels exactly the same.

"I know that. Now. I'm sorry I assumed otherwise." I'm especially sorry that I've ruined the good mood he was in. And that he's no longer touching me. I crawl toward him. "Are you mad?"

He raises his brow and starts to say something, but, after catching the view of me on all fours, seems to change his mind. His eyes narrow. "Yes. Very mad." He uses a tone I've only heard him use in his movies—his dominant tone—and I know he's playing with me in a different way. "Maybe I need to punish you."

I sit back on my knees and bite my lip coyly. "Do you? I'm not sure if I'd like that."

In a flash, he has me on my back, pinned underneath him. "You aren't supposed to like it. *I'm* supposed to like it."

His eyes are dark, his lids hooded, but he's thinking. Assessing.

I'm certain I know what he's trying to figure out. We haven't ventured into kink on or off camera. While I'd marked a willingness to try some kinkier things on the limits section of my contract for *Star-Crossed*, I'd also specified that I preferred not to until later in the show's timeline. It was a comfort issue for me. I'm not new to the more base forms of kink—bondage and spanking and the like—but I've certainly never done anything like that with an expert.

And Logan's an expert. I've seen all of his work—trust me, I know.

So it makes sense that he's cautious now. Because the list of things I'd do for the show doesn't necessarily match the list of things I'd do for Logan. He just doesn't know that.

"You can do it for real," I tell him, giving him permission to play how I think he wants to. "You can punish me."

He raises one brow. "Oh, can I?" but I can see he's finally taking me seriously. He's no longer just deciding *if* but *how*.

The anticipation makes me twitchy and eager and my head bobs when I mean for it to simply nod. I want him so fiercely, want him to take me, to unleash on me, unbridled and tumultuous.

He rocks over me, his expression on fire with lust and I re-utter my consent, giving it even more surely. "You can. I want you to. My safe word is Donald Trump."

Logan freezes. "What?"

I smile, trying not to giggle. "It's a really good safe word, isn't it? I'm proud of it."

"It definitely puts a damper on any thoughts of sex."

And I can see how it's put a damper on *his* thoughts because the mask of pure desire he'd worn a moment ago is now laced with horror.

I wiggle beneath him, purposefully rubbing against his pelvis in an attempt to raise his cock from half-mast to full-mast. "Did I kill your mojo? Bad, Devi. Bad. Maybe I need to be punished for that too."

"Are you taunting me?" Once more, he's asking if I'm sure. And I am. This is one of the things I'd like to explore with him, but I couldn't do it if the camera were on. I'm too new to it. I need the freedom to make mistakes without an audience. And I need to be taken care of as we go. I need to know I've got all of Logan's focus.

I meet his eyes and think he understands me when I say, "I'm not taunting. I'm being very serious."

Then he's decided, and he's climbing off of me, pulling my torso up by my wrists. "You *were* taunting. You've been taunting me all fucking morning. You've been fucking taunting me since we met, and you definitely need to be punished." He's rowdy and rough as he drags me to the edge of the bed. Shifting to hold my hands with one of his, he bends to open the bottom drawer of his nightstand with the other. There, he retrieves a red silk scarf, which he uses to tie my wrists together—securely, but not so securely that it will cut off blood flow.

I love the way the red looks against my olive skin.

I love that my boyfriend is the type of guy who has sex paraphernalia in his nightstand.

Most of all, I love that Logan is my boyfriend.

After I'm bound, he flips me over and pulls me to the side so I'm bent over the bed and my hands are tied underneath me. It's a position meant to make me feel vulnerable, and I do. I feel him behind me, standing, scanning my naked backside, and though I could easily turn and peek at him, I don't. Imagining what he's doing makes the tension thicker, and I like that. I like that a lot.

Since I don't look, and since he doesn't give any preamble, the first smack comes as a surprise. As does the second, following so quickly after the first that I barely have time to yelp. "How. Does. It. Feel?" he asks, spanking one cheek then the other in between each word. "To. Be. Taunted. Cass? Do you like that? Do you want more?"

My ass is fire. My eyes are burning, tears forming at the corners. "Yes," I squeak, and it's barely even a word.

He doesn't accept it as an answer. "Say it again."

"Yes," I hiss. "Yes!"

Logan doesn't just *play* the kink—he makes it real. I believe he's mad in a way that I've never felt with a partner who's "punished" me before. Each strike against my ass is firm and sharp and, though I'm sure he's holding back, that he could hit me harder if he wanted to, it also feels like he's not. Like he's letting everything he has spill out into each stinging smack.

It arouses me to levels I've never been to before.

I'm soaked by the time he breaks from striking to rub the burn out of my cheeks. So soaked I'm dripping and embarrassed because, of course, he knows.

"Christ, Devi," he groans when he slips his hand between my legs. Then he digs his fingers into my thighs and lifts the back half of my body so that my knees are on the bed. "I have to taste you."

A bolt of anticipation strikes through me as I wait for his tongue to find the source of my wetness, for it to ease the ache in my center. I moan when he finally does, and my entire body trembles from the feel of him as he licks around the edge of my hole.

But I want him deeper, want to feel the full length of his strong tongue inside me, and he doesn't give me that.

Instead, he swipes upward, following the line from my cunt to the hole behind it—the one I know he wants to fuck someday, the one I'm desperate for him to inhabit, and nervous too because I know he'll be good there. So good. Too good—it will completely undo any control I have left where he's concerned, and I'm not quite ready for that.

But I'm ready to *play* there. And so is he.

With no hesitation, with a need that's as greedy as mine, he circles my rim with his tongue then plunges inside.

I'm immediately squirming, immediately on the verge of climax, immediately ready to shout *I love you's* at the top of my lungs, and I have to bury my face into the sheets to stifle my cries.

"You like that, don't you?" he asks, pausing his assault to chide me. "You like that and you want to come, but if you fucking come before I tell you, then I'm going to have to start all of this again. Because after I fuck you with my tongue and my fingers, I'm going to fuck you with my cock, and I want you tight and pulsing when I go in there—not recovering from an orgasm. You got that?"

"Then take me now," I plead, certain I can't hold out. "Just fuck me now."

He smacks my ass—hard. "I decide when I fuck you. Ask again, I'll make you wait longer."

He dips a finger inside my pussy and drags my wetness up to that back hole, probing even deeper than he did with his tongue. His other hand strokes up to play with my clit, and then his mouth is on me again, this time at my cunt, stroking inside, igniting the sensitive spot within, and I know that he's set me up because it's impossible not to come, impossible not to be swept into this supernova of pleasure. And now

I'm even maybe convinced of the existence of white holes because what I'm experiencing is completely that—an eruption of energy that is impossible to escape, or get inside or hold on to, and it's amazing and bright and everything, everything, everything.

And while I'm spinning in ecstasy, I'm also drenched in agony. He'll be mad, I know. Because I came. Without his permission. He'll start from the beginning, and there's no way I can bear this euphoria again. It's too much, and any more will kill me. I know this, even as I burn in this bliss.

But to my surprise, Logan twists me to my back and spreads my legs. My ass screams as he drags me across the sheets the couple of inches to the edge of the bed and poises himself at my entrance.

My speech is broken and raspy, my breathing still uneven. "I thought you were going to start over again." I have no idea why I'm provoking him. As glorious as his punishment was, I don't want him to repeat it. I want the punishment he's promising now, the one where he pounds me and assaults me another way instead—inside me.

"I changed my mind when I realized you couldn't take it." He's cocky as he says it. Cocky as he slaps a smarting thwack across my inner thigh. Cocky as he impales me with grunt and a sharp thrust of his cock inside my cunt.

God, his confidence is a massive turn-on. How right he is about me. How well he can read my body's cues. He has a gift to be able to do this as well as he does. I know this. I mean, I truly, truly know it in my head and every part of my rational being, and yet...

And yet.

In my bones, in my skin, in the particles of energy that make up my "soul," I feel like this connection has nothing to do with his skills and everything to do with Him and Me and no one else. As though I were special. As though we were bound by a gravitational pull. As though I were the Earth and he, the moon, and with his orbit he commanded the tidal waves of emotions and arousal within me.

It's not reasonable to feel this way, or even realistic. He's a professional pornographic performer. And yet, I'm a girl who believes she might be something more.

No, not believes—*hopes*.

He takes me while I'm lost in this yearning, drives into me with a bold, frenetic passion that's determined to grind and thrust and fuck, wildly. Mindlessly.

Damn, Logan O'Toole can shatter a girl. I wrap my thighs higher around him, perfecting the way he fits inside me. "Yes. Right there. Right there."

"Squeeze me, Devi. Make your cunt tight and grip my cock."

I clamp around him, clenching as hard as I can then relaxing for just a second before repeating the motion. He groans, his thrusts growing even more frantic. "Jesus, just like that. Do it again. Fuuuck."

He's about to lose himself when he grabs onto the scarf at my wrists and tugs me toward him, bending me in half. He seizes my mouth with his as I cry out, the new position causing him to strike me in the most amazing spot. My vision goes blinding white with the pleasure, and I'm gasping when he breaks the kiss, clawing at consciousness, trying to find something to hold on to so I don't get lost in oblivion. I focus on his face, on his lips, on his eyes, on the crease of his forehead, on the sharp contortion of his features.

I recognize this expression from his movies. It's this crazed, hungry, primal expression that, whenever I've seen it, I've nearly gone mad wishing it were a look I could see in real life.

And now I *am* seeing it in real life, and while it's thrilling and hot beyond belief, I'm keenly aware of how many other people have seen this look on his face. Aware that it's not a look that's special or private or reserved just for me.

That realization pricks at some place inside my chest, pinches and twists it, and when I come this time, my orgasm is accompanied by tears that I'm pretty sure aren't just a component of release.

Oh, God.

I'm so in love with Logan. In deep, deep love.

We lock eyes, and even though I haven't said it out loud, I think he can tell I'm thinking it because his face suddenly turns warm and intense, and then it's not only me falling apart, but both of us. Crashing together like two stars exploding in a blaze of heat and fire and pure light.

The way he looks at me, with eyes that seem to see something heavenly in my appearance, I know—I *know*—he meant it when he said he loved me, and I know he's just as surprised and awed by it as I am.

And I can't help but wonder if he's scared too. Can't help but wonder if the violent way he shudders into me with his release, sputtering and rutting almost like he's angry, is an indication that he senses the same undercurrent of *terrible* within that love that I do.

• • •

"I have to work today." Logan traces a finger along my jaw. "I wish I didn't, but I'll have to get ready soon."

And just like that, the morning is no longer perfect.

It's funny how Logan makes me feel more visible than anyone ever has—like I'm present and *seen*—and yet he also has the ability to make the rest of the world completely disappear. Waking with him, fucking him, lingering in his arms, I'd practically forgotten that we both had jobs and lives and Things besides each other.

I'd forgotten that my boyfriend makes porn. With women that aren't me.

"Editing or…?" I don't know if I want to know what *type* of work he has to do today, but I can't stop myself from asking.

"I'm filming a scene with Bambi Roo." He looks past me to the bedside clock to check the time. "She'll be here in about half an hour."

My stomach drops like a lead anchor. The intensity of my reaction surprises me, makes my mouth taste sour. Makes everything sour. "Okay. I can leave."

I start to roll out of bed, but Logan tugs me closer. "I was going to invite you to stay."

My smile can't be contained. "You were? You're not sick of me yet?" His invitation doesn't completely erase my apprehension, but it certainly helps.

"So entirely not sick of you." He captures my mouth in a blistering kiss. "In fact, for the first time in my career, I wish I could call in sick."

"But you're a professional. You'd never do that." I don't know if I'm testing him or me—trying to feel out whether (a) he'd really ever call off a scene on my count, and/or (b) I'm bothered by the fact that he probably never will.

He tucks a hair behind my ear. "No. I wouldn't call in sick. And that's why I'm inviting you to stay."

I knew he wouldn't cancel. Asking me to stay is a decent compromise, though, one that earns him a decent grade on my test. I, on the other hand, am pretty certain I've earned an *F* because I am for sure bothered by the idea of him having sex with another woman right now.

And what the fuck is that about?

In my head, I hear Raven's voice repeating her accusation from the day before. *"He's always fucking someone else."* She'd called it advice, but she meant it to be hurtful. And it was.

And I hate that.

I hate that she knew it would get to me. I hate that she hit her target. And, most of all, I hate that she's right—that Logan will always be fucking someone else.

And I hate that it bothers me so much. This isn't me. I don't like who this is.

A voice that sounds an awful lot like my mother quoting Maya Angelou, says, *"What you're supposed to do when you don't like a thing is change it. If you can't change it, change the way you think about it."*

So as some sort of silent act of spite, I decide to actually let her words be helpful. Yes—Logan fucks other women. Because that's Logan's *job*. If I want a place in his world, I have to figure out how to deal with it. Starting today.

"Yes. I'll stay. Thank you for asking." Who knows? It might even end up being hot for both of us the way my scene with Kendi was the day before.

Or I'll discover that I'm not as open about sex as I think I am. Considering the direction our relationship has taken, it seems like something I really ought to figure out soon anyway.

• • •

I clean up and dress first. Logan's still in the shower when the doorbell rings twenty minutes later. I expect to come face-to-face with Bambi, but it's a guy's voice that says, "Yo, dude, you moved the key," before I've even finished opening the door.

His brows rise in surprise when he realizes I'm not Logan. Then they rise higher as he skims the length of my body with his eyes. "Oh. You're not a dude."

Maybe I should be offended by his ogling, but there's something instantly charming about him, so, instead, I grin. "Not last time I checked."

"You must be Devi. I'm Tanner. Logan's wingman. Are you…?" He looks around, searching for Logan or Bambi, I don't know which.

I'm pretty sure what he's getting at though. "I'm sticking around to watch his scene today. Bambi's not here yet, and he's in the shower. I'd invite you to make yourself at home, but I have a feeling you're here more often than I am."

He chuckles. "It *is* like a second home. We work together a lot. I assume you've been to the dungeon?"

I shake my head. "I mean, I've seen it on videos. Just not in person."

"Come on, then."

The "dungeon" isn't the most elaborate that I've seen, but it's bigger in real life than it appears on camera. The tight angled shots make it hard to grasp the size of the room, and that it encompasses pretty much the entire basement. A quick glance tells me that Logan's inventory rivals any sex store. He has all the basics—vibrators, plugs, crops, whips, handcuffs—and a bunch of toys that are for the more expert sex enthusiasts. It's an impressive set-up.

And it's hot.

I can imagine myself down here, naked, my nipples clamped, my neck collared, my wrists and ankles strapped to the suspension rings on the wall. I'd be blindfolded and writhing and Logan would implement all sorts of punishments. Naughty punishments. Ones that torture with both pain and pleasure.

I close my eyes and run my fingers through the tails of his flogger.

"What do you think?"

Logan's arrival startles the crap out of me, but I try to play it cool. "I think you've been holding out on me." And then, because I'd been thinking dirty thoughts and because I'm not really ever that capable of playing it cool, I blush.

He studies me with a smile that says he knows exactly what I was thinking, which of course makes me blush further. "Can't show all my cards at once," he says. "You'll get bored too soon and leave me before I'm ready."

I don't miss the raised eyebrows from Tanner at Logan's words, but I'm too thrown from them myself to respond. There are too many layers to his statement. Too many things he could be trying to tell me, and even though it's a flirty line that makes my stomach flutter, I have a feeling there's legit fear hidden beneath it. Is Logan as worried that his job will get in the way of our relationship as I am? He'd been the one to say we needed to find things that made us special. I'd assumed that was for my benefit, but is it possible he's struggling too?

"You've been holding out on me too, man." Tanner adjusts one of the set lights so it will hit a spot on the concrete floor (*he'd make me kneel there; he'd make me beg*). "You told me Devi was supreme, but you didn't let on *how* supreme."

Logan selects a whip from his collection and then crosses to the case of vibrators. "Because I knew as soon as you found out, you'd immediately go watch all her movies, and I might accidentally imagine you jacking off to her, and I'm not comfortable with that." He takes out a magic wand—a powerful massager that makes me shiver just thinking about it.

"Dude, I'm not comfortable with you accidentally imagining me jacking off either. Please don't ever say that shit again."

Logan grabs his crotch and gestures teasingly toward Tanner. "Don't pretend you're such a homophobe. You know you want it."

I laugh as Tanner rolls his eyes. "Do you want two cameras on this, do you think?" Tanner asks.

Logan looks out over the room, and I imagine he's choreographing the scene in his head, which both impresses me and makes me a little anxious for no reason I can explain. "Yeah, two, I think. Leave one on the tripod over there." He points, indicating where he wants it. "Do your thing with the other."

I grin as I watch him because he's sexy like this—he's *always* sexy, but especially like this, all assertive and visionary and passionate about his work. Then my smile fades because I suddenly remember Logan's not preparing this scene for me.

God, why does that thought have to make me so miserable?

I hang back when Bambi arrives, not wanting to disrupt the chemistry they need to perform. I'm suddenly grateful that Logan watched my scene with Kendi first—that way I can take all my cues of how to behave from him. He'd stayed out of the way, so I should too.

But even staying out of the way I'm a mess inside. Every second that passes brings me more and more dread. More and more anguish. It's not fair that I feel this way, not to him. He was totally chill with my shoot with Kendi and, if he'd been upset about my het shoot, he didn't let on. Well, besides the anger he expressed toward Bruce's off-set behavior, but that wasn't the same. He's obviously better at his job than I am. He's older—maybe that helps? He's dated someone in the biz before.

It's me. I know this. All me.

So once again I remind myself that I need to get my act together. I start by trying to rationalize through all the ways that our sexual relationship is different than the sex Logan has for his job.

1. We had sex without a camera.

2. We had sex in his bedroom.

3. We had sex without any money being exchanged—I mean, he'd given me money for *Star-Crossed,* but that didn't pay for what happened between us last night. Or this morning. Or, really, any of it.

4. We had sex when I needed it. When I needed him.

It's not like sex is what makes a relationship, anyway. It takes more than that to make two people compatible. Logan and I have more than just sex between us. We enjoy each other's company. We love each other. We're *in love* with each other. It's the combination of all those things that makes what we have special. We shouldn't have to be monogamous with our bodies to feel like we're a couple.

My head knows these things. Understands them well enough to write a dissertation on the subject of why monogamy is an archaic expectation.

But it doesn't matter what I know. Because my heart feels differently. My heart doesn't get it. Especially when the action begins, and Logan's standing over Bambi, making *her* kneel. Making *her* beg.

My heart is watching the man I'm in love with do very intimate things to a woman who isn't me, and my heart is breaking.

Maybe if I caught his eye like he'd caught mine during my scene with Kendi. Maybe he could make me part of it, and I'd be okay. But I slip out before he has the chance to notice me at all because I can't stand the possibility that he'd catch my gaze, and it wouldn't change anything.

Or, even worse, that he'd get too lost in his performance with Bambi to think to look for my eyes at all.

CHAPTER EIGHTEEN

My phone's dead so, I plug it in as soon as I start my car. I'm still in Logan's driveway when it buzzes with a string of notifications. Down deep, I hope one is from him, hope he noticed I'm gone, and that he stopped the scene in order to come after me, even if only by text.

But I'm afraid to check, in case it's not him. I don't want to find out how much that will hurt. So I start my car, and without looking back, I drive away from his house.

At the first stoplight, I can't help myself—I check my phone's screen. I sort through the messages, quickly determining that none of them are from Logan. Nothing else interests me at the moment, and I start to put my cell in my cup holder when I catch Raven's name in a post that I'm tagged in on Twitter.

@theRealRaven How will this project fit into @number1Toole's schedule with @DeviDare?

Logan's tagged as well, and even before I've finished scrolling to the beginning of the conversation, I'm feeling dread.

The light changes before I find it, and I have to wait until I'm at another red light before I can look again. I find the original post easily—it's a tweet from Raven herself. An announcement.

New project with @number1Toole CUMMING soon. #staytuned #bignews

"What the fuck?" I mutter out loud. I flip through the responses, looking for more info. I'm sure he hasn't seen this or responded to it yet, and I'm dying to know what his answer is as well as what the hell project he has lined up that involves Raven in the first place.

I think back over what Logan said about Raven the night before. He'd seemed fairly irritated by even the mention of her, and definitely pissed that she'd confronted me. It wasn't the type of reaction that led me to believe he'd work with her again. But, did he ever actually say how he felt about her?

He didn't.

And if fucking is really just a job for him, then it stands to reason he might sometimes work with people he doesn't particularly care for. People he once cared for quite a lot.

The thing is—I don't like it.

He'd told me we needed to figure out boundaries; this is one of mine. I don't want him fucking his ex.

At the next opportunity, I flip my car around, intending to go lay this request out for Logan, but before I get very far I remember he's still doing his scene with Bambi Roo. Which is sort of a blessing at the moment, because after I think about it further, I realize that showing up all sorts of pissed about his job only a day after we declare our love would make me look like a petty girlfriend. Especially after skipping out early on the shoot he was doing this morning. I need to make boundaries, but I don't want it to seem like I can't handle his line of work.

And then it hits me—I *can't* handle his line of work.

Oh, God.

This isn't good.

This isn't good at all.

I'm probably just emotional after what happened with Bruce Madden, and with all the intense interactions that have occurred over the last twelve hours between Logan and I. Of course I'm a bit unbalanced.

Except I'm more than a bit unbalanced. I'm upside down and inside out with jealousy. I don't want Logan fucking Raven. I don't want Logan fucking Bambi Roo. I don't want him fucking anyone but me. Period. On camera and off. And, honestly, I'd rather the majority of it be off-camera because I want what he and I have to be just between the two of us. Just ours.

I want him all to myself.

This emotion is so new to me. The unfamiliarity of it is spinning me everywhere, spiraling me this way and that. I'm free-floating with nothing to grab onto, like an astronaut in space whose tether didn't hold. I don't recognize this situation. I don't recognize myself in this relationship.

"What the fuck." It's the second time I 've said this phrase aloud in the last several minutes, but this time it's not a question—it's realization and exclamation. *What the actual fuck?* I'm Devi Dare. I'm a three-year veteran in this world. I'm a person who relies on logic and reason, and there is no logical reason that I should feel threatened by Logan doing the job he's done everyday since I've known him. So what the actual fuck is this goddamned emotion doing inside of me?

At the next intersection, I turn my car around again, this time heading nowhere, just not toward Logan's. As I drive, thoughts of him and the conflict we're facing press deeper on my soul. The cyclone of emotional turmoil inside me whirrs tighter and faster, picking up stray ideas and folding them into the narrative in my head the way loose debris gets caught up in a tornado. What if I can't handle this? What if I'm not capable of being in love with a porn star?

Every few minutes my phone pings with more notifications that people are responding to Raven's tweet. Excited, happy responses. That rubbish finds its way into the cyclone. Then my agent's ringtone plays, and though I reject her call, the reasons she's calling get pulled into the storm as well. What if I can't work in this field anymore? What if I'm blackballed? What if I don't want to shoot porn anymore anyway?

How cowardly would it be to just run away and hide until the storm passes?

Pretty cowardly, I know. And I'm usually a brave girl, like Logan says. But not today.

I turn off my phone and head to my parents'. It's not running away, and knowing them, I'm sure the visit will end in frustration, but they'll let me bitch and vent. And maybe talking about it will bring me some sort of clarity.

Somewhat dramatically, I fling open the kitchen door and, upon confirmation that they are both present, announce, "Everything is terrible."

My father glances up from his hunched position over a backgammon board at the kitchen table. He's obviously playing by himself since my mother is across the kitchen cleaning out her paintbrushes at the sink. "'*When you realize how perfect everything is you will tilt your head back and laugh at the sky*'."

Goddamn Buddha.

My mother turns from the sink and dries her hands on her muumuu. "Oh, Devi! Taste the baghali polo on the stove, will you? And tell your father that it needs more saffron."

I ignore her because, well, she ignored me, and direct my next remark directly to my father. "I'm tilting my head, Dad." I look at the ceiling for dramatic affect. "Tilting my head and there is no laughter because there is no perfection. There is nothing even a little bit like perfection." That's not exactly true—the way I feel for Logan is steeped in a lot of almost-perfect. It's how close to perfect it is that makes the flaws in our relationship so apparent and unbearable.

"Someone woke up on the wrong side of chi. " My mother squints at me. "My word, Devi, you're a cloud of crazy energy! Come sit down, and I'll see if I can straighten you all out."

I fold my arms over my chest and don't budge. "Not right now, thank you."

My father moves a piece on his game and then sits back into his chair. "At least tell us what's so imperfect and terrible about this world." He means well, but I can already tell he's preparing a philosophical argument.

I want no part of that debate, but I do want to talk. It's why I came over here—to unload my burdens, to maybe find some clarity. "All right. I'll tell you." I cross the kitchen and lean against the arch to the den so I can look at them both while I talk.

Then I tell them. Everything. I tell them about Logan and the show, about falling in love, about my idea to do more het porn in order to pay my student loans. I tell them about the day I got overwhelmed looking at the school catalog and about another day when I got a wild hair up my ass and applied to a bunch of universities across the country before I remembered that not having a major was a real problem. I tell them about LaRue Hagen and Bruce Madden, and the likely hit that will have on my career. I tell them about Logan being there for me when I needed him and about being jealous, about not liking the way I feel when Logan's touching other women. About not knowing who I am or what I want.

"Ew. Jealousy. *'Keep yourselves far from envy; because it eats up and takes away good actions, like a fire eats up and burns wood.'*" With that, my father turns back to his game.

Frustrated, I dig my nails into my palm. "At least the quote came from Muhammad this time," I mutter.

Baba tilts his head and studies me. "What's that supposed to mean?"

"Just its nice to know there are inspirational people who aren't Buddha." I'm being unfair. My parents find inspiration in pretty much everything. They've never identified with one religion over another. They love parts of so many faiths and philosophies—Muslim, Buddhist, Christian, agnostic. They're socialists and communists and democrats, and every hippie idea in between. Basically they live by a hodgepodge of good ideas. And I freaking love that about them. I love that they raised me to be like that too.

But today I can't seem to see through the same rose-colored glasses they look through, like someone smudged a handful of mud all over the lenses—Raven maybe, or Bruce Madden. Because every inspirational notion they have seems trite and impossible to embrace.

"Peace comes from within. Do not seek it without." This time I'm the one to quote Buddha, and I do it in my head then follow it up with a few deep breaths.

It doesn't help.

I run a hand through my hair. "I'm sorry. I thought it would help to talk about everything, but I think I just need some time alone."

My mother offers a warm smile. "It will blow over, Boombalee. Meanwhile, alone time is good. Relax and take your mind off of all this bad energy. Do some tai chi and a yoni steam. Just you wait—the universe will give you the answers."

I know her heart is in the right place, but my heart is all over. I've reached my limit. I snap. "Goddammit, Mâmân. No. I don't want to do a yoni steam or tai chi, or have a Reiki session or a Tarot reading. I don't want advice from Buddha or Susan B. Anthony or William Faulkner or the universe. I want advice from *you*!"

I pinch the bridge of my nose and close my eyes and count to ten quietly in Farci in an attempt to calm myself down. *Yek, do, se, char, panj...*

My outburst is followed by silence, and when I force myself to glance over at my parents, the expressions on both their faces reflect shock and alarm. Possibly a little hurt, too. That thought breaks me. The last thing I want is to make them feel bad. I love them fiercely, and I've just attacked everything that they are, simply because my immature ass can't handle my shit.

I lean against the wall and slide down to the floor, wishing I could disappear into the den's lime green shag carpet. Once down there, I decide I might as well go full meltdown. I shift and stretch out fully on

LAURELIN PAIGE & SIERRA SIMONE

the floor. With my arm draped over my eyes, I bite my cheek to keep from crying full out, but I can't prevent tears from spilling down my cheeks. In just a few minutes, I'm lost to my own misery, so it takes me longer than usual to notice the shift in energy around me.

Lifting my arm slightly, I peek out and find both my mother and my father standing over me. The pain I'd thought I'd seen in their eyes a moment before is still there, but now that they're closer, I can see that they aren't hurt *because* of me—they're hurt *for* me.

Whatever resolve I had disappears, and a sob slips out from between my lips.

Mâmân squats down next to me, and like an injured child who desperately needs the embrace of her mother, I sit up and fall into her arms.

"I've been The Fool," I say, like I'm confessing. It's a reference to the first card of the Tarot deck. Or the last card, depending on how you look at it, since every journey ends back where it began. The Fool is exactly like he sounds—foolish. He's the madman, the jester, the beggar. The *majnun.* "I've been stumbling around, carefree, taking risks without worrying about the consequences. And I don't know if I'm at the beginning or the end of this particular journey. I just feel lost, without a guide, and I don't know how long my faith is going to hold out."

Sometimes, with Logan, I'd convinced myself that I was being an adult, that we had a grown-up relationship. And with the naiveté of a kid, I'd let myself fall blindly in love.

And it had been *wonderful.*

But now it isn't anymore. Now I am tangled up and twisted inside. Now I am lost in the dark, afraid to take a step for fear of walking off a mountainside.

"I don't know what to do." My words are muffled in the fabric of my mother's muumuu, but somehow I know she gets the gist. "Tell me what to do."

Mâmân rocks me gently, her hand stroking my hair. "Oh, sweetie. I know it hurts, and I wish I *could* tell you what—"

I know where this speech goes. *I wish I could tell you what to do but I can't because blah blah blah, personal life journey, growth.* All that crap.

But before she can finish, my father, who is still looming above us, cuts her off. "You want our advice, Devi? Let me give you some advice." He's firm and there's enough impatience in his tone to cause my mother to still her sway.

I hold my breath and clutch onto her dress. He has my full attention even though I'm too scared to look at him directly.

"Go back to school. You're a learner. You have a thinker's mind. Go to school."

"But—" I start to deliver all my usual protests—*what will I study? What if I don't choose the right degree?*

He seems to read my mind. "Just pick a major, Devi. If it's the wrong one, you'll change to another. And if that one's wrong, you'll change again. What's the worst that can happen? Higher student loans? Are you really going to let fear keep you from happiness?"

He says it as though money shouldn't be a factor in my decision, which is completely unrealistic. Except I can't really argue with him because, at the same time, do I really want to let my dreams be decided by the current balance of my bank account?

Bâbâ bends down closer to me, and his tone is softer when he speaks again. "You can't know if your path is the right one until you completely become The Fool. You have to take that blind step to see if you're walking on solid ground or if you're falling off a ledge. *That's what you're supposed to do.* You're supposed to be unsure. You're supposed to dare, not stand still. You risk. You take chances. You figure out how to live by *living.*"

I swallow past the lump in my throat. "You mean: *'You cannot travel the path until you have become the path itself'*?" I ask, giving Buddha as a thank you for the perfect, perfect words my father's delivered.

"Yeah. Something like that." He taps my nose lightly with his finger before standing again. "And if it's not school that interests you, that's fine too. Just…is what you're doing now what you want to be doing forever?"

I shake my head.

He raises a brow. "Is it leading you closer to whatever that is?"

This time I don't say or gesture anything because I don't know the answer.

"Well, then," he says, as though everything's been resolved. Then he slinks back to his backgammon board, and I know it's not because he's not interested in what I'm going through. He just recognizes that every fool has to make the journey alone. I'm grateful that he's pointed out the path he thinks is right for me. I still might not choose it, but it feels like he's given me a place to start.

My mother wipes a tear from my cheek with the pad of her thumb. "Look. Everything's worked itself out."

I let out a short laugh. "I wouldn't quite say that."

"Why not? Your father told you to go back to school. So you'll go back to school."

"Mom, do *you* want me to go back to school?" I know she does. It's what she hints at in every Tarot reading she does for me, but it felt good hearing my father tell me what he thought and I want to hear advice from her, too.

"I do." She's confident with her answer, but then she adds, "If that's what you want."

I bite back my amusement. It's the closest she'll ever get to telling me what to do, so worried that she will stifle who I'm meant to be.

I love her for that. So much.

"Thanks, Mom. It's nice to hear you say that." But there's still another subject I'm completely lost on. "And what do I do about Logan?"

My mother pulls back to look at me, her expression slightly perplexed. "It seems like you've already figured that out, haven't you?"

"No, I haven't." Not in the least.

She shakes her head, dismissing my response. "You have. When you really want to see it in your conscious mind, you will."

I know she's figured out something that I haven't yet, either because she's older and wiser, or just because she's wiser in general. Or maybe because she's my mother and she knows me better than I know myself, or because she really is more in tune with the universe than I am. It's frustrating that she can see an answer that's still hidden to me, but I don't press her. Because I trust her when she says I'll see it when I'm ready.

Understanding that doesn't lessen my current anguish.

I peer up at her, suddenly feeling half my age and very vulnerable. My voice is shaky when I ask, "How can I ever hope to see anything when everything around me is so dark?"

"Not *so* dark." She pulls me tighter into her embrace. "You just have to find your North Star. Let that be what guides you."

There's sharp insight in her words and a comfort in the energy she gives, and though I'm not sure yet what—or *who*—my North Star is, I'm reminded of the Tarot reading she did for me not too long ago and the star card that showed up in my future—hope.

And with nothing quite resolved, I cling again to that hope, trusting that the universe will give me the answer soon.

CHAPTER NINETEEN

"Logan O'Toole, you are a god."

My head snaps up. I've been sitting on my couch staring at my hands, my thoughts racing, but Bambi Roo has just walked in the living room, smelling like baby wipes and with her bag slung over her shoulder, and I become aware that I've been sitting like this for almost half an hour.

I give her a weak smile. "Hardly."

"No, really. That thing you did the third time you made me come, when you had me bent over the table? Oh my God, I've never come that hard, I swear."

"Yeah?"

"Yeah," Bambi says, tossing her long, dark hair behind her shoulder with a grin. "I'm telling my agent to make sure I book a thousand more scenes with you."

A couple months ago, this is the kind of thing that would have made me proud, made me a little smug. I like knowing my girls are happy when they leave my set, I like having a reputation as someone who's amazing to have sex with. But right now, all I feel is a churning dread in my gut, a sick feeling of worry and shame—and if I'm being honest, a little bit of self-righteous anger.

"You going somewhere?" Bambi asks, gesturing at me. I'm fully clothed, shoes on and a baseball cap pulled down over my hair, and I've been that way since our scene ended, leaving Bambi to clean herself up while I frantically tried to call and text Devi. She wouldn't answer her phone, and there was no way in fuck I could wait for her to call me back. So I got dressed and I've been waiting anxiously for everyone to leave my house so I can drive to Devi's apartment and figure out what the fuck is going on.

"I'm going to my girlfriend's," I say, trying to make it clear that I really want to go *now* and also trying not to be rude.

But really, lady. Get the fuck out of my house so I can leave.

Bambi looks simultaneously disappointed and excited to hear gossip. "You have a girlfriend? Was it the girl who was here today?"

"Yeah. Her name's Devi."

"She's really hot," Bambi says approvingly.

Something twists inside me. "Yeah. She's pretty much perfect."

"Well, I won't take up any more of your time," Bambi says, and shrugs her bag higher up on her shoulder, walking toward the door. "Oh, and I saw Raven's tweet while I was getting dressed. Congratulations, dude. People will fall all over themselves for that."

Raven's name and the word *congratulations* should not ever share the same space, unless someone is congratulating me on escaping our relationship, and I'm immediately wary and on edge. But I also have to get out of here and find Devi, so I decide to shelve this Raven thing for the moment and make sure Bambi leaves.

"It was great working with you," I say, and I think it sounds convincing because she flashes me a big smile.

"I would say the same to you, except you already know how great it was for me." She winks, and then she waves and walks out the door, blowing me a kiss before she shuts it behind her.

And I'm on my feet in an instant, swiping my keys off the counter, jogging to my garage door. As I get in my car and back out of my driveway, I dig my phone out, thinking I'd have to dig to find this tweet of Raven's that Bambi mentioned, but nope. It's right there in my notifications on my lock screen.

New project with @number1Toole CUMMING soon. #staytuned #bignews

"What the fuck?" I mumble, steering with one hand, my eyes flicking between the empty road and my phone. I swipe at the tweet, opening up the app, and then I see not only Raven's tweet, but the innumerable number of replies, people shitting themselves over Raven's "announcement."

@theRealRaven does this mean you and logan are back together?????

@theRealRaven omfg i can't wait to see you two together again, you guys were my favorite couple.

I can't wait to see **@number1Toole** and **@theRealRaven** fuck again!!!! #bestcouple #truelove

I already feel sick, but this actually sends my stomach clenching, and for a minute, I have to will myself not to puke all over the Shelby's steering wheel. What the fuck is Raven doing? There's definitely no project and there's definitely no chance in hell that I would even consider a project with her, so why the public announcement?

And worse, she's not doing anything to dispel the rumors that we're back together. At this point, the mere thought of dating Raven again is enough to make me go Hulk Smash on the nearest building.

I'm dialing Raven's number without giving it any additional consideration or caution, because fuck caution. I'm pissed as hell, and she's going to know about it. She picks up the phone after only a couple of rings, as if she expected me to call.

"Logan." Her voice is confident, controlled. "How nice to hear from you."

"What the hell are you doing, Julie?"

"You know if you use my real name, I will use yours, and it bothers you much more than it bothers me."

"Thanks for the warning. Now explain yourself."

Raven/Julie lets out a long-suffering sigh. "I was just trying to gauge interest in a joint project. We talked about doing one when I was over at your house, remember? I figured why not toss it around publicly? See how our fans react?"

My jaw is clenched so tightly my head hurts. "*You* talked about doing a scene together. I refused, if you recall."

I can practically hear the one-shouldered shrug on the other side of the call. "You were upset and not thinking clearly. I figured once you saw how much traction a joint scene would get, you'd see that it's a good idea after all. And now that it's announced, you don't want to disappoint all your fans, do you?"

At the last moment, I decide not to take the highway and turn onto Venice Boulevard, driving a little faster and more aggressively than necessary. "You aren't going to force my hand by doing this. My answer hasn't changed. It's still *no*."

"You've changed," she accuses. "You used to put the business first. Now all of a sudden you're too good for it?"

"Don't try that tactic. Even you don't believe it's true."

"Then it's that girl, isn't it?"

There's something raw and exposed underneath her bravado, and suddenly my nausea is replaced with something heavier, something tired. Is that what all this boils down to? Jealousy over Devi?

"You're the one who left me, remember? Why do you care who I'm with?"

There's a pause, and I wonder what she's thinking, what her face looks like. It's funny to think that she used to be the closest person in the world to me, but now there's this insurmountable wedge between us, a wedge so large that I have no idea what she's thinking and feeling right now. And then I remember what she said, that it was my career that was the wedge that drove her away from me, and my stomach knots in fear. I press down harder on the gas pedal, desperate to see Devi as soon as possible.

"She's too young for you," Raven says. "You should have seen her on LaRue's set, Logan. She looked terrified."

"She is none of your business," I say firmly. "And neither am I. I'm done with this—all of it. I'll let you deal with explaining to everyone that there's no project."

"Think about what you're doing," she chastises. "Throwing away an opportunity for what? A girl?"

"No." I stop myself from saying all the angry things that beg to be said, all the threats I want to make if she ever bothers Devi again. Instead I just say, "It's over between us, Julie. Emotionally and professionally. And I'd appreciate it if you could respect that."

And then I hang up, because I'm driving past the airport and getting close to Devi's apartment, and also because I don't think I can keep my temper under control if I talk to Raven a second longer. I turn onto Grand Avenue, trying to process everything that's happened, but unable to focus on anything other than my quest to find Devi.

My Devi. It makes me ache to think of her feeling lonely or unsure or scared on LaRue's set, and I wish that I could have been there, by her side. She is so young, so very young, and maybe I haven't been careful enough of that.

She seemed so certain this morning, so confident, grinning at me in my dungeon as she examined all the toys arrayed around the room. But there was something unsettled in her eyes, a question there that I couldn't find the right words to answer.

The question haunted me. It had settled under my skin and pricked at me as I finished setting up the scene, as Bambi disrobed and we ran through her no list. I felt Devi's eyes burning into me as the cameras turned on, as I slid my hands around Bambi's face and kissed her before pushing her down to her knees. Bambi is beautiful and Latina, with darker coloring like Devi, and so it was easy for me to imagine Devi on her knees in front of me, easy to recall that just a couple hours ago, I'd been buried inside her pussy.

But here's the fucked up thing, the thing I don't know how to deal with. I didn't *have* to imagine Devi to get hard, to enjoy the feeling of pushing past Bambi's plush lips into her wet mouth. My mind drifted between Devi and Bambi as Bambi sucked me off, fantasizing about what Devi was thinking and feeling right then. Was she as turned on as I was when I watched her and Kendi? Was she squirming and wet in her chair, wishing I'd pull her over to me and relieve the building ache in her cunt?

It had made me so hard to think about her watching me, to think about dragging her over to the table and making her kiss Bambi while I took turns fucking them both. I'd wondered if Devi was even touching herself watching me, crossing her legs to squeeze against her pussy or rubbing herself over her dress. I wouldn't have been able to handle it, in the best possible way.

But when I glanced over at her to catch her eye, the chair was empty. Devi was gone.

I panicked. I worried. I even got a little pissed off. And here's the even more fucked up thing—I didn't stop fucking Bambi. In fact, I fucked her harder, faster, forced more orgasms out of her than I normally would have, because I felt that question nipping at my heels, chasing and grabbing at me.

I felt dirty, not in a sexy way, but in the way that I actually felt like there was grime inside my mind, the kind of scum that builds up on shower doors and on the edges of stagnant ponds. I felt ashamed, and yet I also felt angry and unfairly accused of something, even though no accusation had actually been thrown at me. So what if I was fucking Bambi? It was my fucking job!

Except why did I feel weird about it?

Except why did I feeling like I was missing something, something vital, when Devi wasn't there?

And how, with all this weirdness, this feeling of being bereft, could I still keep fucking Bambi? Not just fucking her, but murmuring all my usual sex words to her—*you feel so good,* and *your pussy is so tight,* and *don't you want to make my cock feel good?* They were sex words that I'd murmured in so many different permutations so many different times to so many different women, and they should have felt hollow and wrong, but they didn't. It *did* feel good to pump into Bambi, it *did* feel good to have her suck me off. And at the end, when I wrapped my hand around my cock and shot cum onto her uplifted face? Well that felt fucking good too. How can I feel guilty and good all in the same space? How can I love someone as much as I love Devi, and still get hard for someone else?

God, it's all so fucking complicated. That restless shame, that empty feeling. It makes me horny and agitated all over again just thinking about it. I flex my fingers on the steering wheel before reaching down to adjust the growing bulge in my jeans.

I need to fuck Devi. On camera, off camera, I don't care, but that's the only way to discharge this fucking mess of emotions that I've conjured in the space of a couple short hours. I need her so badly, and we need to fix this, whatever it is. We both have livings to earn, so obviously we have to find a way to make fucking other people compatible with our relationship.

As I turn onto her street, I see immediately that her car isn't around, which could mean she's not home or that she parked in the garage. A pang of frustration almost paralyzes me; I counted on her being here, on being able to start fixing this right away.

I try calling her again as I pull into her driveway—no answer.

I park and I knock on her door—no answer.

I walk around the side of the house and squint up into the window like a fucking creeper—nothing.

She's not here. I get back in my car and call again, leaving a message this time.

"Hey Cass," I say after her sweet voice finishes delivering her voicemail response and the phone beeps to tell me it's recording. "It's Logan. I, um. You left and you're not answering your phone and so I guess I'm worried is all. I love you. Bye."

I deliver it in the short choppy way that a teenage boy calling his crush might, and I don't even care at this point. I don't care if she thinks I'm pathetic. I just need to see her and make this feeling stop.

I wait in her driveway for another thirty minutes, picking up my phone to check the screen every few minutes, even though it would have chimed if she called or texted. But there's no response, and the late afternoon heat seeps into the car, reminding me that I have work to do at home and a phone call with Marieke de Vries at five.

Suddenly, I'm filled with an anger so intense I can barely see straight, my vision going static at the edges and my hands gripping tight around the wheel. It's a fury so displaced and projected and tangled that I'm not sure what I'm actually angry about or who I'm angry with. I'm angry with Devi for leaving and with myself for not realizing she'd be upset watching Bambi and me, and I'm pissed that she won't answer her phone and I'm pissed that there's absolutely nothing I can do about it.

Mostly, I'm angry because I'm scared.

The anger vanishes as quickly as it came and I loosen my grip on the wheel, feeling both empty and pointless. With a deep breath, I reluctantly pull out of her driveway and onto the street, looking in my rearview mirror as I slowly roll away. It's like I'm leaving my heart in her driveway, and all the tendons and veins that attach it inside of my chest are stretching and snapping as I drive away and leave it there to bleed out and die.

Needless to say, it's not a happy drive home. I walk in the door, knowing I need to go to my office, knowing I need to work, but instead I drop my keys on the counter and wander over to my window. Outside in the bright heat, the pool glimmers clear and cold, and I think about watching Devi swim there, moving so effortlessly, the contrast between her dark bronze skin and the bluish water beautiful and perfect and striking.

What if I was right last night? What if that first off-camera sex was the best it will ever be for us? What if it's all downhill from here? What if that perfect moment of shimmering connection can't last? We've defined it now, as love, and maybe love can't bear this many complications, and maybe our baby relationship is already in its death throes.

I scrub at my face with my hands and step away from the window. I can't right now—with any of this. I have too many feelings jumbled too close together, and I can't even begin to sort them out without my Cass beside me.

So instead, I try to throw myself into work for the afternoon, writing and filming my monologue for Bambi's scene and having a ninety-minute phone call with Marieke about *Star-Crossed*. She loves the footage so far, and since Devi and I are getting ready to schedule our last episode for the season, Marieke and I talk about what another season of it would look like. There are a lot of great, sexy ideas tossed around and we finally settle on one, and I should feel energized by all this but I don't.

I feel like my heart is still pulsing in sad, bloody little pulses on Devi's driveway.

I feel like I want to drive back to her house and sit on her steps until she comes home.

I wander downstairs, past the wet bar by my kitchen, and I stop to pour myself a scotch because that is what I do when I'm upset—I process my feelings through my liver. But I don't actually drink it. I just cradle the glass in my hands and watch the sky darken above my pool. And then my phone rings.

I practically drop the scotch answering it, my blood spiking with excitement and dread at the same time when I see Devi's gorgeous face on the screen. I answer, trying to keep my voice from shaking with trepidation and relief.

"Hey, babe," I say, setting the scotch down. "Thanks for calling me back."

"I'm sorry it took so long," she says. Her voice is measured, unreadable. "I wasn't feeling well this morning, so I had to leave. I went to my parents', and then my phone died."

It has the practiced pitch of a rehearsed excuse, and my stomach sinks. I'm pretty sure this means she's upset about my scene with Bambi today, not that she's actually sick.

"Cass, I want to see you."

"Not now," she says. "I'm still not feeling well."

"Later tonight maybe? If you're not feeling well, I can come take care of you."

"I'm going to stay at my parents' until tomorrow," she says, and there's a note of apology in her voice. "I think I really just need to sleep it off…whatever it is that I've caught."

"Devi." I swallow. "Please."

"I'll see you tomorrow, Logan. Remember we planned on shooting in the afternoon? I'll be over at one."

Come over now.

Or let me come to you.

Please, Cass, don't do this.

I don't say these things. I don't say them because I know the right thing to do is to give her space. I don't say them because a good guy would give her the benefit of the doubt and believe her when she says she's not feeling well and needs to sleep.

Most of all, I don't say them because my throat is too tight to speak. I clear it and manage to say, "Okay, babe. I love you. I'll see you tomorrow."

"Love you too," she echoes, and in those three words, I hear pain and confusion fathoms deep. "Goodnight, Logan."

• • •

If I were filming a movie of my own life, I'd be disgusted with it right now. First of all, I'm not exhibiting any believable character growth in response to my obstacles. And second of all, there's no coherence or unity of theme right now. I mean, what am I even feeling? I'm feeling way too much contradictory shit to express in film. No, if I were a director, I would tell my character to pick one thread and stick with it. Am I trying not to cry or am I swooning on my feet whenever I think of Devi? Am I checking my phone constantly or am I trying to resist throwing my phone across the room? If I were a director, I would tell myself that feelings are passive, and to choose actions instead—and then to choose those actions deliberately.

One action at a time.

The idea is appealing to me as I get up the next day and shower. I'm not naive enough to believe I could actually pick one of those feelings and discard all the others, but the idea of cleaning up all these emotions is so deeply attractive. And as I remember Devi's eyes as she watched me prepare for my scene with Bambi, as I remember convincing her that reality is not the antithesis to porn, I realize something so terrible and clarifying that I abruptly stop washing my hair and drop my hands, simply standing under the spray and staring at the wall as I absorb how wrong I've been.

I wanted everything to be together, gloriously messy and unified, because I felt like our palpable love and attraction would make *Star-Crossed* a better project. I thought that blending our personal romance and our onscreen sex would be the answer, not taking into account Devi's youth or the fact that I would end up falling for her so much harder than I ever could have guessed. I wanted everything together, because I thought that together was better, more real—*hyper*-real—but all it did was mix everything up. It cheapened the real connection we had and gave the filming more emotional importance than it deserved.

Fuck. No wonder Devi and I both felt confused yesterday.

The worst part is that this is all my fault. *I* convinced Devi to go down this path. *I* made us blur all the lines. I'm responsible for all our pain right now.

If we want to continue this, if we want to survive with our hearts intact and with our careers thriving, then we have to carve out boundaries now. We have to separate porn from real life, we have to compartmentalize. And I have to take responsibility for what I've done to us.

I just hope it's not too late to fix it.

So when Devi unlocks my door at one, right on the dot, I have an entire speech prepared, practically an entire class to teach on Why I'm an Idiot and How I'm Going to Fix It. But then I see her, and all the words melt away from my mind, because she's so fucking beautiful right now, wearing a short flared skirt and tank top, her long hair in a messy braid that's slung over one shoulder.

The moment she steps in, I'm pinning her against the wall and crushing my mouth against hers, my hands roaming everywhere, aggressive and needy. She kisses me back with an eager hunger, her mouth searching. And then her legs are wrapping around my waist, and we are grinding together while we kiss, and then she pants, "Let's go to your bedroom," and she doesn't have to ask me twice. I carry her, her legs still wrapped around my waist, and we barely make it to my bedroom before her hands are fumbling with my zipper and I'm yanking at her tank top. I set her on the bed, toss her on her belly and then climb on top, flipping up her skirt and yanking her thong aside so fast that I hear the fabric tear. I don't care; another second's work and I'm notched in her cunt, pushing roughly inside.

She's not quite ready, but she's bucking back against me, raising her ass up in an attempt to get me inside her faster, and the friction is fucking unbelievable. Tight and raw and primal. I'm grunting and thrusting hard, the zipper of my jeans scraping against the soft skin of her ass and thighs, her skirt a twisted pink mess of fabric around her waist.

And all I can think is
she wants me
she loves me
she still wants me.

"Make me come," she says, squirming like a wild woman under me. "God, Logan, please. Make me come."

"Anything," I say, dropping my lips to the back of her neck. "I'll give you fucking anything."

I mean it. I reach under her hips and find her swollen bud, and this is another position I rarely film in, because I'm almost completely on top of her, all of the motion hidden by her thick ass and my pumping hips. But who cares how it would look? It feels fucking amazing to take her like this, it feels fucking wonderful to impale her like this, with the rounded curves of her ass pressing back into my hips.

I'm still kissing the back of her neck, stretched out on top of her and bearing most of my weight on my left forearm and my knees, and my right hand is rubbing the throbbing bundle between her legs, and she comes abruptly, catastrophically, keening into the pillow as she shudders and quakes her way through her release.

I feel the sharp heat thrumming in my pelvis already, and the porn star in me wants to change position and slow down, draw this out. But the boyfriend in me wants to go with her, fall together, just like she said two nights ago, and so I let the frantic torrent of desperation and relief carry me over the edge. Deep currents of pleasure unfurl into jagged arcs of lightning, and then I'm pulsing inside of her—still thrusting and ramming hard and fast.

Frenzied.

Relentless.

And finally it comes: sweet relief. All of the pain and worry I've chewed on for the past twenty-four hours bleeds away as I slow my thrusts and my breathing returns to normal, and as she starts to make that purring sound underneath me, my chest constricts with incandescent joy.

"I love you," I murmur.

"I love you," she whispers back, and I want to shout with triumph. I haven't ruined everything after all!

With our clothes still rumpled and twisted around us, I roll us onto our sides, my arms wrapping tight around her torso and my cock still buried deep in her pussy. It's possibly the shortest amount of time I've taken to have sex in years, it's possibly the most spontaneous sex I've had as an adult, but I don't care. Because it was only about us, the two of us, no cameras and no bullshit. I hold her tight and breathe in the smell of her skin, thinking that I'm right, I've finally figured it out.

This is so amazing right now, so perfect, exactly because there are no cameras. And if we carry these boundaries into everything else—if we only think about *Star-Crossed* when we're doing *Star-Crossed,* and Logan and Devi when we're just Logan and Devi—then we'll be able to sustain this peace and satisfaction. Sustain *us,* for the long haul.

Devi's going to love this, I think happily, pressing my lips to her shoulder as she snuggles back against me. She and her parents seem into that Eckhart Tolle mindfulness stuff, and this is basically mindfulness, right? Mindful fucking.

"What are you thinking?" Devi asks.

I answer honestly. "About writing a book called *Mindful Fucking for Fun and Profit.* I could do seminars and speak at corporate retreats and stuff. Make lots of money."

She giggles. "You already make lots of money."

"Pfft. I work hard for that money. I need a plan for when my stamina runs out."

"As if that will ever happen." She shifts against me, and my cock is very eager to prove her right, except we're still supposed to film a scene today, so I tell him to wait. "Look at all the books in here," she observes. "I never noticed them before."

I'm far more interested in licking circles on her shoulder, tracing the line between her tank top and her skin with my lips. "I don't have nearly as many as you do," I say in between kisses. "Was always more of a movie guy. But I think good storytellers should appreciate all mediums."

"Logan O'Toole: fiction nerd."

"Hardly." I glance up at the set of low shelves against the window. "Most of those are poetry collections."

I hear the smile in her voice. "Poetry?"

I feel a little defensive, not because I think she's teasing me but because it's so hard to explain. "It was always my favorite part in English class, when we'd read the poetry. And I knew when I made the choice to do porn instead of going to UCLA like I'd planned, that there probably wouldn't be much poetry in my future. So I started doing this thing where every month I'd buy a book of poetry. I didn't have to like it or even read it all, but I had to try it. Because I think poets come the closest to seeing the world how I see it sometimes. Images. Tastes and sounds. Not always perfectly stitched together, but uneven and unexplainable."

"That's beautiful," she says quietly.

"You're beautiful." And then I'm going to say it—all the stuff I planned on saying—and explain to her how we'll keep our relationship safe and just for us, but then she turns. My cock slides out of her and I can't help the sad groan that I make.

She smiles and bites her lip. "How about we start our scene now?" And all my other thoughts go out the window.

• • •

It feels weird to go back to making "just porn" with Devi. And maybe even *go back* is the wrong way to look at it, since it was never just porn with her. It was always something more; it was always blended with how deeply we felt for each other.

I wish I'd talked to Devi before we dove into the scene's particulars; but once we started blocking and running through what we wanted to do sex-wise, there didn't seem to be a good time to say, "Oh hey, just so you know, I think it's best if we act strictly professional right now."

So I don't say anything. On one hand, it feels good, natural even, to set up the cameras and block the scene like she's just another girl and not my girlfriend. But on the other hand, it feels jarring and bizarre, like waking up to find your house has blown sideways but everything is still perfectly in place. It's hard to stop fiddling with the camera settings when I know exactly how glowing that bronze skin can be in just the right conditions, it's hard to think about what sex positions will translate best on the screen when I know which positions she actually likes the best.

But I manage. It's a mental workout for sure, and there are times before we start that I catch her looking at me quizzically, as if she can tell something is off. *I'll explain it all afterwards*, I think. *After we shoot the scene like this, she'll be able to see how much easier it is. How much better.*

Today's scene is the last we'll shoot for this season of *Star-Crossed*, and I decided to do something a little more intimate than normal. No separate location, no public fooling around. Marieke and I agreed that we should leave the Logan and Devi characters in a happy, loving place, just like you'd leave characters at the end of a romantic comedy. In love for perpetuity.

Of course, we'll shake things up with the second season of *Star-Crossed*, and I smile to myself, remembering I still have to tell Devi about that too. Marieke and I brainstormed some serious sexy, steamy, twisted shit, and I bet my girl will love it.

"What are you smiling about?" Devi asks. She's perched on the edge of the massively fluffy rug I've dragged in from my office, wearing nothing but brightly colored knee socks. The white fluff of the rug is such a stark contrast to her Persian skin that I stop what I'm doing and just stare at her for a minute.

My Cassiopeia.

My queen.

She tilts her head at me, the loose braid sliding tantalizingly over one perfect, full tit, and all I want to do is drop to my knees next to her and kiss her until the stars come out. Have I done that yet? Just kissed her for hours? Made out until we've both forgotten our names, our lives, our histories?

I almost do it. I even get so far as taking a step toward her until I remember, no—that's a boyfriend thing. A boyfriend thought. Logan the porn star loves kissing and will definitely kiss the shit out of her once the camera starts rolling, but it will be kissing for the camera, kissing to make an amazing scene.

Later, I promise myself. *Later, we will have the kissing just for us.* Kissing without a goal or without a time limit…God, the thought makes me hard and excited and warm and melty all at once. How do people handle all of these feelings all at once? How do people stand being in love?

How could I have ever thought that I had been in love before?

This—*this*—is love.

And I have to protect it at all costs, starting right now.

"I'm just smiling because this is going to be a badass scene," I finally answer Devi's question. "Are you ready?"

She nods. And I press *record*.

All in all, it's possibly one of the best scenes I've ever filmed, maybe even ever participated in. We start with her in those knee socks on the rug, grinding on a pillow while I murmur the dirtiest things I can think of, and after she comes against the pillow, her naked stomach visibly tightening, I unzip my jeans and walk over to her, feeding my thick erection through her lips.

Everything is light and bright, with the afternoon sun streaming in and the white furniture and rug, and everything is perfectly staged and seamless. The blowjob transitions to a sixty-nine, the sixty-nine transitions into condom-sheathed fucking, first doggy-style, and then spooning from behind—one of the best filming positions because I can show off her jiggling tits and taut stomach and pussy all at once. And then after she comes a second time and then a third, I pull out, yank off the condom, and then jack myself off onto her stomach. The scene ends with me turning her head back to me for a long, deep kiss while she draws idle circles in the mess on her stomach.

After the kiss lasts what I think would be the right amount of time for a romantic sort of fade to black, I break it off and hop up to turn off the camera. And then I grab a box of baby wipes I keep in one of those ottoman storage cubes (along with lube, condoms and other things I need on hand but also hidden discreetly in case of a surprise Mom and Dad Visit) and trot over to Devi, zipping up my jeans with one hand as I do.

Weirdly, she doesn't look at me as she starts scrubbing at the mess I've made on her stomach. I'm suddenly aware of how quiet it is in here and also how dim—the September afternoon has started to bleed into evening outside, the first pinpricks of starlight piercing the thick sky above my skylight.

I turn on a lamp, and then start breaking down the tripods to put back in my office, watching Devi out of the corner of my eye the whole time. She seems pensive, methodical, as she finishes cleaning up and gets to her feet.

"Are you okay?" I ask as she returns from throwing away the used baby wipes. She's still naked, still in those girlish knee socks with that immensely tuggable braid, and it's so hard for me to focus on anything other than dragging her back to bed. I promised myself that I'd get boyfriend time after we made it through this scene, and now we've made it, and I just want to wrap myself up in her and never let go, but something doesn't feel right. But I can fix that—I'll talk to her, and apologize and explain everything, and then it will be better.

Then kissing until the sun comes up.

"Yeah," she says, "everything is okay." And I can tell that she's not exactly lying, but that she's not giving me the whole answer either. And just as I'm about to launch into the speech I should have given her hours ago when she showed up at my door, she asks, "So this was really the last scene we'll shoot for *Star-Crossed?*"

And then her distance makes sense, because she and I haven't talked explicitly about the future of the series, and I'm so relieved because I get to tell her all the exciting stuff that Marieke and I dreamed up. And she'll be a central part of it, and I know she'll love that we get to keep working together like this.

I button up my jeans and flop down on the couch, patting the space next to me. She obliges, sitting down, but she sits a couple feet away from me, her legs tucked under her and one arm wrapped around the back of the couch, as if she's bracing herself.

"So I know you know that Marieke and Vida are thrilled with *Star-Crossed* and how it's turned out, and we all think it's going to be fucking huge when it debuts in November. They want to do a second season, and I do too. The only real question is if you'd be on board for that."

Her face lights up—but just a little. "Thank you for asking," she says softly, hesitantly. "I think I'd like that. I'll have to think about it though."

It's not a contract signature, but almost.

I grin. "Excellent! Marieke and I are thinking we could start filming in another month or so, just as soon as we line up the other performers."

Her eyebrows rise. "Other performers?" she asks.

I nod enthusiastically. "So just like this season set up 'Logan and Devi' as a couple, this next season will follow another couple. But get this—" I'm so excited I can barely sit still "—we'll be in it too, and there will be a much more complicated dynamic. Threesomes and foursomes and maybe even the illusion of cheating—nothing too seedy, of course, since we want this to be couples-friendly—but edgy enough that there's that illicit thrill, you know?"

Devi looks away, chewing on her bottom lip, and I notice that her hand is gripping the back of the couch. "So we'll be having sex with other people?"

I scoot closer. "Yeah, but we'll still have sex together too. And sometimes it will be combined scenes. I think this has the potential to be incredibly hot and something really different, you know? Like *The Affair*, but porn."

She searches my face. "You're really excited about this, aren't you?"

I blink. She's not angry or upset, but there's something strange in her tone. Strange and cautious, and I'm reminded of everything I still need to say.

But first, "Yes, I'm super excited," I say. I take her free hand because I just can't help it, I want to touch her and feel connected to her. "I love this project. It's porn at its best, you know? Forbidden and hot and a little emotional, a little artistic."

I hear my voice—energetic and full of optimism. Loud in the quiet, dark living room. I lower it as I gesture to the rug and to the camera equipment on the floor. "Don't we have the best job ever, Devi? The best life? We get to *fuck* for a living. We get to feel good and make other people feel good for money. And yes, sometimes it's hard. Sometimes the money is thin and the jobs aren't great. But how many people get to *love* what they do for a living? How many people get to work their dream job? And *Star-Crossed* is exactly the kind of thing I want my dream job to be."

I can see her turning this over in her mind, and it encourages me to be the logical, compartmentalizing guy I need to be right now. "Hey," I say, catching her chin with my finger and meeting her eyes. "I need to say some stuff."

I can see her wrestle with something, and God, I wish I knew what she's wrestling with. "Okay," she agrees after a minute. "I think that might be good."

I lick my lips. I spent a good three years of my life constantly apologizing to a girlfriend who I was never political or intellectual enough for, and so you'd think I'd be good at it by now. But instead I'm insanely nervous. I have to get this right. If I get it wrong, if I lose Devi…

I'll lose everything.

But that won't happen, I tell myself. *I've got it all figured out now.*

"So," I start clumsily. "I, um. I've been doing some thinking since yesterday. And part of it was about how smart you are, how logical and careful you are. And I'm not naturally that way, I guess. I'm more of a 'chips all in' kind of guy, more of a *lover* than a *thinker*. And I'm…"

Devi is staring at me, and I realize I'm babbling. I cast around for the clearest way to say what I want to say.

"I think we should stop mixing our love life and our careers."

Her lips part. "What do you mean?" she asks.

"I think we shouldn't be boyfriend and girlfriend on the camera. I think we should just act like two performers. And then have our personal life completely separate. And that way it won't be like it was when I fucked Bambi yesterday—because I know that hurt you, and because it hurt you, it hurt me too. We'll be able to keep working, keep making porn with other people with zero weirdness, which is what we both want. Right?"

There's no answer. Even her dark gold eyes are still and frozen.

"Devi, right?" I repeat.

Still no answer. My pulse starts to thud in my neck as the silence stretches out, and then I feel my stomach begin to twist as I realize that maybe all of the assumptions I've taken for granted about Devi and me, and what we both want, have been very, very wrong.

CHAPTER TWENTY

I stare at him, silent. There are things to say—lots of things—but I'm not sure where to begin when I'm not even sure to whom I'm talking at the moment.

The Logan who greeted me today, who fucked me with his clothes still on because he was so eager to be inside me, who whispered I love you as I came—that Logan is not the Logan who had sex with me on camera for the bulk of the last two hours. I don't know this version of Logan. He's cold and clinical, and though he was still able to make my body respond to his every whim, he is not the man I'm in love with.

And this bullshit about adding more couples to *Star-Crossed*?

Hell no.

I mean, this show has been one of the special things we've shared, the thing that has just been ours. And he wants to open that up to others?

I don't understand.

I'm not sure I *want* to understand.

I gather my clothes as I gather my thoughts, mulling over everything he's said, trying to figure out how I feel and what to say.

My lack of response seems to make Logan sweat. "Let me back up." He stands over me as I start to dress. "I think I understand why you left the set yesterday and I know how to fix it."

"By being an icy, distant asshole?" My tone has bite, but I manage to keep the volume level.

He laughs awkwardly. "No, no. I should have explained beforehand.

I'm sure I came off that way because you didn't get where I was coming from. See, I realized I haven't thought about us in the right way. I'm learning that from you—you are so good at using your head. And I always do this, I always jump in heart first."

I pull my T-shirt on, then turn to face him. "I *still* don't get where you're coming from, Logan."

"I'm saying I was wrong to try to make it real. The show, I mean. I know it will be good art, but it was bad for us."

I stop, one leg in my skirt, the other in mid-air. My heart thunders in my ears, and there's a bitter taste in my mouth. "You regret that our relationship is real?" He can't mean that, can he? Because if he does…

"No. That's not what I'm saying at all. I regret that I let the real parts cross over into the work parts and now, of course, the lines are blurred. I didn't see that this would be a problem, but I get it now. Right now, you think when I'm touching someone else that it's the same as when I'm touching you. Because of the camera. But it's different, and the way to prove that to you is to take away the camera from the real us. Then you'll be able to see what's the job and what's not."

I step the rest of the way into my skirt and pull it up to my waist, suddenly needing very much to be dressed. "So, in other words, anything that happens with the camera on us would be just for the job?"

"Exactly. They'll be like the scenes I have with any other woman. We should even be formal about it and go through the do's and don'ts each time. I'll wear a condom like the law requires. Just like every other shoot. Then you'll be the only woman I'm with when the camera's off."

He isn't saying anything that terrible. Not really. It's logical. It makes sense. He's thinking about the business in much the way I always have.

Still.

It *sounds* terrible. It *feels* terrible, and, while I'm not quite sure how to refute him, I know I don't agree.

I offer the first thing that comes to my lips. "A lot of our most amazing moments together have happened on set. Lots of very *real* moments. I'm pretty sure I fell in love with you on camera."

"I know, I know." He steps toward me and puts a hand on each of my upper arms. Something about the gesture makes me feel the difference in our ages—makes me feel like *he* feels the difference. Like he thinks he has the better handle on the situation because he's older.

When he speaks next, it just gets worse. "I'm not discounting anything that's happened before, babe. I'm trying to fix things for the future. So that we can keep doing the jobs that we love. And it makes sense, doesn't it? We aren't the first co-workers who've fallen for each other. How do other people do it? I'm sure they have to draw similar lines."

"But most other people's jobs don't require getting naked."

"And that's why we have to make what we do at our jobs different than what we do at home. As much as possible. We need to make things clear. Keep things separate."

Separate.

He says it so easily, so matter-of-factly, that I feel like a jerk for not being able to comply. Or like I'm naive. It's the same way I felt when Raven confronted me. Am I really *that* ignorant?

Maybe we're both that ignorant. Because this solution of his is not a solution I can get on board with.

Maybe this relationship isn't one I can get on board with either.

Don't jump to conclusions, Devi. Talk it out. "Is this really what you want, Logan?"

He shrugs. "I think it's what's best. For us. It will make things easier. It will make it possible for us to keep seeing each other."

I run both of my hands over my forehead, as if I could sort out my thoughts if I just rubbed hard enough.

Logan drops his hands and bends down to meet my eyes. "Devi? Tell me what you're thinking, will you?"

I can't. Because the air suddenly feels heavy and the walls seem like they're pressing down, and what I'm thinking is that I need to run. Which isn't like me at all.

"Air," I say. "I just…I need some fresh air."

Before he can stop me, I bolt through the patio doors to the backyard and stand at the edge of his pool, drinking the night air in deep gulps.

I'm so mixed up about what's happened. When I came over today, I'd been wary, but then I saw him. I saw the way he looked at me, and everything wrong was right again. He'd taken me roughly, yet it was, in every way, making love. We'd been normal. We'd been us. And when he'd held me in his arms and told me about his poetry love, all my worries about us disappeared.

Then came the scene. And everything was different, and part of me wants to tell him that his idea is stupid and ridiculous and can't possibly work, but another part of me realizes that I have no other option to give him in return. Because how things were wasn't working either.

Tears burn at the corners of my eyes. I know Logan's trying to guide me through this. Maybe he's even the North Star my mother suggested I look for. I mean, I hope he is. I love him, and I want to be with him. So maybe I just need to do what he suggests. But how can I, when everything he's suggesting makes me feel even worse than before?

I hug my arms around my chest and look skyward. It's smoggy. Typical for this part of L.A., and it's barely worth looking up. Except just as I do, a meteor shoots across the darkness. It's beautiful and blazing and not unlike how my heart feels at the moment. Like it's on fire, and, even as it burns down to nothing, there's something incredibly exquisite about it's final fall into nothingness.

Like the fool stepping off a cliff.

"Did you make a wish?" Logan asks from behind me. He wraps his arms around me, his body warm and inviting against mine. Not for the first time, I'm aware of how the world around us dims when I'm in his embrace. If only we could live that way always.

I turn my head slightly toward him then look back at the sky. "You know, that tradition started back in ancient Greek times. Ptolemy used to say that it meant the gods were looking down on us, and that when they peeked through the spheres, star matter would slip through and that's what we'd see fall through the sky. Since they were already paying attention to us, it was presumably a good time to ask for whatever our heart most desired."

He brushes his lips against my temple. "I thought I had what my heart most desired. But twice now you've walked away from me, and I can't help but think I should be wishing on that star right now for you."

It hurts to hear him say it because in that one line I can tell both how much he loves me, and how much it's going to hurt when I say the things I'm just beginning to realize I need to say.

So I stall. "They aren't even stars." I casually slip from his hold, needing distance from him to keep my mind in focus. "They're particles of rock burning as they enter the earth's atmosphere. Some of them so small, we'd refer to them as dust. Isn't that funny how we put so much faith and trust into something so common and everyday?"

"Is it really so everyday, though? Dust might be, but catching it at just the moment that it burns up…I bet most people don't look up enough to notice. Maybe the magic is in us taking the time to see it. And then taking the time to voice what it is we really want."

His words strike a melancholy chord, and I turn to face him. Isn't it kind of magic that I get to see Logan as I do? In common ways that burn brightly when caught in the right moment. Isn't that what I have of him that no one else does?

It's almost enough to send me back into his arms, but then he locks eyes with me and whispers, "Devi…" and, just like I know he's voicing what it is *he* really wants, I know I have to voice what *I* really want.

"I can't make pornographic films anymore," I say.

He tenses. "Why? Because of LaRue? Because of Madden?"

"They're a little bit a part of it, yes. But mostly because of—" *you.* That's the word first in my mind, but I think of my heart and that falling star and know the real answer is, "me. It's because of me."

"I don't understand. You don't want to do het porn? Maybe you could go back to girl-girl shoots." There's concern in his tone, but underneath it I sense optimism. He's relieved to hear this isn't a problem with *us*, and now he's probably assuming this conversation is going to be focused on my career.

And it will be. Just, there's more, too. "I could do that. But…well, first of all, it's a dead end if I stick with the work I'm doing. It's not paying my bills and it's not what I want to do for the long term. Staying in it doesn't do anything to get me the future I want for myself."

I pause to swallow before telling him the next part. The *hard* part. "The thing is, you say I'm good at leaving my heart out of things, and I thought I was too. I thought I was a person who understood how to separate the job from the emotions. But I'm not. I can't. I can't help but feel jealous every time you're with someone else. Every time you go to work. I'm torn up and muddled, and I can't even think straight because all I can see is your hands on Bambi—"

"I shouldn't have had you stay and watch. That was—"

I go on as though he hadn't interrupted, thinking of that awful tweet from yesterday. "And your mouth on Raven."

"I will never have my mouth or my hands on Raven again." He's insistent and more than a little bit defensive. "I should have made that clear. She and I are over, and that means I won't—" He pauses, an idea occurring to him. "Is this about the project she announced I'm doing with her? Because she just made that up. I'm not—"

"You're not?" For half a second I'm relieved, but then I realize it's not enough. "Never mind. It doesn't matter, don't you see? If it's not Raven, it's someone else. Because that's what you do. You fuck other people for a living, and I can't deal with it."

He takes half a step backward, his green eyes shrouded with hurt. "So what you're really saying is you can't do porn anymore because of *me*."

"No, Logan. That's not what I'm saying. I can't do porn anymore because I want to be in a committed relationship with someone. I want to be in love and I want only one person in my bed. I don't want to share. I don't want to share *you*. Making work separate and businesslike isn't going to fix that. I can't have sex with other people when I'm in love with you. I can't watch you have sex with other people either."

"You want me to—?"

I cut him off, eager to make sure he understands I'm not asking what he thinks I am. "No. I don't want you to quit. I don't want you to be anything but who you are because that's who I'm in love with. I want you to be happy doing what you do—and you are. And that's why this is about *me*. *I'm* not happy with you doing what you do."

He shakes his head as though dismissing what I've said, an expression of clear certainty settling on his strong, handsome face. "It's because we've been doing this wrong. Like I said. We have to set things up differently between us, and it can work. I know relationships can work in this industry."

"You know this because of your relationship with Raven? Because, far as I can tell, that didn't work out so well."

He tilts his head at me. "That's not fair."

I bite the inside of my lip and sigh. "You're right. It's not fair. And this has nothing to do with Raven or with any other relationship in this industry. Maybe they can work. For someone else. They don't work for me."

"We haven't really given it much of a try." There's a hint of annoyance in his expression, but I get that he's just fighting for me the best way he knows how.

I'm fighting for me too. "I have tried. I've tried enough to know that it's only going to get worse from here on out. It's only going to hurt more, the more I love you. And maybe I could eventually figure out how to be callous and bury those emotions, but quite frankly, that's not who I want to be. That's not who you want me to be."

"Of course I don't want you to be callous. You won't be. You think it's not hard for me too, when I picture you with Bruce douchecanoe Madden? It's horrible. It drives me insane. You can't imagine how I want to claw his eyes out."

A spark of hope ignites inside me. "Really?" If he feels the same way, then maybe there's a future for us I hadn't imagined before.

He steps toward me, cupping my cheek in his hand. "Yes, really. I just need to tell you that more. That's what I meant about setting boundaries." He rubs his thumb over my lower lip, sending shivers down my spine. "And maybe we make up other rules like…" He glances up while he's thinking then back at me. "Like there could be certain words we never use with other people and maybe we always have final approval on each other's costars. Then we find things we never do with anyone else and we make sure that's what we do together. Like we never sleep with anyone but each other—I mean actual sleep. And I want to be the only person who ever takes you to zombie movies."

He's so sweet and adorable and *sure*, and I want so much to be able to let go and trust his conviction.

"I love that you can see a relationship unfolding like this, Logan." It's heartbreaking to say, but it's sincere. "It gives me hope that you'll be able to find someone who will share those special things with you."

"I have found someone." His voice is tight, and for the first time I think he actually senses I might be ending this. He moves his hand to grip behind my neck. "We can be like this together."

I'm already shaking my head. "It's not me, Logan. I can't share the man I'm in love with. That's never going to change."

"Oh, Cass. You're so young. You—"

I pull out of his grasp, my voice sharp when I cut him off. "Don't say that. Don't say that to me right now. It's not fair. Yes, I'm young. But that doesn't mean I don't know how I feel. It doesn't mean I don't know myself well enough to know that this isn't working for me."

In the darkness, it's difficult to make out the details of Logan's features, but I can tell when it finally sinks in. "Devi, are you breaking up with me?"

I can't say it. I don't want to say it. I don't want to mean it, but it's the only answer. I see that now.

So I fold my arms across my chest and break up with Logan O'Toole with just a nod of my head.

His breath catches like I've knocked the wind out of him. It's the single most heartbreaking sound I've ever heard in my life, and I have a feeling that no matter how long I live, I'll never forget it. It's the kind of sound that makes me want to be a different person than I am, makes me want to forsake my own happiness. Makes me want to step forward and press my mouth against his so I can kiss away the sound and the pain.

But I don't move except to wipe a stray tear off my cheek. "I'm going to go back to school. I'd planned to tell you that today. I'm not sure what I'll study, and I'm not even sure what school I'm going to go to. I've been looking at a few. UCLA is still a possibility, but I'm starting to think I need to get out of California. UT Austin, maybe. I was accepted there when I applied in the past."

"You don't have to break up with me to go to school, Devi. I'll support you in that, if that's what you want. You don't have to stay in the business for me to love you. And I don't have to live in L.A. to do my job. I can go wherever you need to go."

My knees buckle. "Don't say that, Logan."

"Don't say what? That I love you? That I'll support you?"

All of it. "If you loved me at all you wouldn't say any of it. You'd let me go."

"No, I'd fight for you. I love you, and I'm fighting for you. And if you loved me, you'd let me."

"Have you considered that maybe the problem is I love you too much?" With that, I've exposed my greatest fear—that the real reason I can't handle our jobs and he can is because I love him more than he loves me.

Before he can respond, I go on. "This is pointless, Logan. We're just dragging this out, and it's already painful for both of us. I'm so grateful for the opportunity you gave me with *Star-Crossed*. I'm so inspired by your work and your passion. And I'm so very honored to have had the chance to—" My voice cracks, and I go to clear my throat.

But then Logan is on me, a hand behind my neck, another tangled in my hair, and it doesn't matter if my voice is working because he's captured my mouth with his. His kiss is searing and aggressive. With his lips and his tongue, he demands, and I want to give into him so I do. For the space of our kiss, I do.

When he breaks away, we're both panting. "You don't want to leave me. You couldn't kiss me like that and want to leave me."

"I don't *want* to leave you." My voice is barely more than a whisper. "But I can't live in your universe, Logan. If there was any way I could, I promise I would."

He leans his forehead against mine and shuts his eyes tight. "Don't do this, Devi. What can I say or do to make you not do this?"

It rips me up inside because it feels like he's asking me to answer honestly, and I want to. So much. I want to tell him the solution that's already staring him in the face. In the same way he asked me to "*make porn*" with him all those weeks ago, I want to plead, '*Don't make porn with me.*" *Don't* make porn. Just be with me.

But I know better than anyone that if he doesn't see that answer, it's because he doesn't want to. And it's not something I'm ever going to ask him to do. I'm not as vain as Cassiopeia to believe I would give Logan a more beautiful life than the one that he has, no matter how much I wish it were true.

"I have to go," I say, pushing out of his arms. *Don't look back*, I tell myself as I head through the open gate of the pool area to my car.

"Devi?"

Despite my self-coaching, I turn. Because I can't not turn when he says my name.

"You should study stars."

For a second I think he's being sarcastic. Like he's referring to himself—a porn star. That he's suggesting I study another porn celebrity the way I studied him.

But he glances up, gesturing to the sky with his eyes.

Oh. Stars. "Yeah. Maybe that's what I'll do."

This time when I turn to go, I don't look back. I don't stop. I step blindly off the cliff into darkness like the fool, and hope, eventually, I'll land on solid ground.

CHAPTER TWENTY-ONE

I almost do it. I almost let her walk away from me. Because I'm so stunned. Because I'm so hurt. Because I can still taste the fire and heat of her kiss, and how could she kiss me like that and then just walk away?

But my feet move before my mind, and I'm jogging through the gate right as she shuts the door of her old VW Bug. She starts the engine but she leaves the car in park as I run over to her.

She rolls down the window, and on her young face is an expression of pain so poignant I can barely look at it.

"You're hurting," I say, bracing my hands against the top of the car's window frame so I can lean down to see her better. "And I'm hurting. Devi, it doesn't have to be this way; we don't have to be hurting right now. Come inside, and we'll talk. We'll figure this out."

"There's nothing left to figure out," she says quietly. "I can't be with you when you can't be with only me."

I slam my hands against the window frame, rocking the tiny car and making her jump. Anger like hot acid fills my words when I speak. "You know it's not like that! My heart would be with only you, so why the fuck does it matter where my cock is?"

"It matters to me," she answers, her voice trembling slightly.

I'm still furious, my hands clenching the window frame now, and I want to tear this car apart, rivet by rivet, until she agrees to stay. "You knew what you were getting into," I accuse. "You knew exactly what it would mean to date a porn star. It's not fair for you to change your mind now!"

Tears catch on her eyelashes as she shakes her head. "I can't be in this porn world anymore, Logan. I can't be in *your* world."

"It's *our* world," I insist, her tears thawing my anger into a messy, guilty regret. "We both live in it, and we both love doing porn."

"No, *you* love doing porn." She takes a deep breath. "And that's why I'd never ask you to stop. I love you exactly how you are, and part of who you are is porn. Doing what you love. Do you think I'm so cruel that I would ask you to give that up?"

"But…"

I don't have anything to follow that word, though. I just know I need to struggle against this, fight for this, salvage something, anything, because Devi is the one thing I can't afford to lose…

Except she's right about me. I can't afford to lose doing what I love either. If I'm not Logan O'Toole, World Famous Porn Star, then who am I?

"It just never occurred to me," I finish lamely. "That anyone would want to quit porn. That porn would be an issue. I thought we both were on the same page. I thought we both loved each other."

A tear finally falls down her cheek, a shimmer racing down her perfect face. "I do love you. More than you love me, and that is why I have to go—and why I'm going without asking you to come with me. Goodbye, Logan."

She puts the car in reverse, and I have to step back so my foot doesn't get run over. And it's not until her taillights vanish around the corner at the end of my street that I manage to whisper, "Goodbye."

• • •

Gutted.

I'm fucking gutted.

The good angel on my shoulder tells me not to call her, to give her space and time, because she needs it and she asked for it, and if I invade her mental and emotional space, then I'm violating her consent in a way, and I don't want to do that.

On the other hand, Devi Dare just broke up with me, and I'm

practically hysterical with betrayed misery. I make it until about two in the morning before I call her, but the call goes straight to voicemail. Like her phone is turned off.

I call her three more times to make sure, and then I leave her a message. "Devi," I say, clearing my throat because her name is the first word I've spoken in hours and my voice is hoarse from crying. "Please call me back. Please."

After that, I finally roll out of my bed and search out my scotch collection. But after I pour myself a glass, I can barely force myself to take a drink. I don't want to be drunk right now. I maybe don't want to be drunk ever again, because it would mean numbing myself to reality, and I can't cheat myself out of one second of feeling this pain. I don't want to; if this suffering is all I have left of Devi, then I'll hold onto it as tightly as I possibly can. I won't disgrace the memory of the perfect thing we had by drinking myself into amnesia.

So I set down the drink and pull out my phone, not to call Devi again, although I want to, but to watch the video I took of her in my pool a few weeks ago. And I watch her swimming over and over again, her hair and her body and the water, and I fall asleep on my couch that way.

Alone. With my phone in my hand and my heart in my throat.

• • •

I wake up, not hung over, not exhausted, but dazed all the same. There's that weird, floating moment between my eyes opening and me remembering, a moment where I feel like something bad has happened but I can't remember what. When I finally recall Devi's tears and her terrible, untrue (does she even realize how untrue?) words, *I do love you, more than you love me, and that's why I have to go,* I'm destroyed all over again.

I call her several more times, I text her pages and pages of texts, because how could she think that she loves me more than I love her? But also how could she think about leaving porn? I text her long, stream-of-consciousness threads of thoughts, about how much I love her, how much I already miss her, all the things I would do to prove it to her, but she never answers me back.

I don't have any scenes booked for today, thankfully, so I drive all the way down to El Segundo to see her. I shouldn't be surprised when she's not there, but I'm devastated all the same, and I wait on her porch step for her to come home. The autumn sun rises high and hot, and I get sweaty and uncomfortable but I don't care. I want to suffer. I want to suffer for her.

She never comes home, though. It's just me and my wretched thoughts until the sun sets over the ocean, and the sky fades into oranges and pinks.

And that's when the ancient Volvo rattles into the driveway. A stocky older man with a black mustache and a full head of thick black hair gets out and then walks around the front to open the door for the woman inside. I recognize her immediately.

It's Devi's mother.

The couple comes up to the door and I stand, wiping my sweaty hands on my jeans and extending a hand to Mrs. Jones-Daryani to shake. She ignores it and pulls me straight into a hug, a tight one. For some reason that makes me want to cry again, but I manage to keep it together.

"Hi, Logan," she says as she pulls away. "It's so good to see you again. This is my husband, Davud Daryani."

"Hi, Mrs. Jones-Daryani. Nice to meet you Mr. Daryani," I greet them back. I look at the car hopefully, even though I already know it's empty. "Is Devi coming or…?"

Sue gives me a pitying smile. "We came to get some clothes for her. She's going to be staying with us for a while."

I want to ask where they live, if I can come back with them, but even in my desperate state, I know that would be crossing a line. So I don't. I just look at the ground and try not to cry in front of Devi's parents.

"Davud," Sue says softly, "why don't you go inside and pack up some things for our boombalee? I want to talk with Logan for a minute."

Davud nods, and before he walks in, he places a heavy hand on my shoulder. It should feel weird, the father of the girl who just dumped me touching me like this, but it doesn't. Instead, I feel just a little bit stronger, just a little bit more clear-headed, as if he's transmitted perspective and wisdom through my skin. And then he pats my shoulder and unlocks the apartment door, walking inside and leaving Sue and me on the porch.

And then it hits me, hits me hard.

This is real life. This is Devi's parents gathering up her things and this is Devi not answering her phone, and this is me left broken-hearted for the second time this year, except this time it's so much fucking worse.

Devi and I are really over.

I sit back down on the porch and put my head in my hands, and I feel Sue sit next me, a musical chiming coming from all her anklets and bracelets as she does.

"Logan," she says, laying a hand on my back. And again, it should feel weird being comforted by my ex-girlfriend's parents but it's not for some reason. "It's going to be okay."

"I fucked up," I say miserably. "I fucked everything up."

"Devi made a point to tell us that you didn't do anything wrong," Sue soothes me. "Porn just isn't right for her. There's a difference."

"I thought I *was* doing the right thing," I say, still staring at the ground. "The right thing for both of us. I was trying to be more like her—more logical and careful—and I thought we could make it work. Have each other and have porn at the same time."

"Let me ask you something," Sue says. "Deep down, is that what you really want? To have both?"

"Porn is my entire life," I say defensively. "It paid for that car and for my house and my 401k. It's the only thing I know."

"That's not what I asked," Sue counters gently. "I asked what you wanted. Pretend that Devi would have been willing to stay, willing to continue doing porn. Is that what would have made you truly happy in the end?"

Yes, of course, I want to snap back, but the response is automatic and rehearsed. Because porn *was* my entire life, until I met Devi, and now I want my life to be more than just my job, no matter how amazing my job is. And I also know the reason I'm defensive right now is because I finally have to look all those haunting questions in the face after avoiding them for weeks, look at those questions and then look at the answers I already know deep down. The answers that I started to comprehend the first time Devi and I made love without the camera.

That I might only want Devi.

That I love her in a way I've never loved anyone else before.

That I want to give her all of me. All of me. Meaning I don't give myself to anyone else.

Sue pats my shoulder again. "Your heart and your head chakra are stronger than before, Logan, which means you're growing and learning. But no growth comes without sacrifice."

And then she kisses my cheek and goes inside the apartment.

I know you want to hear that I stop doing porn right that day, that I swear it off and become immediately celibate, but that's not what happens. Instead, the words Sue said to me only very gradually unfold into an epiphany. And as they unfold, I mindlessly and numbly continue life as before.

Well, not entirely as before.

I give up drinking altogether, sending Tanner home with my magnificent scotch collection one afternoon. I stop posting on social media, because I'm tired of faking a jovial happiness that I'll never have again, and also all I want to do is stare at Devi's feeds, hoping for a single post, a single tweet, one selfie. Anything to connect to. But there's nothing, either from her or about her. When Raven left me, Twitter and Tumblr exploded with people chattering about it, bemoaning it, and yet after Devi leaves me, the fucking love of my life, there's complete silence about it on the Internet, because no one knew. It was only two months. And they were the best two months of my life.

I give up going out, I give up talking to friends. I spend my spare time reading through my poetry collection and reading *The Complete Idiot's Guide to Astronomy*, because reading about space and the stars makes me feel closer to Devi.

I give up texting and calling her, but I don't give up waiting for the phone to ring. It never does though.

I film two more scenes after Devi breaks up with me. The first is with a performer named Candi Hart and the second is with Ginger. I feel itchy and empty after both, even though Tanner tells me that they are some of the best scenes I've ever shot.

"You're so fucking in the zone lately," he says as Ginger and I clean up after our scene. "Damn, you were intense."

I shrug, because what can I say? That I have to completely disassociate myself from all emotion and thought in order to do the scenes? That I'm disgusted with myself as I fuck other women, as I come for them, because Devi is the only woman I want to touch now?

After Tanner leaves, I trudge upstairs to my office. It's been a week since Devi left me, and I've become a hollow version of myself. Even editing and writing my monologues is a terrible chore, and the worst task of all is finishing up edits of the last *Star-Crossed* scene because all it does is remind me of the heartbreak that came after the camera turned off. Every glance of hers in the footage, every pull of her mouth—I can see her confusion and pain so clearly now. How fucking self-absorbed and arrogant was I that I didn't see it before?

I can only watch a few minutes of the footage before the grief and guilt threaten to engulf me, and I have to turn it off. I'll edit my scene with Ginger from today instead.

Except I can't.

I plug in the external hard drive Tanner saved the scene to, and the minute I open it up, I know I can't do it. Even just the still image of me cradling Ginger's face at the beginning makes me cringe, because it's something I used to do with Devi.

No. It's more than that. I did it with Devi because I do it with almost every girl I work with. That move never belonged to just Devi and me, it always belonged to me and the hundreds of other girls I've worked with.

I can't articulate to myself exactly why this bothers me so much right now, but it does. I try to force myself to look past it and press play, but the moving footage is even worse, even when I try to fast-forward to the less personal parts. But seeing my body pressed against Ginger's, my hands rough on her tits while I fuck her, it makes me sick to my stomach with shame. Not Puritanical, anti-sex shame—I'm not ashamed of having sex or making porn—but a deeply personal shame, as if I've betrayed more than Devi by filming those two scenes after she left. As if I've betrayed myself.

Which should be a ridiculous thought. How could I be betraying anything or anyone by merely doing my job? I try to remember all the things I've said before. *It's just a job. It's only sex.* But they don't feel true any longer.

I close out the footage and pace around my office, running my hands through my hair. It doesn't make any sense to me, any part of my life right now. I'm wrecked, emotionally and mentally and spiritually, but I can still get hard for other women, still come for them. How is that? Is it because, like I told Tanner all those weeks ago, porn stars have a more evolved concept of love and can separate it from sex? Or is it because I'm a man, and men are wired to fuck indiscriminately?

No, I don't think that's it either, and not only because Tanner would rant for hours about gender essentialism if I told him I'd even considered that last one as a reason.

No, what I think is that maybe I've been asking the wrong question of myself—not *how* I can still fuck other women, but *why*.

Maybe men and women aren't naturally wired to be monogamous, maybe anyone can turn off their brain and their heart, and let their bodies respond to presented stimuli. But maybe that's what makes relationships different. And special. Maybe that's why people have given up their sexual freedoms for the last several millennia in order to bind themselves to someone else. Because it's the sacrifice, the continued and repeated choosing of one person over all the others in the world, that makes a relationship stand apart, that makes a relationship significant and rare and unique.

So the real question is: why do I choose to share myself with other women when I only want to share myself with Devi? Why do I do this job when it means struggling against a heart that just wants to devote itself to one woman and one woman alone?

I don't know if it's right to change for someone you love, but I do know that it's right to change for yourself, if that's what you want. But is it what I really want? Devi's so young, still so full of energy and opportunity, and it's easy for her to change direction and start a new life. But how can I walk away from something I'm good at, that makes me a lot of money, without having anything certain in my future? What if I give up everything for her and she doesn't want me anymore?

I sit back down in my office chair and stare at the bulletin board by my desk. It's mostly covered in tax receipts and Post-It notes, but I've pinned something else up in the middle, *The Hanged Man* tarot card from my reading with Madam Psuka. I stuck it up there as a memento of my first real date with Devi, but now it seems like more than a reminder. It's a call to action.

No growth comes without sacrifice, Sue said, and isn't that exactly what Devi and the psychic tried to explain to me about the card? That The Hanged Man represented sacrifice and suffering without the guarantee of a reward, because the wisdom gained through the experience would be its own reward?

What would I sacrifice? And what would I gain?

I could leave porn, I think.

It's the first time I've allowed the thought to take form, to establish itself in words, even though it's been creeping around the fringes of my consciousness for weeks.

I let myself say it aloud, just to try it out. "I could leave porn."

Nothing dramatic happens. It's not like a halo comes down from heaven and crowns me, it's not like my office is flooded with golden light and the sound of angels singing. And I don't feel like I'm hanging from a tree Hanged Man style, certainly.

But the words are spoken now and the idea is real, and now it's floating in the office like an invisible fog, making the air thick and cold. It never felt like a real option before, it never even seemed like a possible path, because I loved doing it, because it was my whole life. But now it's there, beckoning to me, unfurling like the new leaves of spring. I could quit doing porn. I could stop being Logan O'Toole, porn star, and go back to my birth name, go back to the dreams I used to have. Going to school, making films.

It's not that easy, I realize with a sinking stomach and a glance around my office. Camera equipment litters the room, unfinished contracts pile high on my desk, old tax forms are banked against the far wall like a pile of red and white leaves. In my email inbox are practically thousands of unanswered emails—projects and scenes that are in every imaginable stage, convention panels that I've agreed to be on, articles I've agreed to be interviewed for. I live so deeply within my own life, and there are so many threads running through it. Tying off every loose end would take months, and the thought of all that work makes me preemptively exhausted. It would be easier to cut and run…or simply stay. Stay and change nothing.

I get up and walk out of my office, trying to walk away from my thoughts. I go for a swim, I tidy up my kitchen. I drive to my parents' house and help them pack up some things for their move to Portland, and as I do, things slowly start to settle into place.

Their packing isn't easy, and there are times when I catch Mom staring at the backyard with a look on her face that suggests she's mentally replaying all those sappy moments from my childhood that parents like to hold on to. There are times that I catch Dad rubbing his jaw and standing in the middle of a room, just looking. They're leaving so much behind, an entire life of memories and moments that fused us together into a family, but they're still doing it and making these huge changes because they have faith. Like The Hanged Man, they know the sacrifice will be worth it.

When I get home that night, the first thing I do is call Tanner and tell him everything, from the moment Devi and I jumped in a pool together at Vida's to her leaving me last week, and I tell him what I've been thinking about today. He mostly listens in silence, only speaking when my ramblings finally come to an end.

"So you think it's wrong to do porn now?" he asks. There's no judgment or expectation in his tone, but I still scramble to answer so that he doesn't get the wrong idea.

"I don't think it's wrong. I'm pretty sure I'll never think that—I still love it, and I don't regret making it for a minute. But I think maybe while it isn't *wrong*, it's not right for me any longer. I think I want something else."

Tanner is quiet for a moment. "So what happens next?"

"I don't know." I use the heel of my hand to rub at my forehead. "I guess the first thing is deciding if I really want to do this. If I really want to leave porn."

"Because there's no guarantee that Devi will take you back," Tanner points out. "So if you do this, then you need to be okay with that outcome."

I think back to all those moments in my life where I've felt that *big* feeling, where I've felt a sense of vision and purpose and creative will. As a kid and as an adult, by myself and with Devi. "I'd be lying if I said I wasn't doing this for her," I admit, "but I'm doing it for me too. When I ask myself what I really want for my life, I can't find a real answer anymore—and I think *that,* in and of itself is enough reason to change."

"Just tell me what you need and I'll do everything I can to help," Tanner says, and I wish I could give him a giant hug over the phone. But I can't, so I clear my throat, find a pencil and some paper, and we start planning the end of Logan O'Toole, porn star.

In the end, it does take a couple months. Doing it right—ending all of my projects and contracts professionally and amicably—is so much harder than just packing up and leaving town. But leaving would have been something an older version of myself would have done—the impulsive, emotional Logan who just wanted love and romance and connection. He would have chased after Devi relentlessly, he would have been showering her with orgasms and gifts and saying *fuck it* to everything else.

And at one point, I thought I needed to leave that emotional guy behind to be the best boyfriend I could to Devi, that I needed to be analytical and logical and even a little callous to keep our relationship strong. But now I know what Devi knew already—that it's not emotion versus intellect or head versus heart. It's both, complementary and balanced and all at the same time. Devi, my Devi, was the wisest of us all along, despite her inexperience and young age.

I can't change what—or who—I've done. But I can change what I will do. And so instead of shutting down my feelings or making a string of rash, impetuous decisions, I am determined that the next time I see my Cass, I will have used my love for her to make smart, determined strides towards a different and better life.

I'm going to show her that the man she knew has come back for her, and he's not going anywhere this time.

CHAPTER TWENTY-TWO

"It was twenty-seven hours of labor," my mother says through the phone. "We're both exhausted. But then at the end, a beautiful baby boy."

She's spent the last ten minutes telling me the details of her and Baba's latest delivery, and it feels like it's been twenty-seven hours of listening. Admittedly, I've only been half paying attention, inserting *uh-huh*s and *oh wow*s when it felt appropriate while I scurried around my apartment getting ready for class.

"Your father didn't even make it upstairs. He's passed out on the couch. I don't know how I'm talking to you right now, I can barely think straight."

"You should be in bed. I can chat with you later." With my phone in one hand, I run my fingers through my hair and take a final glance in my bathroom mirror. God, I look tired, but I've looked tired for the last four months. I can't remember the last time I slept well, the last time I didn't wake dreaming of Logan.

Of course, it would probably help if I didn't fall asleep to a video of us every night. Sometimes I don't even masturbate while I watch. It never completely relieves the knot of tension inside when I do, and it usually leaves me feeling more miserable than when I started. But I like hearing his voice last thing before closing my eyes. I like remembering what it felt like to be with him.

It's kind of pathetic, really. I know I can't live like Majnun forever. Eventually I have to move on. Otherwise, why did I break up with him?

Nothing's changed. His job is still sleeping with other women. And I'm still miserable.

Well, not completely miserable. I do have school.

My mother dismisses my invitation to talk later. "I couldn't miss today. Are you excited? Nervous? Did you fix yourself some of that calming tea blend I sent you?"

I've been in Austin for two weeks now, setting up my apartment and settling in. Yesterday, I went to a new student orientation and a financial aid seminar, and trained for a couple of hours for my job in the bursar's office. Then I met with my advisor. Today classes start, and though I feel a bit unprepared for what's to come, I feel confident that I'm doing the right thing. The undergraduate astronomy program is one of the best in the U.S., and my living expenses are much more affordable than in California.

"I am both excited and nervous," I tell my mother, "and the tea is excellent." I'm drinking coffee at the moment, but I don't bother to let her know that.

And if this is what I look like after already a cup of strong brew, then the bags under my eyes are probably going nowhere. I turn off the bathroom light and head to my bedroom to look for my flip-flops.

"Nervousness and excitement are two sides of the same coin. You can rarely have one without the other."

"I don't know that quote. Who's it from?"

"Me," she says coyly. "See? I can say something useful every now and again."

I smile proudly, even though she can't see me. "You always say something useful, Mom. It's just not always what I want to hear." Kneeling, I stretch to retrieve the shoe that got pushed underneath my bed.

"Good advice never is. Speaking of which, let's do your Tarot before I'm too sleepy to interpret your message. I have a feeling today's going to be an important reading." Every day since I've been gone, my mother has called to read me a Tarot card. That's her excuse, anyway. Really, I think she just misses me.

"Page of wands!" she exclaims. "I knew today was good. There's going to be a boy." We both know when she says "a boy" she really means "Logan." Ever since she saw him the day she went to pick up my clothes from my apartment for me, she's been convinced he'll show up in my life again. "He's growing," she says whenever she gets the opportunity, "you'll see."

But that's my mother. She sees the good in people. I'd like to believe it's a quality I inherited from her. But I'm also practical. And while I think that Logan probably is on a growth journey—because, who isn't?—I can't pause my life while he takes it.

I have too much to focus on right now to bring up the subject of Logan, so I ignore the elephant and say, "Yeah, mom. It's my first day. There will probably be lots of boys."

"Well, one boy in particular is going to be important. Maybe he'll bring you good news."

My mother forgets I know Tarot almost as well as she does. While the page of wands can mean a messenger or a creative man, it is also very much like the fool card. It's more likely my reading represents the new path I'm on, my new beginning.

But I don't contradict my mother's interpretation. "Oh, yay. Hopefully that means my financial aid will finally drop into my account."

"It hasn't yet? Do you need any money, Boombalee?"

"No, no. I'm good." Student loans and my part-time job in the bursar's office will pay for my tuition. Revenue from *Star-Crossed* pays for my basic living expenses and all my textbooks. The first episode released two months ago and is currently Lelie's number one most watched show. Critical response has been just as incredible and preliminary reports show the crossover to non-porn watchers is strong.

I'm proud of it. Proud of Logan. I wouldn't be surprised if he gets an award or two at the AVN show. If he got nominated, maybe I'd attend the ceremony. Surely, by then I'd be ready to see him again.

As of now it's been four months. Four long lonely months.

"Don't be prideful, Devi. When you are—'"

I cut her off before she can finish her Buddha quote. "I'm not being prideful, Mom. I have enough money."

"Good. But I can do a distance reiki to manifest fortune for you if you need it. Just say the word."

"Yeah. I will." I brace the phone on my shoulder with my cheek while I stuff my physics textbook into my bag. "Hey, I have to get to class now. Talk to you tomorrow, okay?"

We hang up, and I take a minute to run through a centering meditation—another useful tool I've gotten from my mother—and then head out for the first day in my new world.

. . .

Do I miss doing porn?

The short answer is I miss the money. (It was really good money for not a lot of work. I could cover the monthly stipend for my campus job with just one shoot.)

The long answer is I miss doing porn with Logan.

It's a long answer because I'd have to go into all the details of how, in my mind, they don't exist separately anymore. Even girl-girl porn reminds me of Logan. Not because he watched me that day with Kendi, but because sex in general is now tainted because of him. Logan made sex better. He made it about all of me, and not just a part of me. Not only my body and what it could do. He made sex a whole experience. Now I can't go back to how it was. It's like I spent my entire life drinking skim milk, and though I liked it fine, I had no idea what I was missing until I drank whole milk. I'm sure it will change one day, that I'll enjoy sex and porn again more fully after time and distance. After I fall in love and have sex with someone else.

But even when it does change, I don't think I can go back to doing the kind of erotic films I was doing. I don't even have an agent for it anymore. Back when I decided to leave Logan, when I decided to go back to school, I wrapped up a few assignments and then politely fired my agent. I'm not sure if I would have had trouble finding more work after LaRue threatened to blackball me, but my guess is that it wouldn't have been the problem I'd feared since he didn't even come after me for lost revenue like he said he would. He didn't really want my money. He wanted me to spread my legs for his films.

Speaking of people who wanted me to spread my legs, I did make a formal complaint about Bruce Madden to the Adult Performer Advocacy Committee. Not that it did any good. He is still offered jobs and the APAC has made no formal investigations. Sadly, women don't have much of a voice in the industry, surprise surprise. At least I did my part.

Logan did his part too. Though it's too painful to watch his videos with other women, I still visit his website from time to time to read his blog and see the latest updates about *Star-Crossed*. One day, about a month after I last saw him, he'd written up a blog post about Bruce and about what he did to the women he worked with. Apparently there were other victims besides me. Logan did his research and put together a pretty in-depth tell-all about the "douchecanoe," as he calls him. I'm not around anyone who would know those things anymore, but based on the comments the blog post got, I suspect Bruce is having trouble getting any big stars to work with him now. I've got to be honest—that makes me feel quite vindicated.

It also makes me feel gooey and melancholy about Logan too, because (a) what doesn't? and (b) I know he spoke out for me. It's proof that he really does love me, but I never questioned that.

Logan is the real reason I can never do porn again.

If I tried, I would be setting myself up for the same situation I fell into with him. Even if I made the rule to not date another porn star, I'm smart enough to know that those kinds of rules aren't always within a person's power to keep. Besides, it would be hypocritical for me to be skim milk when I no longer want to drink it myself. It was fine once upon a time. Not anymore. Not for me. Now I want the real thing. So I'm going to hold out for the whole milk.

As for Logan…

Though I'd never admit it to my mother, I sometimes like to fantasize that he'll change his mind, that he'll decide he prefers whole milk too. But it's not really fair to try to put that dream on his reality. He might actually like skim milk. He might not even be able tell the difference. I can't sit around wishing for him to "fall in line" and show up on my doorstep with a box full of chocolates and a bouquet of roses. That just might not be his future.

But *my* future is the stars. So it doesn't mean that I don't still *hope*.

• • •

After a morning of back-to-back classes, I have four syllabi to go over, five chapters of reading, an essay to write, and a page of math problems.

It's overwhelming and awesome.

I haven't been this happy since…well, since Logan.

School, I decide, is the best cure for a broken heart. That and a busy schedule. Even though I'm eager to dive into my homework, I'm also thankful I have my work-study job in the bursar's office to keep me truly occupied. I'm only scheduled for three hours on Mondays, Wednesdays, and Fridays, but with my full course heavy with math and science classes, I'm sure it will be all I can handle.

The job is easy, thankfully, and even though it's my first day at the counter, it only takes half my shift before my supervisor says, "You've really got the hang of this, Devi. Think you can handle some students on your own while I start working on the deposit for my drawer?"

"Yep. I'm good." Like I said, the job is pie, and Jake's a great trainer.

He's also amazing to look at—tall, dark, handsome, built, and totally gay. He's witty and smart and likes to tease, and since there's no sexual tension, it's easy to tease back. We've only known each other two days, and he's already a friend.

"Coolio. I'll be in the back. Holler if you need anything, I'll be here in a flash."

I don't need anything, but I turn my back to the counter and call after him. "Hey, Jake!" When he rushes back, I say, "Just testing."

He laughs. "You're such a bad girl." *If he only knew.* His expression sombers quickly. "Oh, sorry. Didn't see you come in," he says to someone behind me. "Devi will get you taken care of."

Jake walks off, and I put on a friendly grin and pivot to face the person in front of me. "How can I—" I start, and then my voice cuts off in a sharp intake of breath.

Because the guy in front of me is Logan.

My body reacts instantly, buzzing and itching as if on cue. As if we're in production for *Campus Porn* and our script has us meeting and banging within two minutes. I'm ready to start shedding my clothing and I'm not above climbing over the counter.

But we aren't on set for anything. This is real life, and while I'm thrilled at the sight of him, I'm on pins and needles too.

He locks eyes with mine, a host of familiar emotions present in his intense gaze. "Am I too late?" he asks.

"What?" I ask, even though I heard him. I might even know what he's asking, but I'm still so stunned to see him that I've forgotten how to use words.

"Am I too late?" He glances toward the back office where Jake disappeared just a moment ago.

Damn, he really *is* asking what I think he's asking!

And he's really here. In front of me.

My stomach flutters with nervous exhilaration, and I have to swallow before I can respond. "You mean, are you too late for me? That in the short time I've been in Austin I may have fallen madly in love with my supervisor? Because, number one, he's gay."

"*He's* gay?" Logan tries to play surprised but mostly he sounds relieved.

"Mm hmm." I lean against the counter to be nearer to him but also because I'm shaking like a leaf.

"Huh." He leans forward too, his elbows on the counter, and he's so close I can smell the familiar clean scent of his skin. "What's number two?"

Number two, I'm still madly in love with you.

I almost say it. We're flirting, and it's easy and natural and like we've never been apart. But I'm trying to be cautious because *what is he doing here*?

"Number two, I don't just give my heart to everyone I work with." Speaking of my heart, it's pounding so hard I'm sure he can hear it.

His eyes are back on mine, his gaze deep and penetrating. "I know that about you. It's one of my favorite traits of yours."

It's funny how, out of the hundreds of amazing things he's said and done to me, a simple statement like this can still twist me in delicious knots. Maybe because a part of me had feared that he hated me after I left. That there would never be anything about me that he thought of as his favorite again.

But he doesn't hate me. And he's here. And I've missed him so *so* much that just seeing him makes me all sorts of crazy happy. But if nothing's changed since I last saw him..."What are you doing here, Logan?" My tone is demanding and I don't try to hide the bite of desperation. "You come all the way to Austin like this, and I'm going to start to get my hopes up. Is there any reason why maybe I *should* get my hopes up?"

His eyes fall—nervous maybe? He digs in his back pocket. "I don't know if it's worth getting your hopes up over. But as for what I'm doing here," he pulls out his wallet and flips it open, "I came to pay a tuition bill."

Understanding settles in, and my heart literally sinks. "I don't need you to pay my tuition bill, thank you. I'm doing fine on my own."

I wonder if he talked to my mother or if he just decided to come do this on a whim of his own. I'm not sure how he ever got the notion that I would want this, as if he owed me. As if I were his whore. I'm pissed and my eyes are stinging, and how the hell is it still possible for him to hurt me like this?

But then he says, "Not your tuition, Queen Cass. Mine."

My throat goes dry. "What?"

"Yeah, see," he runs a hand through his hair, and I have to bite my lip to keep myself from doing anything rash like, oh, molest him in a public space. "It took me a little while to get all the details sorted out, but I've wrapped up all of my prior obligations and sold a portion of my production studios to Vida. And as of about three days ago, I'm officially a student at UT Austin." His expression is somehow both bold and boyish. "In other words, you are looking at a man who is no longer a porn star."

In a flash, all sense of propriety goes out the window and I'm crawling over the counter to leap into Logan's arms.

And then we're kissing, greedily, desperately, our mouths clashing awkwardly with eagerness. My ass is still on the counter, but I wrap my legs around his waist, and his hands thread possessively through my hair, and I can't even think because my feelings are so *big* and consuming.

"You're crying," he whispers when I pull away to catch my breath.

"I can't help it. You enrolled in school for me." I watch my thumb sweep across his jawline, too overwhelmed to look him in the eye.

"Hey." With two fingers, Logan pushes my chin up to meet his gaze. "I enrolled in school for *me*. I rented out my house and am living in a one-bedroom in Texas for *you*. Got it?"

Even better. I'm grinning, but I rein it in to give him a look of mock seriousness. "Got it."

He swipes away my tears with the back of his finger then wraps a hand behind my neck. "Awfully convenient that the same school you chose has a fairly decent film program, isn't it?"

"Yeah. Convenient. That's what that was." I like the idea of fate and everything, but I'm not one to rely on it alone. So I nudged the universe a little. Can you blame me?

"You knew I'd follow you here, didn't you?"

My mind flashes to that Tarot's star card, the card that I've held close for all these months. "I didn't know. I hoped."

Logan pulls back to study me. "Why didn't you say that's what you wanted?"

"I couldn't ask you to give up your world for me. You would have resented me forever. You had to choose that for yourself." I'm so proud that he has, that he's thought about this and stayed true to his feelings while taking planned, logical steps that are good for him and his future.

"Hanged man has to hang himself?" *God, I love him.*

"You got it." Then, because it seems like maybe I should be sure he really has chosen what I think he has, that he's really okay with it, I ask, "So you're completely out of the porn business?"

"Not completely." He continues to search my face while he talks, perhaps looking for my approval. "I'm still producing long distance. Tanner's holding down the fort. I'll probably do some directing now and then."

"But no more performing?"

He shakes his head, and it sounds like a promise when he says, "No more performing."

I'm relieved. And, strangely, a little something else. "No more Logan O'Toole films. That's almost disappointing."

He chuckles and the sound vibrates through me. "Maybe, I could come out of retirement for a film or two. But I'll only star with one woman." His voice gets low and serious. "I'll only ever perform again with you, Devi."

I reach up to capture his mouth with mine, kissing him in approval.

But he breaks away after only a few seconds, pulling back with a somber expression. "I'm sorry, babe. Really sorry. I'm sorry I didn't quit before. I know that it hurt you…" He trails off, I think, because this apology is hard for him.

I know he needs to say this, but I need him to know I already know. "I get it. You didn't mean to hurt me. You were doing your job. A job that you loved."

"I didn't really love it anymore when I didn't have you."

Seriously, my ovaries just imploded. Sensitive Logan is *so freaking hot.*

He cradles my face against his hand. "And, besides hurting you, it hurt me. I was in love with you. Even before you left, I knew that loving you changed things. That it *should* change things. I knew that every time I was with someone who wasn't you, I was betraying that emotion, cheapening the moments we shared with these false imitations. I promise I figured it out pretty fast after you left. I'm just sorry it wasn't sooner."

And I'd thought I was done with the waterworks. "I'm not going to lie," I sniffle, "I've been miserable without you. But I think you were probably worth the wait."

He answers with another kiss, one I can feel in between my thighs, and our hands start roving, and if not for the polite clearing of a throat behind me, it's quite possible that our display of affection might have moved from PG-13 to rated R.

Who am I kidding? Rated R would be tame for us.

Like we did when we were caught at the art gallery, Logan and I freeze while Jake, the throat-clearer, opens the drawer on the other side of the counter. "Don't mind me. I just came out for a deposit slip."

I turn and give him an apologetic smile. He returns it with a look that says *we're-good-but-you-better-believe-I'm-asking-for-details* before going back to his paperback.

We laugh in unison.

Then, reluctantly, I say, "While I'd like to keep making out with you, I am on the clock. My new job doesn't encourage heavy petting like my last one did."

"Good. I'd be fiercely jealous if it did." He kisses me once more, chastely, then swats my ass. "Now get back to your side of the counter so I can calm down before I walk out of here. I still need to pay my tuition, too."

"Oh yeah. Let's do that." I unwrap my legs from him and scoot back to my place. "Do you have an invoice?"

"I didn't bring it with me. Can you look it up?"

"Of course." I turn to my computer screen, about to type in his name when I remember that I don't *know* it. Not his *real* name.

He's one step ahead of me. "Last name, Johnson."

"Johnson? But that's—" *a great porn name*, I start to say, but he cuts me off.

"First name, Dwayne."

I'd always known he was embarrassed by his real name, and I always thought I'd be considerate and respectful when I finally learned what it was, but I can't help myself. I laugh. "Your name is *Dwayne Johnson*? Like, The Rock?"

"I'm changing it legally, I swear."

"Do I have to call you Dwayne now?" I'm still laughing as I pull up his account. "Because I just don't know if I can—" I have to pause until

I can gather myself. "I'm sorry, I'm sorry." I'm not really sorry. Not at all. "I'll get used to it. I promise."

"You can just keep calling me Logan, thank you very much."

"Uh huh. We'll see." It's too good to not to use it for as long as it's entertaining. And I have a feeling it will be entertaining for quite some time—at least to me.

It's only a few minutes before I've swiped Logan's credit card, applied the payment to his account, and stamped his receipt *Paid in Full*. Purposefully, I brush my fingers against his as I hand him the printout. I shiver from the spark of electricity that passes through us.

So maybe we're no longer pornographic performers, but that doesn't mean we don't still have the chemistry.

Logan folds his receipt and stuffs it in his pocket with his wallet. "What time are you out of here?"

"Four-thirty." I glance at the clock on the wall. *A whole hour from now.* Logan/Dwayne nods.

A beat passes, and I can tell that he's as unsure of what happens next as I am. As reluctant to leave as I am to let him.

After a minute, he pops the question. "Dinner later?"

"We both know what you're really asking. And the answer is yes."

He backs away from the counter, his eyes still on me. "Hope you're hungry. Because I have quite an appetite."

"I remember. I think about it a lot, actually."

He groans. "You're killing me, Cass." He pauses at the door to adjust himself. "I love you," he mouths.

And I know he does. Maybe even as much as I love him. But I'm not Cass right now. I'm not Layla, and he's not Majnun. We aren't star-crossed lovers who wish for each other across the sky. I'm Devi, and he's Logan (er, Dwayne), and what we have is real and grounded.

I blow him a kiss, and even though I wish he weren't leaving, I'm confident that we'll have plenty of time to make up for the time we spent apart.

When he's gone, Jake appears almost instantly. "Who on earth was that fine piece of manhood?"

"My boyfriend," I answer like it's no big deal that I'm dating the most amazing guy in the world. "His name is Dwayne." Somehow I manage to not laugh this time.

"Lucky, lucky girl." Jake lets out a dreamy sigh. Then he leans in and whispers, "I hope you don't mind me telling you this, but Dwayne looks exactly like this—don't judge me for knowing this—a porn star. Logan O'Toole. He's over-the-top sexy. Totally to die for."

I bite back my smile. "Oh really?"

"Can you imagine what that would be like? Dating a guy who does porn for a living?" Jake practically swoons at the idea. "The things a man like that could do!"

I shrug my shoulder dismissively. "Plenty, I'm sure."

I don't tell him that I'm more than sure of what a man like that can do. Or that I don't have to imagine what it would be like. I don't tell him that a porn star boyfriend is only hot for about five minutes. I don't tell him that Logan O'Toole is much more than just a sex symbol or a status or a "fine piece of manhood."

I let Jake keep his fantasy. He and the rest of the world can have *Logan O'Toole*. I get to have the real thing.

EPILOGUE

"Dwayne, no! Someone will see."

"I better not need to remind you," I say, pressing Devi up against the outside wall of the Frank Erwin Center, "that my legal name is actually Logan now."

"I thought Dwayne would get your attention more," she says but her voice fades into a distracted mumble as I finally manage to slide my hands up her billowing graduation gown and start thumbing at her nipples through her dress. Austin doesn't get freezing in December, but it's definitely colder than it would be in L.A., and Devi's got the goose bumps and stiff nipples to prove it.

I'm determined to warm her up.

"Logan, stop," she giggles as I started nibbling on her neck. I hear people walking and talking behind me as they leave the ceremony and go off to find their cars, but I don't care. I've been desperate to touch my sexy graduate all morning, and I not only had to sit through one graduation ceremony but *two*, and now that we've finally escaped the crowd and our parents, I can't wait a minute longer.

"I can't stop," I breathed in her ear. "You're too fucking sexy right now."

"In my giant black graduation robe?"

"Don't forget the hat, Cass."

She finally succeeds in pushing my hands down and creating enough space between us that she can straighten the aforementioned hat and smooth down the robe. "You need to wait until we're home," she scolds. "We both got accepted into graduate programs here, remember? We will still have to look these professors in the eye next fall, which will be a little awkward if they see you drilling me right after the commencement ceremony."

"Fine," I sigh. And even though my entire groin aches, I help her readjust her garb and I don't even fuss once. I do pull her close and growl in her ear, "You better be ready when we walk through that door, though. I've waited too long to have you already."

With a quick look around us, Devi takes my hand and guides it under her gown. She's not wearing any underwear and so there's no barrier between my fingers and her flesh. She's so wet right now, so slick, and I groan at the thought of pushing myself inside there. "I'm very *ready* for you," she says. "I'd let you fuck me right now if I wasn't worried my faculty advisor would see."

"Like he's hasn't watched every single one of our scenes already," I grumble. But I stop teasing her wet folds and step away, grateful my own graduation gown hides my insistent erection. "Home, Cass. Now."

. . .

The drive to our little Travis Heights bungalow is mercifully swift, and I have Devi out of the car and against our front door in almost no time at all. It makes me smile against her mouth as I think of all the times we've come home this way over the last four years, practically undressing each other before we could even unlock the door. Especially that first year— the transition from fucking for hours every day to listening to lectures on introductory physics and early American lit was torture. Most days I had to text Devi and hunt her down on campus in order to fuck her in a conveniently empty bathroom or in an abandoned corner of the library, and even when I started to acclimate to a porn-civilian's life, I still found myself craving her almost constantly. I left porn in order to be with her, but now that I was here, I found that spending time together was harder than ever. We were both busy with classes and homework, and we no longer had long stretches of our day that we could devote to marathon sex sessions. It didn't take me long to figure out that the only way I could live with that is if we instead devoted long sessions of our nights to making love.

Which we did. Very happily.

There were other strange parts about my new life. For one thing, although I knew my classmates would be a decade younger than me, I definitely didn't expect them all to recognize Logan O'Toole on sight. I still get covert high-fives from the boys and lots of batted eyelashes from the girls, and at least once a day, I get some person asking me for sex advice or an autograph or a date. The date offers are the hardest to deal with, not because I'm even the littlest bit tempted to date anyone other than Devi, but because I'm so laughably *not* tempted that it's hard to be kind when I explain to these girls that I'm not interested. I'm sure they're all nice and smart, but I left a life populated by the dirtiest, prettiest women imaginable to be with Devi; I'm certainly not going to be lured away by a psych major from North Dakota.

The thing is, when I fell in love with Devi, I realized what it is to look up at the stars, and once you've seen the stars, it's impossible to unsee them, to go back to staring at the ground. Devi sometimes says the same thing to me, or at least I think it's the same thing—something about different kinds of milk—but the gist is similar. There's something that happens when you meet someone you love, something alchemical and chaotic and wonderful. That doesn't mean it's been easy—there have been growing pains for both of us transitioning out of porn, there have been fights about money and sex and jealousy. There have been times when loving each other—choosing each other over and over again—means repeated sacrifice and the occasional bout of suffering.

The reward, though, is worth it. Every fucking time.

Like right now, when Devi's burning a path along my jaw with scorching, desperate kisses and I've finally managed to unlock the door and we both tumble into the house. She looks at me with a naughty gleam in her eye and asks, "Want to get the camera?"

"Hell yes, I do," I groan and peel my body away from hers to grab the handheld. I knew when I left L.A. that I never wanted to perform in any scenes that weren't with Devi, and I wasn't sure how interested she would be in ever getting in front of a camera with me again, given all that had happened. But that very first night we were together after I came to Austin she begged me to take dirty pictures of her, and then *Star-Crossed* blew up so big that Vida was begging us for something like it, anything, and that evolved into us having a long-running series under the auspices of Vida's company. It's turned into one of her biggest moneymakers and the most successful thing I've ever done. In a strange twist of fate, Devi and I are more famous for porn than we were when we did it all the time. People are hungry for what we show, I guess—real chemistry, real pleasure, real affection and respect. Sometimes we post edited and cohesive scenes, sometimes we just put up raw footage, and sometimes we have live sessions for people to watch—but it's only ever with the two of us.

Just the way we like it.

And whenever I think that I miss my old life, whenever I hear about Tanner's fancy cinematography jobs, or whenever I see Raven winning industry award after industry award, I remind myself of those final days at home, when I was so miserable and itchy in my own skin that I could hardly stand to be alive anymore. I'm happy for Tanner and I'm even weirdly happy for Raven, because even if I don't always like her, she works hard and she's earned every bit of her success. But I know that life, that world, could have never made me happy in the end, not like it does for them.

My happiness is right here in front me, teasingly unzipping her gown, and suddenly I don't have the patience to finish the more elaborate camera set-up I had in mind. I put the handheld on a tripod, plug in a few cords and click a few buttons, and then the feed is going straight to our website, live for anybody who's on there now but also archived for later.

I unzip my own robe but leave it on, and while I'm at it, I also unbutton my slacks and free my dick, which after a full morning of craving and wanting, is thick and dark. I sit in a chair in front of the camera and pat my thigh with one hand while I stroke my cock with the other.

"Come to Logan, baby," I say, and she doesn't hesitate, pushing her robe off her shoulders and tugging off her dress as she comes closer. All that's left on her body is her high heels and her graduation cap, and this is pretty much one of the biggest fantasies I've had since high school. I'm praying right now that I can last long enough to do it justice.

Devi effortlessly straddles me on the chair and then she's slowly lowering herself onto my waiting erection. She's already so fucking wet for me, but even so, it's a tight fit and her mouth parts in a gasp when the flared edge of my crown finally breaches her entrance.

"Such a good girl putting it inside you," I praise her. "Such a good girl."

Her cheeks and lips are dark-rose with her characteristic sex blush, and her pupils are wide with lust. She slides down another inch, and my toes are curling in my shoes, she's so fucking tight around me, and then with another one of her adorable gasps, she's fully impaled on me.

I lean back a little, admiring the way her plump little clit rubs against me, admiring the way that greedy pussy starts moving and grinding down on me right away. We both watch for a minute, our eyes on the place where we're joined, where the thick base of my cock stretches her folds.

"Bounce on it," I tell her. "Make it feel good."

She eagerly obeys, bracing her knees on the sides of my thighs and then working herself up and down in fast, hard strokes. My head drops backward to rest against the back of the chair, and I hear my graduation cap fall to the floor. I don't care. Instead, I lace my hands behind my neck and watch Devi work, her tits bouncing and her stomach tight and her eyes closed in bliss. And when I feel my balls drawing up, I grab her hips and stop her, changing her movements from the fast strokes to the slow, grinding rolls that I know will get her off. Within seconds, she's falling apart on top of me, the tassel from her cap swinging as her head drops forward and her body shakes.

"That's it," I murmur to her. "Give it all to me."

And she does, her fingernails digging into my biceps as the quivering accelerates, peaks, and then finally, finally subsides. After she comes down, I start thrusting up underneath her again, but she stops me with a smile and a hand on my chest.

"One minute," she says. "I want to give you a graduation present."

I groan. "I love presents, babe, but is now really the time?"

But she's already climbing off me, walking into the kitchen, leaving my cock still hard and aching. But then she returns with a medium-sized tube, and my face splits into a grin. That's lube, and I think I know where this is going, and I love graduation day! I should really try to graduate more often.

Biting her lip in an expression of naughtiness so delicious that I want to devour it, Devi spreads some of the thick, clear lube on my cock. It's cold and I give a little shiver until she curls her strong fingers around my length and gives me a few tight, slow strokes.

"God, I fucking love you," I say hoarsely.

"And I love you. Now finger me."

Those should be our wedding vows, right there.

I spread a dab of the lubricant on my forefinger and do as I'm told, teasing the pleated rim between her cheeks, rubbing and pressing and gradually coaxing it open for me. And after I can easily work a second finger in and out, she crawls back on the chair and positions herself so that my tip presses against her back entrance. I watch her face as she guides my cock into her ass, the intense concentration as my crown passes through the tight rings of muscle at the beginning, the gut-deep pleasure-pain as she lowers herself farther down. Her channel is a tight, hot furnace around me, and the moment she finally buries me and her perfect ass comes to rest on my thighs, I decide I'm in heaven.

She opens her eyes. Goose bumps pepper her skin and a small sheen of sweat glows on her face and chest. We do the occasional anal scene for our series with Vida and sometimes anal just for ourselves, but it's not such a frequent occurrence that Devi's blithely expert at it. Instead, she squirms and groans trying to find just the right angle to ride me, she sweats and shivers every time she moves her ass up and down my cock. It's a constant negotiation between pleasure and pain, and the moment she wins and hones in on the pleasure, she becomes luminescent and beautiful and wild.

I reach up and stroke her face, moving my hands to her hair where I pluck out the bobby pins holding her graduation cap in place. And then I take her hat off and toss it to the floor. (The high heels I let her keep on, for obvious reasons.)

My hands are everywhere, gentle and soothing, rubbing her tense thighs and caressing the full teardrops of her breasts and cradling her flushed face. "Logan," she says, and it's not so much a word as an exhalation, as a prayer.

"Devi," I exhale back. "Come here."

I help her lean forward into me, her naked chest pressed against the white button-down I wore under my graduation robe, and then I tip her face up to mine and kiss her. Rubbing her back and smoothing her hair, stroking her arms and legs, I languorously explore her mouth, give her the kind of slow, luxurious kisses that a queen like my Cass deserves.

And out of all the dirty things we do, out of all the rough, kinky sex we have, this right here is my favorite. The kind of sex that combines dirty and deep, raunch and romance. I know it seems like a contradiction, or maybe even an impossibility, that anal sex could be romantic, but it's an act that requires so much more patience and so much more communication than almost anything else I can think of. It forces you to slow down and look your partner in the face, examine how they're feeling and what they're thinking. To be done right, it requires an incredible amount of trust, and what could possibly be more romantic than that?

My lips slide over hers and our tongues press and twist together. Our breathing unites and our heartbeats pound the same heavy, hot rhythm, and we move together, rising and falling, pushing and pulling. I reach between us and start kneading her clit with the pad of my thumb, and that's how we come—together—kissing and grinding and panting. And when my climax stabs through my balls like a hot knife of ecstasy, when I feel the deep contractions of her own orgasm squeezing my dick, I hold her tight and breathe her name against her lips,

Devi

Devi

Devi,

until we both come down, until I feel her body ease and slump against mine, until my cock stops pulsing inside of her. I lift her off my dick and place her back on my lap. It occurs to me that I'm probably going to have to change into a new pair of slacks for dinner, but I don't care.

"That was a hell of a present, Cass," I murmur into her hair.

Her face is pressed against my chest, and I can both feel and hear her happy humming deep in her throat.

"Are you purring, little kitten?"

She nods lazily, still humming.

I glance at the clock—five in the evening. We're supposed to meet our parents for a big family dinner at seven, which is when I planned on giving Devi her graduation present. But her present to me was so amazing, and honestly, I'd give anything to this naked goddess curled up on my lap right now.

"I have something else to make you purr," I say, standing up and resettling her on the chair. She looks perfect, her hair mussed and her lips swollen, wearing nothing but her heels. I button myself back up and jog over to the small alcove that serves as my office, where I open a filing cabinet and pull out a little box I stashed behind all the files.

I also leave the camera running. I've been looking forward to this moment for years, and I want to capture every naked, sex-rumpled second of it.

My hands start to shake and my pulse starts to race, my heart somehow hammering a frantic beat in my chest and choking my throat all at once. But I manage to walk over to the chair and hand her the box as casually as possible, given the circumstances.

She smiles up at me. "Logan, this better not be expensive."

"I only had to pawn off like half of our sex toys to buy it, it's fine."

She laughs and turns her attention back to the package, which is a small square box with a massive bow on top. She unties the giant silk ribbon and it falls into her lap in sinuous loops. And then she opens the lid to see what's inside.

A ring box.

The moment it hits her, her eyes snap up to me, but I'm already on one knee in front of her.

"Devi Daryani," I say, my voice trembling a little, "I love you more than Manjun loved Layla. I love you more than I love anything else in this life. I know you wanted to wait until we were completely done with school to move forward, but Devi, I can't wait another second. I want to be your husband. I want you to be my wife. I want to be loving you and giving you orgasms until we're too frail to get out of our beds in the nursing home."

She blinks those long eyelashes rapidly, tears shimmering in her amber eyes.

"Will you marry me?" I ask, realizing I hadn't actually said the words yet. "Will you let me be your husband?"

She takes a deep, choking breath and opens up the box. I see the reflection of the diamond in her eyes. For the first time, my vague fears crystalize into an extremely concrete and immediate terror that she'll say no. That she wants to wait or that she doesn't want to ever get married or, worse, that she doesn't love me enough to bind herself to me.

"Please marry me, Devi," I say anxiously. "Please say yes."

She eases the ring out of its box and then she looks up, those tears finally spilling over and tracing streaks down her face.

"Yes," she whispers. "I'll marry you."

My chest expands into that hugely dizzying *big* feeling, and I collapse in relief, my head falling onto her lap. "Thank God," I mumble into the silken skin of her thighs. "I would have died if you said no."

She runs her fingers through my hair. "As if anyone could say no to you."

"You did once," I remind her, nuzzling her thighs.

She parts them for me, half instinct and half banked desire from earlier. "But you had to know that I was still yours, even when I left," she says.

I kiss my way up her thigh to her pussy, giving her clit a gentle, lingering nibble. "I didn't know," I say, pausing in between words to taste her. "I thought I'd lost you forever."

"I think I was yours from the moment I first saw you," she admits, shivering as my tongue finds a sensitive spot. "And that's why I wanted you to be all mine."

"Forever," I say, pulling back for a minute. I take the ring and slide it onto her finger, the vintage rose gold and princess diamond beautiful and brilliant against her skin. And then I move my hand to the nape of her neck and pull her into a long kiss. Our lips move together and my ring sparkles on her hand, and the world is stunning—magnificent and mysterious and big.

Big and *real.*

And then Devi is pulling away, using her hand with its new ring to find the thick bulge in my slacks. "Fuck me like a porn star, Logan O'Toole."

I look over my shoulder at the camera and give it a wink.

Time to get to work.

AUTHOR'S NOTE

It's probably no secret to our fans that Laurelin Paige and I love porn. Tumblr porn, classy porn, kinky porn, whatever. And when we started talking about writing a book set in the porn world, we knew we wanted to be clear about two things: firstly, how sexy, fun, and surprisingly progressive the industry can be, and secondly, how deep cultures of assault, racism, misogyny and de facto coercion still run. Porn, like any other industry—film, publishing, music—is a huge world with both amazing and terrible parts, and so we wanted to make sure we highlighted both.

Pornography right now is grappling with huge issues of consent, performer safety, and piracy, and has been for much longer than Laurelin and I have been researching our story, and it would do a disservice to the very layered and complicated world of porn if we concocted an airbrushed fantasy without addressing the very real issues that threaten performers and producers today. We hope that we've written a story that showcases a realistic portrayal of porn, and we hope that after you read this, you'll be inspired to consume smut more consciously...and more voraciously.

—Sierra and Laurelin

ACKNOWLEDGEMENTS

To our agent, Rebecca Friedman (and friend and cheerleader and soul healer), and everyone at Rebecca Friedman Literary, especially Kimberly Brower. And to our foreign agents at Bookcase Literary Agency, Flavia Viotti and Meire Deis.

To our publicist, Jenn Watson (we don't know how you manage us most days), and the entire team at Social Butterfly PR, especially Shannon from Shanoff Formats and Hilary Suppes. To Kylie McDermott for our cover reveal and Shayna Snyder at Shayna's Spicy Reads for our excerpt reveal.

To Sara Eirew for a cover that we flove, and to Nancy Smay for finding all our mistakes and correcting them.

To our assistants, Melissa Gaston, Candi Kane, and Sarah Piechuta—we would literally be nowhere (online) without you.

To Kayti McGee and Melanie Harlow for loving us, trapped farts and all. To JM who shares our love of (and frustration with) porn. To the women of the Order.

To the authors in our community who inspire and sustain us, especially Lola Darling, Lauren Blakely, Katy Evans, Vi Keeland, Penelope Ward, C.D. Reiss, Kristy Bromberg,

To the readers who met Devi and Logan first and helped to make their story better - Jen McCoy, Liz Berry, Vox Libris, Roxie Madar, Jodi Marie Maliszewski, and the Peen Queens.

To the readers who supported this book as well as the ones before, especially to Laurelin's Lovelies, the lambs in Sierra Simone's reader group, and the Hudson Pierce! Fixed Trilogy group. Our words would be pointless without people to read them. We write for you.

To our husbands and families - we're always amazed when we survive the birth of a book and even more amazed to find you're all still around when we've done so. We actually do love you more than our characters. Thank you for getting that even when we don't show it.

To our Creator—thank you our gifts and talents. We hope we always strive to be worthy of all you've given us.

With over 1 million books sold, LAURELIN PAIGE is the *NY Times*, *Wall Street Journal*, and *USA Today* bestselling author of the Fixed Trilogy. She's a sucker for a good romance and gets giddy anytime there's kissing, much to the embarrassment of her three daughters. Her husband doesn't seem to complain, however. When she isn't reading or writing sexy stories, she's probably singing, watching *Game of Thrones* and the *Walking Dead*, or dreaming of Michael Fassbender. She's also a proud member of Mensa International though she doesn't do anything with the organization except use it as material for her bio.

The Fixed Trilogy
Fixed on You
Found in You
Forever with You
Hudson

With Kayti McGee
Miss Match
MisTaken
Love Struck

The Found Duet
Free Me
Find Me

Falling Under You: A 1001 Nights Novella
Chandler

First and Last
First Touch
Last Kiss

SIERRA SIMONE is a *USA Today* bestselling former librarian (who spent too much time reading romance novels at the information desk.) She lives with her husband and family in Kansas City. She is the author of *Priest*, *Midnight Mass*, The Markham Hall series and the London Lovers duet.

Priest
Midnight Mass (A Priest Novella)

The London Lovers Duet
The Seduction of Molly O'Flaherty
The Persuasion of Molly O'Flaherty
The Wedding of Molly O'Flaherty

The Markham Hall Series
The Awakening of Ivy Leavold
The Education of Ivy Leavold
The Punishment of Ivy Leavold
The Reclaiming of Ivy Leavold

CPSIA information can be obtained at www.ICGtesting.com
Printed in the USA
BVOW06s1425170416

444539BV00033B/869/P

31192020984140